POWER PLAY

PATRICK ROBINSON

POWER PLAY

AN INTERNATIONAL THRILLER

Vanguard Press
A Member of the Perseus Books Group

Published by Vanguard Press
A Member of the Perseus Books Group

Designed by Brent Wilcox
Set in 11.5 point Adobe Garamond Pro

Cataloging-in-Publication data for this book is available
from the Library of Congress.
ISBN 978-1-59315-731-9 (hardcover)
ISBN 978-1-59315-751-7 (paperback)
ISBN 978-1-59315-732-6 (e-book)

Vanguard Press books are available at special discounts for bulk
purchases in the U.S. by corporations, institutions, and other organizations.
For more information, please contact the Special Markets Department at
the Perseus Books Group, 2300 Chestnut Street, Suite 200, Philadelphia,
PA 19103, or call (800) 810-4145, ext. 5000, or e-mail
special.markets@perseusbooks.com.

10 9 8 7 6 5 4 3 2 1

PROLOGUE

The Republic of Karelia runs from St. Petersburg on the Gulf of Finland all the way north to the Arctic Circle. Half of it is pure forest, the other half mostly water, including sixty thousand lakes, two of which, Ladoga and Onega, are the largest in Europe.

Many of its residents are the descendants of prisoners sent by Stalin in the early 1930s to dig the Belomorsk Canal, the inland water route linking Russian rivers and lakes to the White Sea, on the rare occasions when they are not frozen solid.

Petrozavodsk is the capital of Karelia. It stands in the West of the region. And, like so much of this frigid republic, it has a grim history, having been used for centuries by both czars and Bolsheviks as a place of exile, imprisonment, and torture for political troublemakers, a bastion for Stalin's gulag system of brutal banishment.

In the freezing month of February 2018, Petrozavodsk, ice bound on the shores of the frozen Lososinka River, harbored yet another "troublemaker"—not yet captured, not even identified, but a man whose intentions were in direct opposition to those of the quasi-corrupt and ruthless rulers of Russia.

His name was Nikolai Chirkov. He was a thirty-five-year-old *kapitan leytenant* in the navy of the Russian Federation, identified by the two-and-a-half gold-braid stripes and gold star on the black cloth cuffs of his uniform. In a Western navy, he'd have been a lieutenant commander.

He was a tall, blond, athletic-looking officer, assigned to the Northern Fleet, and serving in the nine-thousand-ton Udalov II Class guided-missile destroyer *Admiral Chabanenko*, currently undergoing minor engineering work in the shipyards of Severodvinsk, nearly four hundred miles northeast on the shores of the White Sea. Icebound like almost everywhere else.

Nikolai's present location was in the downstairs bar of the Hotel Severnaya on Lenin Square. Tonight he was in civilian clothes. Despite the relative warmth of the room, he wore his naval greatcoat, collar upturned as he sipped his fruit-flavored vodka. His back was to the long bar and the barmen. His thick fur hat rested on the table beside the armchair. Outside it was snowing like hell.

Six tables away sat a swarthy, thickset English businessman, John Carter, whose six-month mission was to come to this chilly Russian outpost as the representative of an enormous Birmingham paint manufacturer. Petrozavodsk, with its endless, windswept waterfront, more than a thousand islands, and seagoing populace, annually uses more gallons of paint than vodka.

Like Nikolai, Carter still wore his heavy, fur-lined overcoat. Like Nikolai, he was not what he seemed. Despite immaculate travel documents and visa, the "Englishman" was an Israeli, real name Rani Ben Adan, a member of the family of the great Israeli general Bren Adan. An ex-IDF Special Forces officer, Rani was a Mossad field agent and one of the most dangerous combat practitioners in the world, armed or unarmed.

If the Russian authorities had known his true identity, they'd have shot Rani Ben Adan right there in the hotel, no questions asked. Which was why he always sat with his back to the wall, dark glasses shielding deep brown eyes with pure laser vision. Tucked into his leather belt, in the small of his back, was the standard Israeli Special Forces combat knife.

At 6:30 p.m., Lieutenant Commander Chirkov rose from his chair and headed for the exit. He crossed the hotel foyer and pushed his way through the revolving door. The snow was still falling, but the wind had dropped, and he walked almost silently in his heavy sea boots, heading toward Lake Onega along Marksa Street.

Almost a hundred yards behind him, virtually out of sight, Rani Ben Adan followed. He followed for a distance of five hundred yards before the Russian turned left and used a key to enter a low apartment block. He waited for Rani, and both men joined a young Russian couple in the elevator, before disembarking on the fifth floor.

They did not speak until they were safely inside apartment number 506, a two-bedroom inexpensive residence owned by the Mossad, under the cover of a Russian drama coach at the nearby National Theatre. The coach lived somewhere else when Rani was in town.

This policy of complete separateness was familiar to both men. No one had ever seen them together. They sat far apart at the Severnaya bar, walked alone, and never spoke until they entered number 506.

"Welcome, Mr. Carter," said Nikolai Chirkov.

"Lieutenant Commander," replied Rani, bowing his head and shaking the snow off his fur hat. "It's been too long."

The apartment was warm and comfortably furnished, several cuts above the average Russian city residence. Both men stayed here in complete anonymity whenever they met, but never for more than thirty-six hours. Rani had arrived in the city after eighteen hours on the train from Moscow. It had been a long and tiresome journey, but these are the hazards of the trade endemic to a Mossad spymaster operating in the Russian Republic.

He had recruited Nikolai Chirkov three years earlier, but took no credit for it. The young Russian Naval officer had presented himself personally at the Israeli Embassy on Bolshaya Ordynka Street, south of the Moscow River. There, after a three-day debriefing, he had declared to two Israeli "defense" attachés an undying allegiance to the US government.

Riven as these matters were apt to be by almost atomic suspicion and lack of trust, the men from the Mossad decided to give the Russian a few months' trial as an informant before sharing their prize with the Americans. Even though Mossad and CIA field agents frequently work so closely together, it's not always easy to tell the difference.

Which was precisely where Rani Ben Adan came in. Nikolai Chirkov was placed in his care and would henceforth be "run" by the Moscow-based ex–Israeli Special Forces commando. In the ensuing months, the two men became so close there never seemed a reason to have him reassigned to a US agent where there would be, in any event, a heightened chance of discovery.

This utterly unlikely alliance between Tel Aviv and the Russian Naval officer suited all parties. The Mossad shared with Washington every worthwhile detail of Nikolai's information, but decided against revealing their source, particularly since Nikolai Chirkov was a deeply complicated man, part political thinker, part devoted military commander, Russian to his bootstraps, and absolute traitor to his homeland and its government.

Rani believed Nikolai was a tortured soul. Tutored from an early age by his father, Grigory Ivanov Chirkov, a high-ranking minister in the Department of Foreign Affairs, Nikolai understood more about world trade than most members of the Politburo. He understood with crystalline clarity that Russia was an approximate disaster area without its oil and gas reserves.

He understood too that the oil had to be placed on the world market, especially in America. His father believed the new deepwater tanker base near Murmansk was critical to the nation's survival as an exporting nation. And he could not understand the almost messianic fervor with which the Kremlin sought to antagonize the West, or the childlike way they bridled at everything American. Privately, he thought the Russian administration was probably collectively insane.

Their philosophies, their political compulsions, their disregard for the serious business of making money for the nation, and above all their senseless saber rattling toward their potentially biggest customers struck him as the actions of a confederation of nutcases.

He wanted everything good for his nation. He wanted peace and prosperity. He was devoted to Mother Russia but detested the ignorance of the men who ran the place. He could not understand their support for the plainly unstable Islamic Republic of Iran, with its reckless determination to manufacture nuclear weapons. Of course, the Americans would begin strategic moves to relocate their antiballistic missile system just in case they had to crush a threat from Tehran.

What else would anyone expect the world's most powerful nation to do? But Russia's reaction was always so stridently anti-American—threatening this, threatening that, announcing plans to deploy missiles to the West and South of the country, in readiness to take out the US systems— that it was, in the opinion of Nikolai Chirkov and his venerable father, the ranting of imbeciles.

Did anyone in the modern world really want the fanatical ayatollahs of Iran running around with atom bombs?

Lieutenant Commander Nikolai believed the death knell for modern

Russia would be any kind of a military strike against the United States—a guided missile, a clandestine action against a US facility or embassy, an attack on a US warship or naval base, even deliberate cooperation with Iran in its pugnacious threat to blockade the Strait of Hormuz.

Like many a self-appointed political missionary, he felt he had a pivotal role to play in the devious twenty-first-century game of protecting the people from the ignorance of politicians. Hence the visit to the guarded building behind the high walls in Moscow's Bolshaya Ordynka Street three years ago.

And hence his presence here in this apartment, in snowy Petrozavodsk, meeting with the Mossad spymaster. Rani was, in Nikolai's view, the one man in all of the world who could hold Russia's rulers in check; he had the ear of the CIA in Washington. He could warn the United States and NATO of Russia's erratic intentions. And Rani Ben Adan, a Sabra of the blood, had nothing but respect for the knowledge of Nikolai Chirkov. In three years he'd never been wrong about one single Russian Naval operational plan or program. Both men were, one to the other, priceless.

In fairness, Nikolai's information had never been of a pressing nature. But it had been steady and reliable, especially in data about the construction of new and improved Russian warships and state-of-the-art sonar systems. This latest summons to the diabolically cold North, however, was edged with urgency: a coded text message, transmitted on a cell phone, which had been instantly hurled into the ship's garbage crusher on board the *Admiral Chabanenko*.

1800, FEBRUARY 18

Hotel Bar, Czar Nicholas, Lenin Square

As mass confusion goes, that was more or less as bewildering as it gets. Czar Nicholas II had been dead these hundred years, and there's more Lenin Squares in Russia than snowballs in Siberia. Lieutenant Commander Nikolai laid a mean and mystical trail. Rani knew exactly where to go, what time to be there, and how to travel.

His own training was military to the most infinitesimal degree. Born in Tel Aviv, Rani was only three years old when his mother died during the opening days of the 1973 Yom Kippur War. Along with thousands of other young Israeli women, she had raced to the forbidding slopes of the Golan mountains to join the human chain passing shells and ordnance up to the tank commanders on the heights, as they fought to hurl back the marauding army of Syria.

It was stray mortar that did it, screaming onto the upper escarpment and blasting seventeen Israeli girl soldiers to death. Farther up, Rani's father, Moyshe, fought with the legendary Sayeret Golan Brigade, Israel's elite Special Force commandos.

They made the summit of Mount Hernon by midnight and, after a ferocious battle, raised the flag of Israel on the heights shortly after dawn. More than fifty of their number died up there, including their forward commander, Captain Vinnick, who was mortally wounded in the opening engagement but continued to direct his commandos until they carried his body down the mountain on a stretcher.

With the Syrians flung back, and Israeli tanks charging toward Damascus, they promoted the valorous Lieutenant Moyshe Adan in the field. It was two days more before he discovered his beloved wife, Rebecca, was no more. All this was mere folklore to the young Rani, as was the breathtaking raid on July 4, 1976, when his father's Sayeret landed and stormed Entebbe Airport in Uganda and rescued almost a hundred mostly Jewish hostages.

The operation commander, Lieutenant Colonel Jonathon Netanyahu, the bravest of the brave, last man out of the building, was the only Israeli to die, shot in the back, in the dark, by a Ugandan sniper on the roof. Jonny passed away in the C-130 Hercules on the way home, in the arms of a heartbroken Major Adan. This was folklore written in blood and glory. Rani Ben Adan, to no one's surprise, joined his father's old Sayeret Golan Brigade as soon as he was big enough to lift a machine gun.

He was the youngest Israeli trooper ever to complete the make-or-break fifty-mile initiation march under full packs and rifles. They selected only twelve new Golan commandos from that initial intake of four hundred. When the Israeli Special Forces use the word *elite,* they do not joke.

Rani rose to command rank very swiftly. By the age of twenty-one, he was in an Israeli commando battalion that fought with the Americans in Operation Desert Storm. In the second Gulf War, Operation Iraqi Freedom, Rani commanded one of the most secretive battalions ever formed—Israeli frogmen, fighting alongside the Americans, capturing one of Saddam Hussein's most prized possessions, the huge seventy-foot oil rig that towered above the waters of the Persian Gulf.

This was probably Iraq's darkest night of the war. But the ten US and Israeli troops on top of the rig had to jump for their lives, right on time, to escape the forthcoming naval bombardment. It was a long way down, and two of them just froze. Rani seized a US combat officer and hurled him off the rig, holding his arm as they plummeted ever downward, crashing with shuddering force into the waves.

Rani was knocked senseless. And, in the end, they saved each other, the Israeli kept afloat by one of the finest underwater swimmers in the US Navy, before the young American Zodiac crewmen hauled them both to safety.

Like all military friendships forged on the anvil of imminent death, Rani and his American buddy stayed in touch through the years, joined forever by that unspoken bond of utter trust. You have to be a combat warrior to understand the aching, unforgettable grandeur of such camaraderie.

Rani Ben Adan, now in the frozen heart of the Russian Republic, knew why Lieutenant Commander Nikolai Chirkov wished to talk. If the matter had been nonurgent, or involved a wide-ranging international subject, they would have met in Moscow. Only when the matter involved the United States would they both travel to a secret destination to discuss their business. The Russian Secret Police, masters of the black arts, were twenty times more alert for practitioners of espionage if America was in any way involved.

Rani walked into the kitchen and fired up the kettle, reached for the jar of instant coffee, and took a brand-new carton of milk from the refrigerator. There were no servants, orderlies, batmen, or butlers in this game. The watchword was a relentless *FYEO* (for your eyes only), and that included ears, brains, and, if necessary, hearts. He made the coffee very black and tipped a shot of vodka into both mugs, mostly because he suspected a few exposed nerves might need steadying after Nikolai had spoken.

When he returned to the living room, he finally shed his topcoat and sat down on the deep and luxurious sofa. "Okay, old comrade, lay it on me," he said in almost flawless Russian. "To what do I owe this long and arduous journey across the barren wastes of your homeland?"

Nikolai took a sip of his vodka/coffee. "Rani," he said, "you are going to be very cross with me. But not as cross as you would be if I had not contacted you. You see, I do not know what is going on. But I do know something very important is taking place right here in Karelia. And it involves action against the United States of America—in my view, very serious action. I stumbled upon it by mistake, and the security is beyond fireproof."

Rani stayed very cool. He crossed his legs, rebalancing his drink. "Aha," he said. "I know you would not be here if there was nothing."

"Indeed not," replied the Russian officer. "It's more trouble for me to get here from Severodvinsk than it is for you."

"But less dangerous," replied Rani.

"Perhaps so, but what I am about to reveal could get me shot."

"They'd shoot me for breathing if they knew who I was," said Rani.

Both men smiled. And then Lieutenant Commander Chirkov stated, "Rani, I think the Russian government is planning a controlled strike against the USA. Not Armageddon, but a fast missile attack, small and aimed at some kind of critical building in the US defense system."

"You mean like the goddamned Pentagon? . . ."

"Hell, no. You couldn't fire an air rifle at that without being gunned down . . . I mean something far less significant. But extremely important."

"Okay, Nikolai let's go through our usual procedures. Walk me through the phases of your gathered intelligence—like always."

"No problem. And while I speak, remember these truths—the collapse of the old Soviet Union had nothing to do with Russian disarmament. That never happened. They still have thousands of land-based ICBMs, sea launched, air launched, and God knows what else, all armed and targeted at the USA—as if anyone's ever heard of anything that stupid . . . "

"Is security still bad?"

"Christ, yes. Hopeless. A determined terrorist could get hold of a nuclear missile from Russia in about ten minutes, if he had the cash. The Moscow politicians turn a blind eye to the most rampant proliferation of missile technology this world has ever seen. From any angle, Russia's ballistic arsenal is the single biggest strategic threat to the United States of America."

"Washington knows that."

"Well, why aren't they kicking up a fuss about the new Topol-M SS-27? There's almost fifty of them already onstream, and the sonofabitch has a seven-thousand-mile range with a reported 550-kilo ton-yield nuclear warhead. They've got the sea-based version nearly ready—it's supposed to be near impossible to detect, capable of evasive maneuvers at hypersonic speed, with carbon shielding to combat US space-based lasers.

"The whole idea is to penetrate the US missile defenses. And they probably could do it. At least that's what I hear. In the old days, any Russian missile could be crippled by a US nuclear warhead within seven miles of its trajectory. Not anymore. Not with this little bastard. Darn thing's electromagnetic fireproof."

"Okay, let's get right to the point. What are you telling me?"

"Rani, I intercepted an Internet communication confirming the imminent arrival of two missile scientists from North Korea—specialists in medium-range rockets. Russia has given help in developing North Korea's newest missile, modeled on standard Russian SS-N-6 submarine-launched technology.

"I don't know when these characters are coming, or where they're going. But I do know the navy has requested assistance from the state rocket center. That's the V. P. Makeyev Design Bureau—they're the main manufacturers of both land-based and sub-launched ballistics . . . "

"Is that Viktor's crowd?"

"Absolutely. Viktor Petrovitch Makeyev, father of Russia's modern guided-missile industry. They named the fucking factory after him . . . "

"Yeah," interjected Rani. "Probably for inventing SCUD-B—the one Saddam slammed into Tel Aviv over and over in 1991, murdering my people . . . blasting women and children to hell . . . for no reason. One of my closest friends lost his mother and sister . . . Don't mention that bastard's name to me, unless you must."

"I must," replied Nikolai, "because that manufacturing plant is heavily involved in whatever's going on. They're located in the southern Urals, town called Miass, about six hundred miles east of Moscow. And everything fits—the postal code, 456300; the telephone dial code, +7-3513. For all I know, the Koreans are going straight to the factory. But I got something else—maybe in error. It sounded like they were all going to a monastery."

"A WHAT!"

"A monastery. The Russian word's *monastyr*. It could have been a misprint, I guess."

"You got a copy of the download?"

"Are you crazy? Someone traces that to my computer, I'm a dead man."

"I like you better alive, Nikki. No downloads."

"Anyway, then I intercept a new communiqué, usual way, through the ship's link to the Russian Navy's most classified network. It's secure and mostly protected, but if someone gets in, they cannot trace. They can find out and change the codes, but they are not able to locate the hackers. Anyway, I'm cleared for access, because of my work in upgraded sonars."

"Okay. What did you find out?"

"I discovered the Iranians are right in the middle of the plot."

"Surprise, surprise. What happens now? We got the Muslim ayatollahs in the monastery with the Christians, right? All praying for the same atom bomb."

"You joke, Rani, but I'm telling you this is very serious. There are three Iranian scientists coming into Russia this week—the guys who built and refined those Shahab-3 and Shahab-4 medium-range ballistic missiles. They used a lot of Russian technology and systems. But they became experts in their own right."

"I remember, Nikki, the Shahab missile uproar, right after the second Gulf War. Didn't the United States sanction those guys—Russian, Belarusian, and Ukrainian companies—for exporting nuclear stuff to Iran?"

"Correct. The Russians also helped other rogue states, Iraq and Syria, with nuclear programs."

"Well, what's this new Russian-Korean-Iranian *parlez* all about?"

"I picked up a shred of conversation between the naval high command and the Kremlin. Took me hours to get in using a cell phone I had to destroy. But one phrase was clear in my mind: *We'll show these Yankee bastards who's really in charge—kick their nuclear football right out of the stadium, huh?*"

"Pretty fucking droll, for a Russian," muttered Rani. "The Slavic literal mind gone into overdrive."

"I'm sure there's a lot more happening than I know so far. The strange thing is, I have a distinct suspicion that whatever's happening is centered up here in the North. My own ship, the *Admiral Chabanenko,* seems to be involved, moored there on the White Sea."

"I thought you said the action was in the Makeyev factory in the Urals."

"No monastery there, right?"

"I should forget that bit, Nikki. It's obviously a mistake. I just can't see a medium-range missile in the cloisters."

Lieutenant Commander Chirkov permitted himself a deep chuckle. Both men took a couple more swigs of the vodka/coffee.

"Do you have any semblance of a plan?" asked the man from the Mossad.

"Only that I think there is a lot going on, and I seem to have a way to tap into it. I'm returning to my ship tomorrow, and I suggest you stay right here. There's no point going back to Moscow when we may already be in a major Russian black-ops area."

"Okay. I'll park myself here till the end of the week. I have my laptop and two cell phones. Will I see you again this trip?"

"I aim to be back on Friday."

"We got anything to eat?"

"Yup. I bought a few cartons of Tex-Mex at the Sanches Saloon. I've had it before, tacos and stuff. It's good. We can zap it in the microwave. I've got a guy coming in tomorrow to clean up. So you'd better be gone by 0900 and check into the Severnaya, soon as I've shipped out. You're fine there as long as you're not with me."

FOUR DAYS LATER
_____

Severnaya Hotel Bar
Petrozavodsk

Rani Ben Adan had been waiting for almost four hours since the appointed time of 1600. It was now almost eight o'clock, and the bar was beginning to thin out as people headed to the dining room. The Mossad agent was worried. Nikolai had never been late. And when people fail to turn up in the espionage trade, it often means something very sinister, like exposure, capture, or death—even all three.

Rani debated making a break for it, checking out of the hotel, and catching the midnight express back to Moscow. Every time someone entered the room, he half-expected FSB (old KGB) officers direct from the Lubyanka to come striding up to him and demand to see his passport and travel documents.

He did not look suspicious. Rani knew that. His dark complexion and trimmed black hair gave him the look of a Georgian or even someone from southern Ukraine. His clothes were purchased in the West, and his English passport was immaculate. He carried business cards and other literature pertaining to the paint industry in a slim black briefcase. The "factory" that "employed" him as head salesman had an excellent website, which included phone numbers. A check call by the Russian police seeking John Carter's credentials would be routed directly to special operators in the basement of the Israeli Embassy in London.

While Rani sat sipping coffee, Nikolai Chirkov was on one of those interminable Russian train journeys, almost 450 miles from the station at Archangel, all along the southern coast of the White Sea, and then north for the train change at Belomorsk. That's only about halfway, and he still had another 200 miles to go.

The train was late from Belomorsk, and the weather was terrible. When Nikolai finally entered the downstairs bar at the hotel, at almost eight thirty, having run four blocks and a thousand yards through the snow from the Petrozavodsk train station, he was mightily relieved to see Rani still waiting patiently on the far side of the room, his back to the wall.

They went through their deliberate routines, taking care to show no sign of recognition of one another. A half hour later they were back in apartment number 506, where a traditional Karelian meat casserole with potatoes and cheese was awaiting them. Whoever had prepared it was long gone.

Rani scooped the meal onto a couple of plates and zapped them both in the microwave. There was some Russian bread in the warming oven and chilled vodka in the refrigerator. As Russian dinners go, it was pretty good, especially for Nikolai, who'd had nothing all day. Rani had never grown accustomed to the tough meat in what he called "this gastronomic wasteland" and thought constantly of his favorite Tel Aviv steak house on Allenby Street and the fabulous fresh fruits grown in Israel's northern farmlands, especially the pale, sweet peaches of Hebron.

But right now he had bigger matters on his mind. "Okay, Nikki, what's new?" he asked.

"Plenty," replied the Russian officer. "The navy is planning a hit on the USA. I'm not sure of the exact target, because they have not yet tested the missile. I found out it has a range of twenty-five hundred kilometers, and they expect it to be perfected within a few months. They called the missile men in from North Korea and Iran because right now they're having problems with the navigation systems."

"God knows why they want advice from the Koreans," said Rani. "The last four long-range rockets they tested ended up on the beach about a mile and a half from where they were fired. If these ex-Soviets think they can hit any target in the USA without being identified, they're even more stupid than we think they are. The US nuclear defensive shield is light-years ahead of them."

"There's more. The missile scientists from North Korea and Iran have arrived, and they're staying right here in Russia. A new laboratory has been set up somewhere, and so far as I can tell they're working on a new, slimmed-down rocket with a nuclear warhead and a guidance system that makes it almost impossible to track. It's land based, by the way."

"Any idea where they plan to launch from?" said Rani. "If it's land based, it's got a hell of a way to go from anywhere in Russia."

"How about a launch from Canada or Central America?"

"Well, Canada's out of the question. But I guess there might be some banana republic willing to turn its back on a local rocket launch in return for a few pesos. It's very interesting, Nikki, but right now it's pretty vague . . . a phantom strike on the USA, launch site unknown, target unknown, with a missile not yet invented."

"I know that's what it sounds like, Rani. But I have spent half my life in the Russian Navy—and I know there's something big happening, and it's gathering steam. The sheer volume of communiqués would surprise you. I picked up that word *monastyr* again, three times. It could be anywhere, but the foreign scientists are already in it, wherever the hell it is."

"Nikki, I'm not denigrating your information in any way. In fact, I believe there's something highly unusual going on. But I hope you agree with me . . . I can't blow the whistle yet, or even alert anyone. We have nothing nailed down, and the key characters are apparently hiding behind the altar. But I'm confident you'll get some clarity in the near future."

"It's there, and I will most certainly find it," replied the Russian officer. "These poor, misguided politicians will be the death of my country. If they launch a strike on the United States, it could be the funeral for all our economic ambitions. That Uncle Sam. He does not forgive. He'll hit back."

"The Japanese made that mistake at Pearl Harbor," replied Rani. "But right now all we can do is watch and wait. If you've nothing else, I'll take the midnight train back to Moscow. You'd better leave in the morning."

"And my money?"

"Wired into the account in Geneva today, direct from the National Bank in Tel Aviv. One hundred thousand US dollars."

Lieutenant Commander Nikolai Chirkov smiled. "A small price to save the world," he said quietly.

1

Atlantic Ocean, Northwest of Kinlochbervie, Scotland

Captain Gordon MacLeash glanced again at the speedometer of the twenty-five-hundred-ton fishing trawler *Misty*, currently shouldering her way out of a big sea east of the Hebridean islands. The hard nor'wester was right on his bow, and he should have been slowing, but the boat was going five knots quicker than the rev counter told him.

The red-bearded Captain Gordon was baffled. The twelve-cylinder 300-hp Caterpillar diesel engine was set to make eight knots through these choppy waters where the Minch Channel batters its way into the North Atlantic, the Isle of Lewis to port, Sutherland to starboard.

"What the hell's the matter with this damn thing?" he muttered, mindful that his trawl net was full of several tons of fish that the crew was about to haul inboard. This should have slowed him down even more. But right now *Misty* had developed a mind of her own. The speedometer read eleven knots and climbing.

Gordon MacLeash throttled back, and nothing happened. The big, blue trawler, with about a thousand prime codfish in the huge net deep beneath the surface, was making almost twelve knots through the water, straight into a headwind.

"ROY!" he yelled, summoning his first mate to the bridge. *"AND BRING CHARLIE!"*

The two Scottish fishermen came charging into the wheelhouse, alarmed by the anxiety in the skipper's voice. Charlie McLeod, a descendant of five generations of fishermen from the Isle of Skye, did not need his boss to tell him the problem; he looked at the revs and could sense the high speed, none of which made sense.

He cut the engine instantly. Still the boat drove forward.

"Jesus Christ!" he shouted. *"Either there's a fucking great whale hooked up in the net and still swimming, or we've been hooked by a submarine."*

"GET THE AX! SEVER THE WARPS!" bellowed MacLeash. *"ROY, CUT THAT TRAWL NET FREE!"*

"WHAT ABOUT THE FISH?"

"The hell with the fish—I'm talking life and death here!"

Even as Gordon MacLeash spoke, every one of the six-man crew of the *Misty* felt the almost-unknown sensation of the stern hauling downward, only slightly, a matter of inches, but very definitely.

"I CAN'T FIND THE AX!" shouted Roy.

"YOU'D BETTER FIND IT!" screamed the skipper. *"It's always in the same locker!"*

"Not tonight," replied the young crewman. *"It's missing."*

"It's gotta be here somewhere—FIND IT!"

"Oh, Jesus Christ, I used it in the engine room. I must have left it there." Charlie McLeod raced for the companionway and practically jumped down the nine steps. He was back with the big woodsman's blade in moments. And he swung with all of his force at the rigid tautness of the trawl net's warps. It cut, but not deep enough. The massively strong cable held, and Charlie swung again.

Once more it held, and now the boat was plainly stern down, the angry sea breaking over the aft deck in the dark and windblown night. Charlie stood up to his knees in green water, and again he swung, but the boat lurched downward and he missed altogether, embedding the ax deep in the gunwale. It hit with such force the stern light went out.

"HIT IT AGAIN! FOR CHRIST'S SAKE, HIT IT AGAIN! . . . "

Misty lurched again, and her bow rose up. The aft deck was under water. A terrible force was dragging her forward and down, stern first, into seventy-five fathoms of ocean. Roy Morrison, in desperation, grabbed a spanner to unhook the bolts that secured the warps to the boat. Charlie swung his final killer blow, which cut the line.

The net broke free and released the pressure. But it was too late. Too late to launch the small lifeboat, too late to inflate the safety dinghy, too late to live. The waves were crashing over the stern; Charlie McLeod was swept overboard. The water reached the wheelhouse and cascaded in through the open door. The entire engine room was underwater.

In a violent sea, the trawler *Misty* went down fast, heavily waterlogged, stern first, position 58.40N 06.25W, thirty miles northeast of the very tip of the Hebridean islands, the Butt of Lewis.

Not one of the six-man crew had time to jump clear of the boat. *Misty* took them all with her, brave Scottish fishermen, plying that most dangerous of trades in these most dangerous of waters. Captain MacLeash and his crew would not be the last to be lost in this turbulent ocean wilderness. But the vanishing *Misty* made the front pages of every newspaper in Great Britain, because at first there was hope. The men were vastly experienced, and there were no bodies.

Air-sea rescue teams were out searching by midday, when it was plainly obvious that *Misty* was indeed missing. But these northern waters were freezing, and survival was impossible. All day long the rescue helicopters clattered back and forth across the ocean. Other fishing boats arrived in the area to help. Trawlers from Spain and Iceland came steaming to the rescue, but, by nightfall, there had been not one sign of life. Not even a half-sunk lifeboat.

At 1900 the coast guard called it off. The six men, all residents of the little fishing port of Kinlochbervie, were declared "lost at sea, for reasons unknown." And finally, after a twelve-hour wait, huddled on the dockside of the fishing harbor, the families of the fishermen returned home.

This was the worst fishing-boat crisis in Kinlochbervie for more than a half century. All of *Misty*'s crew members were well known in the village. Roy Morrison was the coach of the town's excellent soccer team, Charlie McLeod played the organ at the local church, and Gordon MacLeash, only thirty-four, was a member of the Parish Council. The three younger men were all bred and born in the picturesque seaport where their parents still lived. Fergus Anderson, eighteen, was a son of the local garage owner.

By midnight, the dockside area was busy again, as reporters, television crews, and photographers virtually besieged the village. Mostly the heartbroken families refused to say anything, but the distraught parents of young Anderson handed out photographs of their lost son. Mrs. Annie MacLeash was in shock, and the Morrisons were staying with relatives.

It was not just local publications that turned up. In addition to the regulars from the *Inverness Courier,* the *Ullapool News,* and the *West Highland Free Press,* the big London publications had staff arriving in droves, news reporters, feature writers, and star cameramen trying to re-create the sadness of the fishing port for their readers in the faraway southern metropolis.

Front pages were held, television news bulletins rearranged, stories and pictures e-mailed, clichés collected, and purple prose transmitted:

TRAWLER DISASTER
DEVASTATES SCOTTISH
SEAPORT

SIX TRAWLERMEN DROWNED
IN MIDNIGHT DISASTER

THE TRAWLER *MISTY*
VANISHES WITH ALL HANDS

SIX SCOTTISH FISHERMEN LOST
IN MIDNIGHT DISASTER AT SEA

This was a story that had what's known in the trade as "legs." It could run for several days, while first the basic family heartbreak was recounted, then the sadness of the entire village for its terrible loss, and then the funeral services conducted in steady winter rain—*Even the skies wept for the lost sons of Kinlochbervie.*

Then the "deep" moral issues, praising the men who go down to the sea in ships—*"Oh, hear us when we cry to Thee, for those in peril on the sea."* And the massive "debt of gratitude" the nation owes such men, every time we enjoy a plate of fish and chips.

Finally, the media arrived en masse at the inquest, grilling the coast guard, interrogating the Kinlochbervie harbormaster, quoting the Royal Navy and other local fishermen, and recording the total bewilderment. The newsmen were waiting for someone to come up with something inflammatory. For someone to release a clue that might answer the "Why, Oh, Why?" headlines, which had now been running for the better part of three days.

The clue finally arrived at around lunchtime on Wednesday, March 29, when Stornoway's coast guard chief, Donald Macrae, mentioned to the *London Daily Mail* the possibility of a Royal Navy submarine catching the trawl net and dragging the *Misty* to her grave.

"It's happened before, laddie," he told the young journalist. "And it will probably happen again, although modern sonar makes it fairly unlikely. Unless the submarine is going at one hell of a lick, couple of hundred feet below the surface, and rams right into the cod net. Chances of that must be hundreds to one."

"Don't the fishing fleets request Royal Navy clearance before they start dragging in these waters?" he asked.

"Certainly," said the coast guard chief. "And Gordon MacLeash did so. It was the first thing we checked. He was told the Royal Navy had no submarines in the area last week. And so far as I know, there are no other nations would dream of exercising in those British waters. The Minch is greatly respected . . . "

"What the hell's the Minch?" asked the reporter.

"Christ, laddie, have you no geography or navigation knowledge? The Minch is the famous stretch of water separating the Hebridean isles from the Scottish mainland. It's very deep, almost forty miles across in places. It has rugged headlands on both sides, and the navy considers it the best submarine training water in Europe."

"Well, why don't other European nations want to use it as well?"

"Not many of them have much of a submarine fleet. Hell, the Royal Navy hardly has any fast-attack submarines these days. No nation likes trespassing in foreign waters with submarines, because they're quite likely to be sunk and never heard from again. Submariners don't like foreigners."

"So that more or less rules out the submarine theory, right?" he replied. "Never any foreigners. And no Brits last week."

"On the surface, so to speak," said Chief Macrae, "it does rule it out. But navies do not feel obliged to speak the truth at all times. I very much doubt the first sea lord would be anxious to announce one of his underwater boats had just hooked up and drowned six Scottish fishermen. With the state-of-the-art sonar our submarines use, they would, and should, have detected a two-and-a-half-thousand-ton dragger on the surface above them."

"Not much use to me, then," said the reporter. "I can't just write a story suggesting the navy was responsible when they have categorically stated there was no RN submarine in the area all week."

"No, laddie. Ye canna do that. But I believe something either hit or otherwise sank the *Misty*. She was a very powerful boat, and there was no skipper better than Gordon MacLeash. I just won't accept she somehow sprang a leak and went down or capsized. The sea was rough, but not that rough. We had a force-five gale warning, but Gordon's been through seas like that dozens of times. *Misty*'s last known position was in very deep water. It doesn't make sense."

"Do you object if I speak to the navy again?"

"Absolutely not. Ask them if they're certain. Ask them if they have any other theories. They won't tell you, but you might learn something."

And so the media juggernaut rolled on. For a couple of days, they loved the idea of a submarine dragging down the trawler, and they scoured their files and libraries for other instances when this may have happened. They found around twenty. By the time they'd gotten through with it, you'd have thought all Royal Navy submarines were sharks in disguise, in search of prey.

But the journalists grew tired of the somewhat hollow "story" and inevitably moved on to new pastures, more important "stories," like the latest dresses various members of the royal family wore to some film premiere.

This did not apply, however, to the coast guard station at Stornoway out on Battery Point above the harbor. It was another damp, blustery, cold day. The Ullapool-Stornoway ferry was an hour late, fighting a strong tide, headwind, and heavy seas. The sea was gray. The skies were gray, and the main street seemed gray.

Donald Macrae, with his craggy, windblown face and deep-sea blue eyes, had other tasks. Indeed, he had never heard anything even remotely connected with glamour that in any way affected rugged little Stornoway, except that Donald Trump's mother, Mary MacLeod, had been born four miles down the road from the coast guard station in the village of Tong.

Right now he was staring at a radar screen, checking the progress of the ferry. *And* there had been an emergency call from an Icelandic trawler in some trouble ten miles north of the island. *And* there were six journalists lined up to speak to him on various matters from current sea conditions to the still-warm issue of the *Misty*.

But the most important call was from London. His assistant had shouted the name: "Lieutenant Commander Wenton . . . line 4 . . . "

This was the Royal Navy calling from RN Submarine Fleet HQ, Northwood, west of London. And when they called, it mattered. Chief Macrae muttered, "I wonder what the hell they want . . . " Deep down, though, he knew full well.

Everyone had played down the sinking of the trawler as much as possible to protect the families from unnecessary grief and intrusion. But the professionals did not buy it. Officers in the Navy Department and in the fleet were looking askance at the various accounts of the lost fishing boat. The coast guard knew something sinister had happened.

Fishing communities all over the Western Isles did not accept for one split second that Gordon MacLeash had drowned by accident. Something had happened out there. Everyone wanted answers, but they were damned if they were going to give any to outsiders. Especially journalists.

Chief Macrae grasped the full dimension of the situation when Lieutenant Commander Wenton immediately put him through to a rear admiral who wasted no time with recaps. A cheerful, informal man who had reached his high office because everyone liked him, Rear Admiral John Young, the Royal Navy's submarine flag officer, came straight to the point. "Donald," he said, "did Captain MacLeash make any form of emergency radio contact with any coast guard station on either side of the Minch Channel? And if not, why not?"

Chief Macrae, who, in his youth, had served time as a gunnery officer in a Royal Navy frigate, was fifty-two years old now, but he had not forgotten how to speak to admirals.

"Negative to the first, sir," he replied. "No contact whatsoever. I do not know why that should be so."

The admiral was succinct in his answer: "There's only one possible reason, and it's a very simple one—Captain MacLeash did not have time. I have dismissed the possibility of some kind of suicide pact."

Chief Macrae smiled to himself . . . *Bloody admirals, they're all the same . . . sardonic wee bastards.*

"I agree, sir," he said. "He did not have time. That trawler met catastrophe and death in a matter of seconds, not minutes. Otherwise, we'd have found a body. Not one of the six-man crew had time to jump over-board and take his chances in the water. On a night like that, they were surely wearing life vests, even if the men weren't clipped on."

"My thoughts entirely," said Admiral Young, "which somewhat nar-rows our list of possibilities. Either someone hit her with a torpedo, a mis-sile, or an iron bomb, all of which are hugely unlikely, despite fitting our sinking profile, or something simply dragged the *Misty* under."

"Aye, sir. No other viable solution. And I also write off the torpedo-missile theory."

"So what dragged her down? That's a mystery because even a big minke whale, twenty-five feet long, is not that powerful. It would have taken four of them, working in harness, to haul a trawler to the bottom of the North Atlantic. So what, Donald, does that leave?"

"Only a submarine, sir."

"And we did not have one within five hundred miles of *Misty*'s last known position."

"So where does that leave us, sir?" asked Donald.

"Looking for someone else's submarine," answered the rear admiral. "Which, by the way, we are unlikely to locate."

"Anything particular you want us to deal with?"

"I just want your crews to keep the keenest possible watch for foreign submarines. Particularly Russian. Because we believe they may have been prowling around last week. We actually believe that with their suspect sonar, they may have blundered into Gordon MacLeash's trawler and taken it down."

"I suppose we would nae dare to ask them?" suggested Donald Macrae.

"We'd dare all right, Donald. In fact, we already did. But they refused even to speak to us, and when the Russian Navy refuses to come to the telephone, or to answer an e-mail, you know the lies are just too pro-found, even for them."

Donald Macrae permitted himself a significant chuckle.

"Anyway, keep us posted. Anything shows up, sound the alert as fast as possible."

"You can count on that, sir. We'll be watching."

Admiral Young's car was awaiting him. He left his office immediately and headed directly to the Ministry of Defense in Whitehall, central London, for a meeting with the first sea lord. Again, the subject was obvious: a Scottish trawler had been hauled underwater by a submarine off the Western Isles. It was not a British submarine. There were no RN submarines within hundreds of miles.

The question for both of these experienced naval commanders was: whose damn submarine was it? Their shared opinion was that none of the European Union members would have dreamed of running north through the Minch Channel without requesting permission and giving times and dates for the voyage: certainly not France or Spain, nor any of the Low Countries, or the Scandinavians.

The Minch, in fact, separates the northwest highlands of Scotland from the long offshore crescent of the northern Hebrides. To the south, it is known as the Little Minch and separates the Isle of Skye from the Hebridean islands of North and South Uist and Benbecula. These are intense submarine waters, deep and lonely, used by the Royal Navy's underwater service for generations, both for training and for the workup of new boats.

No other national navy would think of intruding in these waters, except, perhaps, the Russians. And even they'd be pretty darn careful. In fact, they'd probably have touched base with Fleet HQ. As for other neighboring submarine fleets, as Rear Admiral Young told the boss, "Foreign submarines are pretty thin on the ground these days." He then presented the following list:

France—Barracuda Class in new-build program, none yet operational. Six Rubis Class, thirty years old, and four big fourteen-thousand-ton SLBM boats, Triomphant Class, based in Brest. Hardly seen out since *Triomphant* crashed into HMS *Vanguard* by mistake in the eastern Atlantic nine years ago.

Spain—Only one operational. Believed in Cadiz.

Netherlands—Four submarines, one in Somalia, failing to catch pirates, two in refit, and one somewhere in the western Baltic.

Belgium—None.

Germany—A half dozen small eighteen-hundred-ton diesel-electrics. Eight-knots max, flat to the boards. Germans haunted by the memory of deeply hated U-boat fleets in World War II. Nervous to leave Bremen.

Denmark—None.

Norway—Six very small thousand-ton Ula Class diesels. Comparable
  to the Mersey ferry. Not even remote suspects.
Sweden—Three slow diesel-electrics. Ten knots on the surface. Friends
  with US Navy, may even make components. Not suspects.

"Which leaves just our old friends the Bears, correct?" said the first sea
lord. "Though what the hell they're doing in the Minch Channel, in the
middle of the night, knowing they might meet up with a Royal Navy attack submarine patrolling its home waters . . . Well, God knows."

"With due respect, sir, I don't think anyone is bothered about meeting
an RN submarine in home waters. We hardly have any of them operational. And everyone knows it. Nearly forty years of defense cuts have seen
to that."

The Royal Navy boss was silent, his expression a mixture of irritation
and sadness. He knew as well as anyone that the legendary iron shield
the navy provided for Great Britain was no more. There was no aircraft-
carrier strike force. The navy personnel numbers were down to twenty-
five thousand. At times there were no British warships patrolling the
home waters of this island nation, which, quite frankly, he regarded as
the daftest situation even Britain's savagely discredited politicians could
come up with.

The old Trafalgar Class submarines were on their last legs, and the new
Astute Class boats, which had been given formal government clearance,
were running badly behind their production schedule. The truth was the
government did not care about lateness, because that usually meant delays
in the payment schedule, and they really liked that.

The sea lord loved the Astute Class submarines, with their sensational Rolls-Royce PWR2 (Core H) reactors, which never needed renewing
throughout the entire life of the submarine. Only a shortage of food would
bring to the surface these underwater masterpieces of marine engineering.

To a former submarine commanding officer, which the first sea lord
was, the Astute boats were simply things of gigantic beauty, 30 percent
larger than any other Royal Navy attack submarine had ever been, with
one heck of a wallop—thirty-eight weapons on board, guided torpedoes,
plus submerged-launch guided missiles with a range of twelve hundred
miles capable of knocking down a North African mosque from a parking
spot in the English Channel.

That kind of weaponry unfailingly warmed the heart of any seagoing commander, but this first sea lord was more than that. He was a navy politician, expert in the infighting of Westminster, a master at arguing the case for bigger budgets.

And while, after three years, he was severely bloodied by the slings and arrows of half-witted politicians, he was triumphant in his endless campaign to preserve the new Astute Class submarines. They were late, yes, but still under construction at $1.2 billion each. Of the five scheduled hulls, two of them were floating, with three chugging along toward completion in the great dry docks of BAE, Barrow-in-Furness (British Aerospace Electronic Systems, the world's largest defense manufacturing conglomerate).

"You'd think they'd get it, wouldn't you?" mused the boss. "BAE has six thousand people working on the Astute program alone. Imagine the shattering loss if some government canceled it. Imagine the desolation in Barrow, the thousands of skilled men who would go on welfare programs: the loss of confidence, the smashing of morale.

"Not to mention the irreparable loss to the town—because it would quickly become a place that had lost its soul. It does not take long for engineers to forget, for sons of engineers to look elsewhere for work, for an entire industry with a sensational history simply to let their skills slip away. And when that happens, it's damned hard to get them back.

"And pretty soon it's all gone, a great British shipbuilding center no longer in the front line of its profession, highly skilled young British scientists, shipwrights, and engineers looking for work in Korea or Japan. For me it's heartbreaking every time I have to go and fight those numbskull ministers, whose only talent is making fucking speeches. Jesus Christ, it makes me madder than hell."

"As you know, sir, you're preaching to the converted here. But I do wish we had those next three Astutes. I know no one seems to care, but we all love this country, and it gives me the creeps to think of us being virtually defenseless for the first time in centuries.

"We should have three fast-attack boats patrolling home waters at all times, whatever the cost. That way I think we'd both sleep a lot better. Especially with the fucking Russians somehow creeping around our most private seaways. Because they bloody well are, and now it's obvious."

The first sea lord was pensive. He leaned back in his chair and said, "I wonder what they want, or, more pertinently, what they are looking for. I mean, they know the danger of prowling around other people's coastlines. I just cannot understand why they would take those risks, unless they were looking for something specific."

"Beats me," said the submarine flag officer. "But they have been claiming in recent months to have advanced electronic surveillance able to hack into cell phones and even shore-based computer systems. I'd guess they're on the hunt for anything that might prove useful.

"Unlike our own government, they appear to understand that navy personnel get paid anyway, so you may as well put them to work doing something useful. And in our trade, sir, any private information is likely to be precious. Especially electronic."

"I suppose fuel's the only cost involved in running attack submarines around Europe's national waters," muttered the navy's highest-ranked officer. "And these days the Russians have tons of that."

"It still seems pretty bloody weird," said Admiral Young. "Wandering around the Hebrides in the middle of the night and getting tangled up with the stupid cod nets."

"Unless they had a secret objective and believed the answer was somewhere in the Minch Channel."

"You think they might have some idea how seriously the Americans are planning to reactivate SOSUS?"

"I'm not sure even we know that," replied the first sea lord. "But the Russkies might know something. And they might be out there trying to find out a lot more."

"Of course, they always hated it," said Admiral Young. "For years it was the bane of their lives. Just imagine—they couldn't move any big, secret submarine even hundreds of feet below the surface without getting caught. SOSUS virtually negated their whole underwater ballistic missile threat, and they never had a clue about ours, not the Vanguards, and certainly not Polaris."

The subject the two admirals now touched upon, SOSUS, was the simple acronym for Sound Surveillance System, the American deepwater, long-range detection network, consisting of high-gain, long, fixed arrays set in cavernous ocean basins and connected to shore-based listening stations. It was the secret weapon of undersea surveillance, an almost infallible early-warning asset against Soviet ballistic missile submarines.

It utilized deep, horizontal sound channels far below the surface, which allowed low-frequency noise to travel across huge distances with extraordinary effectiveness. It started in quite a small way, but ended up as a multibillion-dollar network of hydrophone arrays, mounted on the seafloor throughout the oceans.

One of the key areas for SOSUS was the somewhat sinister and stormy section of the North Atlantic known as the GIUK Gap—a navy acronym for Greenland-Iceland-UK—the choke point of the Atlantic through which every Russian submarine from the Northern Fleet shipyards must pass if it wishes to steam south into the Western world. Of course, ships of any nationality are at liberty to sail wherever they wish in international waters. But submarines are big, furtive creatures, whose watchword is *secrecy*. They dislike being observed or located, especially Russian ones.

The GIUK Gap has been crisscrossed for years by US hydrophonic wires. No one can even enter those turbulent waters without the Americans knowing more or less what the crew had for breakfast. The system was invented during World War II and underwent a half century of improvements since right until the Cold War was over.

During that time, SOSUS had some amazing triumphs: the electronic trap caught a Soviet submarine as it crossed the gap as early as 1962. Then it located the USS *Thresher* after it sank off Nantucket in the same year. It was SOSUS that loudly flagged the lurking Soviet Foxtrot Class submarine during the Cuban missile crisis—the fabled *Charlie-20*.

And it found USS *Scorpion* after she went down off the Azores six years later. For years SOSUS was top secret, but such was its efficiency that it became almost common knowledge among Western allies. Most people, however, did not understand how it worked, and when the Russian empire caved in, the Americans declassified the system, at which point it slipped quietly into the background.

But it was still there. And so were many of its listening stations, situated mostly on remote coastal sites. There was one on a steep headland on the southwest coast of Iceland, NAVFAC (Naval Facility) Kevlavic; one on the storm-swept coast of Halifax, Nova Scotia; another in Barbados, where they nailed *Charlie-20*.

No one has ever officially revealed the full extent of the SOSUS network, but suffice it to say Great Britain played its part. There was an important US listening station in the remote military station of St. Mawgan,

North Cornwall, with a straight-line radar shot to the North Atlantic, and another on high ground above the Pembrokeshire coast at Brawdy, overlooking the Irish Sea.

The Scottish stations were always secret, but the Americans had them placed in the best possible locations on the west coast, especially where the unseen beams of SOSUS protected the joint US-UK submarine lanes, which led to the Firth of Clyde and the home moorings of the Polaris, and Trident ballistic missile bases at Faslane and Holy Loch. The underwater system could provide early warning too against intruders into the deepwater submarine training grounds of the Western Isles.

There is no record of any Soviet or Russian submarine ever entering those hallowed waters. At least there wasn't during all the years those hardeyed US Naval personnel manned the SOSUS listening stations. But things went very quiet as the 1990s progressed and the twentieth century turned into the twenty-first.

The glinting eye of America's longtime secret weapon became inevitably dimmer. Defense cuts meant many of the listening stations on the eastern Atlantic were surreptitiously closed down. Great Britain's Royal Navy took an endless beating at the hands of political accountants who believed the Silent Service was largely unnecessary.

Aside from the times when there were no warships to patrol the UK's island waters, most of the time there were only a half-dozen warships available for deployment. The start of the second decade of the twenty-first century was approximately the time when the world once more became seriously restless.

And, as ever, in the thick of the ensuing turmoil stood Russia, growing ever richer on the back of its Siberian oil fields and moving steadily backward in its state reliance on a secret police force to keep the populace in order.

Internationally, too, Russia appeared to have learned nothing, standing by the ayatollahs of Iran, supporting the terrorists of Hezbollah and Hamas, inflaming the Israelis, all to the anger of the United States.

Of course, Russia had its own reasons to behave as it did, the close ties to Tehran being one of them. Despite the Kremlin's endless games with smoke and mirrors, one of its absolutely definite modern programs was to raise its aged navy from the dead.

The first sea lord had a brief outline on his desk that showed a rising

Russian underwater force, comprising major improvements to the three near-moribund twenty-six-thousand-ton leviathans of the deep, the Typhoon strategic-missile boats, now once more going to sea. There were plans for a total of eight of the supermodern Borey Class intercontinental missile boats and nine improved Deltas.

The new Yasen Class attack submarines were back on the starting blocks, and ten of the Akula Class hunter-killers were being either refitted or newly built. Sierras, Viktors, and a couple of dozen patrol subs, mostly Kilo Class, were also being brought forward.

The surface fleet was also undergoing a twenty-first-century facelift. After years of decline, there was a major modernization program for Russia's old aircraft carrier the *Admiral Kuznetsev,* the Kirov Class battle cruiser *Pyotr Velikiy* was in refit, and there were multimillion-dollar expenditures earmarked for three eleven-thousand-ton cruisers.

Programs to produce some of the world's most modern frigates and corvettes were well under way. A careful study showed Russia's naval export orders to China were becoming very strong, and they plainly planned to finance their own new, sleek navy with profits from the Chinese.

"And here we sit," growled the first sea lord, "just about the first stop on any southward movement of the Russian battle fleet, and we're on our last legs as a seagoing nation. It was not so long ago the Soviets were scared shitless of meeting Royal Navy warships and submarines on the high seas. It was not so long ago we quietly put one of their noisy old Oscars on the bottom of the Atlantic for straying too close to our shores. *And now look at us! Jesus Christ!*"

"It's also pretty bloody tragic we can't help the Americans much with the reopening of SOSUS," said Admiral Young. "If important data are located in the British listening stations, we just don't have the equipment here to intercept, or intervene, or even to conduct real surveillance. We've lost our teeth."

"It's not that the Americans don't trust us," replied the navy boss. "But they can't really count on us. After all these years, we've just faded out of the picture. The United States knows we're loyal, and they know we're competent. We've just been disarmed by our own side. We can't really help anyone anymore."

"Pretty damn depressing, eh?" said Admiral Young.

"Yes, but the trawler men may not have died for nothing . . . It's about time I had a chat with the US Navy Department in Washington—just to alert them we think the Russians are on the move in more ways than one."

"That'll wake 'em up, sir. They get extremely spooked about renegade submarines, as you know."

Office of the Director
National Security Agency
Fort Meade, Maryland

Captain James Ramshawe, the Australian-sounding but American-born intelligence chief at the National Security Agency, shared his old title of director these days. Since the Chinese and the Russians were suspected of hacking into the Internet systems of the Pentagon, Boeing, Mitsubishi, and other military installations in the early part of the century, a new appointment had been made—commander of cyber warfare.

The immensely popular former West Point lecturer General Harlan Forster had been selected, and while the Pentagon had always hoped the top man at Fort Meade could stand tall over all branches of the secretive spy center—interception, code breaking, cryptology, and cyber warfare— that had proved too difficult.

By 2018 the duties had been separated. Captain Ramshawe, the eavesdropping and spying maestro whose operation intercepted almost 2 billion signals a day, retained his old office on the eighth floor of building OPS 2B, and he retained his old areas of responsibility.

A brand-new headquarters was constructed on the same floor for General Forster, whose duties were wide ranging but essentially defensive. He was provided with a gigantic staff, a brand-new operational building, and a brief to provide the United States, and all of its military and military-related organizations, with protection from any foreign "invaders" trying to launch attacks through cyberspace—hacking, that is, into America's most secret computer systems, listening to the most secretive messages, discovering the innermost workings of the greatest superpower the world has ever known. With every passing year of the twenty-first century, the march of the cyberspace vandals had become more intense.

And one ultramodern objective on an ancient military adage had jumped into focus: to dismantle your enemy, you must dismantle his intelligence, communications, and forward planning. Where once this meant erecting electronic radar pylons on the coast of the English Channel to foil the advance of Hitler's air armadas, now it meant something similar, but about four zillion times faster and ten zillion times sneakier.

And despite the colossal volume of information bombarding the electronics of the National Security Agency, the word *submarine* never failed to cause every nerve in Ramshawe's personal early-warning system to vibrate.

The encrypted message from the Pentagon this morning was pretty lucid: *RN suspects Russian sub operational in Western Isles off the Hebrides— almost certainly responsible for that Scottish trawler vanishing with six crewmen last week. Dragged her down by accident.*

Question: What was Russian sub doing there in the first place? Meeting tomorrow here possible? Assistant to CNO, Navy Dept.

"Good question," Ramshawe muttered to himself. "What the hell were they doing creeping about the Hebridean islands in the middle of the friggin' night?" He'd read about the tragedy days ago, and he'd logged it in his computer to revisit.

It was a constant theme. After years of having their backs rammed against the harbor wall in search of funds, the Russians were nowadays much more solvent. The days were past when dockyards shut down because the government could not pay the electric bills, never mind the workers' wages.

Today the Russian Navy was going to sea and refitting their old boats, which had lain idle for so long. They were conducting sea trials, recruiting to the navy again. Once more slipping into that tiresome old Soviet mind-set, that half-paranoid compulsion to spy on those they perceived as enemies.

"Crazy but dangerous" was Ramshawe's considered opinion of Russians, as he worked his way through the secrets of the world's great military powers. He gave little thought to the stupendous effort made by the United States of America to keep private every single electron in its arsenal and to spend literally billions and billions of dollars annually finding out precisely what everyone else was up to.

It was odd, but the United States even spied on itself. The signal, which had gone to the US Navy's chief of naval operations on the fourth floor of the Pentagon, had already been intercepted by the NSA. Jimmy's staff had read it before the Navy Department even saw it.

Jimmy himself had immediately logged its importance, the clue being that it came from the first sea lord, the former submarine commander who was slated to become Great Britain's next ambassador to Washington. Captain Ramshawe knew that too, before they even told the queen of England. Which slotted in perfectly with the US military chief's desire for "full-spectrum dominance"—land, sea, air, space, information, and presumably the celestial world above.

No wonder his workplace was known in the trade as Crypto City, or, less reverently, "No Such Agency," staffed by thirty-two thousand people who denied its very existence.

Britain's hands-on national security partner made its headquarters on 350 acres of Maryland, fifteen miles southwest of Baltimore, its location being very deliberately clear of Washington, in case the nation's capital was ever hit by a nuclear bomb. The political hub of the United States was judged dispensable in an emergency. The National Security Agency was not.

Which is why Crypto City, with its thirty-two miles of roads and twenty thousand parking spaces, represents one of the largest municipalities in the state of Maryland but does not appear on any map.

The specially constructed exit ramp off the southbound lane of the Baltimore-Washington Parkway is hidden from view by cunningly constructed earth hills and thick trees. Once off the ramp, the employees hit a labyrinth of barbed-wire fences, razor wire, huge rocks placed close together, and heavy concrete barriers.

No one can see the motion detectors and the hydraulically raised antitruck devices. Closed-circuit television cameras sweep the entire area, and there are warnings everywhere forbidding anyone from taking photographs or notes.

Commandos in black paramilitary uniforms armed with submachine guns are seconds away from any area. America's National Security Agency is probably the only place in the entire United States where an illegal intruder could, more or less, be shot on sight. The NSA's supremely trained SWAT teams are an all-seeing force, with information fed into their own HQ from one hundred fixed watch posts manned by the agency's own police officers.

Behind this ironclad, merciless security lies a strange and surreal place, like nowhere else on earth, where the greatest body of international military secrets ever assembled by any organization in history is contained. Since the dawn of the twenty-first century, Crypto City has also become the world's preeminent and most advanced spying operation.

There are almost seventy buildings, offices, laboratories, warehouses, factories, and living quarters. The people who work here do so in absolute secrecy. Most of them will live and die without ever mentioning even to relatives, wives, and children precisely what they do on behalf of the nation.

Every aspect of life inside the perimeters is coded. Even the Christmas party is called something else. No one living anywhere near the vast Fort Meade complex has the slightest idea what happens inside the barricades. When the Maryland county officials placed a rubber cord on the road to try to ascertain the volume of traffic entering the complex, armed guards appeared as if by magic and sliced it into several pieces. Crypto City answers to no one.

The OPS 2B building is a vast rectangle of black glass, and, inside, it contains a huge black granite wall. The great seal of the National Security Agency, twelve feet by eight feet, is carved into the stone, and above, written in solid-gold inlay, are the words *They Served in Silence.* Below, in the eight columns of the Memorial Wall, are the names of almost 160 military and civilian personnel who gave their lives in the line of duty.

The black granite is polished so workers can see their own reflections. This is deliberate, designed to remind them starkly that they too serve, in silence, precisely the same cause as those who died for it.

Personnel usually confirm they work for the Department of Defense. But no one is on record specifying their various areas of collecting and analyzing foreign communications and intelligence. Inside those razor-wire barriers, among the greatest collection of supercomputers the world has ever seen (or, rather, not seen), there are state-of-the-art systems, designed to raise the roof at the slightest suggestion of a cyberspace hacker trying to gain entry to any US government system.

Nothing in Crypto City is quite what it seems. The outside structures actually shield the real building, which lies inside the shell, protected by thick bulletproof material, six inches of sound-numbing space with a copper screen designed to lock in every possible sound, conversation, and signal.

That copper screen is constructed around almost every area of the entire complex, rendering the whole place acoustically impregnable. The aim of America's NSA is to vacuum up every last particle of electronic information on this planet, and far beyond, but not to allow one single atom of its own sounds to escape to the outside world.

There are reputed to be a thousand listening stations on US territory worldwide, almost every one of them hooked up to Fort Meade. But there are also six hundred similar US operations all over the world.

The main one stands in the UK, on the Royal Air Force Base at Menwith Hill Station, in the Yorkshire Dales near Harrogate, approximately two hundred miles north from where Admiral John Young sat with the first sea lord in Admiralty Arch, which guards London's Trafalgar Square.

Like Fort Meade, Menwith Hill irritates the life out of know-nothing left-wingers. The station stands in 545 acres of North Yorkshire and is the largest electronic listening station on earth. On its campus there are more than twenty-three giant Radomes, which look like enormous golf balls. Hidden inside these space-age Titleists are antennas intercepting the world's naval and military signals.

The Menwith Hill technicians form the world's largest spy base, with a vast special area confined to Russia. The entire operation is run by the National Security Agency under the command of the US Air Force's 421st. Airbase Group.

Menwith Hill, nestling in the folds of the Yorkshire Dales, has the strongest possible links not only to the US satellites but also to Buckley, the secretive 3,300-acre USAF base in Colorado, home of the 460th Space Wing, the missile-warning, space-tracking front line of the US military. In the Rocky Mountains near Denver, it, too, displays the gigantic golf balls, linking it to England's Yorkshire Dales.

The Menwith Hill listening station has been under US control since 1954, when the Western world was under the control of the former Supreme Allied Commander in Europe, General Dwight D. Eisenhower, and Sir Winston Churchill, neither of whom believed the Russians could be trusted a yard.

The Texas-born president ensured the Menwith Hill Station answered to no American law, and Churchill absolved it from British law. Also, to this day, it appears on no maps, the largest town in England subjected to this omission. Those, by the way, are three more issues that seriously brass off the lefties.

Occasionally, there are futile protests about the very existence of the mysterious Yorkshire spy base, silent behind its razor-wire fences. Questions are asked and answers demanded concerning this little patch of the United States among some of northern England's most glorious countryside. But no answers have ever been forthcoming. Its secrets are still classified. Less is known about Menwith Hill than any other military operation in Europe.

Menwith Hill, self-sufficient, even owning its own excellent elementary and high school for the offspring of its personnel, continues—unaccountable, beyond the law, sensationally efficient, and the eavesdropping jewel in the crown of America's National Security Agency in faraway Maryland, south of the Mason-Dixon line.

When the signal came in, alerting US Intelligence about the probability of a Russian submarine in the Minch Channel, a thousand lines of communication began to function. And none more urgent than the one from Crypto City to North Yorkshire placing everyone on high alert for an underwater escape, a Russian submarine not heading north through the GIUK Gap but going home, probably south into the Med and steaming on to one of the Black Sea submarine bases—perhaps with sensitive UK-US intelligence gathered up on its electronic intercept antenna.

A northward escape was out of the question at this time of year, the port of Murmansk being more or less ice bound and the White Sea frozen solid. But the sub-chasing networks of the West were stirring themselves for the first time in many years, really since the Cold War ended, and all because of a lost trawler.

There were some hefty ripples left on the surface of the North Atlantic after the *Misty* descended into the endless silence of her grave. And they stretched from Stornoway to central London, from the Admiralty to Fort Meade, and then to North Yorkshire and on to the Rocky Mountains. Whoever authorized that Russian ship into British waters would need a convincing explanation because many hitherto relaxed military minds were now on a very definite high alert.

ONE WEEK LATER

Israeli Embassy
Bolshaya Ordynka Street, Moscow

Rani Ben Adan had been recalled south to Moscow from the frozen lands of the Karelian Republic at just a few hours' notice. He sat in a windowless, white-walled basement, in the presence of two "cultural attachés." They were lean, hard men with swarthy skin, dark stubble, and wary eyes. Neither wore jackets, which left their shoulder holsters exposed on their white shirts. Loaded service revolvers were there for anyone to see.

Rani knew them both well. They were ex–Israeli Air Force colonels whose identities were still classified even within the Mossad, where they now served. Rani knew them only as Andre and Marc. He also knew that Andre was a fighter pilot in the 2006 Lebanon War and almost certainly commanded the air strike when the IAF destroyed fifty-nine Iranian-supplied missile launchers in thirty-four minutes.

Both men had, apparently, taken part the following September in Operation Orchard when the IAF launched a massive strike on a Syrian nuclear reactor and completely destroyed it. Marc's background was even more obscure than Andre's, but word was, inside the Mossad, he had commanded a top secret raid on a convoy of trucks in Sudan in January 2009. It had been headed for Egypt with weapons for Gaza until Marc's air wing obliterated it.

But the strongest unconfirmed rumor was that both men had played command roles in the devastating October 2016 Israeli destruction of Iran's main nuclear plants in the mountains of Qom and Natanz—a military attack that has never been even remotely explained, or indeed been a cause for any nation to become unduly irate. Except perhaps for Russia, whose fabled S-300 missile defensive system was comprehensively shattered by the Israeli fighter-bombers.

In the ensuing couple of years, Russia, while seething, had never uttered one public statement about the strike against their friends the ayatollahs. And Israel had neither confirmed nor denied any involvement in the action. The entire subject of Iran's nuclear capability had gone extremely quiet, and the government in Tehran had ceased to mention the exalted possibility of "wiping Israel off the map."

Yet the significance of that sensational raid—whoever conducted it—had continued into the year 2018. The Mossad's absolute dislike of Russia had never abated—not since the old Soviet Union warhorses armed and then rearmed the Syrians for their murderous bombardment of the Holy Land in the 1973 Yom Kippur War.

In private moments, Andre and Marc had answered a few questions for Rani Ben Adan, who was himself, of course, one of the most revered Israeli battle commanders ever to serve. In the sound-swept security of that very basement operations room, deep in the heart of Moscow, Marc had reasoned, "If I can't trust the decorated Special Forces nephew of Bren Adan, then who is there in this world for me?"

He remembered the assault on Iran's nuclear factories as if it had been yesterday. He remembered the bright moon in the small hours of Thursday, October 6, 2016—the date chosen to mark the forty-third anniversary of the infamous October day when Egypt's Third Army stormed across the Suez Canal and attacked the Israeli nation at prayer.

He remembered the words of the Israeli commanders as the pilots prepared to embark their lethal long-range, heavy-payload fighter-bombers for the journey to Iran: *Tonight you must remember who we are and the endless threats we face. You must attack with all of your courage—because in the end no one will help us. Tonight, as ever, we fight alone—the nation of Israel counts on you alone. Please, God, go with you.*

There were tears in Marc's eyes when he recalled the scene, the howl of the jet engines as Israel's air wings climbed into the night skies—the F-15 Strike Eagles and heavily modified F-161 Sufas with their unprecedented long-range capability and supreme radar tracking for ground targets. The runway lights were glinting on the bright-blue Star of David painted in white circles on each aircraft's wing.

He remembered leading the first attack formation as they hurtled west down the runway, out over the dark waters of the Med, and then banked hard right, back over Israeli territory, before opening the afterburners and flying high and fast over the Golan Heights and across sleeping Syria.

Colonel Andre had led the second wing of sixteen fighter-bombers, completing the thirty-two-aircraft armada, which represented the cream of the world's largest air force outside of the United States. Bringing up the rear were two slower and separate observer aircraft, plus four of Israel's brand-new squadron of Lockheed Martin F35B stealth and Joint Strike Fighters, with their instant VTOL (vertical takeoff and landing) ability.

These were headed for Iran specifically to rescue downed Israeli pilots, as the only fast fighter jet that can land and take off without requiring a runway of any kind. The brand-new, dull-gray *Lightning II* could operate anywhere, including a mountainside or a desert.

Both fighter wings, racing high above the Syrian desert, were tried and tested over the 850-mile distance to the prime Iranian nuclear sites at

Qom and Natanz, each of them situated on the eastern edge of the Zagros Mountains, both of them "dug in" deep, beneath the steep hillsides.

All thirty-two of the Israeli fighter-bombers carried the nuclear-capable Jericho IIB missile as part of its long-range heavy payload. No one has ever admitted whether the warheads were nuclear. Every Israeli pilot was aware of the difficulties they faced. Over the nuclear-enrichment plant of Natanz, they were after the mountain lair that contained a reputed three thousand centrifuges, the huge spinners that hurl the heavy isotopes to the outer edge of the uranium hunk.

This is the facility that caused almost outright war with the United Nations Security Council, whose members considered Natanz likely to be the first Iranian "factory" to develop a full-blooded nuclear explosion—an atomic bomb, that is.

The other target was located thirty miles north of the sacred Shiite city of Qom, where the late Ayatollah Khomeini studied theology, philosophy, and law for fifteen years. Qom is home to the holy gold-domed Astate Shrine and also to a brand-new batch of three thousand Russian-made centrifuges, earmarked to spin relentlessly for several years while Iran settles down to the ignoble art of universal atom-bomb production.

The government of Israel had for years watched helplessly while the world griped and moaned about this clear and wicked defiance of the nonproliferation treaties. And two irrefutable facts slowly became obvious: no one was going to do anything about it, except to apply mostly ineffective sanctions, and Iran threatened no one, except Israel, *to wipe them off the face of the earth.*

Thus, the words of a nameless Israel Air Force lieutenant general were finally heeded on that historic October night in 2016: *There's only one thing worse than attacking Iran, and that's not to attack it.*

Marc and Andre sat silently for a few moments, ruminating on their corner of Israeli history. "We flew very high over the desert," said Marc, "and refueled from our own tankers in Iraqi airspace. Basically, it was a straight shot from there, flying south of Baghdad, directly to the Zagros Mountains.

"We did not expect to run into antiaircraft activity before we got there, and there was none. But once the Zagros Mountains began to slope east, away from us, at first light on that Thursday morning, we were ready to face heavy antiaircraft fire from the Russian missile defense system. So we stayed at high altitude until the force split over the high peaks of the Zagros.

"My wing was to hit the Qom target, and I picked up the railroad that I knew ran up to Arak and then to the holy city. Right there I swerved north and immediately came under attack from the city defenses, which must have been newly installed because of the nuclear factory. One of my pilots was hit and crashed head-on into the mountain. But we kept going, until the underground factory was specially pinpointed on our radar.

"I loosed off my first Jericho II and saw it slam into the mountain. Still under fire, I turned tight and raced back in at supersonic speed, sending two bombs directly into the crater. I saw them both detonate, big bunker busters—looked like they split the mountain in two. My guys were pounding the same crater over and over, just as we had been instructed, and by now, even at five thousand feet, you could hardly see anything for the dust and smoke.

"Suddenly, there was an unbelievable explosion, a white-hot flash, and then a mushroom cloud like those photos of Hiroshima. The whole aircraft shook and shuddered, and I knew it was not about to get much better than that. I gave just one order: *That's it, guys. We're going home.*

"I guessed three of our aircraft were down, but only one had hit the mountain head-on. The other two had a chance, and we had the VTOLs high over the mountains ready to come in after we'd cleared the datum."

"How did the others get on, over at Natanz?" asked Rani.

"A bit better than Marc's wing," replied Andre.

"How come?"

"We think that while Natanz was for many years the prime place of Iran's nuclear enrichment, the huge halls, which contained the centrifuges, were nearer ground level. When the Iranians constructed them, the whole world was not against them.

"It was only in the last three or four years before we hit them that they realized Natanz was vulnerable. And it was so damned difficult to get deeper into that mountain, they more or less started over, rebuilding at Qom. And right there they had a chance to get much deeper.

"We knew that before we started the bombers might have to go in time and time again at Qom. Marc's the best commander in the IAF and the bravest . . . That's why he led them. If anyone could do it, we all knew it would be Marc. My task was much easier. Natanz was less protected. Happily, we had the maestro at Qom . . . "

"Shut up, Andre," said Marc, "and get us some coffee." And then to Rani, "Don't believe what he says. I just did what anyone in our strike force could do . . . "

"Bullshit," said Andre, as he headed for the in-house embassy phone. "He's some kind of genius in that F-161—that's why he nailed the crater with the final killer delivery. It was his fourth attack . . . and he flew past three missiles and intense antiaircraft fire to make it . . . His plane was hit twice . . . God knows how he's still alive . . . It was a sensational piece of flying . . . Don't listen to him. He's a lying little fighter pilot."

By this time all three of them were laughing, and Rani said, "Yes, I believe you, Andre. He is a lying little pilot. I once saw a picture of him with the little red ribbon pinned on his uniform. Even I never thought they gave it to him for his birthday!"

"The Medal of Courage," muttered Andre. "Guess why."

"Will you guys shut up?" said Marc. "This is embarrassing . . . "

"He will. I won't," chuckled Rani. "I have just one more question. How did you guys get through the Russian missile defense . . . that S-300 ground-to-air missile shield? Christ, how many hundreds of semistealth cruise missiles can it track? Can't it take on ten intruders at a time with those mobile intercept batteries?"

"We learned how to neutralize it, that's all," said Andre, smiling.

"Yes, but how? Even now the Russians go on about its success rate at protecting their allies."

"Well, for a start, it's nowhere near as good as the American systems that we have," said Marc. "And we discovered that some years ago."

"Yes, but how did you learn?" asked Rani again. "Was it intelligence, stuff from guys like us working in Russia?"

"Hell, no. We conducted a couple of long exercises against the Greek Air Force; spent days fighting it out with lasers above the island of Crete. We can never tell you how we did it; that's classified. But if you check the map, you'll see Crete is about the same distance from Tel Aviv as Tehran.

"That gave us hands-on experience of the journey, the high-altitude refuel, and the time we needed to circumvent that defense system. We demonstrated to ourselves that an 850-mile distance could be negotiated, and we could fight, beat the S-300, and still get home."

"And I guess it worked."

"Almost," replied Marc. "We lost two of our best guys at Qom and four at Natanz. I'd say that plant was more prepared than Qom, because they'd been working at it for longer. Their factory was not so deep underground, but their missile men were a bit sharper. Don't listen to this clown, Andre, telling you they had an easier mission."

Coffee arrived, accompanied by a tray of small Russian blinis with caviar, and all three men were thoughtful.

Rani spoke first. "Do you think Iran might be preparing some terrible revenge against us?"

"Can't say," replied Marc. "I doubt it. We apparently scared them to death. Whatever they try, we're ready. And if they did launch anything against us, I can tell you it would be the last thing they ever did."

"Well, gentlemen," said Rani, "perhaps you might tell me why I've been summoned back to Moscow."

"On the face of it, this might not seem so important," said Colonel Andre, "but there are a lot of people very interested in a certain subject. And you are known to have the best contacts inside the Russian Navy."

"Aha," replied Rani. "So what's new?"

"Quite a lot these days, mostly involving the continued and improving state of the Russian fleet."

"No argument there," added Rani. "They are on the move. For the first time in maybe three decades, they can afford to set sail."

"However," said Marc, "there is one specific problem that has come to light: the sinking of a Scottish fishing boat out near the Hebrides. What do you know about it?"

"Nothing, except what I heard on the BBC. And I did catch a glimpse of something on the Internet, in one of the newspapers."

"Royal Navy Intelligence believes that fishing trawler was dragged under by a cruising Russian submarine."

"In the Hebrides!"

"Exactly. It seems to us half the world wants to know what the hell it was doing there, which is proving a bit tricky since no one saw it, no one heard it, and the Russians are saying they haven't the slightest idea what everyone's talking about."

"Sounds like a certainty," said Rani. "How did you guys hear?"

"Urgent communiqué direct from HQ. The Americans are already involved. Fort Meade is on the case, practically an open line to London. It's just that it's been so long since the US Navy was chasing submarines through the GIUK Gap."

"And occasionally sinking them, from what I understand," added Rani.

"Precisely so."

"And now it may be starting again. London thinks that submarine was in British territorial waters. It must have been spying on something. The Americans are trying to get SOSUS up and running again, and they are furious the Russkies might be watching them while their guard's down."

"Wouldn't be like Uncle Sam to stop paying attention."

"No, but there's a big fucking difference between paying attention and being on high alert. The Yankees do not like what they're hearing.

"You have been asked here to participate in the discussion. And of course to help us come up with a plan to get inside the Russian Navy's high command, find out precisely what they are up to."

"Okay," said Rani Ben Adan. "I do have a very useful Russian Naval officer, and, curiously, he is convinced they're currently up to something serious. He has a lot of clues, but no hard facts. But he's good, very good. And we pay him well. I'll get to him soonest. I suppose no one's got much idea what precisely it is we're looking for, submarine-wise?"

"Not really," said Marc. "But since the Northern Fleet's pretty well frozen in right now, it probably came from the Black Sea. Right now it's probably chugging home through the Med, and then, on the surface, up through the Bosporus.

"Apparently, it hauled a twenty-five-hundred-ton trawler backward to the bottom of the North Atlantic, so I'd say we're trying to find a very big Russian nuclear boat, probably one of those twin-shafted Oscar IIs, eighteen thousand tons dived. They're a northern boat, but they've been in the Med, and a couple of them were in the Black Sea a year ago."

"And what do we do if we find it?" asked Andre. "Check with the captain about whether he's been running day trips around the Western Isles?"

"Well," said Marc, "the Americans could say they formally logged the boat through the Strait of Gibraltar and that it's the only underwater boat on this planet that could possibly have been involved with the trawler incident."

"I wouldn't do that if I were them," said Rani. "Because that may be precisely what the Russians want to hear."

2

Kyle of Lochalsh, Scotland

Angus Moncrief had worked on the waterfront all of his life. He was forty-eight years old, and he had risen to the significant local position of harbormaster, which made him undisputed master of the busy fishing port of Kyle of Lochalsh, across the channel from the Isle of Skye.

Angus had his own harbor launch, provided by the community, and it enabled him to move easily around the great highland lochs that surrounded his thriving little parish. Moorings, hurricane buoys, jetty space for fishing boats, visiting yachts, tugs, and, occasionally, Royal Navy ships were his stock in trade.

No ship's master or commander either entered or left the harbor of Kyle of Lochalsh without being carefully recorded in Angus Moncrief's monthly logbook. He and his wife, Mary, lived in a sturdy four-bedroom nineteenth-century town house overlooking the harbor, and his office was four hundred yards away, down on the dock.

There had been a deep sense of local continuity for fifteen years, since he was first appointed harbormaster, in succession to his grandfather Rory Moncrief, who had held the office for many years until after World War II

29

and was still remembered by many locals. Angus was perhaps not as popular as his grandpa, being a very serious, somewhat stern Scotsman. He was a teetotaler and wary of those who took a dram of highland malt whisky, especially sea captains.

But he was an excellent keeper of the commercial harbor of Lochalsh, very quick with weather reports, a maestro with the ship-to-shore radios or cell phones, helpful to visiting ships and to local fishermen whatever the problem. He had excellent relations with the Royal Navy and was swift to send out a tug to anyone in difficulties. In his many years working on the waterfront, he understood every pitch and yaw of every possible vessel.

Except for this Monday morning, when Robert McCarver, the local milkman, had called him at home just before five thirty to say he'd just seen a *spaceship* out on the water.

Harbormaster Moncrief did not trust McCarver one inch and assumed he was still drunk. But duty was duty. So he drove out onto the 550-yard span of the Skye Bridge with its wondrous views out toward the open ocean. The sun comes up early in Scotland during August, and the long pink rays, which lit up the waters out past the Crowlin Islands, were a sight that always gladdened the heart of the veteran Scottish seaman.

The morning sun had already cast its pale light high over the broad chain of heather-strewn mountains, which stand guard in the East over the great Alsh Loch and its attendant seaways. It cast its rays over the still tidal waters.

It also lit up, on this day, perhaps the most astounding sight Angus had seen in his entire life—jutting maybe twenty feet out of the water, jet-black in color, was a huge, squarish shape, possibly seventy feet long, rounded at the edges, and tapering back like a ski run, to the water level. Directly behind it was a bulbous protuberance.

Angus stopped the car, grabbed his binoculars, and walked swiftly to the seaward rail of the bridge. The Shape was perhaps a thousand yards away north, and through the glasses Angus could see that both in front and behind, there was a black line in the water.

Angus Moncrief had seen enough. Right here, in the middle of the huge sandbank that guards the starboard side of the channel that flows under the bridge, was a very large submarine, hard aground, and releasing a plume of white steam from its nuclear power source.

The huge fin was a revolution to him, slanting away aft toward the large, round cylinder, which Angus knew must house an enormous electronic towed array.

"Mother of God," breathed the harbormaster. "That's got to be close to ten thousand tons, and it's not British . . . not at all British." For a few moments he stood staring, adjusting his eyes to the brightening gleam of the rising sun on the waters.

Angus was no layman when it came to warships. He knew what Royal Navy submarines looked like. He'd been a guest at the Faslane Base on the Gareloch, 120 miles south on the Firth of Clyde. He'd recognize the tall sail on a Royal Navy Trafalgar Class attack submarine anywhere; the mighty Vanguards were a recognizable boat from five miles distant, and the new Astute Class, with their slightly tapering sail, like a medieval watchtower, would never be confusing for Angus Moncrief.

But this was a major attack submarine, and it was neither British nor American, because they would have alerted everyone if they were visiting. Angus knew not many nations owned a submarine of this size. He also knew the sheer weirdness of the bloody thing almost guaranteed it was Russian.

Angus would not be surprised if the navy impounded the damn thing, took command of the ship, towed it to a harbor, probably Faslane, and took the wee bastard apart. Russia was trespassing in sacred waters, trespassing no different from a common thief, and Angus took a very poor view of that, especially on his bailiwick. He sprinted back to his car and gunned it back over the bridge. He hit the harbormaster's office like a runaway train.

It was not yet six o'clock, and there was no one in the harbor. Angus hit the emergency line to Royal Navy HQ, Faslane, and told the duty officer, "This is Harbormaster Angus Moncrief at Kyle of Lochalsh. I wish to speak to the commanding officer, Admiral Ryan, on a matter of extreme urgency . . .

"Of course he knows me, laddie . . . Do you think I would have called him at this time in the bloody morning if it wasn't urgent? Wake him up."

David Ryan was on the line instantly. "Hello, Angus, what's hot . . . "

"Sir, there's a damn great Russian submarine hard aground, right outside the loch, about a thousand yards from the Skye Bridge. The tide's falling. What do you want me to do?"

"Christ, Angus. You sure it's Russian?"

"Nearly, sir. It's not British, and it has to be ten thousand tons, and a lot more than three hundred feet long, with a strange-shaped sail, tapering aft. There's a towed array sticking out of the water 'bout a hundred feet back. Between them, I can just see the pressure hull."

"Any markings, ID numbers?"

"Nossir. Except for a small red-painted area on the front of the sail. Could have been a name. I couldn't see from my angle."

"That's Russian. No one else has anything that big afloat right now, and no one else has that oddball sail. Sounds like one of their new Akula II Class. She's a nuclear boat with cruise missiles, submerge launch. And you're right about her size. She'd displace close to ten thousand tons dived."

"Well, right now, sir, she's not going anywhere. There was no one on the bridge at the top of the sail. I've a Royal Navy tug in harbor right now. I suppose we could pull her off, right before the tide late this afternoon."

"Angus, look. There's going to be hell to pay over this. First off, why didn't we catch her? Second, what the hell was she doing? Third, should we take command of an obvious intruder in our home waters? I'll have to alert navy security, the coast guard, the Admiralty, and God knows who else. Keep your cell switched on. And be prepared for everyone to get very jumpy."

"Sir, should I take one of the harbor boats out and see if I can raise anyone?"

"No. We'll have a team of Royal Marines in there within the hour. I don't want you to go out there unaccompanied."

"Very well, sir. I'll keep watch from a distance and stay in touch."

Admiral Ryan dressed in a hurry and put an instant call through to FPGRM (First Protection Group Royal Marines). This is a five-hundred-strong group organized into three rifle squadrons and a headquarters guard unit, based at HM Naval Base Clyde (Helensburgh) right on the Firth, west of Glasgow at the south end of the Garelock.

The prime task of this highly trained, classified force is to protect nuclear material anywhere in the area from any form of attack. They are fast-reaction specialists, armed to the teeth with heavy-duty emergency transport to any of the highly sensitive Scottish waters. Their core task is to undertake final denial access and to stand by, in support of nuclear convoy protection.

A specially trained team, within the marines' Helensburgh front-line unit, is available 24/7 to be deployed at short notice in support of the Royal Navy, worldwide. Admiral David Ryan's call represented a five-alarm call to action stations.

Almost before he was off the phone, forty-four fully armed Royal Marines were racing out of the door toward an all-weather, heavy-lift Chinook Mark 3 helicopter, its twin rotors splitting the early-morning air across the sprawling Clyde Estuary. Within minutes they were in the air, climbing to five hundred feet and making 140 knots over the densely wooded mountains of Argyll, up toward Kyle of Lochalsh.

Meanwhile, Admiral Ryan was on the phone to headquarters, commander in chief (fleet), at Whale Island, just north of the main Royal Navy Dockyard in Portsmouth. His words would have frozen the heart of a lesser man, but Admiral Mark Rowan, like every other holder of his great naval office, was one of the toughest commanders in the Senior Service.

The full catastrophe flashed before his mind—the humiliation, Parliament, the Admiralty Board, the rage of the short-fused first sea lord, the ranting of the imbecilic tabloids, the *why oh whys,* the public righteousness: "How could this have happened?"

"Mad question," muttered Mark Rowan to no one in particular. *Everyone in the navy or in politics knows precisely why this has happened. Because our beloved ministers cut the navy budget to the bone, and we haven't got enough fucking ships. Next!*

"Sorry, didn't quite catch that, Mark."

"Oh, nothing. I was just getting used to sitting a few hundred yards from Admiral Nelson's flagship and being told we've been fucking invaded by a ten-thousand-ton Russian nuclear boat, and we didn't even know the bastard was there until it came blundering into some godforsaken Scottish loch. And it's somehow going to be my fault."

Despite himself, David Ryan was compelled to laugh. "I'd be laughing a whole hell of a lot more, Mark, if we weren't in the fertilizer up to our eyebrows," he added, by way of mutual encouragement.

"At least we know what will happen," said Admiral Rowan. "The politicians will rush shamelessly for cover behind a smoke screen of lies and evasions about their own roles in this. And then they'll blame the Royal Navy for not spotting this intruder and probably suggest that since we're so utterly useless, they'd better cut our budget again."

"Don't joke, Mark, for Christ's sake. You speak the godawful truth."

"Sound the alarm. Alert everyone who needs to know. I'll speak to the boss, alert Naval Intelligence, and touch base with 30th Commando."

"Right away, sir."

By this time, the sun was up, crowds were beginning to form near the Skye Bridge, and the Royal Navy was moving very fast. Information was now flooding in. Menwith Hill's satellite links in Yorkshire had a clear picture of the Russian boat on the sandbank and could hardly believe their eyes.

There was an emergency signal from the Garrison Headquarters of 30th Marine Commando in Plymouth, the specialist group that controls the ISTAR program (intelligence, surveillance, target acquisition, and reconnaissance). For years the Royal Navy's lord high admiral, the Duke of Edinburgh, served as its captain-general. And this latter office was not a mere honorarium. Prince Philip was heavily and professionally qualified.

Once voted the outstanding naval cadet of his entry at Royal Navy College, Dartmouth, he served as second in command of HMS *Wallace,* a wartime destroyer, at the astoundingly young age of twenty-one. During the Sicily landings in 1943, with the *Wallace* under heavy bombardment, Lieutenant Philip Mountbatten was credited with great brilliance and probably saved the ship.

For years afterward, when he became consort to Queen Elizabeth II, there were Royal Navy admirals who still referred to him as "Commander Mountbatten." And many senior officers continue to believe he would have risen even more quickly to the very top of the Royal Navy if he had been allowed to make a full-time career of it.

The ISTAR operation was quickly into its stride on this Monday morning, and by 0700 had identified the intruder, the ninety-six-hundred-ton Akula II Class attack submarine *Gepard* (hull number K-335), stationed in the Northern Fleet and claimed at various times by the Russians to be the quietest submarine in the world.

This was a formidable boat, double hulled, single shafted, with noise-cancellation techniques all over the hull. She carried heavy antiship missiles, submerged launch and surface, plus forty wire-guided torpedoes. According to ISTAR, she had been on exercises just north of Murmansk and must have slipped through the eastern side of the GIUK Gap in the past few days.

Certainly, she had not been observed, and this may well have been because she had been nowhere near any Royal Navy patrolling submarine. More nerve-racking, she may have been the most stealthy submarine in all the world, which would now cause both the Americans and what remained of the British submarine service some severe headaches.

By now, all the lines of communication were up—Menwith Hill to the National Security Agency in Maryland, the RN Fleet commander to US Navy HQ in Norfolk, Virginia. At 0200, COMSUBLANT's duty officer could hardly believe his eyes: *An Akula II hard aground in a Scottish loch. Now there's an opportunity to take a real hard look at the damn thing.*

Every submarine professional in the US Navy was aware of the claims made on behalf of the new, improved Akulas. Now was a chance to investigate. The US Navy would be urging the Brits to get hold of the *Gepard* and tow it into a dry dock at Faslane for a thorough going over.

Of course, there was the problem of what spying success the Russians had achieved. No one knew how long she'd been snooping around, no one knew what electronic signals she'd picked up and stored, and no one knew what kind of a handle they'd managed on the very latest UK-US sonar systems.

The American duty officer who sat staring at the signal from London considered the Royal Navy would be well within their international rights to grab the *Gepard* and conduct whatever tests they wished on her hull, her propulsion units, her weapons, and her electronics. "Jesus," he muttered.

With the naval intelligence agencies of the Western world now in full cry, it was left to Admiral David Ryan to contact Russian Northern Fleet Headquarters in Severomorsk on the White Sea and inquire formally whether *Gepard* was in fact carrying nuclear weapons. By now the Russian Navy most certainly knew its submarine was aground near the Skye Bridge and was obliged to confirm or deny the existence of nuclear weapons inside the hull.

Despite the relentless way both submarine services stared at each other, relations between them were cordial. The commander of the Northern Fleet did indeed confirm *Gepard* was carrying no nuclear warheads. They also requested permission to allow one of their own warships to come in from the North Atlantic and enter the wide seaway down to the inner sound where the *Gepard* was parked.

He hoped to tow her off the sandbank and obtain permission from the Royal Navy for safe passage back north out of the sound and into open ocean, from where she would proceed under her own steam to Murmansk. This permission was not forthcoming, and Faslane politely informed the Northern Fleet commander it was rather more likely that *Gepard*'s commanding officer would be arrested and charged with spying, after due consultations with the American Navy.

The Russians did not love that. In fact, the Russians were more worried than the Royal Navy, since they worked for a government considerably more vindictive than either London or Washington. Russian submarine COs running headlong onto a Scottish beach would not be well received back home in the tundra. The commanding officer of the *Gepard* stood a fighting chance of returning to Murmansk as a deckhand rather than a decorated naval captain.

With the outrage simmering among the naval agencies involved, the Royal Marines came clattering out of the skies in their enormous Chinook Mark 3. Angus Moncrief had commandeered the local football field about 250 yards north of the harbor for the landing. He instructed the bells of the Free Presbyterian Church of Scotland to ring out across the town to reassure local people, who may have wondered whose side the marines were on.

They split into two fighting forces, the first jogging down to the harbor in readiness to embark a couple of tugs and escort the harbormaster out to the submarine, the second to march to the shore road and secure the area, ensuring people kept well clear of the *Gepard*, and if necessary to close the left-hand lane across the island bridge.

A detachment of a dozen troops was detailed to each of the tugs, one of which, owned by the Royal Navy, was commanded by Major Ronnie Hughes. Angus Moncrief was in the resident Lochalsh vessel, and they cleared the jetty at 0800.

With the great span of the bridge high above them, they swept out of the loch and drove out into the waters of the inner sound and were now within a few hundred yards of the Russian boat. Through his glasses, Angus could see the name *Gepard* on the front of the sail. He could also see its masts—periscope, radar antenna, radio and satellite comms—and there were now two Russian officers on the bridge. The pressure hull itself was also much more visible, since the water had subsided another couple of feet.

It was difficult for either tug to come alongside, given that neither helmsman wished to find himself stuck fast on the same sandbank as the submarine. And so they both stood off, while Angus Moncrief shouted through his bullhorn, requesting anyone who could speak English to open communications.

The Russian captain, distinctive with the thick gold-braid single stripe beneath one star on his sleeve, signaled by waving his arms that no one on board was able to converse with the British military, and he made significant gestures suggesting all he wanted was a good, solid tow off into deeper water. They'd be just fine under their own power.

The marines, however, had thought to bring along a young lieutenant who spoke some Russian, and after a short consultation with his commanding officer he called out that the *Gepard* was regarded as an instrument of war, that it contained very powerful weapons, and that the captain and the rest of the ship's command should regard themselves as under arrest for trespassing in British waters.

Further, they would not be permitted to leave British territorial waters until it was established beyond doubt they had not been spying or making electronic interceptions during the course of their illegal voyage into forbidden areas.

The submarine would be towed off at high tide, but boarding nets would be required for the marines to secure the ship and take over its command. If the captain did not acquiesce, the *Gepard* would be disabled by means of bombs under her propeller and become the property of Her Britannic Majesty's Government. The crew would then be ordered to scram the nuclear reactor and would be escorted out at gunpoint to face trial for spying and espionage.

The marine lieutenant added that it would be simpler for all concerned for the crew to surrender forthwith until the Royal Navy arrived in force to clean up the operation and remove the *Gepard* undamaged to a safe haven, where formal inspections would be carried out.

Major Ronnie Hughes had not the slightest compunction about treating the captain so harshly. If the situation had been reversed, the Russian Navy would have used every trick in the book to humiliate either the British or the Americans and would most certainly have commandeered any nuclear boat that had strayed into their waters.

They would also have given deep consideration into the possibility of never giving it back, and, would, without question, have dismantled it down to the last rivet to discover its secrets. The major was on the line to Admiral Ryan at Faslane, and they were already into damage limitation.

"Ronnie," said the admiral, "the Royal Navy is going to get the blame for this. The politicians will deny that their defense review had anything to do with it, and they'll say the navy was just too slack. I've spoken to Mark Rowan, and we agree the navy's best bet is to be very harsh with the Russians and to get hold of their submarine and gut the bloody thing for information. That means we have to board the ship and place it under formal military arrest."

"Okay, sir. But what about towing it in? Will we have to bring her down to Faslane?"

"That's possible but not definite, because it really would be a huge pain in the ass to tow her all that way—maybe four hundred miles by sea. And it would be pointless to let her make the journey under her own steam— she'd just dive and charge off home five hundred feet below the surface.

"We're not admitting it, but there's probably nothing wrong with her. I'm flying in a dozen senior submarine engineers and sonar technicians. That way we can take a long look at her weapons, confiscate her electronic surveillance records, and dismantle her towed array controls. We'll also get a grip on her acoustic cladding and see if there's anything to learn. Right after that we'll tell her to bugger off."

Major Hughes laughed at the crisp thought processes. "Right-ho, sir," he replied. "And how about hauling her off?"

"That's under control. The *Sutherland* is in the area, on her way north. She'll be with you in around four hours. You get the captain to surrender his ship. If you have to, threaten to blow the propeller off."

"I've done that, sir."

"What did he say?"

"Nothing, sir. But he went a bit pale."

"Well done, Ronnie. Get in control, ASAP."

The incoming *Sutherland,* a four-thousand-ton Duke Class Type-23 guided-missile frigate, had already cleared the great southern peninsula of the Isle of Skye, past the flashing light on the Point of Sleat, off which the ship had made a U-turn.

The frigate had been en route to the northern Hebrides when the signal had come in to make all speed to Lochalsh. Rather than tackle the

150-mile voyage around the huge island, Captain Allan McKeown elected to swerve hard to starboard and steam straight up the sound into what looked like a dead end.

Every Royal Navy captain knew the shortcut through the narrow waters of Kyle Rhea, with its deep channel sloping up to a minimum depth of around 40 feet as it swirls on a strong tidal pull into the Alsh Loch itself, saving more than 120 miles of the journey to the Skye Bridge.

None of the known Royal Naval routes is marked on any chart, and no Dark Blue personnel ever admits they took this surreptitious cut through the mountains to Angus Moncrief's harbor. The conservationists do not like it, inflamed by the possible dangers to otters and other wildlife. But there was a mischievous turn of mind to Captain McKeown, and he swiftly accepted his new orders: *Make all speed to Skye Bridge, Lochalsh . . . Prepare to tow off Russian submarine "Gepard" Akula, ten thousand tons, and hard aground—then get her to Faslane. RN Submarine Command.*

He gunned the big frigate up toward the tight waters of Kyle Rhea, prepared to scatter the otters and possibly break the Scottish all-comers record for the journey.

As Captain McKeown was charging up toward the mountains, the Royal Marine Fleet Protection Group was issuing final orders to the Russian captain. Boarding nets were to be dropped down the hull for a twenty-four-strong party of heavily armed Royal Marines to climb and enter the ship. All Russian small arms were to be surrendered.

At this point the ship's executive officer and first mate were to leave the *Gepard* and climb aboard the Royal Navy berthing tug *Impulse*, normally based on the Clyde but on standby in Kyle Lochalsh for forthcoming submarine training exercises being conducted throughout these Scottish waters.

Angus Moncrief elected to remain on patrol just off the sandbank until slack water at the lowest point of the tide, at around 1100 hours. His local captain would hold the second tug in readiness in case the marines elected to disembark.

At only 0930, there was a clear Mexican standoff. The Russian captain claimed he was awaiting instructions from his naval attaché in the London embassy and from Northern Fleet Headquarters. Major Hughes instructed his lieutenant to inform the captain he was in no position to

accept instructions from anyone except the Royal Navy since the *Gepard*
had been confiscated and was going precisely nowhere until he gave the
order.

And, should that be unclear, he was ordering the fixing of two "sticky"
bombs, one on the shaft and one on the propeller joint. This, he said,
would most certainly blast the *Gepard*'s only method of propulsion asunder and probably blow all seven of her propeller blades into the middle of
the inner sound.

Meanwhile, the marines would happily wait it out, and when the submarine's food ran out, the crew could send up a flare to avoid starvation
and submit to captivity. Better yet, said the major, they could surrender
forthwith and begin the formal process of getting home to Mother Russia.

Within fifteen minutes the captain saw the sense in this and signaled
that boarding nets would now be placed on the hull. His two officers
would submit to British military custody, and the Royal Marines were
welcome to come aboard and take charge of the ship.

Would the major, however, refrain from fixing limpet mines to the propeller shaft? He plainly had decided that Mother Russia would be quite
sufficiently vexed without that particular expense, and there was no sense
in making a diabolical situation into a disaster.

Major Hughes, a thirty-eight-year-old native of South Wales, thus ordered into action the first boarding party of his career to mount a guard
on the foredeck while small arms were surrendered and then take over the
Gepard, waiting for the tide and the arrival by helicopter of Admiral David
Ryan's submariners. The Royal Navy would then assume command for the
journey to Faslane, in cooperation with the Russian captain, whose name
it transpired was Konstantin Tatarinov, originally from the Republic of
Karelia.

No one broached the subject of how the *Gepard* came to be resting on
the starboard-side sandbank in clear sight of the channel markers, green
buoys on her port side and red to starboard. From her grotesque position,
slewed onto the seabed, she looked as if someone had just left the helm
and allowed the submarine to wallow right, at a slow speed, until she
lurched into the shallows and grounded out.

"I have nae idea how anyone in the whole worrrld could have managed
that," grunted Angus Moncrief in his rich Argyll brogue. "They must have
handed over the helm to the ship's cat."

But while everyone in the Skye Bridge area slipped into calm and co-operative mode, there was absolute hell to pay in London and anywhere else where highly placed naval commanders were involved.

The Royal Navy's first sea lord knew he would bear the brunt of the humiliation from on-the-make politicians and faux-indignant newspaper editors. But, being several times more clever than all of them, he had a plan to defuse the heart of the problem.

Laymen could not possibly understand the complexity of running a submarine protection system around a rugged, rough coastline like that of Great Britain. And they certainly could never understand the system of decoys practiced so assiduously by Russians, Americans, and the home team.

In the broadest terms, a submarine nation trying to spy would likely send in a couple of boats to draw off the defenses, while their main vessel slipped away into forbidden waters. The first sea lord proposed to confirm that a Royal Navy submarine had been tracking at least one Russian in the open Atlantic north of the Hebrides.

And the reason no one had locked on the *Gepard?* The Royal Navy did not have another submarine in the area. The Royal Navy did not have a submarine within four hundred miles. The Royal Navy was desperately short of submarines. And there had been holdup after holdup in the new Astute program.

"We do not have the weapons to carry out these elaborate defensive strategies." That would be the drift of the sea lord's reasoning. And that, of course, was a political problem, not naval. Not naval at all. There seemed no reason for the admiral to go public with those opinions. At least not yet.

However, at eleven o'clock on that Monday morning, he spoke to the prime minister along those lines, reminding him that the Americans were only too well aware of Great Britain's naval weaknesses, and so were the Russians. Otherwise, their bloody nuclear submarine would not be sitting on the beach in Scotland.

The prime minister, who had been perfectly cheerful about his ministers saving money and wielding the ax all over the naval budget, was a great deal more concerned about being remembered as the PM who destroyed the Royal Navy. Looming before him was the possible loss of Great Britain's status as one of the permanent members of the United

Nations Security Council. That type of thing can happen when a former great military nation loses its teeth.

Worse yet, there was the onrushing problem of the press release being prepared by the public affairs department at the Ministry of Defense. Frankly, the prime minister did not care one way or another what it said, as long as it did not reflect badly on him, personally. He wanted no mention of navy budgets, which had been slashed by *his* government: nothing like that.

"Prime Minister," the first sea lord had said, rather succinctly, "you can't defend our hundreds of miles of coastal waters if you don't have enough bloody ships. What can I tell you? Your political defense review is nothing of the sort. It's just a way of taking Great Britain's national defense money and spending it on social benefits for bloody foreigners."

The prime minister's blood ran cold. This idiot could bring down the government. "Well, yes, I understand the navy's point of view. Of course I do," he said.

"It's not the navy's point of view. It's mine," retorted the first sea lord. "The navy's point of view is unrepeatable in polite company. And if it's of any interest, the Americans are extremely displeased about everything. You understand the Royal Navy has been their right arm on the eastern side of the Atlantic for decades."

"Well, yes, I do appreciate their obvious disappointment."

"I should have the MOD phrase that press release very carefully indeed, if I were you," said the head of the Royal Navy. "It will be read widely—in Russia, in the United States, and all points between here and the Middle East. I should not let on how shockingly weak we are—not if I were you, that is."

"No. Absolutely. I will not let that happen."

"Very well, sir. Make sure that press release is cleared by the Royal Navy before it goes anywhere. Let's not be seen publicly to drop our guard. Even if we have, hmmm?"

The prime minister replaced the telephone and murmured, "Damned military. Always arrogant . . . with no idea of my problems."

The press release went out to Reuters, on the main international wire service, at noon. It was relatively short and innocuous, utilizing the skills of four defense department writers to remove all vestiges of the five-alarm international uproar it really was. It read:

A Russian Akula Class submarine has run aground off the coast of Scotland. A Royal Navy frigate is on its way to help tow it into deeper water at high tide late this afternoon. The submarine, the *Gepard*, from Russia's Northern Fleet, is believed to have suffered problems with its rudder, and the Russian Navy has expressed its thanks to the Royal Navy for its assistance.

The submarine is currently grounded on a sandbank off the coast of the Isle of Skye, a thousand yards north of the Skye Bridge. A Royal Navy tug is already on the scene. Admiral David Ryan, commanding officer of the Clyde submarine base, stated, "We are considering bringing the *Gepard* south to Faslane for a routine inspection. We will then assist the Russian captain with repairs to his steering system and send her on her way. The crew will be taken off at Faslane while the work is completed. We enjoy extremely cordial relations with the Russian Navy, which will meet all costs connected with the rescue and repairs."

It was interesting but scarcely exciting. Except for about two dozen British news editors, in print, television, and radio, who practically had a collective heart attack at the sight of such drama.

Was it nuclear? they yelled, most of them unaware of the precise difference between nuclear propulsion and nuclear warheads. *Is it full of missiles? Was it spying? How big is it? How long's it been there? Does the navy have it under guard? What happens if it just floats off and makes a break for home? Can we get a team up there from Glasgow in time for the first editions/evening news/one o'clock broadcast?*

It was not quite pandemonium, but it was close. E-mails were flashed to defense correspondents, demanding details of the submarine and whether its nuclear contents, if any, posed an end-of-the-world scenario for all British citizens within a thousand-mile radius.

The very word *nuclear* is inclined to put journalists on high alert, because before them stands a headline, which might suggest the Isle of Skye may become the next Hiroshima. And *nuclear* can be adapted to pair with so many other newspaper-selling catchphrases . . . *Nuclear Disaster, Catastrophe, Crisis, Terror,* or *Panic.* Closely followed by *Evacuation, Emergency, Hospitals on Alert, Radiation, Danger.*

In London there were almost five hundred phone calls to the Ministry of Defense in Whitehall and another two hundred to the Russian Embassy in Kensington Palace Gardens, many of them international inquiries, especially from the United States, despite the time being only a little after seven in the morning. Russian nuclear boats in any form of accident have that effect on the world's media.

There had not been this much excitement since K-141 *Kursk* went down with all hands in sixty fathoms of the icy Barents Sea north of Severomorsk on August 12, 2000. *Kursk,* an eighteen-thousand-ton Oscar Class cruise-missile submarine, blew herself apart with a powerful explosion in the weapons area. This made it marginally more dramatic than the *Gepard,* sagging slightly to starboard on a Scottish sandbank.

But Russian boats lost in remote Russian waters were one thing. Russian nuclear boats on the beach on the shores of the Isle of Skye were quite another. On whatever the scale, the *Gepard* was way out in front because the ramifications, internationally, were so much greater.

On that subject, the media was absolutely correct. In the United States, the National Security Agency was taking a hard and critical look at itself, because the sensational interceptors, which had enabled them to listen to Osama bin Laden talking on his cell phone to his mother in Saudi Arabia, had somehow failed.

They had not, so far, picked up the electronic footprints of that big Russian boat. Neither had any US Navy submarine picked up its engine patterns in those deep Atlantic waters. Neither had the Brits. And, worse yet, SOSUS had apparently not raised even a glimmer of a warning.

The Russian Navy had been claiming for some time that its new or even refitted Akula IIs were the stealthiest submarines ever built. They were, according to senior command in the Northern Fleet, virtually undetectable, and the *Gepard* at this initial stage of the investigation was proving them right.

Captain Ramshawe ordered an exhaustive search of every possible signal logged by SOSUS and every possible sonar sounding that might have involved the *Gepard.* Within hours three results turned up.

The possible engine lines of a distant submarine, with an unusual seven-bladed prop, maybe fifty miles away, had been detected by USS *Toledo* (SSN-769), the seven-thousand-ton fast-attack Los Angeles Class cruise-missile boat, as she patrolled the deep southern reaches of the GIUK Gap.

There had been no POSIDENT, and the mystery submarine, though likely Russian, was not in the gap and showed no signs of heading north. But the time and date fitted, her position in the water fitted, and the Americans decided to mind their own business.

But then SOSUS came through. The shore-based operation was not as heavily staffed as it once was, in the far-lost days of the Cold War. Data were taking longer to process than they once had. But there was still a US listening station on a remote section of the northern highlands coast, and they had certainly picked up *Gepard*'s engine lines as she traversed the outer wires of the undersea surveillance system.

However, at this time she was headed northeast of the Western Isles. For a while, in the electronic shadow of the Hebrides, she vanished. But then SOSUS got her again. This time a very definite IDENT, but now she was heading along a more southerly course. The US staff did not see any particular danger. Since the Cold War, all dangers had decreased as the Soviet Union faded into the somewhat gloomy pages of twentieth-century history.

Since Russia's acquisition of new wealth, under a government that intended the motherland to be at the forefront of modern geopolitics, things had changed rapidly. Russia had become a militarily expansive nation. Once more it had demonstrated all of its old, inflammatory desires, its saber-rattling personality, along with its traditional stance of *We Dare the World to Object.*

In the West, the only professionals who had cottoned to the dramatic changes in the Russian outlook were the most advanced thinkers in Western society, senior political university professors, high-ranking Pentagon officials, and the resident sages of naval and military intelligence on both sides of the Atlantic.

It seemed that they alone understood the rising threat to world peace from the Near East. But their fears and cautions had not yet spread to the sleeping giant of SOSUS. There was no sense of urgency among the small team of US commanders, who were debating the value of raising it back to the frontline operation it once was.

They were about twelve hours from the real truth, twelve hours from the moment the highest-ranked brains in the Pentagon collectively understood that a streamlined, never-miss-a-beat SOSUS may once more be a matter of life and death. Because now there was a glaring reason for instant restoration of the system. Its name was *Gepard.*

All through that day, Washington discussed the incident with cool concern. But as the afternoon wore on, the evening newspapers came out in England and Scotland. And that was when the full awfulness of the situation finally dawned on everyone.

London's *Evening Globe* proclaimed:

RUSSIAN NUCLEAR SUBMARINE
THREATENS WEST COAST OF SCOTLAND
Royal Navy Forces It Aground on Skye Beach

The *Glasgow Standard* announced:

GIANT RUSSIAN NUCLEAR SUBMARINE
SHIPWRECKED ON ISLE OF SKYE
Royal Navy Tackles Warhead Crisis
Moscow Remains Silent

The *Edinburgh Star:*

RUSSIAN MISSILE SUBMARINE
RAMS THE ISLE OF SKYE
Giant Nuclear Akula II Hard Aground
Radiation Threat to Vast Highland Area

The objective of all three publications was, as usual, to frighten the life out of the population. And there were about a zillion other publications all over the free world preparing to do precisely the same. None with more enthusiasm and barely concealed glee than the US "rolling news" television channels, CNN and FOX.

And now breaking news . . . Reports are coming in that a major Russian nuclear submarine has slammed into the beach of an island in Scotland. Royal Navy warships are racing to the scene as the Akula Class vessel, believed to be carrying cruise missiles with nuclear warheads, lies stranded on the sandbank. . . .

Pentagon sources are admitting huge concern that the ten-thousand-ton submarine somehow penetrated the electronic defensive network, which the UK and United States have operated for decades in that sensitive area of the North Atlantic. . . .

We understand the chairman of the Joint Chiefs himself will chair an initial inquiry later today to discuss an immediate solution to this glaring example of Western naval commanders dropping their guard in the face of obvious and continued Russian aggression. . . .

A rival US channel went straight for the jugular:

US Naval chiefs admit to feeling stunned by the security breach, which permitted a ten-thousand-ton Russian submarine to penetrate electronic defenses and then run aground off the coast of Scotland.

Pentagon officials confirm they have ordered a Los Angeles Class nuclear submarine, out of New London, Connecticut, to make all speed to the Isle of Skye to assist the Royal Navy with one of the most highly embarrassing incidents since the US Air Force spy plane was shot down over the Urals in May 1960.

If the British decide to allow the Russian boat, the *Gepard,* to go free, it is anticipated the American submarine will escort it back to Russian waters. Drastic improvements to US-UK ocean security systems are certain to be announced shortly. . . .

And all this was before the defense "experts" began writing long feature articles pinpointing the blame. This was certain to be aimed at the US Navy, since it was common knowledge in military circles that the Brits were effectively finished.

But that would have been absurd, because of the GIUK Gap, Russia's gateway out of the tundra and into the North Atlantic. Despite being the narrowest point in the entire ocean, it is still a huge stretch of rough, icy water, especially the western part, between Greenland and Iceland. This is the Denmark Strait, 180 miles wide at its narrowest point. The remainder, between the east coast of Iceland and the northwesterly tip of Scotland, the Port of Ness on the Isle of Lewis, is 550 miles wide.

The SOSUS arrays that spread across the entire ocean bottom were laid and maintained by the Americans, and of course the network of listening stations was financed by the Pentagon. But for years the Royal Navy offered immense assistance, both in manning the stations and in patrolling the waters, with surface ships, submarines, and aircraft.

But no more. By 2018 they simply did not have the resources. If the Americans wanted a partner on the eastern side of the Atlantic Ocean, they would need to find someone else. And that may not be easy. Half of Europe was floundering along in near-bankrupt conditions.

America itself had a few heavy financial difficulties, but if the Pentagon wanted to keep a severe weather eye on the scowling military masters in the Kremlin, they would almost certainly have to go it alone. And the *Gepard* had surely heightened that ultimate truth.

Back in Lochalsh, Captain McKeown's frigate was on station out beyond the sandbank, riding at anchor in fourteen fathoms of water. His crew, plus a half-dozen Royal Marines, were fixing towlines to the bow of the submarine, which was scheduled to be pulled off the bank at 1700 hours.

The engineers and sonar men from Faslane had arrived and were already ensconced in the various control rooms of the stranded *Gepard,* inspecting the weapons and finding very little except active wire-guided torpedoes. There were no other warheads on the cruise missiles. There was also no significant damage to the boat, and there had been no gear failure of any kind.

The nuclear reactor was running smoothly, at its lowest pressure, and it was crystal clear the entire incident was due to a classic Russian screwup. They'd misjudged the tide, the distance from shore, the pattern of the channel buoys, and the depth of the water. In fairness to the Russian helmsman and navigation officer, that Skye sandbank rises very steeply 120 feet—80 feet to 15 feet in a few hundred yards.

The contour of the seabed thus sweeps up from deep water to a shallow plateau situated about 36 feet from the surface. On top of this, rising 20 feet higher, stands a narrow ocean mound, about 330 feet long on the chart. *Gepard* had driven head-on into this small underwater mountain and stopped dead.

A couple of Royal Navy frogmen were currently taking a long, hard look at the acoustic cladding on the hull of the submarine. They thought it looked good, very good, but no better than the British or American tiles, which were based on the ones that formed the heat shield around the forward fuselage of the space shuttle returning to earth.

Inside the submarine hull, the Faslane technicians were stripping out any computer hard drives that they believed may contain electronic information pertaining to British or American submarine activities in the area.

For a start, Captain McKeown had driven straight through a critical submarine training area on his way up the Kyle Rhea. Just north of the *Gepard* there was another huge submarine area, either side of the 14-mile Raasay Island, which lies between Skye and the Scottish mainland. This comprises some 50 square miles of submarine country, dark waters, varying in depth from 300 to 1,500 feet, and marked on all charts.

These were clear warnings to fishermen and yachtsmen to take care and to steer either side of Raasay, and stay close to the shore, out of the way of the biggest and most ruthless monsters of the deep. Kapitan Konstantin Tatarinov's navigation staff had misjudged this detailed Admiralty chart when they reached the southernmost waters and careened out of the marked channel, for no real reason except lack of care.

Nonetheless, the Faslane sonar men found a major amount of data in *Gepard*'s computer systems, and they were able to remove it. They were not able to ascertain whether the data had already been transmitted back to Russia. Besides, it all needed to be downloaded, and the engineers also had to dismantle other electronics to ensure that *Gepard* pressed on home without any more spying.

As for towing her all the way back to Faslane, this was becoming increasingly unlikely. There was little more to learn from the boat, which had now been rendered harmless. So in the opinion of Admiral Ryan and the Admiralty, they might as well tell her, in naval parlance, to bugger off home and stop being such a bloody nuisance.

The engineers assessed they had another five hours' work to do, and they proposed staying aboard to finish, while *Gepard* dropped anchor in deeper water at the edge of the channel. The navy estimated she would be released sometime after 2200 hours.

The armed Royal Marine guard stood watch inside the hull while the work continued. The Russians were forbidden to lay hands on any working part of the boat, except for the cooks in the galley, who were busy making soup and toasted sandwiches for the crew and the British visitors.

Angus Moncrief stayed on station until the towing was completed, and this was a major anticlimax. With the blue-twisted steel of the towing lines firmly attached to the submarine bow and the stern of the *Sutherland,* the process was carried out almost in slow motion.

Captain McKeown supervised it personally, ordering his frigate's mighty 31,000-hp gas turbines to take the strain as the lines went taut and then increase speed very slightly. The high water helped to lift the bow as soon as *Gepard* had moved six feet. And then it was twenty feet, then fifty, and suddenly she was floating for the first time in more than twelve hours.

She dipped her bow as the water deepened, and as the stern slipped off the sand, she sagged down in the calm sea, and then came up on the tide. McKeown ordered more power, and the huge submarine dipped forward, along the surface. The danger was that too sudden a pull may have caused her to run faster than *Sutherland* and blunder into her stern. But wily McKeown did nothing sudden. With immense skill he maneuvered her to the edge of the channel and signaled for the towlines to be unhooked and to drop the anchor into eighty feet of ocean.

Only then did the Royal Marines and the Faslane submariners give permission for the Russian rods to be pulled, firing up *Gepard*'s nuclear re-actor in readiness for her long journey home . . . almost two thousand miles, north around the gigantic coastline of Norway, into the Barents Sea, with a sharp right turn down the White Sea to the shipyards of Severodvinsk, where she was originally launched in 1999.

Without even a comment on her plight, the Russian Navy would order her immediately into the enormous workshops on the south shore near Archangel—to repair whatever damage the Faslane technicians may have done to her electronics. Thus far, no one had issued any form of a reprimand, which was unusual for Russia's normally grim Northern Fleet commanders.

By midnight, the saga was over. Line astern with HMS *Sutherland,* *Gepard* had cleared the lighthouse on Cape Wrath, where her escort de-parted. The Russian submarine now dived to two hundred feet, heading north, past the Orkney Islands and into some of the deepest water in the world. On the far side of the GIUK Gap, where the North Atlantic flows into the Norwegian Sea, the ocean is more than thirteen thousand feet deep—that's almost two and a half miles, straight down.

Angus Moncrief had gone home and recorded the day's events in his harbormaster's logbook. The Chinook transporting the submariners and

Royal Marines had already landed at Faslane and was on its way to the Helensburgh base. All was peaceful around the great Scottish lochs, except if you happened to catch the television news, during which you would have thought World War III was about to start.

There were Russians, Americans, British politicians, admirals, ex-admirals, a couple of future admirals, ambassadors, ex-ambassadors, naval attachés, military experts, quasi experts, and various frauds, all nattering away about the threat to world peace that had broken out beyond Angus Moncrief's harbor.

Desperately, Admirals David Ryan and Mark Rowan tried to play it all down. Even the Russian naval attaché tried to assure London's Channel Four there was, so far as he could see, no harm done. It was a minor accident and, if anything, had cemented even more agreeable relations between the Royal Navy and Russia's Northern Fleet.

But the journalists and anchormen had even less interest than normal in the lost art of listening. All they wanted was news of *irate complaints . . . emergency meetings with the United States . . . this shocking breach of security . . . possible expulsion of Russian diplomats . . . spying, espionage, nuclear danger, warheads, retaliation . . . anger . . . fury . . .* and, of course, the inevitable *midnight crisis meeting, United Nations Security Council in New York.*

And in the end the media won the day. There could not have been a member of the public anywhere in the free world who did not have the distinct impression that some kind of truly diabolical international incident had taken place.

Which, of course, it had.

9:00 A.M., TUESDAY, AUGUST 14, 2018

Rotunda Conference Room
The Kremlin, Moscow

The president of Russia, a powerfully built former member of the secret police from the Ukraine, seemed to wear a permanent glare on his craggy, round face. He peered out at the world beneath bushy eyebrows and a thick head of hair, with an unnerving combination of suspicion and general disbelief in his colleagues.

This was, however, a slight misconception, because Nikita Markova was basically a friendly man, although an absolute tyrant when riled, a state of grace occurring approximately now.

He had called this conference personally. And to it he had invited his most trusted ministers to sit in this great domed room on the second floor of the Senate Building on the east side of the Kremlin, among the ramparts of the Senate Tower behind Lenin's tomb. This was the room that, during World War II, had often been the very heartbeat of the Red Army Supreme Command under Stalin. President Markova loved that.

He was a remarkably proud man, with a deep sense of history, who would never utter one word of criticism against the old KGB or its ruthless activities behind the walls of the Lubyanka.

He had believed in the old Soviet Union. He believed in Mother Russia, and he yearned for the old days of the Politburo, and the enormous brutal power of the old Soviet machine, which dealt so swiftly with "trouble" and various "dissidents."

President Markova could not be described as a keen exponent of democracy. Which was why incredible power rested so easily upon his seventy-four-year-old shoulders. He appointed his own deputy, and the prime minister, and all other government ministers. He was deferred to on every subject because every person in the entire government was dependent upon him for a life of luxury.

No surprise, then, that he got along just fine with both houses of the Russian Parliament—the Federation Council and the Duma. President Markova believed in the sledgehammer authoritarian approach of the Soviet Union of old. He could match any Russian leader down the ages for a pure, bloody-minded approach to his nation's problems.

The men who sat at the vast, highly polished rotunda table awaiting his signal to begin the meeting were as follows: the prime minister, Oleg Kuts, from St. Petersburg; the current head of the FSB, Yuri Kasatonov, new, zealous, and only thirty-eight years old; Vassily Levchenko, the minister for foreign affairs, a limited man trying to follow in the footsteps of the great Andrei Gromyko; from the Russian Navy the veteran commander in chief and former C-in-C Fleet, Admiral Vitaly Rankov; the chief of naval staff, Admiral Yaroslav Kietskov; and the Northern Fleet commander, Vice Admiral Alexander Ustinov. There were no secretaries or deputy ministers, but Admiral Ustinov was permitted to bring his newly appointed aide, Kapitan Leytenant Nikolai Chirkov, since, in the end, this was a Northern Fleet matter. Nikolai, however, was there because he was being groomed for a potential military-political career, courtesy of his very influential father. No one at the table wore a uniform.

"Thank you for coming, gentlemen," said the president, without looking up from the bound report he was reading. "And I have to say this entire operation is beginning to give the appearance of a complete foul-up. I realize we all knew the *Gepard* would be caught and apprehended for spying, by either the Americans or the British. But I did not intend for the Russian Navy to be made a laughing stock in front of the whole world."

"She's on her way home now, sir," replied the commander in chief. "And we should perhaps bear in mind that no great harm has been done to anyone. No one's been injured, and the boat is more or less intact except for some electronics."

"I understand that," said President Markova, "but I think we should bear in mind why we sent the *Gepard* south in the first place. We wanted her to steam through the GIUK Gap at a good speed in order to find out whether the American SOSUS system was still working in a highly efficient way. Is that not so?"

"Yessir. Certainly, that was our objective. We simply did not include the possibility of an accident at sea as part of the equation."

"My first question then is this," replied the president. "Is SOSUS working at all these days, or has it been abandoned?"

"It's working at about a quarter of its old potential."

"How do you know? Did the Americans hear the *Gepard*? It certainly did not appear so."

"Sir, they picked her up. Kapitan Tatarinov was detected by a US nuclear boat, probably fifty miles away, and again, twice in fact, by SOSUS. She definitely released a firm signal on the undersea wires, but we have no way of knowing where those signals were picked up. We're not even certain they were picked up, because no one wanted to do anything about it.

"That was why Kapitan Tatarinov proceeded straight into the Royal Navy submarine training grounds between the Isle of Skye and the Scottish mainland. To see if anyone cared one way or another whether he was there."

"But of course that was never put to the test," said the president, "because our Russian navigation team had put the submarine on a sandbank before anyone had much of a chance to react?"

"Correct, sir. We still do not have all the answers."

"The issue here appears to be, Alexander, that SOSUS undeniably still works, but it is being manned less diligently than it once was. They picked up our signature, but failed to act. Which is important. However, the antics of the *Gepard's* navigation team have unknowingly had a profound effect on the future, correct?"

"I do not quite follow, sir."

"Given the enormous fuss the media are causing, do you not think it likely that the US Navy will get SOSUS back on the top line as soon as they possibly can?"

"Very probably, sir."

"So, in a way, the blind navigator has almost certainly answered the critical question for us: do we assume that when we launch Project FOM-2, we must proceed with all due care? Because if we risk a submarine through the GIUK, they will surely catch us. And discovery would be unthinkable."

"Sir, twenty-four years ago they would surely have sunk us."

"If they ever discovered Project FOM-2, they'd fucking well sink us now."

"Well, sir, it seems the most difficult question has been solved. Can we move the nuclear hardware for Project FOM-2 in secret, using a submarine, through the North Atlantic? Answer: No. We dare not. They'd catch us in deep water, lock onto the nuclear content, and almost certainly ram a couple of torpedoes right in our guts, no questions asked, no traces of a lost Russian submarine."

"Before *Gepard* we might have gotten away with it," said President Markova, "but not now. So, we'll use a surface merchant ship and sail, strictly in international waters, straight down the Atlantic to the Caribbean. No one has the right to apprehend us when we're hundreds of miles from shore. Certainly not the Americans."

"Sir, do you wish to interview Kapitan Tatarinov when he returns?" asked the Northern Fleet commander.

"I do not think that will be necessary. But there is one further question I would like to ask everyone in this room: has anyone lost their appetite for Project FOM-2, or are we still of accord?"

No one spoke, and no one moved. This was a moment that required great nerve and steadfastness. At least with this president it did. Russia had received an enormous humiliation on October 6, 2016, when the Israelis had penetrated and then knocked the hell out of the vaunted Russian antiaircraft and missile shield, which was supposed to protect Iran's main nuclear plants.

It was not just a shattering defeat for the ayatollahs, the known staunch allies of Moscow; it represented a terrible setback for the entire Russian international arms industry, which, after oil and gas, represented the nation's most important export.

That October attack by the Israelis, in their US-built fighter-bombers, represented a total eclipse for the fabled S-300, Moscow's revered long-range surface-to-air missile. This had been the great unstoppable specialist antiaircraft and antiballistic system, designed, built, and originated in Soviet Russia and relied upon for defense by so many Eastern European and Asian nations. This was the system that had been ordered by China. And now everything was, in every sense, up in the air.

Russia had armed Iran. The United States had armed Israel. And it had turned out to be "no contest."

"Washington has it coming to them," said Admiral Vitaly Rankov. "We must somehow even the score. And this time there will be no mistakes."

"Just as long as we stay out of submarines, eh?" said President Markova, without even a semblance of a smile.

3

Red Square, Moscow

Lieutenant Commander Nikolai Chirkov hurried through the gathering gloom of the late afternoon. There was treason in his heart, and this, he thought, was one heck of a place to be planning it, directly beneath the great gilded dome of Ivan the Great's Bell Tower, still the tallest structure in the Kremlin.

The meeting in the rotunda had dragged on for several hours while the Russian Navy and its political masters endlessly probed and questioned the events of that day in October 2016, when the air wings of Israel had pounded Iran's nuclear production facilities to a pulp.

It had been a major blow to the Russian defense industry, resulting in several cancellations and even more postponements to international orders for the Almaz-Antey aerospace designs. The vision of the US-built Israeli fighter jets raging through the skies above the Zagros Mountains, avoiding, with apparent ease, the elaborate Russian S-300 defensive system, had shocked many a defense department in countries all over Asia.

And now, in Lieutenant Commander Chirkov's view, he was seeing Russian paranoia on the grandest possible scale. The president was convinced the entire thing was to be blamed on the United States. They had planned the strike, armed the Jews, provided both the hardware and the electronic know-how, and masterminded the operation. Israel had smashed the Iranian nuclear factories because the United States wanted them smashed.

It was a grotesque oversimplification. Israel, surrounded by its Islamic enemies, had *believed* the Iranian president when he'd said he planned to wipe them off the face of the earth. And Tel Aviv was not going to allow Tehran to have an atom bomb with which to achieve that aim.

That was a better simplification. Israel would have hit Qom and Natanz with or without American aircraft and explosives. The United States was perhaps a coconspirator, but by no means a principal. And even if Washington had been up to its ears in the plot, it was never proven. There was no reasonable cause for a Russian president to try to organize a clandestine military strike against the United States.

Yet President Markova was determined to hammer the United States of America, to strike against them, to demonstrate the folly of any nation being involved in any military action against Russian interests.

He was still in that old, tired Cold War frame of mind in which revenge was everything, even if that revenge was justified only in his own mind. In Lieutenant Commander Chirkov's opinion, President Markova was a near-deranged and vindictive old man who would steer Russia into a lunatic confrontation with the United States for no reason at all.

So what if America, with its large Jewish population, was in cahoots with Israel? They always had been, and nothing was ever going to change that. But was that a reason to come barreling out of the shadows and strike at Washington? At the most powerful military nation on earth, on behalf of a bunch of religious maniacs who were essentially dressed in sheets?

Lieutenant Commander Chirkov thought it was madness. And it must surely end in tears. The trouble was, old Markova was so dominant in Russian politics, and thus in military matters, that he could not be argued with. If he wanted to hit Washington, show 'em who's boss, humiliate them in front of the world, well, here we go . . . Nikita Khrushchev all over again, a half century later.

From what Chirkov could tell inside the rotunda, the Russian admirals and generals were going to help the president in his foolishness. That's how it was in modern Russia. One word from the Great White Chief, and it shall be done.

Crazy, crazy people, muttered Nikolai as he hurried across the square. *How could any act of war against the United States possibly do any good for even one person in the whole of Russia? And here they all are—a bunch of very stupid, elderly men, acting like Ivan the Terrible getting ready to conquer Siberia four hundred years ago. And it's not even our damn war! It's Iran's.*

The thirty-six-year-old naval officer pressed on toward the staff car that awaited him. It was raining now, and turning cold, and he wracked his brain to try to understand what the ridiculous Markova was up to. The whole damn meeting he had just attended was conducted in code— *Project FOM-2!* What was that all about? Nikolai had not the slightest idea what anyone was talking about.

And yet . . . and yet . . . he knew it was important. And he sensed it might be something truly earth-shattering, so rigid was the secrecy surrounding it. Even armed as he was with so little information, he sensed he must do something. The only action he could take was to contact Rani. And that might prove very difficult.

When finally President Markova had called the meeting to a close, he had agreed to produce a set of notes for Admiral Alexander Ustinov, who was leaving immediately for a two-day visit to the Black Sea Fleet with Admiral Rankov.

The Northern C-in-C was then flying immediately to Severodvinsk to inspect the work on the destroyer *Admiral Chabanenko,* Chirkov's own ship. It was thus agreed that Lieutenant Commander Chirkov should take the late-afternoon train back to the White Sea and spend a couple of days writing up the Moscow notes, preparing the ground for his new boss on Friday.

Which left him precious little time to blow President Markova's insane plans out of the water. Especially since he did not even know where Rani Ben Adan was. It was almost five thirty, and Moscow was busy. He had to cover his tracks: there were no bounds to the diligence of the FSB, and, as a new aide to a highly placed naval admiral, they may very well track him—just to be certain.

He ran through the rain, trying to avoid the temptation to look back and see if anyone was tailing him across Red Square. He found the navy driver and told him to cover the two-and-a-half-mile journey up to the

Yaroslavskiy railway terminal as quickly as possible, since he was trying to make the Archangel Express and there was not another one until midnight.

But the traffic was heavy. Nikolai finally got out because of a serious jam in Komsomolskaya Square, and he sprinted through the driving rain, past the huge statue of Lenin, and into the Yaroslavskiy entrance with its steep, fairy-tale roof.

Nikolai headed not for the ticket windows but for the intimidating granite bust of Vladimir Ilyich Lenin, which made the old Bolshevik look even grumpier than the statue outside the station. The lieutenant dived around the back of the enormous plinth and pulled out his cell phone, dialing the memorized number of the man from the Mossad.

"Rani, it's me. I need to see you right now."

"Where are you?"

"Yaroslavskiy train terminal, Moscow. Where are you?"

"I'm in the embassy. Just got in."

"Pick a spot. Midnight. I may have been followed, and I need to get on a train. Just in case my driver's checking me out."

"Okay, how about that old restaurant out near Dynamo Stadium— stays open half the night? It's called Novy Yar. We met there, once before. See you there."

The line went dead. The conversation had stayed inside the thirty-second limit regarded as safe within the espionage trade. In this time, government agents who might be listening in Moscow were unable to trace telecommunications even between public pay phones, which might be routed through the Lubyanka.

Emerging from behind Vladimir Lenin's granite glare, Lieutenant Commander Chirkov headed for the ticketing area on one side of the huge central hall. The place was seething, and there were lines at the windows, Yaroslavskiy Station being the final terminal on the longest railroad on earth, the Trans-Siberian Railway, 5,772 miles, Moscow to Vladivostok, half a world and eight time zones away, on the Sea of Japan.

Nikolai Chirkov was not going east, however. He was going north. He swiftly purchased a first-class one-way ticket to Archangel, usable tomorrow. And then he waited to purchase a return ticket up to Sergiev Posad, the old Soviet city of Zagorsk, forty miles northeast of Moscow.

The naval officer's plan was simple. He would join the throng heading for the long-distance trains and find one that stopped at Sergiev Posad, a ninety-minute ride from Moscow. At the very last moment, as the train prepared to pull out of Sergiev, heading north, Nikolai would jump out, walk to the Russky Dvorik Hotel restaurant for dinner, and hope to hell any "tail" was still on the train thundering through the Russian countryside to the White Sea.

As it happened, there was no tail, since Nikolai was deeply trusted as the son of a very senior political figure. But he had a pleasant-enough dinner and returned to Moscow on a suburban-line train, which deposited him back at Yaroslavskiy Station at around a quarter past eleven. From there he took a taxi one mile across North Moscow to the designated restaurant, where Rani was already seated at a small corner table, sipping Turkish coffee.

It was crowded in the Novy Yar, which was excellent. Nikolai waited ten minutes for a table next to Rani to free up, which would allow them to speak quietly yet not appear to know each other. There were so many precautions, and nineteen out of twenty were totally unnecessary. But in Rani's trade no one was bothered about the nineteen. It was the other one.

"I haven't had time to tell you this," said Nikolai, "but I have been given a very important promotion."

"Is this good for us?"

"It is little short of fantastic—I'm the new aide to Vice Admiral Ustinov, C-in-C Northern Fleet."

"You still have access to all those electronic communiqués?"

"A lot more than that, Rani. Today I was at a meeting inside the rotunda with the president of Russia."

"Holy shit!" said Rani. "That's big."

"I heard incontrovertible evidence that Russia is planning a strike against the USA, in response to the Israeli attack on the Iranian nuclear factories."

"Wouldn't it be better to strike against the nation that did it? Why America?"

"Because our president is an old-fashioned Cold Warrior. In his mind there is still only one enemy—the United States. In his mind, Washington is both directly and indirectly responsible for a total humiliation that he cannot forgive."

"Stupid old prick," said Rani inelegantly.

"Stupid and very dangerous old prick, actually," replied Lieutenant Commander Chirkov.

"Well, what's his main gripe? The aircraft, bombs, and missiles, all made in the US of A? Is that it?"

"Correct. But more than that. The Israeli onslaught smashed the Russian S-300 anti–air attack system, which has been sold all over the world and was about to be purchased by China. It was a serious blow to our defense industry, and for that, President Markova blames the USA entirely."

Rani was bewildered by the Russian vitriol. "Did S-300 really fail that badly?" he asked. "The Israelis lost six aircraft, and Iran's antiaircraft guns, on the same system, hit several more."

"I know . . . I know," replied Lieutenant Commander Chirkov. "But the world grasps only one set of facts—the Iranian head of state threatened to take Israel off the map, and he was devoting his life to building his own atom bomb. So Israel decided to obliterate that nuclear threat, just as they once did to Saddam Hussein, and again to Syria. Result: a clear-cut Israeli victory. Which added up to a Russian embarrassment and complacent smiles in Washington. Old Markova cannot take that."

"Since I work for the Israeli government, it would be very valuable for me to know how Russia plans to sharpen up the old S-300 system. Any clues?"

"That's a big part of it. No one knows how the Israelis beat it. It's a long-range SAM setup with NIIP radar to intercept anything incoming—aircraft, bombs, or ballistic missiles. Iran had it all over the place, as a defense for industrial sites, key government offices, naval and military bases. Its aim is to provide total control of any nation's airspace.

"Down the years, it's had almost thirty improvements and upgrades. And it's the pride and joy of Russia's May Day Victory Parade through Red Square, right out there on huge eight-wheel trucks. Its radar can detect a ballistic missile at six hundred miles, and it launches straight up with a forward tip to the target. No need to aim it before launching."

"It obviously did work against us in 2016. Just not well enough, I guess. How many other countries bought it?"

"Many. Eastern-bloc nations, plus North Korea, Syria, Venezuela, Algeria, and God knows who else."

"And all your president wants to do is cause a war with the USA? You're right. He's nuts."

"I just wish I could say precisely what he's planning. But I cannot. The whole subject is in code. But the forthcoming strike operation does have a code, and I've written it down . . . here . . . "

Nikolai handed over a small piece of paper. It contained just one word, three letters, and one number—*Project FOM-2*. "That was mentioned at the meeting several times," he said. "But no one betrayed even the slightest sign of understanding. I watched them all so carefully, and when the president uttered the code, I studied every face at that table. But no one confirmed, denied, or even expressed bewilderment. They just continued the conversation as if they all knew but had no reason to repeat it—Project FOM-2. That was all."

"Did anyone else say 'FOM-2'?"

"Yes, Admiral Rankov did, once. And so did Prime Minister Kuts. No one else."

"Did you have the feeling this was precisely the same subject we discussed before?"

"Very definitely. But more intense. And there was a lot of talk about that submarine, the *Gepard*, that just ran aground on the loch in Scotland."

"They briefed me on that in the embassy earlier this evening. Seems the entire Western world's pretty shaken by the whole incident. The media have gone mad."

"That I did not understand, Rani. But I'll tell you one thing: this crowd in the rotunda was not in the least bit surprised. It was as if they all understood the submarine would be caught, either by the Brits or by the Americans. It was only the accident that took them by surprise. From what I could tell, there is no question of a court-martial for the captain. And in the Northern Fleet, that's almost unprecedented."

"You mean they somehow deliberately sent that nuclear boat to British inshore submarine training waters around Scotland, just waiting for it to be apprehended?"

"That's exactly what I mean. And it was right after that they began to talk about Project FOM-2. I was not supposed to understand. That much was clear. But I'm sure everyone else did."

"You think it's anything to do with that monastery bullshit you came up with last time?"

"Well, I've heard no more. But the nuclear scientists from North Korea and Tehran are in place somewhere. I know that. And just last week I intercepted a Northern Fleet message—it mentioned Solovetsky, which every Russian knows has a very famous monastery."

"Where's Solovetsky?"

"A group of islands somewhere in the White Sea. South. I've never been there."

"Is it a big monastery?"

"Probably about the size of the Kremlin. I think it was once a prison camp."

"That applies to half of Russia," said Rani.

"And if we're not careful, we might end up in one," added Nikolai.

He sipped his coffee in silence, while Rani ordered cheap red caviar and buttered black bread. He'd had no dinner and told the waiter to bring him a large order, since he felt that by midnight Nikolai would want some. He also ordered vodka: "One for me, and a glass for this gentleman who's been talking to me."

The waitress looked spectacularly uninterested and never even glanced at Nikolai, which was precisely as Rani had intended.

Novy Yar was, if anything, becoming even busier and noisier, as late-night Moscow places tend to do. It was just about perfect for the Russian Naval officer and the man from the Mossad . . . anonymous, metropolitan, and indifferent.

"Rani, we have to find out what this FOM-2 is all about." Nikolai was savoring the caviar but pondering the problem. "It's the code for some kind of revenge attack on the USA. I cannot believe they are stupid enough to do it directly and then just stand there and take the blame."

"Neither can I," replied Rani. "The Americans would slam back at them within minutes. Plus, they'd probably stop any incoming attack before it happened . . . but Markova knows that. I mean, Jesus Christ! The US president never moves one yard without his nuclear codes to call in a missile strike at any time."

"And they're more advanced than us," added Nikolai. "They could take out half our nuclear defense shield before we knew what had hit us."

Both men were silent for a few moments, until Lieutenant Commander Chirkov said quietly, "Let's apply normal logic, Rani. How could Russia hit an American installation, military or civilian, without being called to task for it?"

"By doing it in secret and blaming someone else."

"They could do that. But the whole goddamned world has changed. A nuclear strike does not mean what it used to."

"You mean like Armageddon?"

"You can forget all about that, Rani. Military scientists spend their lives trying to perfect much smaller missiles, with nuclear warheads that will obliterate a target with hardly any peripheral damage. The thing about nuclear warheads is they can be made much smaller than a great bomb packing the same power."

"And smaller means less fuel for its journey, right?"

"Less fuel means a slimmer, faster incoming attack, perhaps one that even the Americans might miss. I'm sure that's the game. Trouble is, I cannot find out if this planned strike is imminent. They are too secretive."

"The whole world's pretty secretive these days," said Rani. "I guess it's worth remembering no one found out we were going to hit Iran."

"I know. If we had, it might not have been so easy."

"And now this vindictive Russian president plans to hit back, at the wrong culprit, for all the wrong reasons."

"He does. I am afraid it will end up in blood, sorrow, and tears for the Russian people. I will do anything in my power to stop the stupid old fucker."

"Well, you can start by finding out about FOM-2."

"Give me a break. I only discovered it existed twelve hours ago."

"You also found out a lot more. Sounds to me like that submarine might have been on a trial run. Just to see if it could be used in the real attack."

"Right. And it obviously cannot. Not now. From what I heard, the Americans located it three times, but had no interest in doing anything until the Russian helmsman put it on the sandbank."

"That could mean they've ruled out a submarine. Maybe they'll switch the whole program to a surface ship."

"Who the hell knows?"

"No one's going to bomb, or even attack, big cities, especially with nuclear weapons. It's all changed. It's no longer acceptable. War these days, conducted by states, that is, not fucking terrorists, means surgical strikes on selected targets, almost exclusively military. And if you can do it secretly, and blame someone else, so much the better."

"Is that the orthodox gospel according to Saint Rani? Because if it is, I'll tell you a flaw: Israel never blamed anyone else for Iran . . . "

"Israel said absolutely nothing," growled the man from the Mossad. "And that's *better* than blaming someone else. It's more mysterious, more baffling. And, in my view, if Russia launches something against the USA, they will say nothing. They will merely deny all knowledge and participation."

"Rani, I have come here tonight to suggest we are now in a position to inform the USA to go immediately to high alert because Markova is planning something."

"How can I? We know so little."

"It's definite. Trust me."

"But, Nikki, we know nothing. Not one single detail. I am reluctant to start sounding an international alarm on that scale, until I can come up with a few details."

"I'm just afraid it might be happening very soon."

"Nikki, in this trade, you cannot scare people half to death unless you have hard facts. We have none—except they have a plan in progress. But I take your point . . . You sat there, and you heard it all. More important, you heard the anger of the old man.

"And you have the code, FOM-2. We should make this a priority from now on. I'm going back to tackle the new lead about the monastery. You stick with FOM-2 and stay in touch."

"Okay. We'll share a cab. I'm going back to the railway station and find a way to Severodvinsk. You can take it on to the embassy."

Rani shoved over a handful of Russian rubles for the bill and the taxi. As the senior man—Nikolai's boss, in a way—he always paid. There were cabs in a line outside, and it was still raining. They climbed aboard and set off east toward the Yaroslavskiy terminal.

"Do I get paid for tonight?"

"We'll wire it to Geneva tomorrow. I think 50,000 US dollars, to celebrate your new promotion."

"Thank you very much," replied Lieutenant Commander Chirkov. "Thank you very much indeed."

Rani Ben Adan could scarcely believe his luck. He was running an intelligent, highly placed informer sitting at the right hand of the commander of Northern Fleet and, sometimes, in the company of the president of all the Russians.

"Worth $10 million," he muttered after watching Nikolai run through the rain into the station.

<hr>

8:00 A.M., WEDNESDAY, AUGUST 15, 2018

Israeli Embassy
Bolshaya Ordynka Street, Moscow

The rain was still sweeping across the Moscow River and lashing the wide forecourt of the embassy. Rani could not hear it as he worked his way through reference books and on the keyboard of his desktop computer screen, in the windowless private situation room the Mossad's field agents utilize for research.

Next to his right hand was the small piece of paper on which Nikolai had written *FOM-2*. Next to it he had written the word *Solovetsky.* On the big screen was a color picture of the ramparts of Solovetsky Monastery, which looked a lot like a medieval fortress and nothing at all like a religious building . . . a home away from home for Ivan the Terrible, rather than the Holy Father, Pope Benedict XVI.

The six Solovetsky Islands stand in the southern waters of the White Sea off the shores of the Onega Peninsula. Collectively, they are usually known as *Solovki*—wild, scarcely populated pine and spruce lands, with forbidding granite shores, a zillion lakes, and, on the main island, Solovetsky itself, a network of canals that join many of the lakes together. Generally speaking, the place is better suited to families of polar bears rather than people. The islands are less than one hundred miles from the Arctic Circle and are more or less permanently frozen.

The sixteenth-century monastery, Rani read, was on that main island. It was built within four massive round towers, with walls composed of giant boulders, eighteen feet thick in places. Four more towers completed the aura of Gothic menace that enveloped the place. The only aspect worse than its impregnable, sinister appearance was its history—which makes the Tower of London seem like a backdrop for *Mr. Rogers.*

In 1854, during the Crimean War, a couple of British frigates laid siege to the monastery and demanded its surrender. Nine hours later, after firing sixteen hundred heavy cannonballs at it at point-blank range, they gave up and left, having scarcely cracked the ramparts and killed no one.

The monastery had a shocking record as a prison camp, and while Ivan the Terrible exiled four hundred prisoners to it, permanent notoriety was achieved in more modern times. Both Lenin and Stalin used it as a part of the Soviet system. Alexander Solzhenitsyn wrote about it often and described Solovetsky as "the mother of the Gulag."

Thousands and thousands of political prisoners died there, under the most cruel and brutal conditions—poets, intellects, writers, and philosophers perished, some of them outside, chained up, naked, and frozen to death. The man often known as "Russia's Da Vinci," Father Pavel Florensky, professor of mathematics and physics at the University of Moscow, was incarcerated there before his execution in December 1937.

Solovetsky was the clear and obvious model for the labor camps of the Gulag. It was the first, under Lenin in 1921, and lasted until 1939, when the very name *Solovetsky* became too much even for Josef Stalin. He closed it in 1939.

Rani Ben Adan stared at the screen, at the monstrous fortress before his eyes. *I wonder,* he pondered. *I wonder about that place, about the monastery they mentioned three times . . . and the islands they've just mentioned again . . . and what the heck is the northern branch of the Russian Navy doing talking about it . . . this remote and terrible place, unapproachable, in the middle of absolutely nowhere? As Moses might have asked King Herod, what the fucking hell is going on?*

Once more Rani pulled the map to the screen. He zoomed out to the whole of the White Sea, noting, as a nonnavy man, that it was almost entirely landlocked. There was only one seaway in and out, in the northeast corner, across which ran the line of the Arctic Circle.

Rani picked up the in-house phone and asked for coffee. Mossad men who risk their lives almost every hour of every day in Russia are regarded as gods in the embassy of Israel.

He stared at the map, trying to put himself in the shoes of Russian schemers, to follow their reasoning. Somehow that map, and the melancholy pictures of the monastery, had instilled in him a sense of certainty. Aside from Nikolai's sharp observations, he had only two facts: three mentions of the monastery in communiqués deep inside Northern Fleet command and one mention of the Solovetsky Islands in the same place. This could not be just a coincidence. Rani Ben Adan was sure they were connected, and he could think of no more perfect spot to conduct something truly clandestine, especially something to do with nuclear weapons, than deep within those eighteen-foot granite walls, where even US satellite technology could not penetrate.

They've called in nuclear scientists from two notorious rogue states, and even Nikolai doesn't know where they are or what they're doing. He gazed at his screen, and the answers stood before him. *You don't fly in nuclear scientists for nothing,* he decided. *And we know they're planning to hit the United States. Unless I am fearfully wrong, they're in that fucking monastery. And they're working in probably the remotest, most unapproachable place in all of western Russia.*

So far as Rani could work out, this team of modern weapons maestros must be working on a new, sleeker, and faster missile with which to strike, somewhere in the United States.

He idly scanned through a US military website that pinpointed the main US nuclear response points in the face of an incoming attack. It hadn't changed much since he last visited. But there were some new notes about the president's power and likely speed of reaction. And here there was a very detailed note about presidential involvement—a situation exacerbated by the recent arrest of a Chinese computer technician in Washington. Rani had not read any of it before.

It dealt with the "nuclear football"—the president's emergency satchel, otherwise known as the black box, the nuclear lunch box, the button, or just "the football." It's in a metallic Zero Halliburton briefcase, in an outer leather "jacket." It weighs about forty-five pounds, with a small antenna protruding from the case, close to the carrying handle.

The satchel is kept in the White House but travels with the president wherever he goes. It is always carried by his official aide, one of the five permanent officers representing all branches of the armed services, not one of them ranking less than major or equivalent. The aide on duty is always close to the president and is personally responsible for the security of the satchel.

Every one of the five aides must undergo the most rigorous security clearance and must be familiar with the contents of the satchel in order to brief the president should it become necessary. The supreme presidential command to launch is called the Gold Codes, prepared by the National Security Agency, and carried by the president at all times. It is printed on a plastic card, same size as a credit card, and normally referred to as "the biscuit."

Its principal use is to enable the president to positively identify himself as the commander in chief, with full authority to issue the orders to the National Military Command Center. The United States has a two-man rule, which requires a second person to confirm the president's order—it's normally the secretary of defense. All of the above takes a matter of seconds rather than minutes.

And the Russians want to beat it, muttered Rani. *Good luck, Markova . . . crazy prick.*

Rani read on, experiencing an uncanny feeling he was not supposed to be privy to all this. He had used a classified Mossad password to come on the website and now, somehow, seemed like a spy, which of course he was, but for America, whenever necessary—*never against them.*

If I can help to chop that idiot Markova's balls off, they'll probably make me president, never mind read about his security, he decided, and pressed on, discovering that before he issues his final order, the president must give a "command signal" to the Joint Chiefs of Staff before reviewing the attack options with his aide.

This is the Single Integrated Operation Plan (SIOP). It's contained in a thick binder, inside the satchel. The main headings read: "Major Attack Options," "Selected Attack Options," and "Limited Attack Options." The aide assists the president in transmitting them over the secure satellite phone included in the satchel. Before transmission, the president will sign prepared orders delegating authority to the vice president, should that appear necessary.

There are three nuclear footballs, one with the president, a spare held permanently in the White House, and one with the vice president. As a system, it's as near fireproof as it is mechanically possible to be. The only time it momentarily failed, it took a would-be assassin's bullet to do it—in 1981 when President Reagan's clothing needed to be cut from him by the emergency room's trauma team. The biscuit was later found in one of the president's shoes, on the floor in a corner.

Rani switched off the computer. It was strange, but he had heard that phrase *nuclear football* somewhere in the past few months. But he couldn't remember for the life of him where. He kept almost recalling it, but it always slipped his mind.

But then, ten minutes later, as he prepared to leave the room, it came to him in a rush. Nikolai had mentioned it way back in the winter in Petrozavodsk—after he'd listened in to a cell-phone conversation between someone in his ship and the Kremlin. According to Nikki, he had distinctly heard someone say something about teaching the Americans a lesson and that the Russians would "kick their nuclear football straight out of the stadium."

Someone had laughed, because Rani had remembered saying what a rare matter it was to hear a Slavic joke. And now he understood. It was not a joke after all. When someone had said *nuclear football,* they meant exactly that . . . *the* nuclear football, the American one.

Rani had never heard the phrase before in its correct context. But now he knew, and now he could fit several pieces together, something forming in his mind: a weapons laboratory in the monastery of Solovetsky . . . foreign scientists coming to help . . . the obvious threats against Washington by the Russian president. And now their obvious next step: *If we are to strike against the States, how do we stop their instant-reaction system from destroying us?*

Rani could not answer that. But if the Russians could disable the US president's nuclear football, they would be well on their way—maybe to hold up the entire reaction time by several hours, which might be sufficiently long to deflect American anger from Mother Russia.

He still had very few hard facts, not enough to sound a Klaxon fire alarm in the CIA or the Pentagon, and there did not seem to be a threat against his own country, which had, after all, staged such a sledgehammer power play against Iran.

But he had a straight line of circumstances that interlocked. And he had more speculation to make, which was equally critical, all of it to do with the nuclear football and how to cripple it. Because that is what he himself would have been working on, if he had planned to harm the United States on its own soil.

Plainly, the device, snug in its metallic case, could not be hit by any kind of explosive, because that would almost certainly kill the officer carrying it, not to mention the nearby president himself. Rani understood that very thoroughly. He also knew enough about the murder of presidents to understand that, generally speaking, that should be avoided at all costs.

If that nuclear football were to be put out of action, it would have to be treated as a computer, which it was, with satellite phones attached. It was a communications system, and on command it would send information through cyberspace to the Pentagon and beyond, simultaneously demonstrating that the source of those commands was the president of the United States.

It was also programmed to remove all ambiguity. If its signal ordered "Selected Attack Options" on the SIOP to the US Military Command Center, that would be directly from the commander in chief, backed up by the secretary of defense, with the Joint Chiefs standing sternly by . . . *LAUNCH NOW.*

Rani Ben Adan, sitting all alone in the Israeli Embassy's situation room, sensed he was being drawn into the thoroughly creepy world of cyber warfare, a battleground not entirely unknown to the high-tech section of the Mossad itself. Had they not been blamed for disabling the Iranian weapons plants by that very means only eight years ago?

What Russia, too, must need was a method of "jamming" the nuclear football—by some kind of cyber-related attack from a satellite, controlled from the Russian mainland. "Jamming" was the most tried and tested method. It had been used for many years, both on the battlefield and at tactical level, to disrupt the enemy's communications and to deny opponents the opportunity to listen or watch programs or propaganda.

The problem was the impossibility of "jamming" a radio/telephone without identifying the frequencies being used to transmit. Even then the size and power of the transmitter always determined the range at which it would operate. At ground level, over long distances, it required something close to its own private power station.

The lead country in this ultramodern form of the black arts was China—and the state-of-the-art operation there, both in manufacturing and in marketing the best equipment, was China Shenzhen GSH Technology Corporation, based in the city of the same name directly north and adjoining Hong Kong.

Shenzhen is the world's manufacturing powerhouse. It was the first of China's special economic zones and easily the most successful. Shenzhen SEZ is the fastest-growing city on earth, the pride of the paddy fields, ex–Pearl River Delta village turned industrial metropolis, with twenty-three buildings more than six hundred feet high and a population of more than

10 million. Shenzhen also has the third-busiest container port in China, after Shanghai and Hong Kong.

And there they have perfected the small equipment required to penetrate cell phones, industrial computers, even small communities, and opponents. But they are working on much larger and more powerful technology, for far grander targets.

Every "jamming" device requires an antenna to send the signal, and for a major operation, an external one would be necessary, tuned for individual frequencies. If Russia wanted to hit "the football," it would have to work through Shenzhen. No other cyber warrior, outside of the United States, was so advanced.

Rani knew how difficult this all was. But he knew it in secret. No Israeli, especially a Mossad official, would ever admit to understanding the subject, since any such talk would immediately throw suspicion on the recent activities by the Israelis in this sinister field.

But he did understand it. He knew precisely what Israel had done eight years before, sometime between 2009 and 2010, when a mind-blowing cyber attack had been launched against the Iranian nuclear plant at Natanz, one of the most secure industrial sites in the world.

This was the "mission critical" of the entire Iranian weapons program. In the vast fortified underground bunkers, the Iranians were well into their program of enriching uranium all the way to weapons grade. They had already protected themselves from cyber attack, cutting themselves off from the Internet behind an air gap.

At that point, 2008–2009, the Israelis had not yet considered smashing the place asunder, but rather preferred a high intellectual attack through the computers, which would cripple the Iranian system completely.

The target was the system, which controlled the critical speed of the uranium-spinning centrifuges, the high-tech industrial musclemen that hurl the heavy isotopes to the edge of the uranium hunk during years of fast rotating. The Iranians had around five thousand of them working, with another four thousand being prepared for action.

The problem facing the Israelis, and possibly their American allies, was how to get in there and infect the computers with an effective virus to screw the whole system up. Answer: not possible.

So the Mossad went for the back door. They infiltrated five separate computer companies in Iran, the only organizations that could possibly undertake the endless servicing and repairs at Natanz. These secret cyber technicians introduced a virus onto a USB flash drive and spread it directly to Natanz via the computers of unwitting contractors working at the plant.

It was programmed to hit the Siemens S7-315 PLCs, which controlled the speed at which Iran's gas centrifuges rotated. Once in control, this virus caused utter chaos, alternatively increasing and decreasing the speed of the centrifuge rotor. The attacks were short lived, maybe fifty minutes in duration, recurring every month, until they poleaxed any semblance of scientific order. The uranium was useless, the centrifuges were beyond repair, and the computers were ready for the scrap heap.

The virus was so brilliantly designed that it completely hid the attack from the Iranian plant operators until it was way too late. According to surveillance made by the International Atomic Energy Agency, workers were seen working "desperately"—frantically removing possibly one thousand of the plant's nine thousand centrifuges. The IAEA estimated the number of working "spinners" went down from forty-seven to thirty-nine hundred. Right after that, Gholam Reza Aghazadeh, the head of Iran's Atomic Energy Organization, was forced to resign, "following a serious nuclear accident."

The Iranian president himself was forced to admit in November 2010, "They succeeded in creating problems for a limited number of our centrifuges with the software they had installed in electronic parts." But even he was not about to nail the Israelis, whomever he believed the culprit to be.

But in early 2011, the outgoing head of the Mossad told the Israeli parliament, the Knesset, that by disabling as many as a thousand of Iran's centrifuges, the virus might have set back Iran's ability to produce a nuclear weapon until 2015.

This, however, did not happen. The Iranians launched a titanic effort to repair the damage with a massive program to replace the Russian-built centrifuges.

The Mossad was blamed for a devastating attack in 2011 on an Iranian missile base that killed Hassan Moghaddam, the architect of Iran's missile program. More bomb attacks killed two more missile scientists. But all to no avail. Tehran was determined to proceed with its quest for an atom bomb.

That ended on October 6, 2016, when Israel's air wings demolished

the plants at Qom and Natanz . . . bombs and missiles, this time, bearing
controlled Israeli nuclear warheads. Result: a total wipeout of the Iranian
threat, minimum peripheral damage. Mission accomplished.

Rani smiled at the memory of it all.

He also smiled at the likelihood of a new Russian cyber-research center, working on a method to zap the American president's nuclear-launch
communications system. President Markova would need a site beyond
the prying eyes of the US satellites, and he knew precisely where that
would be—inside those eighteen-foot walls of the monastery . . . the ones
that had withstood a nine-hour cannonball siege, never mind a few laser
beams.

He wondered about the best way to tackle the new myriad of problems
that faced him. He needed instant satellite surveillance of Solovetsky Island, a controlled and regular search for signs of interceptors, antenna, or
radio masts. "Jesus," said Rani, to the empty room, "we ought to be able to
spot that kind of stuff jutting out of a sixteenth-century building."

The photographs he had studied also showed a private docking area,
right below the monastery, and there would be regular lines of supply,
food, and electronic equipment, not to mention nuclear components, as
well as some kind of replicas for the nuclear football, systems upon which
the Russian scientists could practice.

The more he thought about it, the more enormous the problem
seemed to be. He understood the scale of the Russian spy system, the
"spooks" in every embassy, the ease with which they had penetrated some
of the most secure agencies in the world.

But the Mossad were certainly their equals and probably their betters.
Of course, the Israelis, if they knew what he knew, would probably be
tempted to slam a nuclear missile straight at the island and have done
with it.

But this was Russia, not Iran. Not even the United States would be
anxious to pull off something like that, because that was tantamount to
war. And that would be as crazy as old Markova's plan to hit Washington.

Rani was in a quandary. He could contact Mossad headquarters in
King Saul Boulevard and hand the entire thing over. Or he could tip off
the Americans. But Rani had a feeling he should do more, personally, to
bring this problem to a resolution.

Also, he was extremely concerned about blowing the bugle for a five-alarm fire when he could be barking up the wrong tree. He had, after all, no proof of anything, and the last thing he wanted was to be regarded as some kind of a hysteric. In the espionage game, no one ever forgot the field agent who activated a massive reprisal, only to be proven completely wrong.

No, Rani Ben Adan wanted more time to work on this. Lieutenant Commander Chirkov was proving a fantastic ally, and he might just find a way to get closer to the heart of the matter. However, there was one man in all the world he very much wanted to speak to—his trusted American buddy, the man with whom he had jumped off the oil rig in the Gulf.

This was a man as influential as he was in classified Special Forces operations. He had a private cell-phone number in the United States and would probably relish the idea of something this potentially important, this potentially dangerous.

But Rani would need to take the greatest care with the communication. If he was caught, in Russia, trying to make contact with an American military officer, or even "hacked" by the FSB, they would arrest him instantly. What an ignominious end to a promising career, to disappear without a trace into the Lubyanka, never to be seen again.

Rani thought it over. If he spoke to his buddy, who could put various investigations into action, it would not be directly his problem if it all proved groundless. But if he alerted King Saul Boulevard and it all turned out to be rubbish, it would not be regarded as his finest hour—Bren Adan's nephew or not.

The clandestine American route appealed to him more, and he thought it through, long and hard. He could not have the conversations by phone, and he surely could not use the Internet except in the briefest possible way. He would obviously have to meet his friend somewhere where neither would be noticed. He pulled up a map of Europe on his screen to find his bearings.

Then he picked up a telephone and asked for a secure line from which he could dial the United States, much of which was slumbering in the middle of the night. Rani, however, was dialing the West Coast, where it was eleven o'clock. He knew the cell-phone number would first go through a military switchboard at SPECWARCOM, the US Navy's Special Warfare Command, Coronado, San Diego.

He was dialing the home base of the United States Navy SEALs. And at this time in the late evening, it would be answered by the duty officer. The connection was swift.

"United States Navy . . . "

"Could you please connect me to Captain Mackenzie Bedford? I'm a very old friend. Colonel Adan, Israeli Army."

It took a full three minutes to clear the call through to the SEAL commander. But he came on the line and let out a shout of delight.

"RANI! How are you? Where are you? And can you talk?"

"Fine. Moscow. And no."

And once more the terrifying moments of that night on the oil rig stood before them both. Mack Bedford, blood pouring from a wound in his upper arm, trembling from head to foot and just staring down at the black ocean water. Colonel Adan grabbing him and shouting: "We stay here, we're gonna die, Yankee . . . *JUMP! FOR CHRIST'S SAKE, JUMP!"*

And then he had hauled him over the edge. And what a fall it was— *down . . . down . . . down*—before they crashed into the water, Mack still hanging onto the Israeli commando's arm.

"Mack, I must see you."

"When?"

"Now. This might be the most important phone call you'll ever take."

"Christ! That's a hell of an entrance."

"Deadly serious, Mack. How soon can you get to Europe?"

"Quick. We got a flight going to the US military hospital at Landstuhl, Germany, tonight, leaving 1:00 a.m. Picking up some of our guys wounded in Afghanistan."

"I'll fly to Frankfurt."

"Okay. We'll check times later. But I'll have a US military plane pick you up in Frankfurt—you'll be on Lufthansa from Moscow, right? Then we'll fly on over the border into France. That'll lose anyone tailing, right?"

"Great work, Mack. Talk to you later, same number."

Rani put down the phone and sat back in his chair. The situation room was still empty. The computer screen still showed a sinister photograph of the monastery. He shut it down and found himself again wondering about that submarine.

Because of Nikolai's information, it seemed the *Gepard* had been on some kind of a trial run. Those Russians had guessed it would be detected off Scotland and, in these post–Cold War times, were quite prepared to put up with that. Submarines, he thought, have a lot of advantages, like you can't see 'em, mostly can't hear 'em, and you never know where the hell they're going, or even where they've come from. *Furtive little fuckers,* he muttered.

They also had one or two devastating advantages—their reputation for pure sneakiness, unimaginable firepower, and a complete lack of human conscience, which always preceded them. They are, simply, acutely dangerous. They also have a couple of major disadvantages, like no one takes a chance with them in times of war, hot or cold. There is no ship in all the oceans more likely to be hit and sunk by its enemy with no questions asked.

And when a submarine goes to the ocean floor in deep waters, it's just about impossible to locate because of the vast distances involved. Contrary to popular belief, no submarine is in constant touch with its base. It communicates by means of a satellite signal, and for this it must come to the surface and activate its mast, sending its signal and receiving any orders or advice from home.

Most submarines have a "call time" and go through this procedure once every twenty-four hours, usually in the small hours of the morning. If a Russian attack submarine is hit by an American torpedo at 0400 hours, two hours after it checked into Murmansk, no one is going to know. There's no open line. It will be twenty-two hours before it's due to check in again and possibly four more before anyone at home base starts to panic because it's late.

This is a total of twenty-eight hours since its last-known position, and the submarine is known to be cruising at eighteen knots. Therefore, the possible distance between its last-known and right now is more than five hundred miles. And somewhere along that line, it may be located. But . . . it could have changed direction for whatever reason at any point along that line, anywhere it chose.

The submarine hunters had better draw a half circle with a five-hundred-mile radius, maybe a quarter of a million square miles. You want to arrange a search over that distance in the North Atlantic? Good luck.

Which is why submarines have been known to vanish. In Rani's mind, the Russians were considering moving a valuable cargo by submarine, at least they were before *Gepard* ended up on the beach. And now they may have to regroup and move that cargo on the surface.

Everything in Nikolai's dossier adds up to a Russian revenge strike, he thought. *I think they're going to launch from somewhere else . . . They might even be preparing to blame someone else. And they'd have loved to transport everything deep underwater, but they dare not do that now, because the Americans will go on a post-*Gepard *high alert. They'll have that SOSUS submarine-hunt system up and running within weeks, not months.*

Rani shut down the computer and walked upstairs to the travel department and discovered this could hardly have been more awkward. Mack Bedford would arrive in Landstuhl at eleven o'clock at night. So he must get out of Moscow this afternoon and then stay overnight at Sheraton's Frankfurt Airport Hotel.

He texted Mack to meet him tomorrow at 0800 (local) at the hotel. The shuttle would run them both over to the private general aviation area on the north side of the airport.

Within moments he received a text back: *See you then . . . Walk, don't jump. Mack.*

Rani was glad to be leaving Russia for a few days. He looked forward to the flight, and he looked forward even more to seeing Mack. He spent a few hours writing down his thoughts, in an indecipherable code, and had an embassy driver take him out to the airport.

The Lufthansa flight left at 6:00 p.m. and began its 960-mile journey, traveling back through two time zones. The Boeing 737 would thus touch down in Frankfurt at more or less the same time it left Moscow. Its route took it over Belarus and then Poland, directly into German airspace, leaving Berlin to the north, and flying along eastern Germany's southern border to Frankfurt. They landed at 6:15 p.m. Mack Bedford was still out over the North Atlantic.

The evening passed easily, Rani in the Sheraton Hotel, Captain Bedford in the officers' quarters at Landstuhl. There were about sixty miles between them, and the following morning the military flight to Frankfurt took less than a half hour. The two old friends met up with commando precision in the Sheraton foyer at 0800 sharp.

Their short ride to the airport was conducted in silence since both men understood the peril of Rani's position in Russia—fraudulent cultural attaché, fraudulent documents, Mossad spy/assassin, running important Russian Naval officer as a paid informant, and currently engaged in trying to thwart the personal wishes of the Russian president.

Neither man uttered a word until they were safely on the US aircraft bound for the small French airport in the heart of Alsace-Lorraine, which serves the French town of Metz. It lies in rich countryside, twelve miles southeast of the town, which was once German, but now the capital of Lorraine.

After they landed, Captain Mack Bedford requested that the pilot return to Landstuhl and to have them both picked up the next afternoon to return him to the US base and to drop Rani off at Frankfurt Airport, for the evening flight to Moscow.

Not until they were in the air and speeding toward the French border did they finally lean back in their seats and discuss the reasons they had flown several thousand miles just in the interest of trust.

"Well, old buddy, I sure as hell knew you would not have summoned me from San Diego to the French-German border unless it really mattered." Mack Bedford was certain of his ground at least on that.

Rani came swiftly to the point. Before they had even landed he had explained that he was "running" a highly placed Russian Naval officer, who was, in a sense, a prisoner of his own conscience and thought nothing of working against the excesses of his own government.

Mack was all ears. It was not often that anyone managed to hear of the inner workings of a top Mossad operator at this close range.

"And this character actually believes the president of Russia is planning a major missile strike against the United States?" said the American. "Probably somewhere in the Washington area?"

"This character was actually sitting at the table, two places away from the president, when the old bastard was talking about it."

"Who else was there?"

"The fleet commander, who appears to be in charge of the organization. Plus the foreign minister, and the prime minister, and the head of the entire Russian Navy, Rankov himself."

"Fuck me," said Mack. "And where were they?"

"Only in the friggin' rotunda, former Supreme Command HQ of Stalin's Red Army, directly behind Lenin's tomb."

"Holy shit!" said Mack. "You're right. This matters. How the hell did you get this Russian to turn traitor?"

"Nothing to do with me, Mack. He just turned up at the embassy. I debriefed him for a couple of days, and we decided he was genuine."

"And you're sure?"

"Absolutely certain."

"So why not go through the usual channels? Tell your guys in Tel Aviv and have them alert the right people in the CIA and the Pentagon."

"Mack, I'm sure of this, in my own mind. But I'm not so certain that I could not be wrong. And that would be awful, to raise a huge fuss inside both of our countries and then be wrong. I'm just not ready to jump in the deep end. Yet."

"Surprising. I thought you were especially good at that."

Both men laughed. And right then the military aircraft began its descent into the Metz-Nancy Lorraine airport, dropping down across long, sloping fields into superb country east of France's champagne district. SPECWARCOM had touched base with their French counterparts and had booked rooms for both men at Hotel de la Cathedral, a converted seventeenth-century town house with only twenty beamed rooms, antique rugs, and unobtrusive staff.

They were met by a chauffeured car, arranged by the American Embassy in Paris, and taken directly to the hotel. Both Mack and Rani were amazed by the sight of the stupendous Gothic cathedral of St. Étienne, visible from both of their rooms. This enormous edifice dates back to the twelfth century and contains towering stained-glass windows, some more than seven hundred years old and reputed to be the finest in France.

It was a civilized place to speak of barbaric actions. They were directed for dinner to an excellent French restaurant, L'Étude, a half mile from the hotel. This had the effect of turning a potentially arduous afternoon into a kind of overture.

Captain Bedford was a natural-born gourmet, coming as he did from coastal Maine with its sublime fish and lobster, and Rani was starved of excellent restaurants in Russia and could hardly wait to seize the wine list at L'Étude.

Meanwhile, they checked in, ordered a couple of omelets for lunch, and settled down to talk in a quiet corner of the hotel's lounge.

"Okay, old buddy, lay it on me," said the big US Navy SEAL commander. "And by Christ, this better be good."

Rani began his story, beginning with the strange case of the grounded submarine and the odd-sounding intercepts the Russian officer had discovered. He told him about the incoming foreign nuclear scientists, and he regaled him with the mention of the monastery, the site of the monastery, the history of the monastery.

He walked him through the mention of the "nuclear football"—and the onset of cyber warfare, which would be necessary should his theories be correct—and the Russians really did intend to kick that football "out of the stadium," as the naval officer had overheard.

But most of all, he concentrated on the vengeful mind-set of the old Russian president, Markova, and his obsession with America's part in smashing aside the Russian S-300 missile defense system, which the Iranians had purchased from Moscow at vast expense.

He explained to Mack how Markova had been appalled when he heard the ease with which Israel's US-built fighter-bombers had screamed through the skies at supersonic speed, then blitzed the underground bunkers of the nuclear factories, slamming missiles with nuclear warheads straight into the ramparts of the protective mountains.

In the opinion of Rani Ben Adan, President Markova and his closest advisers would never forgive the United States for its part in arming the ruthless Israeli Defense Force. He believed that Mother Russia had been held up to ridicule by the rest of the world and that he, and he alone, the Great Markova, was now tasked by all the Russians to wreak a terrible revenge on the United States.

"Of course, he's fucking crazy," murmured Mack Bedford helpfully.

"So he might be," replied Rani. "But what if he has perfected some kind of new, sleek, very fast lightweight cruise missile, medium range, carrying the massive wallop of a nuclear warhead? And what if they have found a way not only to launch from outside Russia, but to zap the US president's black box, the last-ditch communications system?"

"That would be bad," mused Captain Bedford. "Very bad. Because we could come under attack from an incoming missile from a highly unusual direction and then find ourselves badly delayed in response."

"And then Russia sits back," said Rani, "surveys from long range the death and destruction, and says: *Oh, my God, how awful. Who could do something that terrible? Mr. President, you can count on your friends in Moscow to do everything we can to assist you—and indeed to help discover and punish the culprits for this disgraceful breach of international goodwill.*"

Silence for at least ten seconds. "What then?" asked Rani.

"I'm afraid that's for you to answer, because, quite frankly, it beats the hell out of me," replied Mack. "I'm really new around here. But I'm getting a strong feeling that you're on the right lines, as usual. However, I question, why you are doing this? You're not even American."

"Because, Mack, if they can hit the United States with some kind of an advanced new missile, they can persuade Iran to turn it on Tel Aviv or Jerusalem . . . The carnage in our cities would be unimaginable. Meanwhile, we have to think, what can anyone do? If asked, the Russians will deny everything, which, hypothetically, would leave the Americans with just one option . . . "

"Which is? . . ."

"They'd have to hit the goddamned monastery," said Rani flatly, "and hope to Christ to destroy the entire program—high-speed missiles, cyberwarfare equipment, satellite comms, masts, antenna, computer systems, technicians, scientists, the lot . . . "

"But they will not do that," interjected Mack. "Nothing is going to persuade the US government to nuke a remote sixteenth-century monastery in the far north of Russia because it might have a fucking bomb in the cloisters. That's not going to happen. Because that would bring us as close to World War III as October 1962, when Khrushchev decided to plant ballistic missiles in Cuba . . . DEFCON 3 . . . ninety miles from Miami and all that."

"Then there's no point mentioning any of this to any government," said Rani, "because no one's going to believe us sufficiently to take action. That means it's up to us, to work in the background, investigate, research, utilize my spy, and sound the alarm at precisely the right time."

"Rani, I'm afraid it's mostly up to you."

"Will you help, Mack? Provide intelligence backup? Maybe surveillance? Get the CIA involved? Alert the Special Forces, if we need to move?"

"Affirmative, Rani. Affirmative to all of the above."

4

L'Étude Restaurant
Metz, Alsace-Lorraine

"Could you tell me precisely where you want to start?" Captain Bedford had the US Navy SEAL's yearning for precise and clear orders, identical to the ones he always issued in combat.

Rani Ben Adan was from a military background and had no problem with that. "Gotta get satellite surveillance on the island of Solovetsky . . . because they must have heavy-duty electronics, out in the open. Darn walls are so thick, no beams of any kind could possibly penetrate."

"Okay, and what else are we looking for?"

"Arrivals by sea. There's no other way in. And there has to be incoming freight, to supply the nuclear program. There will be a steady stream of Russian Naval vessels, small craft. It's not deep water inshore. I'd say we're watching for night landings."

Mack Bedford had studied the map. In addition, he knew, more or less from memory, the programs of US surveillance satellite passes over northern Russia. He thought it unlikely that America's space photographic department had much of an interest in the north end of the Onega Peninsula—a sincerely desperate place, aside from the paralyzing cold weather.

The Onega is sparsely populated, with a few tiny coastal fishing villages and some logging in the Southeast. The peninsula is a wilderness, one hundred miles long with high, snowcapped hills and a half-dozen rivers hurling, occasionally, melted ice into the already freezing White Sea.

"For months at a time no one can get to it," said Rani. "And with a major scientific program ensconced there, I would guess there are helicopter deliveries to the monastery."

"We'll have heavy satellite surveillance," said Mack. "Especially on the Russian Navy bases to the north in Murmansk and Severomorsk. The same Big Bird will photograph to the south—shipyards in Archangel and Severodvinsk. I doubt it catches the Solovetskys. That will take an adjustment."

"Can that be done?"

"Yup, I'll get that fixed. What else?"

"Look, Mack, a strike on Washington would be terrible, and it must be prevented. But I am even more worried about Russian interference with the president's black box. We know the Russians have it on their minds, because it is the one thing that can screw up their crazy plans and initiate a possibly fatal US strike against the motherland. Also, my man in the rotunda heard them use a reference to the nuclear football. And I do not believe that was a coincidence."

"But you don't have much else on that, right?"

"Only my brain, which might not be good enough."

"Well?"

"Mack, the clear leaders in the race to cyber warfare are the Chinese. They're ahead in the technological stampede to hack into other nations' comms systems. It's happening in Shenzhen, a city that transformed from a Pearl River Delta farmyard to China's Silicon Valley in about an hour and a half."

"And what happens there?" he asked.

"It's high-tech central. And there's one corporation that stands supreme—China Shenzhen Technology. I have a gut feeling that inside that place, there's a Russian connection. If I wanted to clobber America's nuclear football, that's the first place I'd go. Just because they're the acknowledged world experts."

"And . . ."

"We want to know if any of their guys make the journey to Solovet-sky—because if they do, that's game, set, and match to us. *Hackers Supreme enter Honorable Monastery to help Russian Maniac kick the shit out of American capital city.*"

"What am I supposed to do about that? Kill them on the Solovetsky dock?"

"No, Mack, but I hope you will alert the CIA to a possible cyber attack on the nuclear football, which may be masterminded in Shenzhen Technology. They'll have guys in there. Jesus, the Mossad has two. I just want Langley to watch out for a connection between the cyber center of the world and what I believe is a new intercept laboratory on those islands."

"Can your man help us? You'll keep us posted if he hears anything significant?"

"Affirmative to both, sir."

"Okay, Rani. I'll talk to Bob Birmingham and get some kind of surveillance. He's damned well good at all that undercover crap."

"He must be, otherwise he'd be damned well dead. We know all about that Bobby. Same racket, right?"

For a few moments the two men sat sipping wine and studying the menus. Rani went for escargots and steak au poivre, Mack for *moules à la marinière* followed by coq au vin. Rani chose a 2010 St. Emilion, Château Canon Fronsac.

"I am about to place myself in a very delicate position, which I'm not used to," said Mack finally. "This sounds to me like a serious Russian threat against Washington. I do not doubt anything you have said. But I'd better not misjudge it—because right now I'm all there is."

"Even if I alerted my top commanders, I'm not sure they'd carry it forward to the Americans. It's just too tenuous, and all of us are afraid of causing an uproar over nothing."

"In my game we kinda specialize in causing an uproar," said Mack. "But the most I can do is alert all of the key players in the Pentagon and the CIA that the Mossad believes something truly dangerous is going on. We need to step up surveillance, sharpen up the satellite cameras, and get SOSUS back in the front line. That's likely to be the toughest part.

"Because however good the electronic sensors are, none of it matters if you don't have warships or planes to arrest or destroy an intruder. We can't count on the Brits anymore—they don't have the hardware.

"Christ knows, the Brits were our guys. And they were the best; top-class officers, top-class crews, top-class ships, weapons systems, and aircraft. Now they're like some fucking banana republic. No strike aircraft, no carrier force, hardly any destroyers or frigates. And their submarine force is just a shadow of its old self. It's a goddamned shame. And it's the end of our trusted right arm on the eastern side of the Atlantic."

Rani nodded his agreement and understanding. And they dined together speaking mostly of old times. Mack Bedford was hours away from returning to the high-pressure environment of Coronado, home of the US Navy SEAL training program and strategic planning for US Special Forces missions.

Since his promotion to captain, Mack had moved his wife, Annie, and young son, Tommy, out to California for the remainder of this tour of duty. They lived in extremely comfortable officers' quarters, but it was right on the base and almost impossible to escape the long friendships and camaraderie of his calling. But it was a grand and healthy way of living in almost perpetual sunshine, and Annie was just thrilled her husband was not required to lay his life on the line in active combat every other week.

SEAL Team 6 was also back at Coronado, and Mack's vast close-quarter combat experience was constantly used by all the base commanders. Returning home to Coronado was never a hardship, however hard the training and the work.

Rani, on the other hand, led a cold and lonely life in Russia, as the eyes and ears of his nation, shouldering enormous responsibility and often working alone for weeks on end.

Before the two men parted, Rani alerted the American to the Russian code word for the probable forthcoming attack. "Listen out for *Project FOM-2*," he said. "That's the code they used at that meeting in the rotunda. And they used it more than once. No one even told our man at the table what it meant. Which I guess put it under the heading of 'Top Secret.'"

The two men finally parted the following morning. Mack headed toward the huge military aircraft that would transport him nonstop from Landstuhl to California.

Rani boarded a smaller US military aircraft for the short flight to Frankfurt and then a return to the shadows of Moscow, and the sinister regime that ruled the place.

His outlook deepened as the Lufthansa flight made its way over the Central European plain toward the Russian capital. He understood his objective had been gained. Mack Bedford was about to get the right people onside in the United States. If Mack said the surveillance should be stepped up, and he advised the satellite observations to be adjusted and instructed the CIA to investigate Shenzhen Technology, then it would be done.

But deep within Rani's soul there was a fear: that things were moving faster than he understood, that Nikolai might find himself behind the eight ball, and that Moscow was even further advanced with this plan than either he or the Russian lieutenant commander realized.

For now he could only wait, and watch. But his heart was heavy as the Lufthansa Boeing came screaming down, over the flat fields to the northwest of Moscow, toward Sheremetevo-1 Airport.

TWO WEEKS LATER
FRIDAY, AUGUST 31

Solovetsky Islands

Nikita Markova was one hell of a long way from home, his vast Kremlin apartment he regarded as a temporary pied-à-terre in Moscow. His real home, in his own mind, was a picturesque small town near the Crimean coast of the Ukraine, Massandra, famous for its wine making, its fabulous Louis XIII–style châteaus, and its subtropical climate fanned by warm breezes off the Black Sea.

President Markova could perhaps have been forgiven if he'd gone into acute shock as he walked through the cold rain, fourteen hundred miles from his homeland, almost as far north as possible that one could go and yet still be in Russia. To his left stretched the chilly White Sea. Beyond that the even colder waters of the Barents Sea and then the Arctic ice cap.

President Markova, wearing one of those dark-green Australian cattle drover's raincoats over his heavy sweater, plodded gamely through the mud, crossing the long dam between the two islands, flanked by his staff and by Admiral Ustinov and navy chief Admiral Rankov. There were at least twenty more members of this working party, all walking, heads down into the rain. The wind came in from the North, and the Russian president, from the warm South, felt like a total stranger in his own land. But his heart was alight with anticipation.

Up ahead, trundling over the rough causeway built by monks two hundred years ago, was a large army truck, high and wide, with a major construction on its rear bed. For anyone who had ever attended Russia's May Day Victory Parade through Red Square, it was an unmistakable sight—the Mobile-TEL, the Red Army's most advanced missile launcher. Clearly visible were the conical heads of two medium-range rockets: the business end of the top secret Russian 9K720 Iskander SS-26, their most lethal tactical ballistic missile.

Up ahead of this slow-moving convoy was the cold, desolate island of Bolshaya Muksalma. Behind them was Solovetsky Island. Just out of sight, back through the pine forest, was the Solovetsky Monastery, where many of the walkers had lived for the past eighteen months.

The mobile-theater Iskander system had been for many years in almost perpetual stages of development and improvement. The missile was always world class and appeared to have not only a cluster-munitions warhead but also a fuel-air explosive-enhanced blast version, plus an earth penetrant for bunker busting.

It hurtled into its target at supersonic speed, following a quasi-ballistic path, with brilliant evasive maneuvers if necessary, pulling up to thirty Gs to evade an antiballistic missile. It flew a relatively flat trajectory. At speeds of almost four thousand miles per hour, it traveled low, never leaving the earth's atmosphere.

The Iskander was twenty-four feet long and weighed close to four tons. Its accuracy was near legendary among the world's missile technicians and scientists. The Americans had a better one, but not that much better. No other nation had a missile anything like the latest Iskander. With its superb accuracy, reliability, and ability to launch virtually from anywhere, it brought a whole new approach to precision bombing, even in the face of superior enemy fighters and air defenses.

The Iskander was designed to destroy anything. It had a near-flawless, failure-proof record both in launch preparation and in its automatic-computation flight. The transportability of its system vehicles made it unique among ballistic weapons for every friend of Russia.

There was only one glitch. International treaties for guided missiles ban nations from increasing the range of the unmanned rocket-propelled flying bombs. The Iskander-M was for years restricted to a distance of between four and five hundred kilometers as the principal system being used by the Russian armed forces. But rumors abounded that Russia had the capability for flying the Iskander much farther.

Development for the top secret K-model was perhaps the most highly classified area of the entire Russian arsenal. For the past couple of years, there had been silence. Hardly anyone, even deep inside the Russian defense industry, knew when and where the system was being improved to provide the intermediate range the Russian government desired.

However, within the Russian Navy there was one man who guessed what was happening. His name was Lieutenant Commander Nikolai Chirkov, and unhappily for the Kremlin, he did not approve. And now there were two, because Chirkov was a committed spy, and his "contact," Rani Ben Adan from the Mossad, agreed with him.

If you counted Mack Bedford, there were three, because Rani had guessed Moscow was looking for a slimmed-down nuclear-warhead missile to fly at high speed and for longer than any other missile of its type had ever done. And Mack had believed him.

The two guided missiles, jutting out from under their tarpaulins on the back of that truck rumbling over the rough, rain-swept causeway between Solovetsky and Bolshaya Muksalma, represented months and months of work. The warhead had been worked on, and the aerodynamics had been updated. The letter *K*, in *K-model,* stood for *Krylataya,* meaning "winged," which sounded awfully good to Nikita Markova.

The scientists were pleased with the progress. The Iskander-K was no longer a five-hundred-kilometer short-range cruise; it was programmed to travel more than three thousand kilometers, possibly twenty-one hundred miles, before pounding into its target with a nuclear warhead packing megatons of explosive power, way beyond the comprehension of ordinary men.

If the forthcoming tests were accurate and running concurrently with the blueprints back in the monastery, this was the breakthrough for which Markova had been praying. This morning he would know. Both missiles had been preprogrammed for speed, distance, and guidance. A massive target had been jettisoned from a Russian Antonov-AN225, the world's largest and heaviest jet aircraft.

Adjustments had been made to the forward loading ramp, since the "target" had been dropped from below the nose cone of the aircraft while flying at high speed. A half-dozen parachutes were used to guide it through the ice-cold air, way beyond the North Pole, over which the new missile was scheduled to fly.

The target itself was a long wooden structure with steel-ribbed base beams to protect it from the impact of the landing. Right now it stood high, wide, and frozen on the tundra, six hundred miles beyond the pole. It had no doors or windows to avoid the possibility of a family of polar bears making an entry and finding themselves blown to high heaven by the entry of the Iskander-K.

Its latitude and longitude numbers had been fed into the missile's computer, although this was not so much a test of accuracy as one of distance. There was no point continuing with the missile experiment if the hardware could not fly far enough.

The rain-battered convoy reached terra firma on the far side of the causeway, where they stepped onto Bolshaya Muksalma, the lonely spot upon which the launch would take place. Not even the US satellites probed here, since there was no human life and no military presence of any description. Until now.

The Mobile-TEL howled in protest as it jolted over the rising ground, its rear wheels spinning in the deep mud as it lurched on, bearing the enormous weight of the launcher and almost eight tons of solid missile, fueled up and armed with high explosive. This may have seemed excessive, as they were only aiming to locate and blast a Russian shed.

The scientists, however, had insisted the voyage of Iskander-K be thoroughly authentic: weight, speed, fuel, warhead, under the atrocious weather conditions that can occur anytime over the polar ice cap. The regular single-stage solid propellant, which drives the missile, had been modernized to a supreme degree. And they were almost ready.

There were just a few hundred yards more to march in this wet and freezing hellhole to watch the launch of the missile that would put Mother Russia back where she belonged in the world pecking order: number one.

When finally the Mobile-TEL swerved to the right onto rough, soaking ground, a young army officer walked in front, holding a GPS and a compass. He signaled the huge truck into position, keeping one eye on the flickering indicator as it searched for magnetic north. When he was satisfied the launcher was aiming in the correct direction, he signaled the driver to raise the hydraulic gear, lifting the first missile into launch position, aiming due north.

President Markova watched from a distance of one hundred yards, standing in a small group comprising Admirals Rankov and Ustinov, plus the presidents of the Belarus corporation VirusBlokAda and the Moscow-based Kaspersky Corporation, both world experts in the field of cyber warfare.

With them was an unannounced guest, a Chinese executive wearing a massive raincoat and constantly wiping off his rain-lashed spectacles. In answer to Admiral Rankov's discreet question about the man's identity, Admiral Ustinov had replied, "Computer interception. He's here from some Chinese consultant firm. A guest of Vassily Levchenko."

"Do you know his name?"

"I think it's Wang or Yang. I didn't quite catch it. But he smiles a lot."

"All Chinese smile a lot, just before they rip you off blind and copy all your designs."

Ustinov chuckled. "I got the impression we were after his designs, not the other way around."

"Never know with wily Orientals," replied Admiral Rankov, borrowing a phrase he had learned, and treasured, years ago from his old American friend Admiral Arnold Morgan.

In fact, Mr. Wang/Yang was a great deal more interesting than that. He was head of technical design and development at China Shenzhen GSH Technology Corporation. He was the man who would create the satellite beam that would attempt to zap America's nuclear football.

President Markova had paid a fortune to have Mr. Wang/Yang move into the Solovetsky Monastery for a month. He and Foreign Minister Levchenko were the only two people who knew the true identity of the Pearl River Delta scientist.

Mr. Wang/Yang had cost the Russians 5 million US dollars, which had subsequently been divided equally with his home corporation. Which was probably why, despite the weather, he was smiling broadly at this unusual view from the pig's back. It was, after all, the year of the dog. The pig was not scheduled to take center stage until next year, 2019.

All eyes were fixed on the Mobile-TEL. Technicians punched in final numbers on the computer screens in the truck. The Iskander-K's course and speed were set.

SYSTEMS GO!

With an ear-shattering roar, the ballistic missile edged slowly up and then thundered skyward, flame blasting from its stern exhaust, scorching trees growing peacefully forty yards in front of the launcher.

Houston would have said coolly, "We have liftoff."

President Markova jumped up and down in his sea boots, clapping and cheering, as the rocket accelerated into the leaden skies, visible for only a few fleeting seconds before it ripped into the low, gray cloud base and hammered its way into the northern heavens.

They could still hear it, faintly growling and crackling in the no-man's-land of the earth's middle atmosphere, adjusting its course, making Mach 6—more than thirty-five hundred miles an hour—and now on a beeline for the North Pole, twelve hundred miles from Bolshaya Muksalma.

The men from the monastery were glued to their cell phones, speaking to the "spotters" posted in two observation posts in northern Russia, watching for Iskander to come streaking through the skies overhead on its deliberately low trajectory, if possible below the clouds, below any radar's line of sight.

And now it was flashing through clearer skies over the White Sea, driving north at its cruising speed of four thousand miles per hour, knocking off the ninety-mile crossing from Bolshaya to the south shore of the Kola Peninsula in one and a half minutes. The Russian Naval spotter, on the cliff close to the little seaport of Olenica, caught it in the southern sky four miles out, and it was past him in five seconds. He had no time even to raise his camera.

Across the peninsula the Iskander blazed its trail, covering the almost two-hundred-mile span of wilderness, tundra, forest, and low mountains in precisely three minutes before ripping over the headland of Teriberskij, forty-five miles east of Murmansk, on the shores of the Barents Sea. The navy spotter on the headland had even less time to make a proper observation, but he saw it, clear as a shooting star and, he thought, a hell of a lot faster.

He snapped out the agreed wording on his cell: *Teriberskij to Bolshaya . . . Isky running low and fast . . . on time and on course . . .*

The missile hurtled north over the Barents Sea, covering the distance of more than four hundred miles across the broad and lonely acres of one of the world's coldest oceans in less than seven minutes. By now it was level with the largest of all the Norwegian islands, Spitsbergen, the only populated place on the Svalbard archipelago, the final outpost before the polar cap. North of here, there is only the permanent ice shelf of the Arctic Ocean.

Iskander-K left the Land of the Midnight Sun nearly two hundred miles to its port side. Its course now took it over the eastern headland of the neighboring island of Nordaustlandet. Staring hard to the south was the Russian Navy spotter, standing next to a navy helicopter.

Like the other two, the young officer barely had time to focus, never mind act. He took no photograph, and he uttered no words to the copilot before the revolutionary Russian missile had flashed across the sky in the blink of an eye.

Nordaust to Bolshaya . . . Isky running low and fast . . . on time and on course.

The helicopter's comms were permanently connected to a Russian satellite. His words came through, clear and welcome to the launch group still standing in Bolshaya's drenching rain. President Markova and the visiting Mr. Wang/Yang were still smiling cheerfully. Iskander had been in the air less than twelve minutes.

Now the missile made a slight course adjustment and headed straight for the North Pole, five-hundred-plus miles and a little more than eight minutes away. An automated Russian weather station was programmed to pick it up and did so with the effortless robot efficiency of these high-tech radar installations.

The missile was logged flying south, past the pole, and now searching for its target, the huge wooden shed parked incongruously on the ice shelf.

From the pole it was another five minutes' flying time, and by now Iskander-K was locked onto its target, losing height but not speed and streaking through the icy air. Ten miles out, there was no longer a doubt. Russian Naval spotters, just over two miles away in a parked helicopter, saw it in a clear sky, and then it was over.

The ballistic missile hit that wooden shed with stupendous force, exploding with precision, courtesy of its computerized timing device. It actually detonated five feet above the roof, possibly because it was about one-millionth of a second early. Not that this mattered. This kind of weapon would have knocked down Yankee Stadium.

The shed almost went into orbit. Planks, struts, and beams blew into the Arctic air, over a radius of more than a mile. Timber was blasted into space. Some of it rained down on the tundra; some of it seemed to have vanished forever.

There was a gigantic hole in the pack ice, revealing a "floor" around seven feet thick. When the missile hit, a huge spout of freezing water gushed out of the ocean below and, under breathtaking compressed power, jetted more than a hundred feet high as the shell of the Iskander-K plummeted to the bottom of the Arctic Ocean.

If the missile had kept going for another couple of hundred miles, it would have run out of gas somewhere on the ice just west of Canada's Queen Elizabeth Islands in the extreme North. Gone a little farther, it might have splashed down somewhere near the Amundsen Strait, in the middle of the Northwest Passage, just before Canada's Beaufort Sea.

It had been a supreme piece of engineering to have sent a new, improved ballistic missile that far, that fast, and that accurately. The Solovetsky team members were immensely pleased with themselves.

There was, of course, no need for the second Iskander to be fired. It had been brought to the launch only in case of a major system failure of the first. And now they were returning to the monastery, that huge Mobile-TEL rumbling across the muddy ground, its industrial-level four-wheel drive forcing it on.

The observation party, in company with the Russian president, plodded along behind, and their spirits were high. The test firing of the new missile had been a resounding success. The Iskander-K had lived right up to the designers' hopes, and the president of Russia was ecstatic.

For his proposed strike on the United States, his greatest worry had been that he might have to launch from Russian soil—a course of action fraught with danger. Now he could look anew, and a wonderful possibility had opened up—that he could launch from a Central American country aiming straight at a major US East Coast military installation.

No one could possibly accuse him of being the perpetrator, at least not very quickly. That Iskander-K fired from the western Caribbean would accomplish its task in secret and near silence. It could fly over water almost all the way, low across the ocean, and then keep going north after it passed Florida, flashing up the Eastern Seaboard, making four thousand miles per hour—a thousand miles in fifteen minutes.

Nikita Markova had rarely experienced such elation. The words of his favorite Russian anthem from the eighteenth century cascaded through his mind . . . *Let thunder of Victory sound!* Deep in his soul there awakened the strident chorus of the enormous Red Army Choir and the greatest national music on earth—the sacred music of Alexandr Alexandrov, the anthem of Russian domination, which has reduced her sportsmen and sportswomen to tears of pride on a thousand rostrums in the world's Olympic Stadia.

Nikita Markova could feel it now as he plodded through the mud, in company with his admirals and his scientists, following the symbolic power of the future—the steel-pointed Iskander-K that would surely smash open the gateway to undisputed world leadership.

At the end of the causeway they stepped back onto the island of Solovetsky, where three army jeeps awaited them for the short ride back to the monastery.

And eighteen hundred miles away, scattered over a vast distance of the pristine white ice cap north of Canada, there were endless hunks of timber of no use to anyone, because no one lived within a hundred miles of the debris. And soon they would be covered, and buried, by the winter snows, and no one would ever know they bore such testimony to the ambitions of a distant president of Russia.

Except, perhaps, for a couple of night-shift technicians working in the air-conditioned photographic section of a US Defense Department complex, in deep, dark countryside, twenty-four miles west of Washington, DC.

0400 (LOCAL), FRIDAY, AUGUST 31

National Reconnaissance Office
Chantilly, Fairfax County, Virginia

Aside from a couple of branch offices of the New York and Chicago Mafia, and one or two California pedophile rings, the NRO stands unchallenged as the most secret organization in the entire United States of America.

It was established at huge expense in 1960, and despite a zillion requests from the media to reveal its purpose, it took the US government thirteen years to admit it even existed. And that was an accident perpetrated by a careless Senate committee.

The National Reconnaissance Office, in the broadest terms, is US satellite central. It designs, builds, and operates the US spy satellites, or, more officially, US space reconnaissance systems.

The NRO works hand in glove with the National Security Agency, the Central Intelligence Agency, and US Navy Research in all international matters. It employs three thousand people, and its annual budget would, more or less, finance the whole of Africa south of the Blue Nile.

Among its closest working partners are Buckley Air Force Base at Aurora, Colorado, and Menwith Hill, in Yorkshire, England, both highly classified aerospace-data facilities.

While building the US space grid, the NRO launched more than thirty major spacecraft, a couple of them nearly as big as NASA's Space-Lab. Each of them contained more than sixty miles of film and was able to photograph the streets of Moscow as if the cameras were two feet above the sidewalk.

These data were for years so secret that the use of any electronic system was strictly forbidden—*outer space to earth,* that is. This represented intensive cloak-and-dagger operations extremely difficult to carry out. The data were dropped down to the Pacific in "space buckets" with parachutes, and huge C-130 US Air Force planes came thundering in and snagged them with grappling hooks.

On one occasion, ten years previous, a spacecraft had failed and had to be returned to earth with all of its classified data. At first, an uncontrolled reentry into earth's atmosphere, with a warship ocean pickup, was considered, but upon reflection discarded. The data were too valuable to run any kind of risk.

The NRO finally settled for total destruction. The spacecraft was obliterated by a guided missile from a US Navy cruiser on February 21, 2008.

By 2018 there were almost a thousand satellites circling the earth, almost all of the major ones controlled by the NRO, the result of its sudden and aggressive launch schedule conducted in the eighteen months leading up to 2012. For so many years this clandestine branch of the Defense Department enjoyed such universal domination in space that it seemed to develop a driven ego of its own, as if demanding the necessary funds to outclass any and all of the world's rising nations and whatever power plays they intended.

So the United States continued its huge lead in space technology, and very little occurred on the geopolitical stage to cause it concern.

This changed during the week of August 31, when a series of instructions had come through directly from the Pentagon: satellite surveillance was to be widened in the area of the White Sea in northern Russia.

This applied specifically to the Solovetsky Islands, north of the Onega Peninsula, all the way up to the coastline east of Murmansk. At the same time, there was a very similar request from the CIA, expressly asking for enhanced surveillance in that same area.

Everyone in the satellite surveillance departments "rogered" that—*understood, will comply*—but no one asked why. The creed of all sixteen secret agencies in the US Defense Department is never to ask unnecessary questions and never to provide answers. Except to the chairman of the Joint Chiefs and the commander in chief.

US satellites were strong in northern Russia. Murmansk and its deep-bay neighbor Severomorsk were "home" to the Northern Fleet and included Russia's biggest submarine base. Less than four hundred miles to the southeast were the massive shipyards of Archangel and Severodvinsk.

The US satellites, twenty-two thousand miles above the earth, had for years made a half-hourly pass over this area. But the photography only just clipped the eastern edge of the Onega Peninsula, principally because there was hardly anyone there, and it was possible to get better pictures of Arctic bears and reindeer from wildlife magazines.

The satellite cameras now panned over the Solovetsky Islands. Captain Mack Bedford had been comprehensively believed, especially by Rear Admiral Andrew Carlow, commander in chief SPECWARCOM, and Bob Birmingham, the CIA director.

Strings had been pulled at the highest level of the Defense Department, where there was already consternation that one Russian submarine, and possibly two, had penetrated the GIUK Gap without being challenged earlier this year.

Rumors of Russian aggression, with its better-funded twenty-first-century navy and its continued high-income stream from West Siberian oil and gas, had been noted. SOSUS was being tightened up, listening stations reopened.

Captain Bedford's high-quality information, via a Russian Naval spy and an ultrareliable Mossad field agent, had been acted upon. Director

Birmingham had ordered two more agents into the Shenzhen cyber-warfare plants. Security had been tightened on the president's emergency communications system and codes changed, which meant a brand-new "biscuit."

As a direct result of Admiral Carlow's warnings, Mack Bedford's observations were widely circulated. US armed forces were all shaken out of the comparative relaxation of DEFCON-5 and ordered to DEFCON-4.

This was most unusual in a time of apparent peace in the free world. The DEFCON system (Defense Readiness Condition) had been America's alert-posture gauge since it was first developed, by the Joint Chiefs, under President Eisenhower in 1959.

It marked the grades of increased severity. DEFCON-5 is normal; DEFCON-4, Double Take (Green), signifies increased intelligence watch and strengthened security measures, above normal.

The United States went to DEFCON-3, Round House (Yellow), increased readiness, for 9/11, the Yom Kippur War in 1973, and the first day of the Cuban Missile Crisis, October 22, 1962. On the second day, for the only time in US military history, strategic air-strike forces went to DEFCON-2, Fast Pace (Red), next step nuclear war.

There has never been a call for DEFCON-1, Cocked Pistol (White), nuclear war imminent, maximum readiness. But in 2018, DEFCON had been relaxed for so long, the formal call from the US Defense Department to go immediately to DEFCON-4 was taken extremely seriously. Captain Bedford was given freedom to depart for Europe at will, to touch base with the man from the Mossad.

All this was before Nikita Markova decided on blastoff from Bolshaya Muksalma. And the newly organized US satellites caught the launch almost before the Russian president had time to cheer.

It was nonetheless such a surprise that there was hardly any formal military language or observation commands at the moment of truth, which provoked a total split-second reaction in front of the NRO screens.

"WHAT THE FUCKING HELL'S THAT?" snapped the duty officer, deep in the surveillance labyrinth of America's spy-satellite headquarters. It was exactly 4:00 a.m. in sleeping Chantilly, Virginia. And, right before his eyes, the officer could see a tiny blip moving north on the camera of the orbiting White Sea watchdog.

He instantly called for a second opinion. He zoomed way out to get a better perspective. His screen now showed the entire area from the Solovetsky Islands up to the Barents Sea. The Russian naval port of Severomorsk was now in the top left-hand corner of his screen.

Whatever the "paint" was, it was not a regular aircraft, not at this speed. There was not even the semblance of a landing strip on this tiny island of Bolshaya Muksalma. This was some kind of a missile, or even a spacecraft, because it had been fired into the air from a standing start and was now moving at supersonic speed under its own power.

The duty officer called for every kind of technology to lock onto its guidance system, to try to identify what was plainly a ballistic missile of some description. It was not an emergency situation, since the missile was going nowhere important, just due north, headed over the Kola Peninsula and across the Barents Sea toward the permanent ice cap that covers the Arctic Ocean.

But it was making four thousand miles per hour, and unless it changed direction or stopped altogether, it would reach the North Pole in about twenty minutes. *After that, God knows.* Right now the first satellite was running out of real estate, and the NRO technicians were switching to new pictures. There was a substantial satellite gap over the North Pole, but there was surveillance over northwestern Canada, Alaska, and west to the narrow Bering Strait, which divides the North American continent from the far-eastern limit of Russia.

The NRO computer estimates, now operational, suggested the missile would eventually travel due south down longitude 130 degrees west. If it stayed on that course, it would cross the Beaufort Sea and head south across Alaska and straight out into the Pacific.

No one in the Chantilly ops room, however, thought it could possibly last that long at that speed. And twenty minutes later, during which all eyes in the now-crowded ops room were concentrated on the screens, they watched the tiny "paint" vanish as it honed in on the pole.

For five minutes there was nothing. Then it showed up again, now flying south, still very fast, before, quite suddenly, it dived nose first, straight into the tundra, smashing straight through the ice floor of the Arctic. There was a substantial explosion, which caused the screens to go fuzzy . . . and then everything went quiet.

The conclusions were obvious. The Russians had test fired a small, very fast ballistic missile, which had traveled approximately eighteen hundred miles under its own power, and then blown up on the ice in a deserted stretch of the tundra known as the Alpha Rise. No harm done. Yet.

The interesting aspect of this was the launch site: a tiny island in a southern corner of the White Sea, a place cut off from the mainland for several months of the year, a place ten thousand miles from absolutely nowhere, except for another slightly larger desolate island upon which there was nothing except a sixteenth-century monastery that, eighty years ago, had been one of Stalin's prison camps.

There was no runway, no lights, no control tower, no radar installations, or even a launch scaffold. By any standards, even Russian, this was the skid row of the space world, about a million light-years from the slick professionalism of the Cape Canaveral AFC, home of US Air Space Command's 45th Space Wing with its two-mile runway.

The missile, however, in the opinion of the Chantilly experts, was almost certainly a variation of Russia's 9K720 Iskander. The big surprise was its range. No one had ever seen these twenty-four-foot ballistic missiles travel that far before, not even half that distance.

This morning's flight had probably been illegal under international law, but it had been launched from the very spot designated last week by the US Navy SEAL commander Captain Mack Bedford. Of all the millions of square miles in Russia, the updated Iskander-K had taken off in the shadow of Solovetsky Monastery. And that was a coincidence too far. Someone, somehow, needed to get to the bottom of this.

It was a military matter. After all, the Russians were not threatening anyone, at least not publicly. But the warning of the man from the Mossad, the urgency of his call to meet his trusted friend Mackenzie Bedford, could not be ignored. Something was going on. Captain Bedford thought it was highly sinister, and the anonymous Rani Ben Adan was certain there was a diabolical plot inside the Kremlin to hit, and hurt, the United States and probably Israel as well.

The director of the NRO, a US Air Force general, was awakened by his staff at 0430 and was sufficiently concerned by the Bedford-Solovetsky coincidence to issue an instant alert to the Pentagon and the CIA. He also fired an e-mail to Admiral Andrew Carlow, for whom it was only 0130 in Coronado. Andy was sufficiently on edge to phone Mack personally and tell him the Russians had launched a brand-new ballistic missile from *"that fucking little island you were going on about."*

Big Mack came hurtling out of bed the way you'd expect a SEAL to do. He woke up Annie, and Tommy, as he charged down the stairs to locate his encrypted cell phone. He called Rani, who answered swiftly, but had to call back because he was on his other line, talking to Nikolai Chirkov, who was on yet another cell phone, facing the wall in a deserted bus shelter in the remote fishing village of Solza, twelve miles along the coast from Severodvinsk.

Nikolai knew less than Rani, who had been in the embassy when the Israelis had detected the launch on one of their own satellites. They were not quite so advanced as the Americans and had not yet pinpointed the launch site. But they knew a ballistic missile was in the air, "from somewhere in the south of the White Sea." Nikolai knew only that his boss, Admiral Ustinov, had gone by navy helicopter to the Solovetsky Islands.

Rani knew also of the presence of a director of China Shenzhen Technology arriving in Russia and leaving Moscow by military aircraft, destination unknown. Lieutenant Commander Nikolai believed he would understand much more in the next twenty-four hours since his boss was due back on board the *Admiral Chabanenko* later this afternoon.

It would, however, be impossible for Nikolai to get away to Moscow, or even Petrozavodsk, for a rendezvous with the man who paid him so handsomely. They would need to meet somewhere in the North, close to the Russian warship. Rani would have to do the traveling. Nikolai could take off, but he could not be gone for longer than five or six hours.

Rani said quickly, "Sunday afternoon . . . call me on the secure cell, two thirty to three o'clock. I'll give you directions. I'll be close." Then the line went dead.

The Israeli agent, using his embassy's encrypted line out of Moscow, immediately called Mack in Coronado. He was not surprised to learn how much the SEAL commander actually knew about the launch—the make of the missile, its name, speed, route, and crash landing. And, above all, where it had come from.

Rani was succinct. "Mack, I'll know a lot more Sunday night. We'd better meet on Monday. I may be pushed for time, but I'll get there. Frankfurt Airport, midafternoon. Call me."

"Roger that."

Rani went immediately to his private apartment in the embassy and began to pack for a minimum of four days away. He gathered up his "John

Carter" documents, passport, and clothes, warm for the North, and summoned an embassy driver to get him to Yaroslavskiy railway station ASAP.

Running through his mind were all the steps that a master spy should follow—the main one being "unobtrusive," an art form in itself, the paint salesman traveling by train from Moscow to Archangel, a twenty-four-hour haul, more than seven hundred miles. On board the train he would speak to no one unless compelled to do so. He would travel first-class, a normal procedure for visiting Western businessmen, sleeping in the warm, comfortable compartments the Russians have perfected for long-distance travel.

He would have liked the instant speed and convenience of a private jet straight up to Archangel and back. But there was something ostentatious about that: a businessman flying into a very sensitive area, on a Learjet, which the Israeli Embassy favored, parking it overnight, and then flying out.

Archangel was only twenty miles from the "closed" port city of Severodvinsk, which was forbidden to foreigners, mostly because of the secretive nature of the Russian Navy. It was also the home base, for the moment, of Lieutenant Commander Nikolai Chirkov.

Rani wanted nothing about his arrival or departure to attract any attention, which was why he had elected to spend an entire day on a train. The embassy travel staff had booked him into the Zelyony Hotel, a couple of miles from the Archangel train station. He planned to spend the night there, since, even then, it may be several more hours before a rendezvous with Nikolai was possible.

However, boxed into another meeting with Mack Bedford in Frankfurt on Monday, he would need to move fast when his business with the Russian officer was concluded. And he would need a private plane to transport him directly from Archangel's small commuter airport, Vaskovo, situated a dozen miles southwest of the city, to Moscow's Sheremetevo-2 on Sunday night.

But that was a far less obtrusive procedure. He would arrive at Vaskovo completely unknown and blend in with the rest of the passengers in the private section. There would be no customs or passport control for an internal journey, not even check-in. He would board the just-arrived Learjet and take off immediately. No one at that airport would have the slightest idea who he was, just another Western businessman in a hurry.

Meanwhile, his driver was fighting the Friday-afternoon traffic in Moscow, trying to weave his way to Yaroslavskiy Station. They made it just before three thirty, and Rani purchased his ticket with his embassy American Express card for the long journey north, nearly three hundred miles up to Ivan the Terrible's old hometown of Vologda and then on through the mountains and lakes of northern Russia to the White Sea.

He spent a lot of his travel time trying to think of a suitable place to meet Nikolai, but Archangel was a place of enormous shipyards and state-of-the-art nuclear plants, many designed to produce propulsion power for Russia's newest submarines. It was a place where he would need to tread very lightly, because the FSB watches this area with immense diligence.

Anyone seeking to unearth Russia's innermost secrets in naval nuclear development would surely head directly to Archangel and then try to make it into the naval dockyards of Severodvinsk. This was known to be a graveyard for foreign spies, no place for the careless, and really no place for Rani. Except he was likely to hear more priceless information from Lieutenant Commander Chirkov than the last twenty foreign intruders had learned collectively.

Eventually, he decided they would meet at the bigger Archangel airport, Talagi, where neither of them planned to get on a plane. They could sit in a quiet corner, facing the wrong way, and chat. Then leave in separate cars, Nikolai back to the *Admiral Chabanenko,* Rani to Vaskovo Airport.

Meanwhile, Rani settled himself into his empty compartment, removed his jacket, and pulled on his regular traveling gear—a heavy, ribbed-knit olive-drab wool sweater with shoulder patches made of matching suede and buttoned epaulettes. It was the kind of universal sweater used by many national armies, as well as by many hunters and shooters. It was V-neck and made by Sturm of Germany, whose label appeared inside.

He decided to have dinner at the second sitting at around eight thirty and then sleep for as much of the night as possible. Rani slept intermittently through the night and had a halfway decent breakfast in the dining car. They arrived late afternoon, more or less on time, in Archangel, where he removed and repacked his sweater. The cab took only five minutes to run him down to the Zelyony Hotel. Waiting in his room was a note informing Mr. John Carter a private aircraft was due to land at Vaskovo,

Sunday night, at 7:30, and would be ready to leave immediately, or any time during the night suitable to the passenger.

The restaurant in the Zelyony had the highest reputation in the city. It was thus unnecessary for Rani to move until the following day. Nikolai came through on the cell phone right on time, Sunday afternoon at two thirty.

"Talagi Airport, Archangel, six o'clock. if that's okay with you," said Rani.

"See you there." Click.

Espionage, on the periphery, is mostly conducted in spoken telegrams. The rest of the time there is an atmosphere of suspicion, unrest, and nerve-wracked wariness. But Rani was comfortable with Nikolai and was anxious to see him.

They arrived in the Talagi Airport lounge at almost the same time. Nikolai went to a nearby counter and came back with coffee and a plate of sweet Russian pastries. He had much to impart, but he could stay for no more than an hour.

"The admiral's back, and he needs me later," he said. "I have a car with me, but I'll have to leave by seven o'clock."

"Not a problem. Where do we start?"

"The submarines. There were two sent into Scottish waters. One hit a trawl net, wrecked the boat, and drowned the crew. As you know, the other one wound up on the beach. But I discovered something. They were both transmitting on their sonar. They expected to be detected.

"The sub that dragged the fishermen under switched off everything after they realized something very serious had happened and made its way home. But the *Gepard* kept on transmitting until they ran out of water.

"I found out these were both trial runs to test the British and American SOSUS. Admiral Ustinov thinks they found out exactly what they needed. FOM-2 requires them to transport and deliver some serious hardware somewhere into the western Caribbean. As a result of *Gepard*'s antics, this will not be done with a submarine. Everything will be transported in a surface ship."

"Are we talking radioactive nuclear stuff?" asked Rani.

"These are four of the most modern, fast nuclear-warhead ballistic missiles ever produced," replied Nikolai Chirkov. "These are the weapons that will be fired at the United States. These are FOM-2, and I now know what the code stands for . . . "

"This can't be real . . . You are kidding me!" replied Rani.

"While the admiral was out I took a careful look at his computer, which he had not shut down," said Nikolai. "I didn't need his passwords. *FOM* stands for 'Fort Meade'; the *2*, as always in military weaponry, stands for 'nuclear.'

"Markova and the admirals are intending to smash America's National Security Agency in Maryland . . . destroy their code-breaking and communications systems with at least two missiles into the main headquarters building.

"They realize the Americans will respond at high speed. However, they intend to zap the nuclear football exactly at H-hour, rendering the US president helpless, and giving themselves a lot of time to deny all knowledge of the attack."

"Holy shit!" breathed Rani. "Was that the missile they tested on Bolshaya Muksalma on Friday morning?"

"Correct. An updated Iskander-K, with a possible range of around two thousand miles. They think this smaller, streamlined bird cannot miss and that it will fly too low for the US antimissile system to catch it.

"Also, remember that first missile we discussed six months ago in Petrozavodsk?"

"The Makeyev design?"

"Yes. They bailed out on that. And then they all worked together on the Iskander. The Makeyev was always too big and kind of obvious. Its new slimmed-down version was not giving them enough range to hit Washington. The Iskander very definitely can."

"This is unbelievable," muttered Rani. "Are these guys insane?"

"Very probably. That's why I'm sitting here."

"Can you get into that computer again?"

"I'm not sure. It was very dangerous. If he'd walked in that door and seen me, I'd have been court-martialed and then shot."

"How did you know he wouldn't?"

"Well, I knew where he was . . . on the bridge, checking some electronics. And there was a call for him from Moscow, and I had it switched through to him. That's when I got into the computer. I was pretty sure I had ten minutes."

"One thing, Nikolai. Was this information fragmented? Or was it in one file?"

"One file, which was not in any way fragmented. Everything was edited together into one complete document. Like a corporate plan."

"What was the file called?"

"'FOM-2.' And it had its own password . . . 'Natanz.' I managed to check that on the way out."

"Jesus. Did you get the feeling this was a file that all the main guys had? Or was it just for Admiral Ustinov?"

"Funny you should mention that. But I did have the feeling this was some kind of a master file that everyone had. Somewhere in there was a list of Admiral Ustinov's team, but I had no time to find it. I think Ustinov is the mission commander. This will be a Northern Fleet attack, when it starts. I think the admiral updates it personally and then circulates it."

"Why does he want you tonight?"

"No idea. But I wouldn't be surprised if he needed help with that FOM-2 file—bringing it up to date as a result of the test firing on Friday. There was no mention of that. And he does like to pace the room and dictate his reports."

"Directly onto the computer?"

"Right. And he prefers me to do the typing, because I can correct his language and spelling as we go along. Matter of fact, I think that was one of the reasons he hired me."

"Thank Christ he did. We might yet save the world," said Rani. "Could you get a copy of that file?"

"No. He's careless. But we have a full-time Internet security team on board. And they check everything and everyone, from the admiral down to the lowest seamen. I'm worried already they might know I've been into the file."

"What are they targeting at Fort Meade?"

"The tallest building in the complex. It's known as OPS 2A—eleven stories high, black glass, the place where they process the intercepts and cyber systems. That building goes up in smoke, the US of A will not know where the hell it is for probably six weeks. At least that's what our man in the Pentagon reckons. The entire US armed forces would lose their way."

"Is OPS 2A where the boss sits?"

"No. He's in OPS 2B. Eighth floor. Most of the NSA high command is in there with him."

"And Markova's maniacs have no plans to hit that as well?"

"No. There was a note on that in the file. Seems they all agree that's a step too far—murdering the most important intelligence and surveillance officers in the United States. They think, with some justification, the president might just take Moscow off the map for that. And that Markova might be remembered as the man who ended life as we know it."

"That might still be his fate," muttered Rani thoughtfully. "The Americans are capable of getting seriously pissed off—you push 'em too far."

"That's another reason we're sitting here," said Nikolai. "This has to be stopped."

"Trouble is, we can't stop it without getting fucking executed or something," said Rani. "Only the Americans can stop it. Which, I guess, makes Mack Bedford the most important man in the world. I'm seeing him tomorrow afternoon."

"Oh. Where?"

"It's a need-to-know situation . . . but not in Russia, obviously."

"Right. There's a major Chinese situation involved in all this. I don't know enough, but I do know there's a Dr. Yang here in Russia, possibly in residence at the monastery. He was going to the launching on Friday."

"And who's Dr. Yang?"

"He's the director of design development at China Shenzhen Technology, the cyber-hacking kings in Guangdong Province."

"Is this the critical path to the nuclear football?"

"Without a doubt. The Chinese are involved in this, much more than we know."

"How did you find out?"

"There's a section on them in that file. It was unclear, but they're going to be involved in the launch of the missiles. God knows how. China's farther away from Fort Meade than Russia."

"I thought you said they were taking the missiles down to the western Caribbean?"

"They are. And that's where China is going to help. But I can't see how, and certainly not where."

"What did the file say?"

"It was very disorganized on this subject. But there was an assessment by Admiral Rankov that went into the danger of launching an attack without nailing the president's football. He suggested that unless that emergency comms system was dismantled, those missiles could represent the most deafening suicide note in history. Rankov says the Americans would react so fast, no one would know what had hit them."

"Yeah," said Rani, "but they wouldn't know who to hit, would they? They got a couple of missiles coming at them from fucking Honduras, or Belize, or Nicaragua, or some other third world outfit, they can't fire back, can they?"

"No," replied Nikolai. "But they could, with some ease, identify the Russian-built Iskander-K, knock both missiles out of the sky, and then draw a bead on a major Russian Naval base like Murmansk or Severomorsk."

"Hmmm," said the Israeli. "Has China got any influence in Central America?"

"Not as much as the USA, except for maybe Venezuela."

"Then I guess we're back to square one," concluded Rani. "But that does not diminish Beijing's involvement, both with the cyber attack and the missiles aimed at the NSA. You've seen this material with your own eyes, and now we've got Dr. Yang standing at a top secret missile launch with the most prominent men in Russia."

"The one thing I couldn't work out was a time frame," said Nikolai. "The only fact we have is they won't launch until they can put that nuclear football out of action. And for that, they'll need some really advanced data. Plus the codes, which I could tell we don't have."

"We're talking months, not days or weeks," said Rani.

"Correct. Months during which they'll make even more perfections to the Iskander and probably increase its range."

"And nail down the perfect site from which to launch it. I guess you'll have to keep your ears open at all times to find that out, Nikki. And yes, I know you need to go. Your money will be on its way tomorrow."

"How much?"

"Have I ever let you down?"

"Never. But I'm putting my life on the line for this. How much?"

"A lot of money."

"How much?"

"For this? Probably a quarter of a million—if we can save Fort Meade."

"What if we can't?"

"One hundred thousand. This is very valuable."

"I was thinking more."

"Nikki, you are being paid very well. A grateful America will reward you in time. But you may have to defect, if you ever want to spend it."

"I know. But then I'd be on the run from the FSB for the rest of my life. They'd try to hunt me down."

"You have already taken that risk. And I believe you had a higher purpose—to save Mother Russia from nuclear mutilation by the Americans. And that you will probably achieve."

"Do you think I could survive in Russia? I mean, go on with my navy career?"

"I hope so. But if you want my personal opinion, I would say it's unlikely. This will get much deeper. We may have to get you out of here. But for now you appear to be safe. Just don't get careless."

"I understand. But there are so few people who know about this. Admiral Ustinov must realize I am one of the few. If they ever found out there was a spy, a Russian spy at that, and a trusted naval officer, well . . . "

"Nikki, they may never find out there's a spy. They may just decide the Americans were one jump ahead all along—they are, after all, the maestros of eavesdropping."

"And that's the main reason Markova wants to put their National Security Agency out of action. Funny how things go around in a circle, eh?"

"Always, but the main thing is to work safely. Take the greatest care when you contact me. And always give consideration to those times when no one else could have known except for you. That's what often betrays a spy: when he spilled too many beans."

"There's something else as well. A girl. I'm hoping to get married next summer. She's from my hometown, St. Petersburg. Our families have been friends for years. She's twenty-four years old and very beautiful."

Rani smiled. "What's her name, Nikki?"

"Anna. Anna Melnikov. She's a musician, a violinist, with the Kirov Ballet and Opera."

"In St. Petersburg?"

"Yes, the Marinsky Theatre is home to the Kirov."

"I think you are a very lucky man . . . but I have to ask, does she know about this? And your views about the present Russian government?"

"No. And if anything should happen to me, she must never know why. Her family would never get over the disgrace."

"And yours?"

"The Chirkovs are rebels. My father agrees with everything we are doing. He thinks Markova should face a firing squad."

5

Talagi Airport, Archangel

It was cold now, overcast, and growing dark. Across the parking lot, the sallow-looking man in the black leather jacket was still astride his dark-red Ural Wolf motorbike, a 750-cc V-Twin Russian-made powerhouse. The handlebars were high, wide, and gleaming chrome, and the rakish-looking rider had the gear to match: studded leather trousers, cowboy belt from the US Midwest, and ex–East German border-patrol guard boots, black steer hide with a steel horseshoe running right around the heel.

Kurt Petrov had spent the past half hour taking photographs of the distant mountains. And now, with the light fading, he was still snapping, still staring into the distance. But only with one eye. The other was focused on the main entrance to the airport, the only way in and out of the passenger lounge.

At 6:45 p.m. he saw what he'd come for—the uniformed Russian Navy lieutenant commander Nikolai Chirkov exiting the building in company with a smartly dressed foreign visitor, about whom there was nothing re-motely Russian, from the cut of his suit to his Burberry overcoat and leather briefcase.

He leaned down low in the saddle and aimed the long lens of the

111

camera straight at the two men, over the roof of the nearest car, firing off shots in quick succession.

Then they turned their backs, shook hands, and parted. It was all very swift. Kurt put down the camera and watched the Russian officer head for a black automobile and climb in. He took three more shots, then two more as the car pulled away, zooming in on the Russian license plates. He made no attempt to follow the car. No need. He knew precisely where it was going.

He then watched the foreigner, walking toward a waiting taxi. He kicked the Wolf 750 into life. He stowed the camera into the left-side holder behind the saddle and gave the cab a five-hundred-yard start before roaring out of the parking lot in effortless pursuit. He tracked it for several miles, all the way down to Vaskovo Airport, where the cab driver collected his fare and drove away.

Kurt Petrov parked and went immediately to the reception desk, where he showed his identifying badge and card. He was immediately escorted to a staff-only area with a straight view out to the private jet short-term parking area. And there, ten minutes later, he photographed Rani Ben Adan, in company with his pilot, making their way out to a waiting Learjet.

He never got a decent shot of either man's face, but combined with the other set of pictures, taken at the other airport, he had most of what he needed. He also had a record of the tail numbers of the Learjet, and on his cell phone he requested details of the owners. The charter company was not relevant, but the organization that rented the aircraft was.

Kurt Petrov, field agent (FSB), worked for the one organization in Russia that answers only to the president. He now knew one impressive fact: that Learjet was currently chartered to the Israeli Embassy, Moscow. The passenger had signed in as a Mr. John Carter of Birmingham, England. The embassy was not at liberty to disclose any further details and indeed pleaded diplomatic immunity from so doing.

The Russian agent watched the aircraft take off and bank around to the south before he fired up the Wolf 750 and headed back to Severodvinsk. He wondered what the Russian Naval officer was doing in secret company with anyone from the detested Israeli Embassy.

Still, it was not the forty-nine-year-old FSB man's job to find that out. He was a specialist in surveillance at the highest level, for Russia's Federal Security Service, the counterespionage and border-protection force, now reputed to have more power and freedom to act than the old KGB ever had.

Kurt had been involved a dozen years before in one of the FSB's most ruthless actions—when they finally located the "mad Muslim" Shamil Basayev, mastermind behind the Russian theater disaster and the Beslan school massacre. The FSB simply lured Shamil toward a truckload of high explosive and blew both him and the truck to smithereens. Questions were asked, but the reply was simple: the FSB had legal power to carry out targeted killing at its own discretion.

Kurt Petrov was accustomed to FSB autonomy and brutality. He had no idea what would happen to the naval officer, although he understood one thing: Nikolai Chirkov would require some very fast talking to get out of this one.

Things had moved very fast, and very unexpectedly, since the hour between eleven and midnight the previous evening. And neither Lieutenant Commander Chirkov nor "John Carter" knew one thing about it.

At ten o'clock the Internet security team, led by Lennart Weinert, had made a routine check on the desk computer of Admiral Alexander Ustinov. They had found a discrepancy—the system had revealed an update to his most protected file at 9:35 in the evening.

The team had not been able to look at the file, since they did not know the password, but they could see there had been "editing" at that time. Problem: Admiral Ustinov, commander in chief of the Northern Fleet, had not returned to the ship before eleven. So who had done the "editing"?

Lennart Weinert reported to the admiral as soon as he returned to his quarters and informed him that someone had been into his computer ninety minutes before his return.

The admiral was mystified and told the security guys there must be something wrong with the hard drive.

"This is not a discussion," he told the highest commander in the fleet and almost certainly the next chief of Russia's Naval Staff. "Someone went into that file. Otherwise, the information could not have been saved."

"Well, the only person would be my personal assistant, Lieutenant Commander Chirkov. He has access to the office. But not to that computer, certainly not to the most sensitive documents."

"I am proposing to call in an FSB officer and discuss the matter further," said Weinert.

"I am not ready for that," replied the admiral. "And I forbid it. However, the lieutenant commander has informed me he will be off the ship for a couple of hours in the late afternoon, tomorrow. You have my permission to follow him. If there is guilt, we must find it. But I would be very surprised if Nikolai Chirkov had committed any kind of indiscretion."

"As you wish, sir," replied Weinert. "I will undertake that. And report to you as soon as possible."

One hour later, FSB HQ, in Lubyanka Square, Moscow, had officially sanctioned a "tail" to be assigned to a Russian Naval commander, a man working personally with one of the two or three most auspicious men in all of the Russian Navy. It was not unprecedented, but it had not happened in recent years, certainly since the KGB had been formally dismantled in November 1991.

Thus, Kurt Petrov was hurtling around the shores of the White Sea on his motorbike, trying to find out precisely what Nikolai Chirkov was up to. And, by any standards, he'd gotten very close to achieving that on his first day at work.

He returned to the FSB private office inside the enormous waterside sprawl of Zvezdochka Shipping and Engineering, the world's largest shipyard, in Severodvinsk, where the *Admiral Chabanenko* was still laid up after more than six months.

He printed his pictures, selected the best ones, and called in to report that the Learjet's flight plan was direct to Sheremetevo-2 in Moscow. The FSB was mildly interested in the program of the Englishman, John Carter, but not sufficiently to arrest him and risk a blazing row with the British Embassy. All they really wanted was to know who he was, and why, as a paint salesman, was he apparently in cahoots with the Israeli Embassy?

As the somewhat bored duty officer in the Lubyanka said, "They're probably redecorating, right?" The route of the private jet suggested he was leaving Russia anyway, and Kurt had noted that Carter and Chirkov had met, perhaps by accident, at the Vaskovo Airport. Yes, they had left together, but separated immediately and gone in totally different directions.

There was a naval inquiry scheduled for 9:00 a.m. the following morning, Monday, and Kurt needed to have his pictures ready. Admiral Ustinov was chairing it himself, since any aspersions cast upon his personally selected assistant would reflect very badly on him.

Alexander Ustinov, a bull-necked, bald-headed former nuclear submarine commander, had a towering reputation in the Russian Navy and had also commanded the eight-thousand-ton Sovremenny Class destroyer *Nastochivy* in the Baltic. He was a native of the city of Volgograd, which sits on the convergence of the Volga and Don Rivers and was the scene of the bloodiest battle in human history, July 1942, when the city was called Stalingrad.

Admiral Ustinov was fifty now, but he was an expert on that and many other aspects of World War II. His grandmother had died in the German bombardment, and his grandfather was one of the six hundred thousand Russian troops who also died. Alexander Ustinov had a total of twelve relatives killed in the siege of Stalingrad almost thirty years before he was born.

But to him, it was last week. The Northern Fleet commander was a Russian, through and through. He had nothing but contempt for any other nation and was indeed certain that no other nation in the annals of the human race could have withstood what the Russians endured in the face of the German army and then crushed them.

Every year he made a pilgrimage back to his hometown, and there, in company with his two army officer sons, he would walk up the long slope of the hill that serves as a plinth for the largest free-standing statue on earth, the *Mamaev Kurgan* . . . Mother Russia, in battle mode, sculpted to commemorate the most triumphant and tragic event in Soviet history.

The 236-foot female warrior, her sword brandished another 36 feet above her head, caused his heart to beat and his tears to flow as he stared across the distant Volga River. It was as if Alexander Ustinov was renewing sacred vows of devotion and, if necessary, valor. There was no military officer in all of Russia more suited to help President Nikita Markova fulfill his dreams of a dominant Russia.

Admiral Ustinov held his inquiry in the wardroom of the *Admiral Chabanenko.* He sat at the head of the table, surrounded by Weinert and one other member of the Internet security team; by Kurt Petrov, the man with the photographs; and by two officers of the FSB. Lieutenant Commander Chirkov was informed five minutes before proceedings began that he was required to attend.

But only when the admiral was finally seated did he realize this was about him and that he faced a possible charge of high treason against the state. Nikolai was terrified, and he tried to scramble his thoughts into line, asking Admiral Ustinov over and over what he was supposed to have done wrong.

The C-in-C informed everyone he would conduct the inquiry personally, and if anyone had any specific questions, they must be addressed to him alone. If he thought Nikolai Chirkov should answer directly, he would indicate his approval. Admiral Ustinov was accustomed to total command.

"Lieutenant Commander," he began, "it has been brought to my attention that my personal computer was used by persons unknown during my absence from the ship on Saturday evening. The log on the hard drive showed a record of editing carried out at 2135 hours. I ask now, was that you?"

"Of course it was, sir. I entered the office to bring you the notes about the missile, and I noticed your machine was still switched on, although the screen was blank. I hit the space bar to wake it up, and it jumped instantly to the page you had left.

"The headline had a major mistake. It referred to an improved range for the Iskander of two-hundred-plus miles. I knew it should have been two-thousand-plus, so I added a comma and a zero. Saved it and shut it down."

"Thank you, Nikolai. Weinert, what else?"

"Nothing on that, sir."

"Very well." Admiral Ustinov studied Kurt Petrov's report. "Now, Lieutenant Commander, you left the base on Sunday afternoon, traveling by car. Where did you go?"

"Archangel, sir. To visit my aunt."

"In the town."

"Yessir. Gaidara Street, near the park. She's Ludmilla Volkov—my father's sister."

"Lieutenant Commander, I put it to you that you never went anywhere near Gaidara Street, or the park, or your father's sister. As a result of the

computer confusion, you were followed by officers of Russian internal security, and you were 'tailed' and photographed at Vaskovo Airport."

Nikolai Chirkov's mind raced. If he was caught lying, seriously lying,
he could be shot at dawn. He needed a story.

"Sir . . . this is hugely embarrassing. I did not wish you, or anyone else,
to know the truth. But this is a very private family matter . . . "

"In your own interests, I am afraid I must ask you to inform us of
the truth."

"Sir, Ludmilla Volkov is still attractive and very wealthy. She has been
seeing some kind of a mysterious foreigner, intermittently, and both my
father and her children are afraid this man is after her fortune. After weeks
of persuasion, she finally provided us with his name and phone number.

"He's English, younger than her, and a director of an industrial paint
company. My father arranged for me to meet him at the airport and try
to find out his intentions toward Ludmilla, who is, needless to say . . .
smitten."

Everyone in the room smiled at the vision of the wealthy widow and
the plainly rakish paint salesman fortune hunting in Archangel.

"Then why lie to us?" asked the admiral.

"Sir, surely everyone can see this is not something my family would
want made public, especially as Ludmilla might suffer a fit of pique and
marry him . . . "

"Well, yes, I see that. But to tell deliberate untruths to a naval inquiry
such as this is punishable by a very long term in a military jail, or by an instant dishonorable discharge. For matters involving espionage . . . "

"Sir, this is about as far removed from the affairs of Russia's navy as it's
possible to get. Surely, I get some leeway to deal with a family problem,
and try to keep it private?"

"Well, I see no reason to act in a completely inhumane way," replied
the admiral. "And your service record is quite outstanding. I would be inclined to drop the whole matter, pending Ludmilla's broken heart. But the
FSB must make their own decision whether to check out the story."

"Sir," said the resident FSB field officer in Severodvinsk, "with your approval, we will discuss this further and then decide."

"Very well," said Admiral Ustinov. "You make your decision later. For
the moment this inquiry is suspended, and, I should record, with no
blemish thus far on Lieutenant Commander Chirkov's record."

Everyone left the wardroom except for the admiral and his assistant, who had a huge amount of work to do, recording the official version of the test firing of the Iskander-K.

"I really am very sorry about that," said Nikolai. "I probably should have told you the story before I even left."

"You probably should have. But I think it will be fine. Except for poor Ludmilla. You probably frightened this Mr. Carter to death, turning up at the airport in naval uniform—he'll probably never come back to Russia."

"I suppose not . . . but still, anyway, I expect you want to start the full report of the test firing. Will I meet you in the office in ten minutes?"

"That'll do well."

"Yes, sir," snapped Nikolai, saluting his boss, in deference to his exalted rank. At which point he left the room, unsure whether to (a) take his service revolver and commit suicide, (b) run for his life, or (c) try to contact Ludmilla.

Only one thing was certain. He was finished, in the navy and in Russia. The FSB would check out his story and find it was a pack of lies. His father would not have the slightest idea what they were talking about, and neither, for that matter, would Ludmilla Volkov. The "spooks" probably already had a phone tap on the landline in Ludmilla's house and probably on his father's. Neither of them had a cell phone, which rendered him just about powerless.

He could contact no one. The only area of confusion would be Ludmilla's whereabouts. He happened to know she was on vacation somewhere down on the Black Sea. There would be no one at the house on Gaidara Street. Not even the housekeeper.

But the "spooks" would find her. It might take a couple of days, maybe three. But they'd locate her, and she would listen in amazement to the absurd tale of the British fortune hunter. At which point they would know the whole story was a fabrication, and a warrant would be issued for his immediate arrest.

If they were very smart, which they normally were not, a new question would leap to the forefront: who precisely was this John Carter? He clearly had not come to Archangel to see Ludmilla Volkov, who'd never heard of him. So whom, precisely, had he come to see? Lieutenant Commander Nikolai Chirkov?

If they got that far, the FSB might very well pinpoint the Israeli Embassy and burst in demanding answers, whether or not Rani was still in the country. Right now, Nikolai needed to get hold of Rani, on a cell phone, and make arrangements to get out of Russia. Luckily, he did have money.

He returned to his quarters and gathered up his gear—laptop, notebooks, pens, and Iskander-K missile-component guide. He reported to the admiral's office and started mapping out headings for the missile report. He could tell Alexander Ustinov was busy because he was uncharacteristically late. When he did come in, he was preoccupied on the phone.

Eventually, he produced his hardcover notebook, opened it, smoothed out the page he wanted read, and told Nikolai to make a start on the report, following his own jottings in the book.

"Try to read my writing, and lay it out as well as possible. I'll set aside a couple of hours right after lunch, and we'll knock it into shape and then circulate it. I'll see you around 1400 hours."

The admiral walked off down the corridor, quietly singing the uplifting anthem of his hometown, "The Song of the Volga Boatmen": *Mighty stream so deep and wide, Volga, Volga, our pride.*

He was unaware, of course, of the hard-angled attack the FSB was mounting on his office, and on Nikolai, who was effectively his chief of staff. He was certainly not aware that his closest colleague was a master spy who worked for the West and regarded the Israeli Embassy as his second home. Had he done so, he would have shot Nikolai Chirkov dead, no questions asked.

When Ustinov had left, Nikolai picked up the notebook, scanning it for further information. He realized he was in the last hours of his navy career—somehow he needed to get through to Rani and to arrange passage out of Russia. Slowly, he turned the pages of the book, stopping every few moments to make notes on his laptop.

There was a fund of knowledge in Admiral Ustinov's pages, stuff Nikolai had never heard of, detailed accounts of progress made at China Shenzhen Technology, even more detail about a twenty-nine-year-old Russian lawyer living in Washington, DC, Nina Muratova, who appeared to work for a European bank.

He spent a half hour on the book and then left the administrative area. He collected documents from his cabin, stuffed them into his pockets, and prepared to leave the ship for the last time. He dared not take a bag of any kind, for fear they were already following him. If they could track him to the airport in Archangel, they sure as hell could track him out of the Zvezdochka dockyard, carrying even a small suitcase.

It was eleven thirty in the morning, and he had no idea where Rani was, since that destination had been on a strictly need-to-know basis. He walked along to the gangway that led to the shore and disembarked. The gatekeepers saluted him, and he walked away along the usual route to his car. Somehow he had to get away, far away, but he was nerve-wracked about this familiar vehicle, and whether anyone might track it. How far would he dare drive? How long did he have before he was missed?

He scanned the surrounding area and saw no one paying him the slightest attention. So he climbed into the driver's seat and took off, making for the main gates to the dockyard, the town, and the fast route south down the M8. Happily, he had filled up with gas on the way to the airport and now faced a quick seventy-mile run down to a country road, leading over the mountains, to a little place called Emca, where there was a railway station on the main line to Moscow. Nikolai had no idea where he was going, only that he had to get away.

The first part of the journey was simple, straight down the freeway, checking all the while for any car that may be tracking him. For all he knew, there was a tracking device already fixed to his car, and then to the satellites, but he did not believe he was under quite that degree of suspicion.

At a quarter of two, he swung off the highway and headed for the mountains. He realized that sometime in the next few minutes there was likely to be a bellow of rage emanating from the admiral's office when he discovered his assistant was either late or AWOL.

The thought made Nikolai doubly nervous. He ran the numbers through his mind and decided the FSB guys had already drawn a blank over at Ludmilla's house. But he did have a chance: if he was lucky, they would merely wait around, or make a few inquiries, and discover she was away, maybe for a few days.

However, if they concluded that John Carter had come to Archangel from Moscow but not to see Ludmilla, then they would swiftly work out he came to see someone else . . . almost certainly Lieutenant Commander Nikolai Chirkov. Kurt Petrov had photographed them together.

That, in Nikolai's mind, was the key. Would they refrain from getting aggressive for maybe another couple of days, or would they conclude that Ludmilla's absence confirmed that Nikolai's second story to the inquiry was a total pack of lies?

If so, all his dreads would come true, and he would be hunted down in this vast country by professionals who were supremely gifted at this type of relentless cruelty. Nikolai drove on between the hills, and he crossed the many rivers that cascade through this part of northern Russia.

By now it was almost two thirty. He was within striking range of Emca and was almost certain there would be a major alert for him in the Zvezdochka Shipping and Engineering yard. He had left no indication of leaving the ship permanently. His cabin was shipshape, and aside from his documents and his greatcoat, he had taken nothing. He hoped they would be baffled, but the most urgent matter on his mind was his current dress. If the navy had put out an emergency alert to locate this missing lieutenant commander, it was plainly not smart to be walking around in uniform.

He needed clothes, but he did not want to start a trail in a small-town shop where he might buy new trousers, shirt, and sweater. The heavy overcoat would blend in with other dark coats in the chill of the Moscow night. If he got there.

The road was winding and slow. Nikolai was stuck behind a large agricultural truck for six miles, and he did not drive into Emca until around ten past three. He went past the railway station and parked on a deserted piece of land at the north end of the town. He took a screwdriver out of the tire-changing pack and unscrewed the front and back license plates of the vehicle.

Nearby was a pile of old building material, and he leaned a piece of flat wood on the rear end of his car, covering the empty space. Then he walked to the station and purchased a regular ticket to Moscow. The train was due at 4:00 p.m., forty minutes from now.

"Change at Vologda," said the clerk. "You want the 11:00 p.m. express to Moscow, arriving Yaroslavskiy Station 7:00 a.m."

Nikolai purchased a newspaper and walked back to the car, dumping the license plates in a trash bin without breaking stride. He only wanted to avoid being noticed, and this did not include a half-hour wait on a station platform where anyone might see and remember him.

He started the engine and ran the heater against the chill of the late afternoon. The newspaper was not especially interesting, though it did have a story about a possible missile test over the White Sea three days ago. The reporter knew about one-tenth as much about the incident as Nikolai did.

At ten minutes to four, he locked the car and strolled back to the station, where he walked to the far end of the platform, still pretending to read his newspaper. The train was only three minutes late and not very crowded. Nikolai found a near-deserted part of the passenger car and settled down, making sure his greatcoat covered his uniform. He removed his Russian Naval tie and opened his collar, which made him carelessly unlike a military officer.

For six hours he slept fitfully, trying to cast from his mind the scale of the uproar he must by now have left behind in the Zvezdochka shipyard. He was certain that by now the FSB officers had contacted the Israeli Embassy and once more insisted on knowing the identity and whereabouts of "John Carter."

Equally, he knew they would never be provided with that information. Nikolai thought it likely that Rani would be warned off Moscow altogether and transferred back to Tel Aviv. For himself, there was an extremely difficult path to take—principally, to get out of Russia forever.

The FSB was not anxious these days to launch operations in other countries. The president did not like it and considered it bad for Russia's image—too much of a reminder of what the world saw as "the bad old days." Markova himself regarded them as the very best old days, when a steel-edged Russia had growled at a nervous world from behind the Iron Curtain.

Nonetheless, the FSB would be relentless in their operations inside Russia. They would search to the end of the tundra and back to find the naval officer they believed had become a traitor. God knows what his father and Anna would think. Even Ludmilla might look askance.

Over and over, the roads led to only one solution: he had to get out of Russia. There would be a cordon around airports, railway terminals, and bus stations. This was becoming a nightmare, despite the presence of almost a half-million dollars, with more to come, in Geneva.

On reflection, he would be lucky to get out of Yaroslavskiy Station without being arrested. He was certain the FSB would have covered all major railheads. And now he had no car. His only chance was a private plane, and the only person who could possibly help with that was Rani, who had temporarily vanished.

Nikolai understood it would be hopeless to try to contact the Israeli Embassy, because that would be asking them to shelter a fugitive. He thought it likely the FSB would be encamped outside the place, just waiting for him to show up. As far as he could tell, Moscow was just about the worst idea possible for him. He was safer in a remote, provincial city where the FSB had few resources.

He looked at his train map, and he checked his wallet for the credit card no one knew about, the one with one hundred thousand dollars' worth of credit on it, backed as it was by his Swiss bank.

With Rani's help, he could fly out. He had two false passports, one British, one German. Rani had insisted on these as soon as they began working together. If he could just find different clothes, he had a chance. If Rani would answer his phone, he had a better than good chance. But Nikolai knew the pilot must never be aware of his true identity.

With the northern Russia southbound local still clattering through the night, Nikolai made a clear-cut decision. He was getting off the train at Vologda at 10:00 p.m. and not getting on the Moscow overnight express.

So far as he could guess, the Russian railroad system represented a potential valley of death. When he reached Vologda, he would try to find a hotel and contact Rani. Failing that, he would take a taxi out to the airport, six miles out of town, and try to charter a flight either to Helsinki or at least to the Russian airport at Brest, hard against the Polish border.

LATE AFTERNOON

Frankfurt Airport, Germany

Rani had made his flight connection. He and Mack Bedford were at a corner table in the Goethe Bar, and they were very serious, Rani having already heard from the embassy in Moscow that officers of the FSB were looking not only for John Carter but also for Lieutenant Commander Chirkov.

Rani had his encrypted cell switched on, in case Nikolai called. He also understood it might now be too dangerous for him to return to Russia.

Mack listened gravely to the ever-increasing conundrum facing his two prize contacts.

"Okay, let's not dwell on the working problems facing my Russian officer," said Rani. "Let's get up to date with FOM-2, because we now know a lot about it."

"It stands for 'Fort Meade,' and the 2 means 'nuclear.' These guys aim to slam a couple of these new Iskander-K missiles right into Building 2A at the National Security Agency."

Mack stared incredulously at Rani. "They wouldn't dare."

"That's what they're planning, and those plans are very far advanced."

"Well, we saw the new missile in action," said Mack. "It was very fast, and it went way more than eighteen hundred miles, and blew the bejesus out of the polar ice cap, right?"

"Worse than that. The Russkies dropped a massive wooden structure on the ice with parachutes. That missile blew every last plank into the stratosphere. They can hit that, they can hit the NSA."

"So give me the plan as we now know it."

"They decide to whack America and somehow hide behind a bunch of lies and evasions. First step was to build a new missile with the correct range, propulsion, and payload. The new Iskander-K that we saw last Friday possessed all three of those qualities."

"Right."

"We know they worked in secret at a monastery on the Solovetsky Islands. All kinds of international-class nuclear weapons guys turned up from North Korea and Tehran. A presidential party walked out to see the launch last Friday. No bullshit."

"Okay, that's all clear."

"However, Mack, there is still a gray area, and that's the launch site. Our man at the table heard them repeatedly discuss the possibility of Central America. A two-thousand-mile range makes everything possible from that area. If they can somehow launch from the narrow land between Mexico and Bolivia, they can stand well clear of the blame.

"And this brings us to the nuclear football, which I believe is the most complicated part of the deal. The Russians have to shut it down, and you'd think it would be easier from Central America than from Russia, forty-five hundred miles away.

"My man has the distinct impression they intend to transport the whole setup—missiles, launchers, jammers, computers, code breakers, and people—by surface ship to wherever they are going."

"You dismiss the possibility of a submarine?"

"Yes. When the *Gepard* hit the beach in Scotland, that was the end of it. Especially now that SOSUS is returning in a big way.

"The Kremlin has no appetite for a Russian submarine to sail through the GIUK Gap and somehow be apprehended by the Americans with all that Russian intelligence on board. They've settled on a surface ship."

"And we cannot get a handle on the place they might launch . . . "

"Not yet."

Right then Rani's phone rang three times and then stopped. There was no one there. The Israeli agent was nearly certain it was Nikolai trying to get through—as it happened, from a train in the middle of nowhere.

"I'll just have to wait," he said. "He'll get into a good reception zone sooner or later."

Mack was a great deal more concerned about the National Security Agency getting hit by a nuclear missile than about anything else. So far as Mack knew, the agency had its own police force and SWAT team right on campus. He did not, however, know whether there were antiaircraft missiles and artillery on the NSA roof to shoot down intruders.

The real problem was the part they knew least about—the jamming of the football. It was possible that Bob Birmingham's boys would find something inside China Shenzhen Corporation in Guangdong Province. Meanwhile, they could do no more than have all the codes changed and hope to hell the Russians did not have hot intelligence operators deep inside the Pentagon or even the White House itself.

"We can match them militarily any day of the goddamned week," said Mack. "It's this tricky stuff with computers, and all this code shit—that's what bothers me. Also, I wish to hell we knew where this proposed strike against us was actually coming from."

In the years since they had half jumped, half fallen off Saddam's oil rig, Rani had always followed the career of the man he regarded as a blood brother. He never really knew what the legendary SEAL commander was doing, but he had an instinct, as if Mack Bedford left his personal signature on certain operations. When a busload of jihadist terrorists was blown up in an operation that made the state of Connecticut literally shudder, Rani knew. When four of the most dangerous al-Qaeda men on earth were hunted down and "eliminated" somewhere up the Khyber Pass, he knew. But when an entire town of Somali pirates was obliterated in brutal battles, both at sea and on land, Rani Ben Adan could not help himself. He shouted to an empty room, *"That's gotta be Mack!"*

And now they were together once more, plotting and scheming in this German airport, trying to make sense of a Russian president who thought he was a twenty-first-century Peter the Great. They knew almost enough, but not quite. At this point Russia had done nothing to break international law, except maybe a mildly illegal but harmless missile test firing.

They had nailed down the significance of the monastery, site of the new missile development. They knew its projected target, although not from whence it would come. They also knew that Nikita Markova would not dare hit the United States in any way until they had cracked that nuclear football. Equally, they knew one of the world's leading cyber-warfare specialists was in the Solovetsky Islands, helping with the program that would temporarily castrate the president of the United States.

Mack was already inclined to "slam the friggin' monastery" with either a SEAL attack or a very large bomb. But that would solve the problem only in the short term. Markova would simply start over, or, at least, he might. A far better plan would be to wait until this entire FOM-2 operation was ready to go and then somehow obliterate it and hang Russia's government out to dry, universally accused of planning crimes against humanity.

So far as Rani could make out, there were two priorities. They had to find out the precise launch site of that Iskander-K and then discover the precise method by which this Dr. Yang was proposing to "jam" the football. If it were by way of a Chinese or Russian satellite, the United States would knock it clean out of the sky, probably with a supersonic missile launched from the Colorado Rockies.

But these were tomorrow's refinements that would move onto the front burner as soon as Mack was back in San Diego. Right now they had a serious situation developing. Their master spy, Lieutenant Commander Nikolai Chirkov, was in danger, being hunted down by his own side. And, worse yet, the Russian was probably carrying the priceless information that might make the difference between success and failure of their bid to crack and eliminate FOM-2.

There was nothing either he or Mack could do except sit and wait for the phone to ring and hope to hell it was Nikolai with some kind of scheme to get out of Russia and join them in the West. Rani himself was waiting for instructions from Mossad HQ. He already knew it was unlikely he would return to Moscow, but he would still be effective, as long as he had access to Nikolai's vast knowledge of FOM-2.

Mack, too, was unable to return home until the Nikolai problem was cleared up, especially if the fugitive Russian officer needed rescue. Captain Bedford was good at that type of stuff, considered a world expert, even in the slick and ruthless environment of SPECWARCOM.

Right now they were both bored sideways with the enormous airport and decided to get a cab into the city, check into a hotel, and try to leave phone numbers on Nikolai's text service—anything to provide the Russian with options to communicate.

10:00 P.M. (LOCAL), SAME DAY, MONDAY, SEPTEMBER 3

Vologda Station
Northern European Russia

The southbound local from Archangel ran into the slow approaches to Vologda with a rattling and clanking of railroad points and locomotive brakes. They were down to a speed of 10 mph a half mile from the passenger platforms, trundling past the outskirts of the twelfth-century town, which sits astride the Vologda River, 250 miles north of Moscow.

It was very dark now, and the tracks were not well illuminated. Nikolai Chirkov was standing in the train's corridor and never saw the parked helicopter, standing somewhat incongruously in the dark on a playing field at the edge of the town.

In fact, there was nothing incongruous about that helicopter. It was one of the great military warhorses of the world, the Mil M8T 260-mph twin-turbine transport and gunship used almost universally by every Russian satellite armed force. It possessed a wonderful track record, on and off the battlefield, going back deep into the old Soviet Union.

This particular one, with two armed navy guards in attendance, was virtually brand new, blue and white in color with a sixty-nine-foot rotor span. It was built at the world's largest helicopter plant, in Kazan, Tatarstan.

It had taken two aircrews and an engineer to ferry four FSB agents in this big military transporter south from Severodvinsk, on what was a routine line of inquiry—just checking the main railroad stations for the missing lieutenant commander, sometimes following a mainline train, sometimes not. It was a dull and laborious task without much hope of success, especially as everyone thought Nikolai Chirkov would keep going all the way to Moscow.

The M8T was formally owned by the Russian Navy's Northern Fleet, but right now had been seconded to the FSB, although Admiral Ustinov had insisted his own men operate it for as long as it was on loan. The agents had not yet arrived at any station in time to search the train's passengers, and in any event this type of behavior was not encouraged.

The one aspect of his near-totalitarian rule that made Nikita Markova truly jumpy was any accusation of bullying and harassment. He might have been all in favor of such tactics, but he had no plans to make that public.

Which was why the four FSB agents were sitting quietly in the Vologda Station, reading, dozing, or chatting, waiting to see if anyone interesting disembarked from the train. Failing that, given the late hour, they would board the helicopter and fly to check out Yaroslav. After that it was Moscow, a routine check-in at Lubyanka Square, and then to the FSB hotel where all the agents stayed.

Nikolai climbed down from his car, buttoning his greatcoat around him and joining a substantial number of visitors from the North who had also been traveling all evening. He walked down the station platform to the main station concourse, which had a tomblike atmosphere with hardly anything still open. He asked the ticket collector for directions to a hotel or café and was told, "Café Lesnaya, three hundred yards that way, or Hotel Vologda, just up the street. Both open until late."

Nikolai, who had been too nervous to eat anything all day, headed straight up the side street that led to the Lesnaya and found it agreeably warm, cheerful, and fairly crowded. He ordered coffee and a couple of cream cheese and caviar sandwiches. He had ceased to worry about the cost of anything, only the possibility of leaving Russia at dawn tomorrow.

He used his cell to call the Hotel Vologda and book a single room, and then, restored by the excellent sandwich and coffee, he moved outside and into the shadows of Galkinskaya Street, which seemed deserted, with the time now around a quarter to eleven.

The two men who had spotted him at the station, and then tracked him all the way to the Café Lesnaya, were now into Galkinskaya but had lost sight of him. They moved quicker on soft rubber-soled boots, coming swiftly down the street and listening at the same time.

They heard him rather than saw him and ducked into a doorway perhaps fifteen feet from the shop entrance into which Nikolai had retreated. They could hear him speaking on the phone. They heard the name Rani. And they heard "Frankfurt," and then "Brest," the town on the Polish border. Within seconds they heard "Ustinov." They scarcely needed to hear more. Their orders were succinct.

9:45 P.M. (LOCAL), SAME DAY

Holbein's Restaurant, Frankfurt

Rani's phone rang just as they finished dessert. He almost dropped his final spoonful with the pure excitement of seeing Nikolai's number come up on his cell-phone screen.

He covered the mouthpiece and hissed to Mack, "It's him. Can't see where he is . . . "

"*Hello, Nikki . . . Where are you? . . . Where the hell's that? . . . Okay, I got you. What? You need a plane? No problem. Going where? Where's that? . . . Christ! You have his notes? Whatshisname? . . .*"

Right then Rani heard the shot, the bullet that smashed through the back of Nikolai's skull.

Pedro. He's Pedro Miguel . . . Those were the last words the Mossad field agent heard. And then there was a loud clatter as the phone hit the sidewalk and another *crash!* as the dying Nikolai slammed the heel of his leather boot into the fallen telephone, resolutely ensuring the phone had surrendered its last secrets.

Rani did not hear the second shot, which shattered once more the dark quiet of Galkinskaya Street. This bullet cleaved into Nikolai Chirkov's just-beating heart. Then there was nothing.

The agent reholstered his service revolver and tapped the buttons on his own cell phone. Within one minute a Vologda Police Lada Priora came hurtling around the corner, with no sirens or flashing blue lights. Two officers jumped out and bundled the somewhat messy remains of Lieutenant Commander Nikolai Chirkov into a black body bag and stowed it, with some difficulty, in the trunk.

The two FSB agents climbed into the backseat, and the Lada swerved out of the downtown area and headed for the waiting helicopter, which now had its main rotor running. They loaded the body bag on board and lifted off, bound for Moscow. A couple of hours later, the deceased Nikolai would be in the morgue of the Lubyanka, where the agents would discover incontrovertible evidence that he had indeed been a master spy of the very worst type.

They would find his extra passports, the notes written down from Admiral Ustinov's logbook, his credit card with the hundred-thousand-dollar limit, and his Russian, Swiss, and German driver's licenses. And a lot of rubles. This was a Russian insider, and he was selling secret military information to the West.

There was, however, no record of his contacts, no trace of Rani's name, no mention of the Israeli Embassy, no record of his most recent meetings, and not a word about the mysterious John Carter he had met in the airport at Archangel.

Nikolai had been careful and very professional, but he was planning to make the final break, to get out of the country he had betrayed. And for that he needed documents and cash. No need to try to conceal them. If he was caught, he would be a dead man, as he now most certainly was.

9:55 P.M.

Holbein's Restaurant, Frankfurt

The line to Nikolai Chirkov had gone dead for the last time. Rani still held the phone in his hand, but there was, plainly, no connection. He'd heard the shot and knew that his contact and friend was gone.

"They got him," he said quietly. "As I guess they were bound to do. He never had a prayer getting out of Severodvinsk. There's hardly any roads, one railway line, and I imagine the airports were cordoned off. I didn't really hear where he was."

"What about this Pedro Miguel? Who the hell's he?" asked Mack. "That's a Latin American name—sounds like Pedro's somehow mixed up with the launch site."

"I think you are right about that," said Rani. "I know that was Nikki's priority—to get us the precise area where they planned to fire those missiles.

"He'd already established Central America. And that was important to him. He was a lifelong military man, and he knew we'd have a ten-times better chance of intercepting those Iskanders if we just knew where they were coming from."

"What do we do if we find Pedro? Kidnap him and find out what's going on?" Mack Bedford was, as ever, practical to the last degree.

"Well, there's probably about 17 billion Pedros in Central America, so that'll take the rest of the century."

"Yeah, but if this guy's a president, or at least a minister of defense, the NSA will find him."

"They'd better. Or they might be off the map. A nuclear warhead on one of those missiles would nearly level Fort Meade."

"Look," said Mack, "let's get back to the hotel. It's only four o'clock in Washington. We can get on a landline and talk to someone at the NSA, brief them, and get the right people on the case. That'll give me a chance to talk to Andy Carlow—and you probably want to find out where you're going to live."

"Guess it'll make a change from hiding in some Moscow alley trying to make the cell connect," said Rani. "I'll tell you something: I won't be sorry to be out of Russia. Two years is enough for one lifetime."

They were back in the Intercontinental Hotel, on the banks of the Main River, within ten minutes. Mack Bedford opened up the line to the NSA in Fort Meade, asking to be connected to the director's office.

When someone answered, he went very official. "US Navy SEAL Captain Mackenzie Bedford, SPECWARCOM, speaking . . . personal to Captain James Ramshawe. Tell him to use the encrypted line."

"Hey! G'day, Mack. Where the hell have you been?"

"Well, right now, Jimmy, I'm in Frankfurt, Germany."

"What the hell are you doing there?"

"Just had some kind of apple strudel, since you ask. But I have stuff you need to know."

"Lay it on me, Mack."

"Can I assume you are well briefed on this Russian problem—Solovetsky Islands and so on?"

"As well as I can be. Not many hard facts, though."

"Well, here are some for you. That missile test last Friday—in the Arctic . . . "

"Yup . . . I got it."

"We encrypted right now?"

"Affirmative."

"Okay. They're planning to hit Fort Meade with that Iskander-K. Their working code's FOM-2. Stands for 'Fort Meade—nuclear.' Building OPS 2A."

"Christ," said Ramshawe.

Mack continued, "We don't think anything is going to be fired directly from Russia. Our source thinks South America. Unhappily, he was just shot by the FSB earlier this evening."

"Jesus Christ, this is like the Wild West."

"Tell me about it. But there's something important. He was on the phone to my contact when he died. And he was trying to tell us about the missile launch site. He was saying the name of some guy in Latin America. And I think we need to locate this character, real quick."

"That's my part?"

"Hope so."

"What's his name?"

"Pedro Miguel."

Captain Ramshawe said, "Pedro Miguel's not a person. That's the name of the second big shipping lock at the Pacific end of the Panama Canal. It's the Pedro Miguel Lock. Named after the little town on the waterway."

Mack saw the funny side of the discussion. "How the heck do you know that?" he said finally.

"I'll tell you, mate. It's why I'm sitting here in the big chair and you're fucking about eating apple crumble with the Third Reich."

Mr. and Mrs. Ramshawe had bequeathed their son the outrageous humor of the Australian Outback. And he'd mastered the art of saying the worst thing he could think of at the hands of his mentor, Admiral Arnold Morgan.

But now he was extremely serious. "That missile they fired was the most advanced rocket they've ever launched," he said. "I'm talking speed, accuracy, and range. You want to stop something like that, every second matters. You guys detect any Chinese involvement in any of this?"

"Some," replied Mack. "They're helping with a cyber-warfare action to jam the president's nuclear football. They got a guy from China Shenzhen Technology ensconced in the fucking monastery . . . Why'd you ask?"

"Well, China does have an involvement in the running of the Panama Canal. They have a major interest in the ports at either end. If they are in any way involved in this FOM-2, it would make sense to launch from somewhere along the canal. It's kind of quiet, with a lot of jungle. They launch from in there, no one would ever know."

"When they test fired from Solovetsky," said Mack, "they used one of those regular vehicles. It sure would make life easy for 'em, if they could off-load a launcher through a Panama gateway port. Then just drive it into the jungle."

"When are you back?" asked Jimmy.

"Tomorrow sometime. I'm getting a ride from Landstuhl."

"Check in with me, will you? I'd like to compare notes. Meanwhile, I'll get guys active in the Pedro Miguel area . . . By the way, am I going to read about your buddy who was shot?"

"I doubt it. That's not the type of stuff the old Russkies issue these days. Anyway, I'm one removed. Don't even know his name."

"Poor bastard."

0900 (LOCAL), TUESDAY, SEPTEMBER 4

Russian Navy Main Staff HQ
St. Petersburg

Admiral Vitaly Rankov, C-in-C Russian Navy, stood in jackbooted splendor in his new headquarters. The move from the old Kremlin offices in Moscow to the majestic and historic Admiralty Building on the shores of the wide Neva River had delighted the entire Russian Navy.

This was reflected glory in its most dazzling form, beneath the epic gilded spire of the old Naval Academy, with its time-honored golden weather vane, a Russian sailing ship of the line, swiveling quietly, the focal point above the central area of St. Petersburg.

Housed in a great building of the empire style, rows of white columns, and statues, the subject of a book by Vladimir Nabokov, the very embodiment of Russian Naval power, rising now from the hard-up ashes of the old Soviet era and into the new, prosperous, oil-rich glitter of the twenty-first century.

Admiral Rankov, a former Russian Olympic oarsman, presided over a dark-blue service comprising 150,000 active personnel, a burgeoning blue-water fleet, and a desk full of wonderful reports revealing updates on new and brilliant nuclear submarines, plus nuclear-powered aircraft carriers, Russia's first. The latest guided-missile destroyers and frigates were being constructed along the river, just as they always were in Russia's maritime history, when this building was for so long the hub of the navy, the old HQ, until the 1917 Russian Revolution.

Rankov was one of the first Russian Naval chiefs ever to stand on the brink of such overwhelming improvements. Before him stood a man whose star was plummeting to earth, as surely as Rankov's was rising to the heavens. Alexander Ustinov, despite his status as patriot, fleet admiral, and heir apparent, had the appearance of a defeated warrior.

His face was crestfallen, his expression was resigned, and there was a slouch to his shoulders. His very bearing suggested the end of the line. But Vitaly Rankov had known him for many years and had long admired his clear grasp of Russia's problems. When the chips were down, when the dockyards were falling apart, when the old government could not afford to pay the dockyards' electric bills, Admiral Ustinov was a power in the land.

He had kept the shipyards open. Even as a rear admiral, he had fought and argued for his men to be paid, and when they weren't (which was often), he issued great patriotic speeches, imploring his captains not to give in, promising that Russia would rise again, reminding them of the times Russians had stood alone in the face of unprecedented human onslaught. And, above all, telling them that they were the best, that a united Russia was unstoppable. Mother Russia must be protected . . . *If not by you, who?*

Admiral Rankov had never forgotten this martinet of the Northern Fleet, and now, for the first time in his long career, he was witnessing the man at his lowest level. But Vitaly was a sportsman. He understood the levels of performance required to stay at the very top. And he knew about days when everything went wrong. His mighty heart went out to his longtime colleague Alexander, the peerless commander who had been compromised by a cheap little traitor who had tried to sell everyone down the river.

Rankov, a massive man, an Olympian, and, like Alexander, a patriot, smiled and said, "Sit down, old friend. Let me pour you some coffee."

Admiral Ustinov sank gratefully into a chair. He watched the all-powerful Vitaly tilting the coffeepot, and he knew that on his huge mahogany desk there was a document demanding his own court-martial for dereliction of duty, allowing the Northern Fleet to be infiltrated by a spy for the West and failing to protect documents of a vital nature. He was further accused of endangering Russia's homeland security and of willful neglect of duty.

"Have you read the charges?" asked Admiral Rankov.

"I have."

"Will you plead guilty?"

"I don't know."

"I'll tell you what you'll do," added the boss. "You'll plead not guilty to every one of those charges. Because they're trumped up, cobbled together by a bunch of fucking politicians who, as usual, know nothing. There's not one senior admiral in the entire Russian Navy who believes you should be court-martialed. And, in the end, you will be tried by a Navy Board of Inquiry, and I'm the fucking head of it, and I won't put up with it."

"That's kind of you, sir."

"It's right. That's what it is. That lieutenant commander could have gotten inside any part of the Russian Navy. He had a flawless record, he was from an important family, and he was destined for the top. He could have worked for me, and I would never have known what he was doing."

"Sir, I do understand the damage he may have done. And I do accept the responsibility for what happened on my watch."

"That's still no excuse for some kind of political witch hunt. Alexander, times have changed. Modern communications, computers, and cell phones have made it near impossible to intercept a really determined infiltrator. Until he makes a mistake.

"However, to court-martial a fleet admiral for the unforeseen actions of a trusted Russian officer is the height of folly. First of all, because the whole matter will rapidly become public, which we do not need. But, mostly, because it does us no good. If they were to find you guilty, we lose the best fleet commander in the Russian Navy—for no good reason whatsoever."

"Again, sir, I thank you. But what happens now?"

"I'm speaking to the president this afternoon. I'm having this whole bullshit court-martial thrown out. I have asked you here because I need a few facts. And the first is, how much did Chirkov find out about FOM-2?"

"Too much. He was in the rotunda when we had the most important meeting. No one revealed the meaning of the code, but I still think he could very quickly have put two and two together. The president kept mentioning his desire to strike against the USA."

"Alexander, with you on Solovetsky, he must have known the missile we test fired was the selected weapon chosen by the president for the strike."

"Sir, he also knew the president was there at the launch. He took the call, which informed me of the lineup at the monastery. So he must also have known of the presence of Dr. Yang, but I don't think he could have known what he was here for, nor where he came from."

"Do you think there's any possibility he could know what *Operation FOM-2* stands for?"

"Well, I have never written it down, nor seen it in any document. If he found out, which I doubt, it must have been from somewhere beyond Northern Fleet Command HQ. You have my guarantee the words *Fort Meade* do not appear anywhere in my office, or on any computer. Not even my deputy has that information, and, as you know, he's a vice admiral."

"And how about the launch site? Could he have found that out?"

"Sir, that's more of a problem. I did write it down in my notebook, but I did so as if it were a person. *Pedro this, and Pedro that. Pedro has to understand* . . . That type of thing. Chirkov could have copied the name, but I would be very surprised if he understood the implication."

"Alexander, did he have permanent access to that notebook?"

"Absolutely not. But in this case I used a clip to show him the significant pages because I was under pressure to write up the Northern Fleet's official report of the test-firing operation."

"And Chirkov was to draft this?"

"Yes, from my notes. He was very good at getting hold of reams of rough notations and turning them into ordered, well-written reports, with all the correct headings and source notes . . . He was actually the best I ever knew at it."

"I'm not sure that is very helpful right now," said Admiral Rankov wryly.

"No. I understand that. But you want the truth. And I must give it to you."

"So, at this stage, he almost certainly found a way to inform the Americans we planned a revenge strike in return for the Iranian debacles at Qom and Natanz. But he probably was not specific about the target, and certainly not about the launch?"

"Correct."

"Can you estimate how great an opportunity he had to transmit knowledge to his contact on his way out of Russia?"

"Well, he was driving fast for the first three hundred miles in an area notorious for its lack of cell-phone reception. Then he was on a train for six hours, surrounded by people. It seems to me his first attempt at contact was in that shop doorway in Galkinskaya Street, in Vologda.

"The agents were hiding within fifteen feet of him, and they heard him say only three words, *Brest, Frankfurt,* and *Ustinov,* before they took him out."

"Any clues who Chirkov was talking to?"

"'Fraid not. His phone was dropped and smashed. They tested it, but nothing worked."

"And how about his pockets?"

"Just what you'd expect from an escaping traitor: extra passports, British and German; cash; driver's licenses; and his notes."

"Copied from your own?"

"Correct. Specific reference to the test firing."

"Anything incriminating?"

"Not really, except for 'Pedro Miguel.' There were two references."

"But he never had a chance to relay them to anyone in the West?"

"I don't think so, sir. And neither do the agents. They swear to God his phone would have been dead all the way from Severodvinsk. Mostly because their own cells would not work until they reached Vologda."

"Then there is just one further matter. This afternoon, I will have this court-martial stopped. After that, in association with the Lubyanka, you will devote your entire energies to tracing this John Carter.

"I don't care if you have to ransack the Israeli Embassy. I don't care if they close it. But I want to know the precise identity of this fucking paint salesman from England."

6

The Russian Embassy
Wisconsin Avenue, Washington, DC

The press room was typically quiet in the early part of the afternoon. Russia did not actively encourage inquiries from anyone in the great imperial capital of the United States. Various attachés and press officers spent these peaceful hours pouring through the US newspapers and magazines.

Tamara Burda, who was preparing to move into the heartland of America as a trainee field officer, was an unusually alert young woman from the Urals, age twenty-six, and she had been tasked with discovering a definite location for the president of the United States on a given date in the summer of next year. Preferably out in the open air.

Skimming through the *Denver Post*, she found what she was seeking. At 11:00 a.m. on Friday, June 28, next year, 2019, he would attend a military ceremony in the city of Littleton, south of Denver, Colorado. The event was a biannual presidential occasion when the commander in chief honored his decorated Navy SEALs, the bravest of men who had died in action on foreign soil.

The ceremony in Littleton would be to honor Navy Gunners Mate 2nd Class Danny L. Dietz, whose bronze statue in full battle dress, M4 rifle at the ready, stands in a small park on Berry Street. Danny died, along with two of his comrades, in Operation Redwings, a battle in the Afghan mountains, on June 28, 2005. He was awarded the Navy Cross posthumously for courage beyond the call of duty in the face of an overwhelming enemy.

The only eyewitness account put the number of Taliban and al-Qaeda warriors at 150, against four SEALs. Danny Dietz was still fighting after being shot five times. He was a native son of Littleton.

The park, where the statue stands, is flat and tree lined, and the *Post* carried a photograph of the grassy surrounding area. In the background were the snowcapped shapes of the towering Rockies, the great craggy peaks that had turned Danny Dietz into a mountain man. He was a natural expert among the massive escarpments of the Hindu Kush in Kumar Province, where he finally went down fighting.

The current president was an emotional man, visibly moved by the families of those who died in action on behalf of the United States. He never missed this particular ceremony and took great pride in giving the address, and he always wrote it in his own words. The story in the Denver newspaper suggested that Air Force One would land at 10:00 a.m. at Buckley Air Force Base and that the C-in-C would go directly to Littleton, where he would host a luncheon for SEAL commanders.

And right there Miss Tamara had it. She had pinpointed the time and place of the president on a specific day next summer. Her task was completed. Better yet, she had been asked to try for a hillside town if possible, though the reason for this had not been made clear.

She sent an e-mail with her information directly to the Foreign Office deep in the Kremlin, and within moments it was relayed to the office of the Northern Fleet commander, Admiral Ustinov, thankfully now rid of the threat of court-martial.

The admiral was now in supreme command of Operation FOM-2, and the message from Washington was hugely welcome. There had been a lot of roadblocks on this black operation, and now, for once, there was some plain sailing. Tamara's words had clarified many things, like time and date of attack. They provided a critical path to the most important Russian strike for many years—and they carved out a timing chart for the missile production, the establishment of a "jammer" for the football, and the date the Russian ship must clear Murmansk.

The communiqué also made clear the date by when the ship must land in Central America and off-load her cargo. Plus, it specified the time frame necessary to transport the huge generator up to Colorado. The presence of Dr. Yang had already presented them with details of the machinery necessary to put that football out of action, but this new message laid out exactly how long they had either to buy it or to make it.

Dr. Yang considered it impossible to devise a program to get into the Pentagon computer systems and somehow insert a virus that would cause chaos and thus disrupt the nuclear football programs, making them unreceptive to the presidential codes that activate them. In the jargon of US security, those are the "Gold Codes" to the nuclear launch signal.

Dr. Yang's principal objection was the difficulty of penetrating the exquisitely designed US system. His view was, "It will take forever to achieve a specific time, and anyway it's not really possible. You take very successful mission, like when Iran centrifuges were in chaos, no one knew exactly what time the disruption would occur, or even for how long. Only that it *would* occur. Computer virus very crazy. Not good for you."

Dr. Yang was correct. The cyber-warfare route was too unreliable. And anyway the nuclear football was a system for satellite telephones. There was nothing high-tech about it. The president simply needed to punch in the codes. The US Command Center would do the rest.

The solution required a powerful "jammer," a device that could be activated on demand to go straight in and knock all of the efficiency out of the football and render it useless, unintelligible. That meant positioning the Russian device in precisely the correct place and switching it on at precisely the right moment, timing it to the split second.

"That way you cut off president's balls," disclosed Dr. Yang helpfully.

But he confirmed such a "jammer" was difficult to make, because it needed serious electronic power, and for that it required either a US power source at exactly the place it was situated or a very large generator.

There were a zillion complications, but at least the most critical one— the path—was now clear. Admiral Ustinov sent a navy helicopter three hundred miles south to Solovetsky, to fly Dr. Yang to Severomorsk in order to lay out the engineering requirements to make a large electronic jammer with its own mobile generator that could somehow be transported up the Rocky Mountains.

When he arrived, Dr. Yang made no attempt to sugarcoat the dimension of the task. "All jammers need to know the precise frequencies your enemy is using for transmission. Your effectiveness to cripple him will always depend on the size and power of your transmitter, because this basic electronic muscle will decide the range it will operate from."

He explained that if the admiral hoped for a distance of three or four miles from the target, that would require a generator the size of a small room. "You want very small, unobtrusive 'jammer' you stand right next to target, and shudder president's balls when you turn it on."

Admiral Ustinov politely informed the electronic doctor that he thought two or three miles would be ideal.

"Okay. No problem. Generator will be in a very large truck and will need a supply of diesel to keep it running. How long you want it?"

"Once we've deactivated the target, we'll want it to keep working for a couple of hours. Making sure the football will not transmit the critical codes."

"With big generator, transmitting on the exact right frequencies, that football will not work until someone gets it out of your range."

"Do you think we'll need to make it here in the navy yards, starting from scratch?"

"No. I think we buy big industrial generator, with its own radiator control panels, compressor, pumps, and appliances. We can find one in a manufacturer's warehouse. Then we fly it here, work on it, and build the jammer around it. We want the most powerful, ready-made jammer from China Shenzhen Technology, and then we make changes to it, so it jams what we tell it.

"This thing very heavy—maybe build it on back of truck that transports it."

"Dr. Yang, we lift and transport warships around here. Lifting generators is no problem. Can you supply me with a list of requirements? This is a classified program, so I will make the documents myself."

"Good plan. Don't want information leaking to spies, huh?"

Admiral Ustinov unsurprisingly agreed with that. He reached for his notepad and pen.

"Okay," said the doctor. "First thing, we need antennas, big ones. And they have to be external. We fix them to 'jammer' and have them jut out of truck roof. High, tuned accurately to frequencies we specify when we find out what they are."

"Where do we get 'em?" asked the admiral.

"China Shenzhen. But we don't order until we know size. You have very good electronic warfare team in monastery—they make good plan. Shenzhen fly parts in here very quick."

"Thank you, doctor. What's next?"

"We need a large voltage-controlled oscillator."

"No problem. We may even have one here." Admiral Ustinov understood very thoroughly that any "jammer" sufficiently powerful to work at a three- or four-mile distance would require an electronic circuit producing a repetitive signal of similar penetration to that on a major transmitter.

He also knew the function of this oscillator would be to create the electronic carrier wave, which would be so much more efficient if transmitted above ground level. It was Admiral Ustinov himself who had always briefed Russian military staff in the United States to seek out hilly ground for the mission.

"Recommend you have Shenzhen build special one. No mistakes," replied Dr. Yang. "That oscillator life-or-death situation. That's what sends the radio signal that will ruin phone signal."

Admiral Ustinov continued to be amazed at Dr. Yang's capacity to say precisely what he meant in a language that was plainly foreign to him.

"Next component is a special tuning circuit, which must control the frequency," said Dr. Yang. "This jammer can only broadcast its signal by sending the exact correct voltage to the oscillator."

Right here, the Chinese doctor lost the Russian admiral, who looked up, raised his eyebrows, and said, "Don't worry about translating that for me. Just tell me how we get the tuning circuit."

"We get it from Shenzhen again. They make parts compatible, not leave much testing to do here. But we will test, make sure this thing hits hard at four miles, working above its target. No mistakes."

Admiral Ustinov smiled. "Next," he said.

"We need a noise generator, a device that generates white acoustic noise, in the speech frequency range of 250–4,000. These things are not very big in Shenzhen, and not much range. We may have to enlarge it, give it more power, maybe attach it to our own jammer.

"But one idea for you—why not have a couple of your people in the target area carrying these things, just as backup? They could also hit home on the football at the appointed time. When we finish, football might never work again!"

"I like it," said the admiral. "Anything else?"

"We will need extra RF amplification."

"We will?"

"It's not too difficult. Just means boosting the radio-frequency power output to levels sufficiently high to jam a phone signal. And we will have a very big generator to make that simple."

"How do we know when it's high enough?"

"Admiral, I'm sure you have heard a small radio station being drowned out by a major national network. That usually means the small station must look for a new frequency. It's the same all over the world. The big transmitter will choke out the lesser signal.

"That's what we're trying to do. Just send out one powerful beam, make president's nuclear football useless. We get jammer well tested and in right place. We can manufacture in very few weeks. And, of course, missiles and launcher are ready."

The admiral was thoughtful for a few moments, and then he asked for advice. "Dr. Yang," he said, "I understand the effectiveness of this electronic hardware can vary. Do we need to consider stuff like the proximity of towers, buildings, and landscape, or even temperature and humidity? I mean, factors that could increase or decrease the range of the jammer?"

"Very definitely. We should select a three-mile launch site for our beam and make sure it's four-mile effective. That way we'll be okay. It will all be much better if we can get the electronics high, looking down on the target area."

"There's no possibility of laser beams to zap the football, is there?" asked Admiral Ustinov. "I did read somewhere the military was using them to disrupt and destroy enemy electronics."

"That's true," replied Yang. "My own corporation is leader in this field, especially target acquisition. But lasers require line of sight, most effective as a ground-to-air or air-to-ground weapon. No good for us. We cannot get too close to president security. They find anything, US military first get rid of our generator truck, then Moscow, in that order. Very bad. No lasers."

The visit of Dr. Yang had concentrated the admiral's mind. It was now clear to him that the puncturing of the presidential football would require troops on the ground. Well, spooks, not troops. This operation needed constant intelligence about the surrounding environment, and Russia needed to make a start very swiftly. That June 28 day already seemed pressing, and it was only September.

Planning was everything, and work must start this day designing a replica "football" based on whatever intelligence was available. Everyone needed to conduct rehearsals. Failure at any level could result in a hostile nuclear exchange between the United States and Russia, and the United States would win. So far as Admiral Ustinov was concerned, that was a possibility, even if Operation FOM-2 was successful. An elementary mistake in execution would be unforgivable.

He spent the rest of the day in conference with naval procurement departments, placing the electronic orders with Shenzhen Technology, knowing that Dr. Yang would personally ensure that top priority was given to everything connected to FOM-2.

His staff had located a huge industrial-size generator in a warehouse in Sofia, Bulgaria. A navy freighter was flying it in tomorrow, complete with six technicians to ensure it functioned properly. Naval engineers would make the adjustments and additions.

Admiral Ustinov had at least fifty skilled men at his disposal in the shipyards of Severodvinsk and Severomorsk.

At five he contacted the naval attaché in the Russian Embassy in Washington and tasked him with finding the frequency numbers that were normally utilized by the president's aides. This, Admiral Ustinov knew, was not so daunting a problem as it seemed.

There were more than 3 million Russians living in the United States, many of them members of that shadowy group once known as "the Soviet sleepers"—men and women known to the Russian authorities who had been encouraged to join major US telecommunications and electronic companies with contracts with the US Department of Defense.

This Cold War mind-set was routine in the old Soviet era, when technicians from behind the Iron Curtain routinely infiltrated any and all US corporations that were involved in design, manufacturing, and servicing the Pentagon's vast communication networks, both in combat and in peacetime.

There were still "sleepers" throughout the electronic industries in the Washington area, and they were people with considerable knowledge about Pentagon equipment. Many of them had risen to important corporate positions and were regularly involved in live tests throughout the world's largest office complex.

It was by no means certain that the Pentagon was, even now, free of the myriad of "bugging" devices and other software "intruders" capable of totally disrupting the network. Soviet spymasters, working behind the high walls and armed security guards on Wisconsin Avenue, tended to be uninterested in where information came from, only that it flowed steadily.

The CIA occasionally nailed a US citizen spying for Russia, and there have been some shocking cases, but the United States, of course, has at times been equally as devious. In the 1980s the Russians were reluctant to move into their new headquarters, the biggest embassy in the United States, because of a tip-off from a US traitor that the Americans had constructed a secret eavesdropping tunnel underneath the entire building!

The secret tunnel is still there, and if federal agents ever reluctantly admit this, it's usually dismissed as a minor reprisal for the KGB's inserting bugs into every wall in the new US Embassy in Moscow in the 1970s, an escapade that caused the United States to fly in American construction workers and lop off the top two floors, replacing them with new secure premises.

No details of the tunnel have ever been formally released, but it was built, and it has been widely accepted that the man who betrayed its existence was the notorious FBI spy Robert Philip Hanssen, who spent twenty-two years selling US secrets to Russia in return for hard cash.

When Hanssen was arrested by the feds in a park near his Virginia home in February 2001, he had just taped a bagful of lethal, classified secrets to the underside of a wooden bridge in readiness for his handler to collect. In return for this outrageous climax to a stupendously dishonest and treacherous career, he was sentenced to life in prison.

In addition to the unseen army of "sleepers," there was a new gateway into American communications. A major new Chinese international electronics company, Pearl River Satellite Systems, was making inroads all along the East Coast. They had strong support from their government and were gaining a significant foothold in sensitive US institutions, working, often, deep inside the nation's infrastructure. It was hard to avoid the obvious truth: Pearl River was placing itself in a perfect position for deadly espionage.

The corporation's activities had been so invasive that US senators were expressing concerns. They had, after all, seen how Huawei Technologies Co., Ltd., had gained a $140 million contract to provide a huge access network and transmission center to British Telecom's twenty-first-century operations. It had escaped no one's attention that there were 3.6 million Chinese living in America and that Huawei might very soon make a move to enter the US market staffed principally, and with some ease, by its own nationals.

The Russo-China alliance was seen as a potential threat to the United States—two very large and burgeoning economies, with giant egos at their heads, all driven by a burning desire to reduce America's prominence as the world's leader, banker, and policeman.

Meanwhile, Admiral Ustinov was studying yet another significant observation e-mailed to him from Solovetsky by Dr. Yang. It pointed out that the entire team of presidential protection and support staff—drivers, aides, secretaries, politicians, White House staff, Air Force One crew, and so on—were all linked on a cell-phone network to form one instantaneous contact grid.

It was a substantial support staff. At times it seemed half the US government was in attendance. But that's the way modern presidents travel, with all hands on deck, as if they had never left the Oval Office.

These people always deployed with laptops and ancillary equipment for immediate communication with Washington. I advise we disrupt everyone and everything while we are on the case next June. Yang.

"If he wasn't a scientist, we could use him in the FSB," murmured the admiral. "Some kind of a grasp of new subjects—never really met anyone like him."

Office of the Chief of Naval Operations
Fourth Floor, the Pentagon

Admiral Mark Bradfield, who had been made commander of a guided-missile frigate at the unimaginably young age of twenty-nine, now occupied the highest office in the United States Navy. An urbane and educated graduate of the Naval Academy, Annapolis, he was widely regarded as an excellent CNO, as good as there had been in recent years.

He enjoyed a close working relationship with General Zack Lancaster, chairman of the Joint Chiefs. Both men had experience under fire and were smooth and erudite negotiators. Also, they were both capable of sounding like seasoned gangsters if things were going against them in any debate.

Weaker members of US Navy hierarchy were visibly cowed by both men when the chips were down. Thus, things did not look great for the future for those who felt intimidated. Everyone knew Mark Bradfield was next in line for the top job when the craggy ex-Rangers C-in-C retired at the end of next year.

Admiral Bradfield did not possess the built-in mantra of the US Navy SEALs: that almost every one of the world's most pressing problems could probably be resolved best by high explosives. He was a hard-assed negotiator and a versatile strategist. His natural instinct was to think his way through obstacles rather than kick, punch, and flatten them in the time-honored manner of men like SEAL Team 10 boss Captain Mack Bedford, who sat quietly before him.

In his big office on Corridor 7, off the Pentagon's great internal highway of E-Ring, Mark Bradfield was seriously flummoxed. For two weeks he had been studying the numbers of brand-new and rebuilt warships scheduled to join various fleets of the twenty-first-century Russian Navy.

It made extremely impressive reading if you happened to be Russian, but the list made the US Navy boss grit his teeth. There were five ten-thousand-ton Delta IV ballistic-missile submarines returning to the Northern Fleet after long refits, two new Borey Class nuclear boats of similar capabilities were returning to the Pacific Fleet, and two more Sierra Class submarines were just out of refit and headed for Severomorsk. Three new Oscar IIs, Russia's fourteen-thousand-ton biggest attack submarine, were out of refit with brand-new missile systems and headed home to the Northern Fleet.

The main export submarine, the near-silent, diesel-electric Kilo Class, was being built for extensive overseas orders—nine to China. But a whole group of brand-new Kilos, already under production, was scheduled to join all four Russian fleets, Northern, Baltic, Black Sea, and Pacific.

There were four new aircraft carriers under construction, and the forty-six-thousand-ton *Admiral Kuznetsov,* with its total refit complete, was expected to begin fleet exercises in the North Atlantic off Norway early next year. All three of Russia's big Kirov battle cruisers were scheduled to complete refits within eighteen months, and the cruiser *Marshal Ustinov* had arrived back in the Black Sea after extensive modernization.

The biggest program, however, was for Udaloy Class guided-missile frigates, several of which were scheduled for each Russian fleet, including the Caspian Sea flotilla.

There was nothing about the update from Russia that pleased Admiral Bradfield. Suddenly, at least in his own mind, America's trusted SOSUS grid was back on the front burner. The electronic guardian of the GIUK Gap needed to be reactivated in the North Atlantic and probably improved.

This program had been activated almost as soon as Captain Bedford had returned from his meetings with Israel's Moscow spy. The information he had imparted was priceless, and everyone in the Department of Defense was now working on strategies to protect the National Security Agency should Russia go ahead and carry out its threat to strike against the Maryland hub of US surveillance.

One problem was that no one in Russia was ever going to admit one single thing. There was nothing to negotiate or threaten simply because the time-honored Russian tactic, when under verbal assault, has always been to say absolutely nothing. It was not worth considering even a president-to-president conference. The wily, old Nikita Markova would simply claim he had no idea what the American was talking about. The only course of action would be to install a new antiaircraft and missile system at Fort Meade, increase all-around surveillance for any incoming attack, and alert every possible US field agent in Russia.

The information Admiral Bradfield had was strong but not infallible. The biggest gap was no date for the attack. Not even the month. The second biggest was no direction, no clues from where the strike would launch.

Perhaps the most valuable intelligence was the Russian abandonment of a submarine as transport. With SOSUS running at only half efficiency, this had given Mark Bradfield precious months in which to put SOSUS back on the top line. And even then he was by no means certain that his navy could zap the oncoming ship from the Arctic that might be carrying the entire paraphernalia required for a full-blooded attack on the US mainland.

And the problem was there for all to see—and it involved the modern, not-so-great Britain, that once all-powerful island nation that had once conquered half the world, but now sat gloomily in the damp northeastern Atlantic, engulfed by immigrants, still swamped by its old Labour Government debts, and with a navy that would have trouble defending the Staten Island Ferry.

There was a deadness about that great stone fortress in London's Whitehall that houses the Ministry of Defense. Years and years of financial cuts, decades of cutting back personnel, cutting back the fleet, failing to replace critical parts of the armed forces, had left a terrible mark on the morale of the services, as if they felt no one gave a damn about them and their problems.

In a nation where a sizable percentage of the population had never worked, did not even *know* anyone who had worked, and furthermore had no intention of ever working, the armed services understood two things: there was never any money for what they believed they needed in order to willingly fight and die for their country, and there were millions and millions of pounds to give away to a bunch of bone-idle wasters claiming benefits, most of them foreign. That may not have been accurate. But that's how it felt to them, inside the granite walls of the ministry and on the far-flung battlefields of the world where they were constantly deployed.

And when America came calling for assistance to resurrect SOSUS, the result was nothing but evasion, pleas of poverty, political considerations, local objections, and lack of interest.

Admiral Bradfield had already faced it. If the United States was once more going to electrify the GIUK Gap, and police it, Washington was going to have to do it alone.

America, while forging ahead, as ever, could see its most modern military science was usually several years ahead in its thinking and development. But it missed those alert Royal Navy eyes on the far side of the North Atlantic.

In the opinion of Captain Bedford, Russia's proposed nuclear slam of the National Security Agency in Maryland was being so well planned, with such a large budget, that the odds had to favor them to pull it off.

"Our best chance has to be to grab the archer on his way to the battlefield and kick him straight in the balls." That was Mack's assessment. "And for that," he added, "we need to catch him way out in the Atlantic. And, if necessary, sink him."

"You sure he's coming down the Atlantic?"

"Dead certain," replied Mack. "My man in the Mossad is sure of that. They will launch from Central America, and it's looking like Panama. For that they need some heavyweight gear—missiles, launcher, and so on. It's a naval operation, so they'll use a ship for transport, probably a converted warship rigged out in the livery of the Russian merchant fleet, painted dark blue with red lines and flying the flag of the Russian Federation, diagonal blue cross on white."

"What about this half-assed attack on the president's emergency comms?" asked Admiral Bradfield.

"In my opinion there's not going to be anything half-assed about it," said Mack. "They've recruited the Chinese to help, probably with a satellite connection and a state-of-the-art jammer."

"Can they pull this off, Mack?"

"Damned straight they can," replied the SEAL captain from Maine. "And unless we get on the case real quick, they will. Russia is a huge, powerful, and now wealthy country. If they set their mind to something, they will almost certainly succeed. But that applies to us as well. Our job is to stop them before they get a chance to do anything."

"One in the cobblers for the friggin' archer, right?"

"That's the stuff, sir. Straight in the cobblers."

"Well, Mack, our problems with the Royal Navy have been very serious."

"They didn't just tell us to forget about it, did they?"

"No, they just seemed helpless. We asked about reopening St. Mawgan in Cornwall. That was always one of the best stations, with a great SOSUS hookup, but all they talked about was no budget for this kind of stuff. Basically, they could not afford to lift a finger to help us. And you know how hard it is to operate in a foreign country unless you have 100 percent backing and a joint financial involvement."

"Sure do. You get all this local bullshit whenever they see our trucks. They don't even seem to care if we use local labor for the project."

"It was actually worse in Wales. We tried to get that secret place down on the Pembrokeshire coast reopened—NAVFAC Brawdy. But that came down to town meetings, and God knows what else. And the Brits would neither help nor invest. Kept saying Brawdy had been deactivated for twenty years, and it would cost the earth to get it back into action. It was just too difficult."

"What's there now?" asked Mack.

"Strangely enough, it's another electronic warfare setup—headquarters of the 14th Signal Regiment, which is a very advanced British outfit. It seemed we might have a perfect fit right there, maybe dovetailing our navy surveillance with very sophisticated British electronic equipment. But, like I said, it was just too darned difficult."

"How about Scotland? That place always seems to be the hub of Russian submarine intrusion."

"Scotland was not much different. We tried to get Machrihanish back onstream. You probably know it—a Royal Navy Air Base up on the west coast of the Mull of Kintyre?"

"I've always heard there was a US SEAL base up there. But it was all very secret. Even now we don't hear much, except it has a two-mile runway, the longest in Europe, so I guess someone thought it was significant."

"Guess so, Mack. I was disappointed when we got the Machrihanish brush-off," said Mark Bradfield. "It was just the perfect place for a listening station, gazing out from lonely country, straight to the Atlantic. The other place we tried up there was the Royal Air Force Base at Kinloss, out on the Moray Firth. It used to be a specialist hunter base looking for Russian boats coming south through the Norwegian Sea. But it's pretty quiet up there now, and despite all we said, the RAF was even more uninterested than the Royal Navy. No dice there.

"The only other place we tried was the old HMS Sea Lion Base in Northern Ireland, way north, near Londonderry, on Lough Foyle."

"You draw a blank there too?"

"You can say that again," said Admiral Bradfield. "The Ministry of Defense had sold it a few years ago to a developer in Dublin, who turned it into a housing estate."

"So where does that leave us?"

"Somewhere between helpless and destitute," said the admiral. "The United States needs a base somewhere in the Northeast Atlantic, and we've never had to worry about it before, because we always had the Brits. And that's no longer possible."

"In an ideal world, Admiral, what would be your solution?" volunteered Mack.

"We need a new ally, as savvy, brave, and clued up as the Brits used to be."

"Is that possible?"

"No. There's no real firepower in the Baltic except for Russia. And it would be politically impossible to go into partnership with Germany or France or Spain or Italy."

"What do you think we need from such a new ally?"

"We need a base where we can park a couple of submarines and maybe a couple of frigates. Also, it would be useful to have a fueling area for an aircraft carrier."

"Then you're talking one helluva lot of waterfront property. Plus some pretty serious ocean depth. And we'd need accommodation for a lot of people."

"Maybe not to start. Not while we sort out this Russian crap."

"I suppose, when you think about it, the cost of reparations to Fort Meade, and the amount of money we'd need to rebuild our entire surveillance system, would run into billions. The price of a new US base somewhere in Europe would be negligible, if we could head off this Russian attack."

"That's all true," replied Mark Bradfield. "I've thought about it a lot. We should get moving on this. How about a meeting with Simon Andre, see what he thinks? How about this evening?"

"Can't. Got an 8:00 o'clock dinner date in Washington. You can come if you like. But I wouldn't bring anyone else."

"Where is it?"

"Can't tell you. But you'll enjoy yourself. And you'll get a darned good dinner. And we'll both learn things."

"Okay, Mack. Where you staying?"

"I'm at the Mayflower, one night only, leaving for San Diego tomorrow afternoon."

"Okay. I'll pick you up at 7:45, and I'll fix it for us to see Simon Andre here tomorrow morning at 0900."

"You have an idea where we might build this base?"

"Sure I have. It's a bit of a long shot, but it would be great if it worked."

"Can I know the location?"

"How about Ireland? They got a huge deepwater Atlantic coastline."

"Those devils! They'd probably want the whole of the state of New York in return."

"How about if we paid off their debts and made 'em the fifty-first state?"

It was one of the few occasions in naval history when Captain Mackenzie Bedford had been nothing short of dumfounded.

SAME DAY

Office of Northern Fleet C-in-C
Severomorsk, Russia

Admiral Ustinov, in conference with six of his officers, had finally come up with a sufficiently large ship to transport the hardware for Operation FOM-2 across the Atlantic. Two hours ago he had ordered the forty-seven-hundred-ton large amphibious landing ship *Korolev* (Ropocha Class Hull 131) to be completely repainted in civilian colors and livery.

Work began this day on removing her 76mm guns from the for'ard and aft decks and blanking out the rocket launchers from either side of her hull. The objective was to make her look like a big, old merchant-marine ship, moving slowly down the middle of the Atlantic Ocean at around twelve knots to make the most of her six-thousand-mile range. The hull would be painted out and her waterlines painted red. The principal hull color would now be dark blue, with white upper works.

She would fly a Russian flag and make the journey from the northern Black Sea port of Sevastopol to Murmansk as soon as her new image was completed. At her top cruising speed of sixteen knots, she would take a little under three weeks to complete the seventy-seven-hundred-mile voyage.

Korolev was a thirty-year-old warship, stationed most of her working life in the Ukraine. But she had always been well maintained in the warm waters of her Black Sea home and would have no problem with the long trip to Panama once she was loaded.

Admiral Ustinov intended to keep her regular crew for the Atlantic crossing, since she would be heading into near-tropical waters and, in the end, steaming essentially through rain forest.

The selection of a cargo ship for the FOM-2 mission was a make-or-break decision. The admiral intended to use the very latest TELAR (transporter erector launcher and radar) to fire the Iskander-K surface-to-surface missiles on their way from the remotest regions of the Panama jungle to Fort Meade, Maryland.

He intended to fire four of them, fast, one after the other, with only split seconds between them, no time to reload. And this meant two enormous TELAR vehicles rumbling through the rain forest. It also meant two mighty launchers had to be transported across the ocean to Panama.

The Chinese port authorities would land them, but thereafter they needed to be in top condition and ready to move off, westward along the waterway. The ship that carried them thus needed to be more than capable of the task. The *Korolev* could carry ten battle tanks if necessary.

And she was a ro-ro (roll-on, roll-off), with a wide tank deck running the length of the ship. From one of the enormous military loading docks in the Severomorsk yards, the heavily armored TELARs, with their high mobility MZKT-7930 Astrolog 8X8 chassis, would roll aboard the former landing ship under their own steam—brand-new 1,000-hp Yamaha diesels, which would provide a road speed of fifty-five miles per hour.

The TELAR vehicles chosen for this operation would carry every possible extra—including the new TADAGAR system (target acquisition, designation, and guidance radar) and a heavy rotating turntable, to allow maximum aim accuracy, however awkward the jungle vegetation may be.

Once launched, it was difficult to see how the Iskander-Ks could possibly miss their target: a black glass building that jutted up out of the essentially flat campus of America's National Security Agency. Admiral Ustinov favored a night firing to avoid inflicting heavy casualties on the US technicians who manned the giant surveillance complex 24/7. But the NSA was the Crypto City that never sleeps. There would be casualties. Admiral Ustinov knew that, but he also knew the nuclear warhead, which would destroy all the US communications, was especially designed to detonate under tight control, inflicting as little peripheral damage as possible. The objective was an unstoppable intense explosion, tailored to incinerate only the immediate area that surrounded it. That was the modern way. President Markova liked that.

When eventually the *Korolev* cleared the Murmansk channel bound for Panama, she would carry a sizable cargo. Aside from the two TELARs and their four missiles, she would also carry a third truck to transport the giant generator and heavy fuel tanks plus the jammer itself and high antennas, with boxes of electronic spare parts.

The forty military staff personnel required to conduct the jungle section of the operation would disembark at Cristóbal Harbor, on the outskirts of Colón, at the Atlantic end of the canal.

Another fifteen electronic technicians to operate the generator and the jammer would travel the length of the Panama Canal with the generator truck before disembarking at the Port of Balboa, right opposite the old Rodman US Navy Base at the Pacific end of the canal. They would travel on a commercial flight from Panama to Houston, where they would change to Delta Airlines and continue to Denver.

The truck, bearing civilian livery but containing the equipment that would nullify the president's emergency comms, would swing through Balboa and cross the Puente Centenario Bridge, a colossal cable-stayed span sweeping 262 feet above the canal. This is the continuation of the Pan-American Highway, known only as CA-1 all the way through Central America, from Panama to Mexico.

Admiral Ustinov did not consider his career was on particularly shaky ground, but that court-martial threat must have been noted in the Politburo's inner sanctums. Certainly, the president and his senior ministers knew about it. But Rankov had been very persuasive, insisting that it must all be shelved and forgotten. In his view, Ustinov was the man for any major naval project.

And FOM-2 was just about the biggest project around. Another screwup was out of the question. The operation had the highest possible priority. If it went wrong, Alexander Ustinov would not look forward to a long and peaceful retirement or exalted government position.

Nossir. He'd be breaking rocks in outer Siberia. Thus, he did not care what FOM-2 cost, or how many people it took to make it succeed. He only knew he had to win. The main building in Crypto City must be destroyed.

Mayflower Hotel
Connecticut Avenue, Washington, DC

The US Navy staff car pulled to a halt outside the most majestic hotel in Washington. The doorman moved swiftly to the rear passenger door and recognized the head of the United States Navy sitting inside.

"G'd evening, Admiral," he said crisply and stepped back to allow the uniformed Captain Mack Bedford to enter. The doorman closed the door of the long black Buick, with due deference. The SEAL commander issued quiet instructions to the driver, who drove swiftly up Connecticut Avenue to a point three miles out of town.

And there they swung into a fortress of an entrance and pulled up before a pair of tall iron gates, Admiral Bradfield staring ahead at the striking stone building, with its great archways, Middle Eastern architecture, and wrought-iron accessories.

"Who the hell lives here?" asked Admiral Bradfield. "Ali Baba and the forty thieves?"

There was no time to reply because two armed guards came to the driver's window and requested the names of the visitors.

"Admiral Bradfield and Captain Bedford," he replied.

"They're expected. Carry on," replied the guard. "Will you be waiting or coming back for them?"

"I'll wait."

"Okay, park over there. We have a chauffeurs' room. I'll take you over."

Almost immediately, a young military officer appeared and said, "Admiral . . . Captain, welcome to the Embassy of Israel."

He led the way into the wide central atrium for which the embassy is famed, and they crossed the enormous carpet, which had been specially woven for the building and features the deepest-held traditions of the Holy Land. They walked together up a short flight of stairs to the ambassador's residence and there stepped through two wide mahogany doors into an unpretentious but superbly decorated room, a portrait of David Ben-Gurion on one wall, one of General Moshe Dayan above the fireplace.

The Israeli officer sitting on the far side of the room stood up and walked toward them, smiling to offer a brief, warm bear hug to Mack Bedford, who in turn faced the US Navy's chief of operations.

"Admiral Bradfield, I would like to introduce you to Colonel Rani Ben Adan, who has, as you know, been very, very helpful to us."

Mark Bradfield shook his hand warmly. "I really am delighted at this," he said. "My country owes you its gratitude."

"Sir," replied Rani, paying immediate deference to the American's high rank, "it is my opinion that we have reached the point where I need to tell you everything I know. May I suggest a glass of wine and we can talk before dinner?"

"Perfect," replied the admiral.

Rani walked to the sideboard and poured three glasses of Israeli wine from the southern town of Richon-le-Zion, the place where Baron Edmund de Rothschild first established some of his greatest vineyards at the end of the nineteenth century.

They sat down in three plush, dark-red velvet armchairs, and Rani began by explaining the contact who had disclosed such remarkable intelligence involving both the United States and Israel.

"There is no possibility, I suppose," offered Mark Bradfield, "that this Russian Naval officer is a double agent playing one side against the other."

"I'd be inclined to doubt that," replied Rani. "Particularly since the FSB shot him dead a couple of weeks ago."

"They did? Jesus!" said the CNO.

"There's no doubt, this was the most important traitor Russia has had for some years. He was the personal assistant to the highest-ranking fleet admiral in the Russian Navy, Alexander Ustinov, C-in-C, Northern Command. This man, a career officer and a lieutenant commander, was so trusted he sat in on the last major meeting on this subject in the Kremlin's rotunda, two seats from the president."

"Have you yet told everything to your own government?"

"I've told them quite a lot. But, you see, I've been given no hard facts about a strike against Israel. Only America. The Mossad is happy to help you in any way we can, but it is important you now know everything there is to know, and that's why we're having this dinner. Because this thing is real. If we don't stop them, they will hit Fort Meade."

"How soon did you realize it was Fort Meade?"

"It took months. No one ever mentioned the true name, only FOM-2. Then Nikolai found it in the pages of Ustinov's personal notebook, pages he was not supposed to see."

"No wonder they shot him."

"Very quickly everything fell into place. Nikolai had fingered that monastery on the Solovetsky Islands as the kind of remote place where they might set up the research and development systems for the new missiles and the radio jammer. We were mystified for months about the identity of the monastery, which they kept mentioning in meetings—but they never put a name to it."

"Then the missile test launch?"

"Yes, but Captain Bedford had already alerted the US satellite surveillance system, based on Nikolai's accurate suspicions."

A white-coated butler emerged and summoned them into a small dining room, where they dined lavishly, beginning with Israeli eggplant salad made with tahini, and then progressed to shaslik of spiced lamb with crispy fried *mallawah* bread.

Rani was an excellent host and served with the lamb a deep-red Israeli wine from the fabled Domaine du Castel in the Judean Hills. Mark Bradfield, who considered himself well beyond the novice stage in his appreciation of fine vintages, was astonished at the deep, rounded quality of the Castel Grand Vin, and commented, "Rani, this is really good—I didn't even know Israel had a wine industry."

"No, it's quite a new development," chuckled Rani. "Just for the past twenty-five hundred years. What d'you think they drank at the Last Supper—Budweiser?"

Mark Bradfield and Mack Bedford laughed, partly at the wit, but mostly at the mock-doleful expression on the face of the Israeli agent.

"You didn't have to buy this, did you?" asked Mack.

"Hell, no," said Rani. "This place has a great cellar, all Israeli bottles. And since the ambassador's away, I thought I'd raise the corkscrew for my country."

"Good call," replied Mark. "And I'd like to thank you. This, I hope, will not be our Last Supper."

"I'll drink to that," answered Mack Bedford, raising his glass. "Confusion to our enemies—may all their missiles fall on stony ground."

"I'd have said, 'May all their goddamned missiles fail to launch,'" added Mark. "I was just beginning to forget how serious this is."

Before they sampled the dessert, Admiral Bradfield suggested that Rani give them a quick rundown of what precisely was factual and what was educated guesswork.

"No problem," said the Israeli. "First, we know that Markova has requested his senior naval commander to prepare a missile attack on the US surveillance headquarters. We know these missiles, the improved Iskander-K, have an increased range and can carry a nuclear warhead. We photographed the test launch from space, and we know the precise distance the missile traveled.

"Number two, we know where the research and development is being carried out. We also know there have been several visits by top foreign missile scientists, including those from Iran, China, and North Korea.

"Number three, we know Russia does not intend to launch at Maryland from anywhere inside the old Soviet Union. We know for certain they have always intended to attack from Central America—presumably because of the reduced distance. We now know their chosen launch site is Panama, and the last words Nikolai Chirkov uttered before he died were *Pedro Miguel*."

"Remind me," said Mark Bradfield. "How do we actually know that?"

"I was on the line talking to him when he said it."

"That's decisive," added Mark. "Obviously, he was referring to the small village and the huge lock at the Pacific end of the Panama Canal."

"That was our surmise," replied Rani. "But the Panama connection was very strong, especially with Markova's friends the Chinese in such an influential position with the government of Panama, and I would say we may safely put that under the fact column."

"I agree," said the admiral. "But we'd better adjust the satellites to keep a survey on Pedro, right?"

"Done," said Mack. "I reported it to Admiral Carlow, and he's already taken care of it."

"Okay, what else do we know for sure?"

"A great deal," said Rani. "And the first thing concerns that Russian submarine. Nikolai established it was a trial run to check whether SOSUS was still working and whether it was still possible to bring a big underwater boat through the GIUK Gap, without being harassed or sunk, by the British or the Americans.

"The test failed. *Gepard* was detected twice, possibly three times. From that moment they decided all the hardware was going by surface ship. We don't know which one, or indeed what it will carry as cargo, except for the missiles. But Nikolai did think it was based in the Black Sea somewhere and that extensive repainting and dockwork were required, before it set sail for Murmansk."

"We got that in hand, Mack?" asked Admiral Bradfield.

"Yessir. I sent a note to Admiral Carlow, and Bob Birmingham is on the case at Langley."

"Rani, do you think they're shipping those damn great launchers, or will they fire from a standing start they'll have to build in the jungle behind Pedro Miguel?"

"We think they'll take the mobile launchers," he replied. "Those Iskanders have always been a little sensitive—always required their own specialized launch and radar. They had one of them out on the Solovetsky Islands, right? God knows how they got it there."

"So, we surmise we'll be looking for a couple of huge TELAR mobiles making their way to Pedro Miguel, sometime before the launch."

"Admiral, we also surmise they'll arrive and fire immediately. The Russians won't take any chance on US surveillance. They'll know that if they're seen from the US satellites, the United States might just make a preemptive. They threatened to do it to the Russians in Cuba; they sure as hell won't think twice about upsetting Panama."

Just then the butler arrived with a spectacular-looking wide plate of Israeli baklava—the classic Middle Eastern dessert of baked phyllo pastry and chopped pistachio nuts dripping in aromatic sweet honey. Mark Bradfield considered it probably the best thing he'd ever tasted. And Rani added to the overwhelming feeling of dining in paradise by serving a silky, sweet dessert wine, which the Israelis use principally for ceremonial occasions but usually produce for VIP guests.

It all provided a perfect atmosphere for a sense of genuine trust among the three men. And it was Admiral Bradfield who finally stated what they all knew: "Colonel Adan, your long friendship with Captain Bedford has proved to be critical in this very dangerous time. And I speak to you as one of my country's best friends. This is my question: would you favor slamming into these Russian gangsters right now, taking out the Solovetsky plant, sinking their fucking freighter, blowing the hell out of the missile launchers in Severomorsk, and taking Pedro Miguel off the map?"

"I cannot fault that line of logic," replied Rani. "As you know, we were faced with a similar decision over the potential atom bombs in Iran. I have to say we dealt with it much as you just suggested, but equally we maintained an element of mystery. We struck at their cyber structure; we trained and practiced in total secret. We told no one else, we came into the attack from out of the blue, and we pressed it home with massive security. No one actually knew it was us. And we've never said it was us.

"You, Admiral, have a bigger problem. If you carried out the program you just outlined and beat Russia about the head and shoulders with the kind of military clout you are considering, there would be absolute hell to pay, for one simple truth: no one can hit as hard as the United States.

"If you blew their freighter out of the water, obliterated their missiles on the docks, vaporized their monastery, and then smashed into the launch site at Pedro Miguel so hard you'd probably knock out the Panama Canal for six months . . . well, the whole world would know who'd done it in about seven seconds. Because no one else *could have* done it. That's the reality. And the USA would be accused of mounting an absolute power play."

"And that would not be true, would it?" murmured the admiral. "We would have acted in self-defense—the power play is theirs. And then, I guess, the Russians would throw up their hands and deny all knowledge."

"That's the truth of it, Mark—may I call you Mark?"

"Certainly you may—Rani?"

"Of course. I'm just trying to point out that for us to stop these Russians, there needs to be an element of stealth and secrecy. That means we'd better let them pull this together and then hit them all at one go, hopefully someplace far from the crowds."

"You mean like the middle of the Atlantic?"

"That's what I'm leaning toward," said Rani. "Maybe nail their ship with all the hardware on board and put it on the seabed. So no one would ever know what happened. It would be justice, because, after all, it's the Russians striking the first blow, with no prior warning. And they will deny all knowledge if their own attack succeeds in hitting Fort Meade."

"I'm with you there," interjected Captain Bedford. "Although a mission like that is not without its problems . . . "

"Before we start on that," added Mark, "may I just ask about the nuclear-football part of this equation?"

"Definitely," replied Rani. "Nikolai heard them use the phrase twice, but did not think twice about it. He thought it was just some figure of speech. But, months later, it came up again, in a context that seemed to beg for clarification. He did the simple thing and Googled the words. And out it popped, the US slang expression for the presidential emergency transmitter, the one that launches cruise missiles, instantly, against a hostile enemy."

Mark Bradfield's eyebrows raised, and he said, "I bet a whole lot of pieces suddenly fitted together when Nikolai worked that out."

"Hell, yes," said Rani. "He already knew something was going on when he found out there was a Chinese scientist from Shenzhen at the launching of the Iskander-K . . . "

"Jesus, are we looking at a cyber attack on the presidential communications system?" frowned Mark.

"I think we were," replied Rani, "but not anymore. Nikolai heard them take a serious swerve away from that. He thought that the Shenzhen scientist Dr. Yang had advised against, on the basis that the nuclear football is basically a telephonic device. It's not a computer; it's what the C-in-C uses to communicate the critical computerized code numbers. Which gives you two options: first, you can get inside the system, probably controlled at the Pentagon, and screw up the sequences, so the wrong numbers are fed in—a lot like when we confused the centrifuges to death in Qom—or, second, you can merely jam the satellite phone, before it even comes out of the big leather bag we call the nuclear football. Then it doesn't really matter whether the code words are right or wrong, because the president is going to be unable to communicate them. One major part of the issue is that the Gold Codes need to be transmitted to the US Command Center, direct from the actual football device. Just so there are no misunderstandings.

"The Russian answer is, at this stage, to jam up the football, so no one can work it. And while you're at it, you could jam up the communications grid of the entire presidential party. That would close down everything for at least an hour, possibly two . . . "

"Which would give those fucking nutcases from the Russian Navy sufficient time to vaporize Fort Meade and then sit back without any chance of a nuclear reprisal coming in from the US of A."

"Precisely," said Rani. "Very neat, right?"

"Too goddamned neat," said Mark. "Don't write off that first option—for us to beat 'em up so badly, and so quickly, that they won't feel like trying anything like this again."

For a few moments Admiral Bradfield ruminated. And then he took another sip of his sublime Israeli wine, which, for a fleeting second, reimbued him with that steel-edged resolve of the embattled desert nation.

"We'll do it, if we have to," said the head of the US Navy.

7

The black US Navy staff car pulled out through the high gates of the Israeli Embassy shortly before midnight. For the first time, Mark Bradfield considered he had a firm handle on the Russian problem.

He now understood precisely how it had happened, why it had happened, and where it would happen. None of it changed his opinion that President Markova and his band of thieves in Moscow were not much short of international gangsters.

"Thank Christ for Rani Ben Adan," said Mack Bedford. "If not for him, we never would have known."

"I meant to ask you sooner," replied the admiral, "is he related to Major General Avraham Adan?"

"Yup. Nephew. His own father commanded the Golan Brigade on the heights in 1973. His mother was killed on the shell line."

"You've known him a long time?"

"Yes, I have . . . He saved my life on the oil rig."

The navy car swept through the dark northwestern suburbs of Washington, and the two men rode in silence, until Mark Bradfield broke it.

"Where will he go now, Mack?" he asked.

"I think back to Tel Aviv. He hasn't been home for a while. There'll be a lot of people who want to talk to him."

"I suppose so. Is he married?"

"Only to Israel. He's a real Sabra of the blood: born there, Orthodox, and prepared to die for Israel, anytime, even if he's the last man standing."

"I guess it runs in the family. Bren Adan was probably the greatest Israeli field commander in history. And there's been a few."

"I don't see him that often. But we're never out of touch. I count him as one of my closest friends."

"Well, he's sure put us straight. We got the satellites in a line watching all the critical points—Severomorsk, Black Sea, Panama, GIUK Gap, and Solovetsky. We got NSA interception and the National Reconnaissance Office and the CIA on the case. Anything breaks, we're on it."

"Just one thing worries me," said Mack, "and that's our lack of hardware. If we spot something big, the Brits do not have a warship or even an ASW aircraft to deal with a problem. We may or may not have something in the area. But our problem remains constant. We don't have big warships, or SEAL teams, or ASW aircraft, or top surveillance, in the northeastern Atlantic. And if we did, we don't have anywhere to put 'em."

That silenced the CNO. And just then the car pulled up outside the Mayflower Hotel.

"Gives us both something to think about, right?" said Mack as he climbed out. "See you tomorrow, 0900 sharp, with Simon Andre."

Office of the Chief of Naval Operations
Fourth Floor, the Pentagon

A meeting such as this would normally have been carried out on the third floor, in the office of the most senior man, the world-traveled, geopolitical, intellectual secretary of defense, Simon Andre. However, this was all a little too close to "Action Stations." The office of the CNO was much more of a navy ops room than the political hub of the Pentagon. In the entrance was a serving lieutenant commander, assistant to the CNO, plus a labyrinth of communications to US warships, bases, and all significant government departments.

The Harvard-educated Simon Andre was a veteran US ambassador, having, by gross personal miscalculation, ended up in the embassies of Iraq, Saudi Arabia, Iran, Nairobi, Zagreb, and Beijing, drawing the comment from General Lancaster, "Poor bastard's seen more high explosive than Rommel."

He was a calm and assured man, and he had been very thoroughly briefed on the FOM-2 operation, even before this first meeting with the principal US informants and advisers, Admiral Mark Bradfield and Captain Mack Bedford.

No one understood better than he the gravity of the loss of the Royal Navy. He also understood the breadth of the Russian problem and the obvious increase in its naval ambitions. No one was more clued in on the sly and disconcerting relationship Russia had with China. And few men knew with more certainty that Markova was a throwback to the old Soviet Union, a hard-eyed and ice-cold devotee of the KGB, currently disguised as a modern president.

Simon Andre had no doubt about the validity of the Russian threat, no doubt they would carry it out precisely as planned, given the chance. His many diplomatic contacts had long advised him how angry Moscow was about the humiliation in Iran.

And now it was time to act. Andre was the first of the three principals into the Pentagon that morning, looking forward to his new briefing by Mark Bradfield and talking to the best known of all Coronado's SEAL commanders.

The question was, could anything be done before Russia made its opening move? And where, if anywhere, could the United States find a new naval station, with submarine facilities attached, plus a SOSUS listening station? This was the topic that occupied Bradfield, Bedford, and Andre for almost the entire morning. It was quickly agreed that the cerebral issues involving surveillance, electronic spying, and satellite strategies could probably be dealt with if the United States was prepared to offer 100 percent financing to countries like Norway, Denmark, Holland, or even France or Portugal.

But some of these were financially unstable, no place to invest, in Simon Andre's opinion. Besides, all of them were reluctant to permit docking space to park regular surface US warships, never mind submarines. All these peripheral countries seemed to live in dread that, sooner or later, the United States would upset someone so badly, they themselves would become targets for retaliatory aggression. None of them had that tough old British attitude that all other nations were ultimately inferior to the United States and United Kingdom—and they could take their nervous little concerns and shove 'em right up their jumpers.

They were well into the meeting when Admiral Bradfield played his surprise card for the first time. "It is my opinion," he said, "that we have one standout country for all this—and I speak of a nation that traditionally loves us, feels we are a part of them, and may welcome us with open arms . . . Gentlemen, I refer to the emerald paradise of the North Atlantic, the Republic of Ireland."

Mack Bedford had fleetingly heard this before. But Simon Andre was astonished and looked up sharply. "Ireland?" he said. "Well, how about that?"

"How about it?" replied the CNO. "Our first requirement for a new US Navy base is obvious—deep water inshore, an Atlantic vista, hopefully a nation that speaks English, and a coastline with a lot of bays and anchorages. It needs to be long and varied, cliffs and beaches, and a willing, educated workforce that will push hard if you pay 'em."

Simon Andre, whose French ancestors had never set foot in the Republic of Ireland in ten thousand years, asked only one question: "How long is their Atlantic coast?"

And that did not stump Mark Bradfield. "It's more than two hundred miles from Cape Clear in County Cork to Killybegs, a fishing town in Donegal in the North. If you can't find a place somewhere there, you're not looking hard enough."

"And does all of that coastline face the Atlantic?"

"Every last yard. In the South you have deep indents cutting into the land in Cork and Kerry, then there's the Shannon Estuary and County Clare, then Galway, Mayo, and Sligo. Donegal's top left with a huge coastline that includes about a thousand bays and the highest cliffs in Europe."

"How do you know all this?"

"My parents go there almost every year for a couple of weeks. Mom's family is from Kerry. I spent a lot of time over there when I was a kid."

"Mark," said Simon Andre, "are you really serious? Do we actually think it's possible to build and staff a new US Navy base in southern Ireland?"

"I am serious. We need somewhere of our own in the eastern Atlantic. Ireland has better credentials than anywhere else; geographically it's easily the best, educationally it's the best, as a nation they love us, and, most important of all, they're broke."

"It's also got a mild climate, I believe," said Simon Andre thoughtfully. "And if you're blasting and building right on the Atlantic Ocean, that's a consideration. A west wind gusting off the sea is a relative pain in the ass, but it's twenty times worse when the wind is freezing, and it's about to bring in a blizzard, and there's ice everywhere."

"That's not Ireland," said Admiral Bradfield. "You get palm trees in many parts of the country because they don't have any serious cold."

"Look, I accept the theoretical merit of such a plan," mused Simon Andre. "In many ways, it would be ideal. But what the hell is the Irish government going to say when we call and suggest we'd like to build a modern version of the Norfolk Navy Yards in the middle of Galway Bay?"

At this point, Mack Bedford was punching the keyboard on his laptop, pulling up various maps of the west coast of Ireland. "I'll tell you something, Admiral," he said. "The northern part of that coastline is farther north than Newfoundland . . . Are you sure it's warmer?"

"I know it's warmer," said Mark Bradfield. "And it's because of the Gulf Stream, which flows across the Atlantic and washes onto the first shore it reaches, and that's the west coast of Ireland."

Simon Andre looked up and said, "Listen, gentlemen, it is clear to me that the United States must have either a base or a very strong ally in the eastern Atlantic. It makes no sense for us to be thousands of miles away from the Russian Navy's highway into the rest of the world.

"Let's look at this Irish situation, just exploratively for the moment. But let's take on board the three salient issues: geographic, political, and economic. That should give us three sound directions in which to proceed: first, a short list of places where we could put a new base; second, how we propose this to the Irish government; and third, what it will cost in terms of building and persuading Ireland it's a good idea."

It was not difficult to see how Simon Andre had been a mainstay of US overseas policy since his early thirties. It would not have been a big stretch for an average bureaucrat to have made 374 points about this particular naval proposition, spanning about seven thousand pages with notations, flotations, rotations, and God knows what else.

Simon Andre had it wrapped up in three short sentences. And he achieved it with an effortless certainty. No one in the room was in any doubt of the task that stood before them. All of them had seen the engraved copperplate writing, framed on the wall behind the defense secretary's great mahogany desk. It read: *Let me see a complete reorganization of the North Atlantic fleet's defensive strategy against Nazi U-boats. And if it won't go on one side of one sheet of paper, it hasn't been properly thought out—Winston Churchill.*

Simon Andre was a devotee of Great Britain's World War II prime minister. He owned every book Sir Winston ever wrote and was a board member of the Churchill Society, which meets every year in Independence, Missouri, 120 miles west of Fulton, where the great orator made the immortal speech on March 5, 1946: *An Iron Curtain has descended . . . dividing Europe into East and West.*

The prospect of a new and vitally important naval project on the far side of the Atlantic was precisely the kind of grandiose scale that Simon Andre liked to ponder. He was a realist and a romantic, and he was one of those Americans who believed this granite-hewn nation should never drop its guard.

Simon Andre was not so much an admirer of Churchill as he was a disciple. He believed that when the mighty bulldog of Britain's Parliament bowed out in 1955, the beat of its heart was never the same again. And today, more than a half century later, America's political head of defense often ran a military problem through the back of his mind, just checking, wondering whether Winston would have approved.

And one thing he knew for absolute sure and certain—a new modern US Navy base, tucked secretly into a clandestine and lonely bay on the west coast of Ireland, glowering unseen at the Russians, packed with electronic venom, firepower, and seagoing efficiency, above and below the surface: Winston would have loved it.

"I may be second-guessing you, Mack," he said, "but I imagine you would like this new place, wherever it is, to be built with a US Navy SEAL training area?"

"I think so, sir," replied Mack. "One of our biggest problems has always been quick deployment. We are all set East Coast and West Coast, Virginia Beach and Coronado. But when you think about it, they're both a long way from the rest of the world.

"You remember all that fuss we had with the Somali pirates—just because it took us so darned long to get to the middle of the Indian Ocean. It would be terrific if we could deploy direct from southern Ireland. Save us hundreds of hours of preparation."

"Well," said Secretary Andre, "there is obviously an element of intense secrecy about all this. I think you should be tasked with the preliminary geographic study of Ireland's west coast with a view to locating suitable harbor sites. I don't think Admiral Bradfield will object?"

"Certainly not," said Mark.

"I will personally investigate the political procedures, and perhaps, Mark, you could look into the costs of building such a structure on a virgin coastline, bearing in mind that basic materials like steel and concrete must be shipped in from somewhere. Not to mention labor."

"Affirmative," replied Admiral Bradfield. "Time frame?"

"A week," said Andre. "I expect Mack here wants to get back to base this afternoon, and there's not much we can do about the Russians except to keep watching. So why don't we break until next Monday, September 24, 0900, right here?"

So the meeting broke up. Assured the US satellites were watching with the greatest possible vigilance, each of the three returned to his own domain, Admiral Bradfield checking in with Captain Ramshawe at the NSA to keep them both posted if any suspect pictures came into Chantilly.

Mack hitched a ride on a navy flight returning to San Diego from Andrews Air Force Base. With a three-hour time gain, he made it back by late afternoon and reported to Admiral Andy Carlow, the SPECWAR-COM commander, for a thorough debriefing about his immediate tasks.

That proved to be an agreeable meeting because the emperor SEAL had long fretted about the US Navy's lack of an exclusive base in or around the UK. A brand-new facility in western Ireland would be a terrific asset, and if they could find the right place, Admiral Carlow would heavily back any attempt to do the deal with the Irish government.

All of this flying around as some quasi spy/diplomat had taken a minor toll on the fitness of the commander of SEAL Team 10. The following morning he was out of bed at 0430 (0730 on the East Coast) to greet his men on the grinder, pacing around while his instructors shook the class into action before sending them down to the Pacific beach to complete eighty push-ups before the morning running.

Mack did the push-ups effortlessly, as he did every morning, whether he was in the Mayflower Hotel or the Hindu Kush. He once set about this most punishing of exercises in a back alley in North Baghdad after being motionless as a sniper all night and was very nearly shot in the backside by a wandering terrorist, age twelve.

But a SEAL's merciless training regime lasts for all the days of his service. Anytime, any day, regardless of rank or length of time spent in combat, a United States Navy SEAL may be called upon to "go to Action Stations." That means right now. Nothing else. It means everyone in the team. And it may mean that you will be required to die in the not-too-distant future. The fitter, the faster, and the stronger you are, the better your chances of survival. Every SEAL agrees with General George Patton's eloquent summation: "There's no darn glory in dying for your country—the idea is to make the other poor, dumb bastard die for his country."

Peak fitness means peak speed, peak reaction time, peak awareness. The supreme tuning of the combat warrior's body signifies wild-animal strength and agility. To face a hard-trained Navy SEAL is to face a crouched mountain lion with an M4 rifle and a combat knife.

That was why the battlefield veteran Captain Mack Bedford was pounding along the sand for four miles with the new class of hopefuls, running hard on the outside of the pack, bounding along with the instructors, pushing it, taking it to the limit with every stride, with no other ambition, except to be the best. Always the best.

He did not join in the oceangoing training involving the rubber boats and the rowing, and capsizing and swimming, dragging the heavy hull up over the rocks opposite the famous Coronado Hotel. He adjourned to the huge SEAL swimming pool back in the main complex, near everyone's living quarters, and completed fifty laps in quick time.

He had lunch in the officers' quarters, just a sandwich and fruit salad, and retired to the campus library, where he delved into the chart drawer and pulled up the ones from the British Admiralty that provided infinitesimal details of the waters that surround the long coast of southern Ireland.

He sat at a wide table and decided to work his way methodically around the Irish coast, starting with the vast natural harbor of Cork City—known in Gaelic as *Cobh*—the Harbor of Tears, the last sight of Ireland seen by hundreds of thousands driven from their homeland in the nineteenth century by famine and poverty. The ship that carried Patrick Kennedy, the great-grandfather of President John F. Kennedy, left from here, bound for Boston in 1848.

The headquarters of the tiny Irish Navy is located in this harbor, but for Mack Bedford it was too enclosed by cliffs and hillside. Basically, it faced the wrong way, southeast, toward northern Cornwall in England, not to the dark reaches of the GIUK, away to the northwest, across the land.

The simplest place to begin excavating for an American base was almost certainly the spectacular coast of West Cork, with its long and picturesque bays, lonely countryside, and many natural harbors. But again they were apt to face too far south.

Mack studied and rejected wondrous Irish seascapes all along that stretch of coast that encompasses the Old Head of Kinsale, Clonakilty Bay, Glandore Harbor, the islands before Skibbereen, Roaring Water Bay, and the near-irresistible harbors of Crookhaven and Barley Cove. There was Dunmore Bay, Bantry Bay, and the Kenmare River, all with deep water, all with anchorages and deserted coastal land, all facing the wrong way, southwest now, jutting directly toward the Azores.

The rest of Ireland's southwest corner was composed of the mythical Kingdom of Kerry, the Shannon Estuary, and County Clare. Mack had never been anywhere near that area, and, surrounded by guidebooks, photographs, and charts, he pondered the places of great Irish legend, the Ring of Kerry, the Lakes of Killarney, Dingle Bay, and the pinnacled Skellig Islands, where mystical tales go back a thousand years before Christ. He read about the Viking raids and the long-abandoned monastery (*Jesus! Another one!*).

He read how Dara Down, king of the world, rested there on Skellig in the year AD 200 before sailing on north across the bay to Ventry to do battle with the giant Finn MacCool. This was a terrible conflict that, records show, lasted one year and a day, as might reasonably be expected by any enemy tackling MacCool, the chieftain of Irish legend who built the Giant's Causeway.

The more he gazed at photographs and film of Kerry's endless beaches and coves, the more he coveted the land. But the more he studied, the more hopeless it all became. Kerry, all the way north to the seventy-mile estuary of the River Shannon, was one of the world's great tourist areas.

Mack scanned the list of hotels, built specifically to accommodate every last one of the 80 million Americans who claim Irish ancestry and may wish to gaze upon the land of their forefathers.

"We can't build a base down here," he decided. "Not even in northern Kerry, where the land looks more west. It's just too busy, too many people wandering around, too many harbors, boats, and, I guess, buses."

He checked out the county town of Tralee, which is sited up the River Lee with an excellent seaport ten miles west along the north shore. But the problems remained. It was all too busy, "civilized," and sophisticated.

"For crying out loud," muttered Mack, "Tralee Golf Course was designed by Arnold Palmer. We'd probably have to make him an admiral. And I guess he'd be a darned good one. But Southwest Ireland's no place for a US Naval base."

County Clare, which stands modestly between the two more celebrated counties of Kerry and Galway, is the site of the Cliffs of Moher, which is one of the most majestic sea-cliff spectacles of the world. Mack thought Clare had possibilities, except for its starry neighbors to the north and south, and the attention they inevitably brought to the area. But the coast was very rugged, and the water looked like it would be rough and exposed.

However, the Isles of Arran are part of County Clare, and these might suit just fine according to the Royal Navy's Admiralty chart. Each of the three islands is really a limestone plateau, rising up from the sea at the mouth of Galway Bay: Inishmore, Inishmaan, and Inisheer converted to Christianity in the fifth century and are, to this day, places where time has almost stood still.

Mack studied the long lists of local shipwrecks down the years, the obvious slashing violence of the Atlantic on this rocky outpost. He noted the near-total lack of electricity, and the reliance on the steamer bringing supplies from Galway across that rough water, and decided this was a backward step too far. A new US Navy base could not be on an island because it would probably require more mainland supplies than all the rest of Ireland put together.

Northwest of the thriving city of Galway, deep into the ancient province of Connaught and along the untamed and wild coast up to Connemara, were the most realistic possibilities Mack had yet encountered. It was suitably desolate, with low population at any time of the year.

He studied the demographics, and he stared at the photographic evidence. So far as he could tell, there were miles and miles of peat bogs above which he could see black lakes, which gleamed in the sun. There were lonely valleys with no signs of life, and high above, there arose the pale-gray mountain peaks of the Twelve Bens.

The coastal road running west out to Slyne Head twisted and curved around small bays and inlets. Miles of this corrugated coastline consisted of high, steep cliff faces. It was, however, the lack of population that was most striking. Mack estimated it would take about seven thousand years to put in a new dock.

"US Navy Station Connemara? I don't think so."

Heading north, the Irish coast runs up to sad and lonely County Mayo, jutting out into the Atlantic, its desolate beaches protected by places like Achill Island, the enormous Blacksod Bay, and the Mullet Peninsula. Again, it's mountainous country with its best harbors mostly quiet.

Mayo, once described as "poor, dying Mayo" with its endless peat bogs, deserted beaches, and myth-shrouded peaks, never recovered from the mid-nineteenth-century potato famine, which devastated its population through starvation and mass emigration.

Every account Mack read pointed out the problems of this prolonged shortage of people. During the famine, Mayo's population fell 29.5 percent in nine years, from 389,000 to 274,000. This was a time when 1 million Irish people died of starvation and another million emigrated. But County Mayo represented the most shattering misery and despair in all of Ireland: its people were 90 percent dependent on the potato for existence, and the crop failed. Twice. Even today, there are still only 130,000 people in Mayo, Ireland's third-largest county.

Despite the geographic advantages of the place, its perfect coastline from which to hook up with SOSUS, Mack Bedford rejected it on the basis of its obvious lack of manpower. "US Naval Base Mayo" had the wrong connotation, and the last half hour's reading had induced a sadness in the SEAL commander that refused to leave him. He suspected this universal melancholy might affect others if the United States decided to move in.

Which brought him even farther up the coastline to the top left-hand corner, County Donegal, which looks as if it should be a part of Protestant Northern Ireland but isn't.

Donegal has the longest coastline of any Irish county. If it were measured in dead straight lines, it would be more than two hundred miles. If you counted every one of the deep inlets, bays, estuaries, and harbors, it would probably be twice that. Its coastline is mostly spectacular, grandiose, but it has its share of superb harbors studding the contours of the coast all the way from Donegal Bay to the border of the never-ending coastline near Londonderry in the North.

Mack Bedford gazed at this colossal expanse of seascape and seaways and wondered where to start, dazzled as he was by the Irishness of the coastal names—Drumanoo Head, Rossnowlagh, Dunkineely, McSwyne's Bay, Dunmore Head, Inishfree Bay.

He looked at the giant peninsula in the North, Inishowen, the largest in all of Ireland, with Malin Head jutting north into the Atlantic Ocean, the most northerly point in the entire country.

Mack noted that Inishowen was bordered by two giant sea loughs, to the east by the seven-mile-wide, twenty-mile-long Lough Foyle, and to the west by the narrower but twenty-five-mile-long Lough Swilly. "Captain Bedford," he muttered, "if you can't find a place for a US Navy base somewhere in all the miles and miles of coastline around Donegal, you probably should resign."

For the next two hours, he pored over the charts, checking ocean depths, accessibility from the main roads, closeness of population, nearness of a sizable local town, but above all deserted coastal landscape where a huge building project could take place without upsetting local people.

In the end he had a short list of four, all of them completely suitable and geographically sound. All of them were ideal places for the SOSUS hookup. But one stood out, and Mack kept returning to it, a long seaway cutting back, deep into the land, at the eastern end of Donegal Bay, toward the south of the county. It was called Inver Bay and was protected by the most unlikely narrow finger of rock, ramming its way southwest out into the main bay for almost six miles and ending with the lighthouse on St. John's Point.

This Donegal promontory seemed to Mack like the longest headland in Ireland, with a village at the mainland end, Dunkineely, and practically nothing all the way down to the lighthouse. He measured the promontory at about nine miles west of Donegal Town, with its population of twenty-five hundred and its majestic fifteenth-century castle, now rebuilt, having been torched by the local chieftain, Rory O'Donnell, in 1607 to prevent the English from getting their greedy little hands on it.

Mack thought that might have been a bit hasty—and would personally have favored a quick retreat in the face of the English army, but a return in the dead of night: *SEAL Team 10, in the Zodiacs, heavily camouflaged, rowing ashore and blasting the enemy to hell before they could locate their weapons.*

"Not sure about this Rory character," he muttered, in reference to the O'Donnell clan chief, now dead for more than four hundred years. "Might not have what it takes to command one of the teams. Probably wouldn't have passed BUD/S."

Say what you like about Captain Bedford. He could always relive a battle and nearly always win it.

Now he was preoccupied with an ancient but at the same time extremely modern problem: water depth in harbor approaches. And Donegal Bay represented a blue-water mariner's wildest dream. Coming in off the Atlantic, there was almost 200 feet of water all the way.

Right off St. John's Point the chart showed 171 feet. Moving northeast along the estuary the water was 120 feet, shelving up to 75 feet. The deep water ran almost the entire length of Inver Bay, except for the last mile, where it still showed 50 feet, to a point well beyond the ideal site for the proposed US base.

Tight inshore, there were shallow areas, but nothing that could not be quickly dredged, or built on, with industrial-size jetties and docks. He selected the spot on the chart and made his mark, informing the librarian he would be taking it with him and they could either make a copy or order another.

Office of the Director
National Reconnaissance Office
Chantilly, Virginia

Air Force general Jack Myers had two reasons to be baffled this morning. The first was a picture of some Russian monastery with a giant golf ball on top of a sixteenth-century chapel. The second was a picture of a large Russian freighter turning out of the Black Sea into the fast, narrow waters of the Bosporus, the waterway that divides Europe and Asia.

The first was the biggest puzzle. General Jack, a forty-nine-year-old former fighter pilot who now presided over this top secret arm of the US defense system, had simply never seen anything like this. The golf ball was about fifty feet in diameter and was parked on the chapel roof, surrounded by religious spires and symbolic statues. To the layman it looked as if some celestial adman had gone berserk.

But Jack Myers knew better than that. For the past three or four weeks, he had been preoccupied with a new space laboratory being launched in the next few days. But he still had read the memos detailing how a huge fortified monastery in North Russia was being converted into the main target of the US surveillance system in that part of the world.

Here was final proof that something was going on. General Myers did not know what the massive white and rippled sphere contained, but he was sure it was something to do with satellite communications.

The second photograph showed something unusual rather than mystifying. The freighter turning into the Bosporus had been tracked by US satellites all the way from the northern ports of the Black Sea. But this one was from a Russian Naval harbor, outside Sevastopol in the Ukraine. The ship was civilian, around five thousand tons, and it had made a beeline north to south across the Black Sea, straight to the Bosporus.

This was the unusual part. Russian Naval vessels rarely left the Black Sea these days, conducting exercises and workups for newly refitted warships right there in the 168,000 square miles of this inland ocean, which is 7,000 feet deep in parts and 800 miles wide.

For a civilian ship to come out of a Russian Naval yard and head directly for the only Black Sea exit was unusual. The Russian Navy traditionally did all of its own fetch-and-carry work. General Myers wondered what this five-thousand-ton freighter was carrying when it pulled out of Sevastopol.

He asked for details and was quite surprised to be told an hour later there was a good chance it was carrying nothing, it was riding so high in the water. It was moving at sixteen knots and picked up a Turkish pilot as soon as it crossed the unseen line across the northern entrance to the Bosporus between Fort Rumineleferi to starboard and the headland of Anadolu on the left.

General Myers instructed his ops room to keep a weather eye on the ship, and he sent a signal to the Pentagon, alerting them he was tracking a large, empty merchant freighter out of Russian Naval Base Sevastopol, making its way through the Bosporus Strait toward the Mediterranean. Its name was *Koryak,* presumably after the Siberian Mountain range north of the Kamchatka Peninsula in the northern Pacific.

Everything about it was unusual. It was almost unheard of for any Russian merchantman to leave the Black Sea with no cargo. It was doubly unusual that *Koryak* came from a navy port, and there was absolutely no record of its going into the Sevastopol Base, which suggested it had been in the dockyard for many months.

General Myers had been specifically instructed to keep a keen watch on anything out of the ordinary that took place in or around Russia's Black Sea Fleet, and this fitted the profile. US satellites would track that ship to the end of the earth if necessary.

1130, FRIDAY, SEPTEMBER 21, 2018

Office of the Northern Fleet C-in-C
Severomorsk, Russia

The news from the monastery was not wonderful. A serious question had been raised about the Iskander-K's guidance system by one of the North Korean nuclear missile scientists. And Admiral Alexander Ustinov knew better than to argue with very smart Far Eastern rocket men.

The technician in question, Dr. Chon Nam-sun, was on loan at hideous expense from the government of North Korea, and he was concerned about the Russian missile's reaction to sudden landmasses as it flew over water. This involved the most sensitive areas of radar guidance and had bedeviled missilemen all over the world for decades.

The most common issue was in the radar of the fire-and-forget cruise missile, or SAM (surface-to-air). With the radar beams aimed out over open water, the system worked perfectly and could detect any incoming fighter-bomber or missile in very good time. The problems always arose when the radar scan flashed onto an island, or even the mainland, and momentarily the screen would fill with "snow," fizzing out the picture.

Nowadays it usually cleared, but many operators recall the old days of twenty-five years ago when, on certain systems, it never cleared. It seemed the sudden change from sea to land confused it, and while the problem has been removed from some modern Western missile systems, there are often traces of the old flaw. This was likely to cause a rush of blood to the heart of any missile scientist.

Dr. Chon Nam-sun, working deep in the underground laboratories of the Solovetsky Monastery, had seen something that alarmed him. He spoke to the lead Russian project director, pointing out the blip on the screen when the computer fed in a landmass to the fictitious virtual missile. "Just imagine," he had said, "that missile flying at Mach-5 across the Caribbean, suddenly is faced with the Florida peninsula up ahead, swerves, and smashes straight into downtown Miami. With nuclear warhead, that flatten very big city, and bring you very bad war with Americans—goodnight, Moscow."

"Doctor, we can take no chances," replied the Russian. "But I ask you one thing: how come the test went so well, no problems of this kind?"

"Sir, there were two problems, so small hardly anyone recognized them, but I was looking at the screen and for single second there was a blip, very early on when the missile reached the Kola Peninsula, and another when it crossed above the polar ice cap northeast of Spitsbergen.

"I said nothing at the time, but I did study the playback. I showed the main-screen technical observer, and he also had noticed the two blips, and one of them was distinctive, blocking the screen for maybe one and a half seconds."

"Is this serious?"

"I don't know. But I'm concerned about the missile suddenly running directly at very warm land, like Florida. We can fix it, but I need to know it's not going to happen before I sign off the final documents that express my satisfaction with the work we have carried out."

"How do we find out?"

"We run a new test, and this time we will try to fly a similar course to the real thing."

"That's predominantly over water. The Panama launch will send the missile straight out over the western Caribbean," replied the Solovetsky project chief, at the same time pulling up a computerized satellite picture of the area.

He studied it for a few moments and said, "It's ocean all the way for the first 800 miles, and then the missile needs to fly straight over the narrowest part of the Cuban jungle. From there it's a 300-mile slingshot up past the Bahamas, logging 1,140 miles off Miami."

"How far off Miami?" asked Dr. Chon.

"I'd say close to 100 miles, but far enough for them to miss seeing us, with luck."

"At supersonic speed we make Maryland in under fifteen minutes, flying the ocean all the way," said the doctor. "That's nice. Very nice. I'm not worried about the range, only the swerve if that radar scanner blips on us. Florida has many, many people on east coast. Many important people. No swerves, okay? I sign nothing 'til chances of swerve eliminated."

"You may do whatever it takes to perfect the Iskander's guidance system," replied the Russian formally.

"Sir, it would be simple if we could fly higher," said Dr. Chon. "But my orders are to stay low as possible, maybe fifty feet above water surface. Always under American radar."

"When will you be ready for the new test?"

"Two days. We launch same place but spotter locations different. Must be very accurate."

"You want it made open to VIP visitors?"

"Not this time. Very quiet. Just in case I am not satisfied. Because it may all look fine, but I know there is a very small flaw, and I must kill it."

Dr. Chon had spent the next hour plotting the new route, trying to fly straight over possibly the coldest ocean in the world in order to fly very fast over one of the warmest.

Russia's deadly Iskander-K would blast off vertically, locking onto its route with a huge swing to the northeast and then ripping across the White Sea, straight up to the only seaway in and out of this landlocked northern ocean.

Three hundred miles, in four and a half minutes, would see the missile cross the Kanin Nos headland, which guards the White Sea at the very tip of the long and desolate Kanin Peninsula, to starboard for exiting ships.

Now over the Barents Sea, the Iskander would streak another six hundred miles before crossing the glaciers on the huge island of Novaya Zemlya, the old Russian nuclear-testing site that separates the Barents from the Kara Sea.

Dr. Chon plotted a forty-five-degree swing north just to keep the missile low over the water up to the permanent ice shelf of the North Pole. From there he did not much care where the missile went, so long as it stayed on course and crashed into the ice. He intended no explosion, since he already knew the warhead was well tested and fail-safe.

The route he mapped out had three landmass crossings over the peninsula, twice over Novaya Zemlya and then the ice shelf, which may or may not count. And all the way, Dr. Chon would keep his eyes glued to that screen, watching for the blip, the fizzing snow that he was certain he could eliminate before blastoff.

Admiral Ustinov studied the report from Dr. Chon and agreed with every word. The consequences of a malfunction that might cause the missile to hit a US city were too calamitous to ponder. And the admiral could not work out to whom such a disaster would prove a worse fate—himself or the North Korean nuclear expert.

The admiral himself had never been in the middle of a true catastrophe, except for the Chirkov spy disgrace, but he guessed Dr. Chon had, since North Korea's diabolically unreliable test missiles had made more big but unscheduled splashes into the Sea of Japan than the local bluefin tuna.

But Dr. Chon was a warhead specialist, with a secondary interest in rocket range and guidance. His opinions were valuable on either subject. Admiral Ustinov was more than happy to grant formal permission for the second test, and, frankly, the less everyone knew about it, the better.

Office of the Chief of Naval Operations
Fourth Floor, the Pentagon

Admiral Bradfield read Mack Bedford's detailed report about his findings in northwestern Ireland. He liked what he was learning. And he smiled at the sheer scale of the plan's title: US Naval Base Donegal.

Simon Andre had stopped by earlier in the day and had astounded him at the continuing scale of Irish debt on the international markets. It was currently running at $2.3 trillion, which worked out to around $500,000 per head! Ireland stood sixth out of 188 countries in terms of external debt—that's the total public and private debt owed to nonresidents.

On the other hand, the United States owed $15 trillion, but its vast, rumbling economy meant that was a mere $47,000 per citizen. The UK owed $9 trillion, and that was $144,000 per head of population.

Ireland also had the second-highest household debt in the world and had suffered several credit-rating downgrades by Standard and Poor's, damaging its reputation and branding it a high-risk nation. Simon Andre said Ireland would be lucky to hang on to a single-A rating in the next few months.

Secretary Andre thought this was all absurd. Ireland had been trying extremely hard to manage the debt. In the years since 2012 when it seemed the roof might fall in, they had cut back government spending and done everything they could to improve the situation.

If there had been a world table for pure effort, Ireland might have finished on top. And, unlike most other countries, their situation was visibly improving. The Irish were a savvy and hardworking nation, and there was no question of a default on the international market.

"But," said Simon Andre darkly, "what wouldn't they do to get out of that debt situation?"

That was the question that could very easily settle the issue of a new US Navy base in northwestern Ireland. There were many forms of assistance that the United States could offer to the fiercely independent nation across the Atlantic, but was there one that Ireland might be unable to refuse?

Simon Andre believed the answer to that was a resounding yes. "The crash of 2008 took them completely by surprise," he said. "They were the first country in the European Union to enter recession. Their very solvency was brought into question.

"The main trouble was far beyond the comprehension of ordinary people. It was caused by reckless banks lending astronomical amounts of money to property companies. This created a major oversupply in both residential and commercial buildings.

"Worse yet, some of the largest Irish institutions like pension funds were exposed to what became the biggest property crash in Irish history. They just ran out of customers. No one wanted to buy anything. Banks had to start waiving the covenants, just to enable the borrowers to pay back the interest—it was touch and go whether the entire Irish banking system caved in. And they have not yet been able to get out of it."

"But they keep trying?" added Mark Bradfield.

"Yes. And with some success. The Irish government has shown an admirable determination to do whatever may be necessary to put the economy right. And, hopefully, that may be where we will come in."

"You mean step in and pay off Irish government debt?" asked Admiral Bradfield.

"No need to go that far," said Secretary Andre, "because they are making progress. But I see a scenario where we might take over the ultimate responsibility—perhaps form a brand-new partnership with Ireland as a trading nation."

"How about making them the fifty-first state?" asked Mark Bradfield. "That way we could pump in some cash to the banks in return for ownership and build a new base in Donegal, which would be a substantial boost to their economy, since everything in that base would be Irish made."

"I've heard worse ideas," replied Simon Andre. "And there's a hell of a lot more Irishmen living in the United States than there even are in Dublin. An Irish-American nation-state would be a great benefit to everyone involved . . . and they just might spring for it."

"I can think of a few Americans who might not be overjoyed."

"Yes? Who?"

"Ireland's full of American corporations that went there mainly because of the very low corporate tax rates." Mark Bradfield was thoughtful. "If Dublin was suddenly part of the United States, they'd all have to pay the full whack."

"Do you know how long it would take a Senate committee to think of a way around that?" said Andre. "I'll tell you. About four and a half seconds."

"Okay, sir," replied the admiral. "What's our next step?"

"Plainly, to get someone over there, just to take a look around Donegal, study the roads and the land along the shore, hire a boat and take a jog around, see if there are any serious problems we need to get around."

"Okay, who do you have in mind, or will you leave it to me?"

"I thing Mack Bedford's the obvious candidate. He's spent God knows how long studying the maps and charts. He'd give us the best insights of anyone. Plus, we will need a SEAL base, and Mack's a frogman. He'll want to check out those inland waters at the head of Donegal Bay. Eliminate any surprises."

"Good call, Andre. Let's send Mack to Ireland."

MONDAY AFTERNOON, SEPTEMBER 24

Andrews Air Force Base
Prince George's County, Maryland

Captain Mack Bedford saw it coming from way out, the giant, new Hercules C-130 turboprop freighter, flying in from California, bearing the members of SEAL Team 2, which was deploying once more to the Middle East.

He'd made that journey many times himself, and the refueling stop at Andrews was always poignant because it may be the last time any of them ever saw American soil. SEALs never go anywhere that is not highly dangerous. They are always going to fight an enemy of the United States; otherwise, there's no point sending them.

Andrews Air Force Base, now jointly in the hands of the USAF and Navy, was a place of the deepest military folklore. It was here that the body of the slain thirty-fifth president, John F. Kennedy, was returned from Dallas on November 22, 1963. Andrews is still the home of the enormous Boeing VC 25A Air Force One.

Operational since May 1943, the base has been the first and last stop in the United States for almost every foreign king, queen, president, prime minister, pope, and military leader. Mack stared out at the seven square miles of the airfields and could see his own aircraft much closer now. He watched its shimmering descent to the eastern runway, which was more than two miles long, and he watched it come howling into focus, four big engines in reverse thrust, dragging it down to manageable speed on the ground.

It came to a stop as close to the naval terminal as possible, and Mack saw the fuel trucks moving quickly toward it. He picked up his bag and walked out to the stairway that was already being wheeled into place. He saw the door open and the navy lieutenant standing ready to greet him.

The aircraft was packed with guys he knew, many of whom had trained under his explicit instructions. The hold of the aircraft was packed down with their essential gear: heavy weaps (machine gins), M4 rifles, SIG Sauer 9mm pistols, pigstickers (combat knives), ammunition belts, grenades, and medical and communications equipment.

Mack climbed the stairway and shook the hand of the young SEAL lieutenant. And as he entered, there was a well-rehearsed roar of *"HOO-YA, INSTRUCTOR MACK!"*

He threw them a good-natured salute, slung his bag into one of the enormous freighter's high netting, and settled down into a large seat made of the same material. Most roving ambassadors or representatives of the US government on a highly classified mission would have had a heart attack at the pure discomfort of traveling like this across the Atlantic.

Mack could not have cared less. He had nearly always made the journey like this, and if it was good enough for his boys, sprawled out all over the aircraft in various hammocks and sleeping bags, then it sure as hell was good enough for him. These guys were about to put their lives on the line. How could he possibly deserve more than they?

With the refuel complete, the Hercules immediately rumbled back down the runway and then thundered skyward into a gusting southwester. The pilot banked left over the Potomac and then climbed high above Chesapeake Bay, crossing Maryland's eastern shore and flying out over the Atlantic Ocean.

The aircraft was scheduled to make a fairly civilized landfall at Landstuhl at around seven thirty (local time), but Mack's requirements meant a stop in Ireland at some ungodly hour like five. However, nothing could be done about that, and the SEALs continued to josh around, eating sandwiches and drinking coffee and telling unlikely stories long into the evening.

Mack slept until the copilot came back and told him they were into their descent to Shannon Airport, running up the north shore of the estuary, the delta to Ireland's longest river. The Hercules flew straight up the middle, through the dark dawn, and slid down through the early mist to the runway. It landed with an almighty bang, the sure sign of a pilot who had spent much of his life putting down fighter-bombers on the flight decks of US aircraft carriers.

They taxied the Hercules right up to a gate, dropped him off, and left immediately. Mack said good-bye to the SEALs and walked into the arrivals hall, which was almost deserted, except for two military attachés from the US Embassy and an Irish customs official who put a sticker on Mack's bag, never bothered for a split second with his passport, and said,

"Welcome to Ireland, sir." All three of them accompanied him outside the main terminal, where there was a large black Mercedes-Benz awaiting him, complete with an Irish driver from the US Embassy in Dublin.

"Good morning, sir," said the chauffeur. "I'm instructed to drive you anywhere you want, for as long as you want, anytime you want," he said.

"Well, that's downright Christian of you," replied Mack. "Any idea where we're going?"

"Yessir. I've booked you into the St. Ernan's House hotel, a coupla miles down the road from Donegal Town."

"How far from here?" asked Mack.

"Close to 150 miles, I'd say. Straight up the coast past Galway. It'll take us around three hours. Be there for your breakfast, sir."

Mack glanced at his watch. It was 0515. He spoke briefly to the attachés from the embassy, noted phone numbers and contacts if he needed them, and accepted an envelope that contained a US government American Express card for his personal use, all charges to be picked up by Uncle Sam. Then he climbed aboard the Mercedes, asked the driver's name, which was Michael, and instructed him to wake him when they reached Donegal.

The Mercedes pulled out of the airport and turned up the main N18 north to Galway. Mack settled into the backseat and became almost instantly unconscious, while Michael sped through the darkness, wishing to hell the sun would come up and wondering who was his obviously important passenger.

They rode in complete silence for a couple of hours, and then Mack awakened and inquired, "Who's this guy St. Ernan? Was he a local saint?"

"Yessir. He was a Galway saint, an abbot, I believe. Had his own monastery. From what I hear, he was a person of great note."

"What's his hotel like?"

"Oh, it's a grand place," replied Michael. "The ambassador sometimes goes there for weekends. It's on a private island, surrounded on three sides by water. I think you'll like it."

"Michael," chuckled Mack, "by definition, an island is *completely* surrounded by water."

"Well, this one couldn't be, sir. It has a causeway where you drive across to it."

"Then it's a peninsula, not an island."

"Nossir. It's an island alright. It's an island with a causeway, stops you getting wet before you check in."

Mack knew he was going to love this place, with all these crazy people. "You think they'll give me something to eat? I've been on a plane all night, with just coffee and a few cookies."

"I'll fix that right away," he replied and reached for the car cell phone.

"Is that Ernan's House? . . . This is Michael O'Malley, the US Embassy driver. I'm about thirty minutes away, and I'm bringing in an American naval officer who's spent the night in a bomber over the Atlantic. Can you make sure you have a fine breakfast for him . . . Irish bacon and sausages . . . Hold on a minute . . . "

"Sir, how do you like your eggs?"

"Sunny-side," replied Mack.

"Sunny-side . . . and I'll call when I'm five minutes away . . . I will . . . Good luck now."

"Thanks, Michael," said Mack. "By the way, where are you staying? I'll be here a few days."

"I'll be just along the road in Donegal," he replied. "Staying with Uncle Seamus. My own family comes from south of here—Castlebar, County Mayo. Sure, I've uncles and aunts all along this coast. I'll be about five minutes from Ernan's House."

Mack looked out to his left and could see they were driving around a wide bay with several islands and inlets. It really was a soul-stirring seascape, with the sun rising from out of Donegal's mountainous heart and casting a glinting light on the calm, lapping waters.

"Is this all part of Donegal Bay?" asked Mack.

"It's the absolute back end of it," said Michael. "The bay's about twenty-five miles long, and it ends right here."

"Were you brought up on this coast?"

"I was, sir. Not on the water. Castlebar's inland. But everyone in Mayo has a connection to the water, and we've a few historic seaports—Mulrany, Newport, and Westport. Half the population of Mayo tried to get out through those harbors when the crop failed . . . but a lot of them starved. Thousands of families just died in the fields after the English evicted them from their farms . . . "

Mack was silent and slightly shaken by the way this Irishman could talk of the Great Famine of the 1840s, almost 180 years ago, as if it were last Thursday.

"A couple of my relations, boys about seventeen, made it out, stowed away on a four-master going to Boston," Michael went on. "But they got caught, and four sailors tried to heave them overboard. But Patrick and Tommy O'Malley fought to the death, killed two, and then took the sailors' knives—and defied anyone else to attack them . . . "

Michael paused as he made a right turn. "By God," he said, "the lads were very brave that day . . . "

It was still last week, thought Mack. *And it always will be.*

"I've cousins in Boston, even now," said Michael. "They're still O'Malleys. Patrick became a professional boxer. But a couple of the new generation went to university."

"Have you been to see them?" asked Mack.

"Oh, no. They're educated people now. Wouldn't want anything to do with the likes of me, I doubt. But they're still relatives. And they always send a Christmas card. They've done that for 180 years. Never missed."

"I think they'd treasure you and the family here a lot more than you think," said Mack thoughtfully. "Everyone needs roots. Even Americans . . . especially Americans."

Michael made the call, and a few minutes later they crossed the causeway into the picturesque grounds of the St. Ernan's House hotel. Mack grabbed his own bag and asked his driver to meet him in a couple of hours, *Right here, ten o'clock.*

He checked in and was taken immediately into the dining room, where he was served a breakfast fit for a SEAL commander—bacon, sausages, fresh eggs, baked beans, and toasted Irish soda bread. They brought him a copy of the *Irish Times* and a guide to the area, which included the information that this country house had been built in 1826, by a nephew of the Duke of Wellington, victor of Waterloo.

"Can't beat that," muttered Mack as he walked up to his room and unpacked his gear, including a frog suit and flippers, which he expected to be utilizing before the week was much older. But not today. This was strictly recce.

Michael arrived with the car right on time, and Mack instructed him to drive around the head of the bay and then take the road down to

Mountcharles and Dunkineely. They stopped in each village, and Mack walked around the shore and down to the water and stared out into the bay. He noted the very small number of houses and the good access road. He also noted the small village stores that seemed well stocked with every kind of food and supplies.

He told Michael to drive on down to the end of the peninsula, all the way to the St. John's Point lighthouse. And they stopped frequently to allow the American to walk around, as if testing the wind, which indeed he was.

"The eastern side of the headland gets a lot of shelter," he said. "The weather mostly comes in from the ocean, I guess."

"It's nearly always westerly," replied Michael, "straight off the Atlantic. Can be a bit gusty, but you're right, the landward side of this headland is well sheltered."

"And the water's deep out there?"

"Oh, Christ, yes," said Michael. "There's very narrow shallows close to shore, and then it shelves straight down. That's not the case farther along this north shore of the bay where there are good beaches. But right here, it's a steep falloff."

They drove back from the lighthouse and continued west down the main coastal road, and Mack spent most of the afternoon in Ireland's busiest fishing port, Killybegs, which so far as Mack could see was a virtual blueprint for all that he and his team wanted to achieve.

Killybegs had always been a busy fishing port, but the harbor authorities had put in a new fifteen-hundred-foot deepwater dock that enabled huge freighters and fishing factory ships to moor alongside. It made Killybegs probably the most important seaport outside of Dublin, with ferries, tour ships, and every other kind of merchant ship finding an easy and efficient home on the wild shores of Donegal.

The part that interested Mack the most was the cost of the new pier, $65 million. He quickly assessed that the new US base in Inver Bay would require probably two of them, plus a couple of covered dry docks. The basic construction would come in at around $400 million for the jetties and buildings, at which point there would be a live, working US Navy base.

When the infrastructure was added—cranes, couple of tugs, harbor launch, gangways, water lines, fuel tanks, electronics, office equipment, accommodations, forklift loaders, ammunition storage, much of which could be shipped from Norfolk—the bill would probably approach $1.4 billion. In major military spending terms, very little, not in return for a brand-new, secret base in a different country, northeastern Atlantic, right on the edge of the GIUK Gap and its SOSUS guardian.

"Not bad," muttered Mack Bedford. "Not half bad at all."

0700, SAME DAY, TUESDAY, SEPTEMBER 25

Solovetsky Island, Northern Russia

It was much quieter this time as the transporter erector launcher lurched across the causeway to the tiny island of Bolshaya Muksalma, headed for the clearing from where the second Russian test launch would take place.

There were, again, two Iskander-K missile cones protruding from above the tarpaulin warhead covers, and the big overhead swing doors were tightly sealed. Behind the TELAR there was one jeep containing a team of just four missilemen, all from the monastery. Inside the cab of the TELAR were four launch technicians, two of whom would not be required so long as the first Iskander-K lifted off correctly and swung onto its homing course.

There were no guests, no VIPs, no one who was not absolutely essential for an accurate and trouble-free launching. Dr. Chon himself was in the main laboratory with Dr. Yang, both pacing, watching the screens, praying there would be no blip when the lead missile streaked across the Kanin Peninsula and then ducked south and north for its two crossings of Novaya Zemlya.

The driver maneuvered the TELAR into place, facing northeast, and the missilemen punched the final numbers into the rocket's guidance system. The gates to the launcher opened, and the first Iskander-K rose slowly upward into a vertical position.

The technicians moved swiftly into the countdown phase, and in the soft, cold early-morning light, the Iskander-K ignited. With a deafening roar of pure combustion, it moved at first slowly and then accelerated toward the heavens, cleaving its way into the rose-colored sky, its afterburners leaving a fiery red trail in its wake. The few onlookers stared as it swerved and then settled on its course of zero-four-zero, racing northeast, straight for the narrows that lead directly out of the White Sea.

Back in the basement of the monastery, Dr. Chon watched white-knuckled as it cleaved its way across the screen, running at four thousand miles per hour, directly at the Kanin headland. He knew the missile's built-in system was scanning the empty skies, flashing out the radar beams, watching for any form of impediment.

And now it was scanning the high land all around Kanin Point, where the Russian Navy spotter had his camera aimed high, with his cell phone open directly to the monastery.

The missile hurtled through the skies right above him, and he snapped three pictures. Back in the lab, Dr. Chon's wide Korean face was split by an enormous grin. There had been no blip on the screen; the radar on the Iskander-K cruise had made no distinction between sea and land.

This looked like a triumph. Twice more, and it would be perfect. Within moments, the second and third tests were under way, and the results were the same. No change. The radar flashed onto the Novaya Zemlya landmass without breaking stride, and then it did it again.

The Iskander-K, the modernized veteran of a thousand battlefields, was setting the pace into the twenty-first century. Dr. Chon knew precisely the adjustments he had made, and now he was watching living proof of his success.

"Yes," he told himself, "that is a job very well done. If the Russians get this thing into the air somewhere along the Panama Canal, there is no way the Iskander-K can miss the biggest building in Fort Meade."

He turned once more, with satisfaction, to the tiny paint flashing across his screen. He watched it change to a more northerly course, up toward the ice cap. He watched it racing over the Arctic Ocean, now making a beeline up the forty-degree easterly line of longitude.

Dr. Chon saw it race over the final Arctic waters and then flash across the ice floes, with their peaks and valleys, rippling ice fields and ridges, flying critically low at the highest possible speed. "That's a very nice missile," he murmured to himself. "Very obedient, very well prepared. I'd be surprised if even the Americans could stop it."

8

Killybegs Harbor, Donegal

Captain Bedford had been shopping in the local diving store and purchased a couple of dark-blue scuba tanks, mask, and air line, all of which he wore with the practiced ease of an underwater professional.

In the normal course of his duties, the hefty tanks strapped to his back would signify the imminent destruction of a foreign warship. The SEALs' great hallmark of achievement is, after all, known as BUD (basic underwater demolition). As Mack himself was apt to illuminate, *No bullshit.*

But today was more relaxed. None of the large freighters moored alongside were in any danger. The SEAL commander was just sightseeing, chugging out of the harbor with driver Michael O'Malley at the controls of a twenty-foot Boston whaler.

They were headed around the lighthouse at St. John's Point and into the outer waters of Inver Bay. Somewhere along that north shore, Mack planned to go over the side and take a careful look at the ocean floor, especially down near the village of Bruckless, where Donegal Bay becomes, very briefly, McSwyne's Bay.

This was the place Mack Bedford was recommending for the new base. There were a couple of hundred people in Bruckless who might not think much of it. But Americans were highly skilled at making people rich, and, generally speaking, the poor Irish residents of this near-bankrupt country, even those who had a nice view of McSwyne's Bay, would jump through seven hoops in exchange for a million bucks.

They chugged on along the leeward side of the six-mile peninsula. Mack was amazed at the clarity of the water. It had an Atlantic chill to it as autumn approached, but it was so clear, and inshore it was like crystal, all the way to the bright, sandy bottom.

Three times Mack went over the side, kicking downward with his big SEAL flippers, and now as he prepared for his fourth dive, they were right off the village, with a clear view of the ancient round tower in the grounds of St. Conal's Church.

Mack glanced up, then tipped over backward, out of the boat and into the bay. There was some swaying eel grass toward the shore, but the water remained clear and unpolluted. Mack thought it was the best ocean water he'd ever dived in. And the seabed was not littered with trash.

There were no wrecks, no discarded bikes or machinery. In fact, this ocean floor was pristine. No other word did it. Mack swam around underwater for twenty minutes and returned to the surface with an unmistakable feeling of mission accomplished. If the US Navy could not build a new base here, they probably couldn't build one anywhere.

He climbed back into the whaler and stripped off his wet suit and flippers. Dressed comfortably in a sport shirt and dark-blue Aran Islands sweater, he took a drive along the coast road to the distant headland of Glen Bay. Far from finding himself stumped as to a suitable location for a SEAL base training area, he found it hard to locate anywhere that wasn't almost perfect.

The land on the north side of Donegal Bay had everything: Long sandy beaches, most of the time sparsely occupied. There were undulating country roads and lanes to run and train. A little farther inland the twenty-two-hundred-foot Blue Stack Mountains rose almost sheer from the long, wide flatland below.

As a place to maintain the fitness of US Navy SEALS, it could scarcely have been better. Mack decided that this was some kind of omen, that he had stumbled upon the greatest SEAL training landscape he had ever seen, and it was pure destiny, since he had been searching for something else.

As he and Michael were driving home at the end of the afternoon, he stumbled upon something that proved his journey to Donegal had indeed been touched with stardust. In the little town of Mountcharles, midway between Donegal Town and Inver, he ran headlong into the world head-quarters of one of the biggest stone-quarrying operations in Ireland. In this half-pint village were the offices of the nationally renowned Mc-Monagle Stone, the largest importers and stonemasons in the business, proprietors of five Donegal quarries.

Mack could not believe his luck. *"STOP THE CAR!"* he yelled, and Michael was so startled he almost ran into a bus.

"What's happening?"

"Nothing. Lemme out."

Mack charged across the street and into the offices of the giant stone corporation. He scanned a handful of brochures and shoved them into his pocket. The headline on the brochure stuck in his mind: *A product riven from the rugged landscape adjacent to Ireland's Atlantic coastline.*

Mack charged back across the street and dived into the Mercedes, explaining briefly to Michael O'Malley, "When you're building harbors, you gotta have stone, right?"

"Well, I think that would be correct," said the driver.

"And it's the main subject been bothering me for a couple of days," replied Mack. "I mean the distances we might have to transport it. And right over there, I can see enough natural stone to repave the city of Washington." He stared out at the beautifully chiseled stonework on the Mc-Monagle campus.

Mack decided he'd seen enough and would return to America tomorrow. Michael drove him back to the hotel, and he checked in with Admiral Bradfield's Pentagon office, requesting an airline booking, Shannon to Washington, unless there was a naval flight going to Norfolk, Virginia, which could pick him up.

Mack spent the early part of the evening writing up his notes and marking the chart he had hijacked from the SPECWARCOM library in faraway Coronado. He dined in the hotel's excellent restaurant—Irish smoked salmon and then a local shellfish concoction cooked in a creamy white sauce, mussels, lobster claws, and clams.

The SEAL commander from Maine believed he might have eaten better seafood, but certainly not in living memory. He took a phone call at around nine o'clock informing him he was booked, business class, on an Aer Lingus flight to Washington, leaving Shannon tomorrow at 1:00 p.m.

He did a couple of swift deals with the proprietor, to leave his scuba gear here until he returned, probably with several other naval officers. He ordered Irish sausages, eggs, and bacon for 7:00 a.m. and summoned Michael with the car for a 7:30 nonstop, south to Shannon. He slept the sleep of the righteous, with the sound of Donegal Bay's quiet waters lapping outside his window.

THURSDAY, SEPTEMBER 27

Eppley Airfield
Omaha, Nebraska

Tamara Burda's Delta flight from Washington touched down on the long runway just west of the Missouri River shortly before noon (local). It was her first day's assignment beyond the high walls of the Russian Embassy after more than two years of training.

At twenty-six, she had served her time and was now a qualified Russian field agent (spy). She was obeying one of the cardinal rules as they applied to agents working alone and far from base: *Never, ever, travel directly to your ops area.* Always get a ticket to somewhere different, and make your final approach from an unusual direction, thus confusing the life out of your own paper trail. *Where's Tamara? God knows, she wasn't on a regular flight.*

Which was why this dark-haired Slavic beauty was standing somewhat bewildered in the airport of the biggest city in Nebraska, hard on the Iowa border, more than five hundred miles from where she was supposed to be, the city of Littleton, Colorado, in the foothills of the Rocky Mountains.

The embassy's Midwest Desk, down on the lower floor of the building, had arranged her trip, and in her briefcase she carried a document that contained the most valuable information—provided by two of the Russian "sleepers" who had worked servicing the electronics in the Pentagon since 1990.

These two comparatively low-grade technicians had revealed the precise frequencies of the nuclear football, wherever it was being used in the United States. Not the Gold Codes contained on the "biscuit." No one had ever seen them. This was just the doorway to the unseen radio highway along which the presidential messages and instructions would always travel.

The numbers were stamped onto what looked like a perfectly harmless, normal credit card. If Tamara should be searched, for whatever reason, no one would dream those figures, stamped where every cardholder's long number is engraved, represented the key to the frequencies, the ones that kept the innermost secret of the US government private.

Tamara understood the scale of the task to which she had been entrusted. Her training had taught her to tackle each subject, one at a time, as she went through a mission. She had a clear and definite objective: to locate the local radio operator who was to accompany her on the next phase of her journey. They were to rendezvous at the selected car rental desk, prior to leaving for the mountains.

Even that long ride had an element of deviousness about it. She was not to take the direct highway to Denver—Interstate 80 straight across Nebraska, with a left swing to Colorado's I-76 and into the Mile High City. Tamara's instructions were different. She would turn off Interstate 80 shortly after leaving the capital city of Lincoln and drive due south to Kansas, making her approach to Denver on I-70, straight across Kit Carson County and over the Big Sandy River into Arapahoe County.

None of this meant much to the Russian girl as she stood on the airport concourse, but she understood it was important and that someone, someday, might attempt to follow her trail across the United States. A major part of every spy's mission is to make utterly certain that cannot be achieved.

Tamara met up with her technician within ten minutes of her arrival. He was a thirtyish immigrant from Bulgaria, medium height, with the short-trimmed, curly black hair not unusual among those born close to Turkey's Black Sea border. His name was Josef, and he'd been in the United States for seven years.

Tamara handed him the printed sheet that gave him the directions, and they walked down to the car rental area, where they picked up a dark-green Ford station wagon booked in the name of Joseph Popescu.

The drive took eight hours, and it was after nine when they drove into the wide, sprawling city of Littleton and checked into the Sheraton Hotel. They'd driven mostly in silence because Tamara had been told the less Josef knew about her mission, the better. She was told to be polite, but remote, to mention nothing of the purpose of her visit. When she had selected the precise place she wanted, she was simply to give him instructions.

They were not to have breakfast together, or to indulge in unnecessary conversation. So far as she was concerned, Josef was a workman, and he must do his job and then deliver her back to the airport in Omaha. And so they met in the hotel parking lot and took a drive around the town until they located Berry Park.

Tamara got out and took a walk over to the statue of Danny Dietz, scanning her eyes over the surroundings, staring out west to the Rocky Mountains, all the way to the distant Mount Evans, which rises more than fourteen thousand feet, stark against the morning sky.

She took several photographs, made her personal notes, incomprehensible as instructed, and climbed back into the car, telling Josef to drive out of town. She told him to start north on the Santa Fe road, a stretch of which had already been renamed Navy SEAL Danny Phillip Dietz Memorial Highway, to commemorate forever the young warrior whose statue she had just photographed.

From there they were to head west out toward Indian Hills, and Tamara kept her head down as if there may already be dark forces in search of her. She neither noticed nor registered a road sign that told her Buffalo Bill's grave was very close by.

Tamara was actively uninterested in historic graves. She had been born and raised in the city of Yekaterinburg, which lies 1,130 miles east of Moscow, on the eastern slopes of the Urals. That city of 1 million people is a bright, airy, modern place, constructed like St. Petersburg, with public buildings in fawn-and-white stucco, a place made famous for its graves.

In a Yekaterinburg basement on July 17, 1918, Czar Nicholas II, his wife, Empress Alexandra, their little boy, Alexi, and the four grand duchesses Marie, Olga, Tatiana, and Anastasia were gunned down and then bayoneted by a Bolshevik murder squad. Years later, the actual house was bulldozed on the personal orders of Leonid Brezhnev, but the stain of that bloodbath remains.

The very word *Yekaterinburg* still evokes the memory of that shocking mass slaughter of the Russian royal family, just as Dallas will always be grimly associated with the assassination of President Kennedy. Tamara Burda was well accustomed to using the name of her hometown with care and discretion, because of the graves.

Buffalo Bill's last resting place, on the western slopes of the Rockies, simply did not register with the brand-new spy from the Urals. She kept low in her seat, watching carefully as they reached the rising ground and the Ford wagon gradually tilted its nose toward America's most formidable mountain range.

She was watching her GPS and trying to judge when they were sufficiently far above the city, and the trees between her and the distant buildings were sparse and low. Finally, they reached a grassy area with a wide, empty space on the left-hand side of the lonely road.

Tamara immediately ordered Josef to spin around and park facing Littleton, which was now spread out below them, maybe seven miles away. Tamara took out her powerful 8X30 BPC Russian military binoculars of the 1950s, which were rapidly becoming priceless, developed as they were by the Red Army after they captured the world-famous Zeiss-Jena factory in Germany. The victors had taken the optics, technology, and tooling back to Russia and subsequently created the finest long-distance lenses the world had ever seen.

Tamara focused fast and stared down at the ultrasharp image of Littleton's rooftops. Then she summoned Josef to bring his equipment and start tuning. She handed him the "credit card" and instructed him to locate the correct, available frequency, operating in the bandwidth of a narrow-band jammer—embassy advice suggested somewhere in the range of 250–500 MHz, targeting the proposed electromagnetic spectrum.

She watched Josef, who was operating against the protection of the car, earphones on, right-hand fingers twisting a dial slowly, listening to the frequencies, trying to find his electronic range, searching out the unseen tracks for a future beam to come lasering down off the low mountain and slice into the president's nuclear football, rendering it silently useless.

It took him about twenty minutes before he looked up and said, "I have a frequency. I'll write it down for you, and then you should take one of these headsets and transmitters down to that park, and I'll speak to you from here."

Tamara nodded, and Josef placed her electronic equipment on the passenger seat. "Switch that on and use the headset. We'll be about seven miles apart, but I'm higher than the town, and the air is very clear. We have a straight shot between the two transmitters. It should be fine."

Tamara drove back down the hill toward Berry Park. Once there, she walked back to the statue of Danny Dietz and wore the headset. Immediately, she heard the voice of Josef: *Testing . . . one-two-three-four . . . Testing . . . one-two-three-four.*

She replied as prearranged: *Receiving . . . Receiving loud and clear. Over.* And then she walked back to the Ford wagon and returned to the hill to retrieve Josef. Without another word, they headed north across Denver and picked up Highway 76, the direct route back to Omaha's airport.

The frequencies were fixed. When the Russian technicians raised those giant antennae on June 28 next year and aimed the jammer's laser at Berry Park, there was no way the president's nuclear football could ever work, not until the Russian jammer was turned off.

Tamara knew the frequency number. She knew the GPS numbers for the parking place. And she knew precisely how to get there. As first assignments go, hers had gone without a problem. A vital component of President Markova's grand plan to humiliate the United States was well and truly in place.

0900, WEDNESDAY, SEPTEMBER 26

Atlantic Ocean, Two Hundred Miles West of Portugal

The *Koryak* (formerly *Korolev*) was through the Mediterranean and steaming up the Atlantic, having successfully traversed the Strait of Gibraltar, which was, as ever, swept by UK and US radar. No one had approached the five-thousand-ton Russian freighter, still riding high in the water and moving as fast as its twin-shafted turbines would take it.

The *Koryak* gave every appearance of a civilian ship, transmitting no military electronics. Nonetheless, her captain was pleased she had attracted no specific attention and had been ignored by the Spanish coast guard. If no one had bothered her in the strait, the captain considered no one would trouble her as she ran south down the Atlantic, on her forthcoming journey to Central America.

Of course, no nation has rights of arrest and search against any ship traveling in international waters, except in the detection of nuclear materials. Should these be identified, either through the hull or from the satellites, under maritime law, any ship has the right to demand the offending ship stop and be searched.

The manufacture and transportation of nuclear material are everyone's

business, as the North Koreans found out when a Spanish warship apprehended and captured a cargo of weapons-grade material, plus brand-new
missiles, on its way to Saddam Hussein.

If the *Koryak* set off next spring for the Panama Canal, she would
steam as a simple Russian merchant ship. On board she would carry the
two Russian TELARs and one huge civilian truck transporting a large generator attached to the electronic jammer, essentially a mysterious piece of
equipment, likely to bemuse customs officials. The truck would bear the
livery of a major French manufacturer of heavy-duty industrial electronic
equipment, Lyon Generateur l'Électronique. There would be flawless doc-
umentation accompanying the generator, proving it was being delivered
to a hospital in Colorado.

Should there be any attempt by a foreign navy, especially American, to
intercept and search the ship on its journey from Russia, its officers would
find nothing. A false wall was right now being constructed in Severomorsk
that would shield the TELARs and the missiles from an examination.

The two nuclear warheads were being encased in heavy lead and would
be stored deep in the ship's hold, constructed to appear like a part of the
hull. It was completely unlikely that anything could be detected from the
outside to betray the presence of the weapons-grade nuclear material.

The *Koryak* would become a freight-carrying miracle and would dis-
play nothing to suggest a Russian warship, which had been built originally
to land troops and heavy armored vehicles onto a foreign beach. In its new
battle mode, it could only be perceived as an innocent commercial vessel,
plying an honest trade through Central America. Certainly not carrying
an entire operation designed to wreak absolute havoc with America's defensive systems and enable a hostile enemy to blast asunder the most important building in the entire Fort Meade surveillance network, probably
killing several hundred people in the process.

And that French civilian truck, on its journey north through the United
States, well, who would ever suspect the industrial generator on board,
with paperwork for the Colorado hospital, was anything but a second-line
emergency protector for the sick, ready to kick in if there should ever be a
major power outage?

So far as Kapitan Sergei Gromyko was concerned, every possible detail
concerning his ship had been thought out. He greatly looked forward to
his forthcoming journey across the Caribbean, confident in the proper

standing of his cargo on the high seas. Even the military men aboard, and the scientists and technicians, would be attired in formal Russian merchant navy uniform, with insignia.

Kapitan Gromyko was confident in his senior commanders. After all, he had just passed a serious test, steering his ship through the Strait of Gibraltar. The entire area was notorious for very officious US warships, containing very suspicious US Naval officers, working in cahoots with the Royal Navy, in the rough ocean waters that surround this British overseas territory.

By any standards, Gibraltar remained the gateway to the Mediterranean. It's been British for more than three hundred years. For generations, ships of the old Soviet Navy that strayed close to the Gibraltar coast en route to the Black Sea could be stopped and questioned. There was still a natural wariness among foreign ships leaving the Med for the Atlantic whenever a US destroyer came rolling over the horizon.

Kapitan Gromyko felt he had run the gauntlet, driving his five-thousand-ton Russian Naval vessel straight through, heavily disguised, and unsuspected by the British and American authorities.

But he was only half right. The *Koryak* was permitted free passage through the strait for one excellent reason: the Americans did not wish to alert the Russians for a New York minute that anything was suspected. But they'd been tracking the *Koryak* all the way from Sevastopol. Big, silent US satellites, whispering through the stratosphere, had recorded her progress through the Bosporus, across the Sea of Marmara, through the Aegean, and into the Mediterranean west of Crete.

Kapitan Gromyko may have believed he was moving unnoticed across southwestern Europe. In fact, he was being tracked more closely than any Russian vessel since the Cold War ended. North in the GIUK Gap, there were alerts sounded in two Los Angeles Class submarines, informing them of the *Koryak's* speed, course, and last-known.

The *Koryak* was at present steaming over one of the deepest parts of the Atlantic Ocean: the Iberian Basin, west of Portugal. It was eighteen thousand feet from keel to seabed here—that's almost three and a half miles, straight down. There would be no time between now and when she turned into the Murmansk inlet when *Koryak* was not observed by the eagle eye of the United States Navy.

Another little Russian secret was also being kicked around Chantilly, Virginia, with less reverence than that usually bestowed on the baseball scores. The satellites had seen and photographed the second missile test as ordered by the North Korean Dr. Chon Nam-sun, and they had tracked it from takeoff, right from the moment when the Iskander-K had hurtled into the skies above the island of Bolshaya Muksalma and then blasted its way across the White Sea, en route to the polar ice cap.

Air Force general Jack Myers had a detailed report in front of him, and the only significance he could see was the missile had taken a very different course, going northeast over water almost all the way and then traveling three or four hundred miles farther than the first Iskander had done. Also, it had not detonated with the same explosive force of the first one. In fact, it did not appear to have detonated at all.

Which meant, so far as Jack Myers was concerned, that this test was strictly about guidance and range. As a member of the US military's inner circle, the head of the National Reconnaissance Office was well briefed on the possibility that Russia may launch a controlled strike on the United States from the Pacific end of the Panama Canal.

He also understood clearly that the missiles would be newer, faster, and more accurate than other Russian missiles had been in the past. A fast cruise, with a "shaped" nuclear warhead, needed testing. And it was no surprise to the air force general that they were rehearsing, for the second time, the rocket's performance, flying low over water, and its final-approach target accuracy within sight of its objective.

They did not need to blast the ice cap to smithereens to make sure the weapon exploded. They'd already nailed that down. This was a routine range and guidance test, and the US satellites were well aligned. Nothing of importance was going to happen in that monastery, on the island of Solovetsky, or in the airspace above the cloisters, without the United States knowing.

SAME DAY, WEDNESDAY, SEPTEMBER 26

Office of the Chief of Naval Operations
Fourth Floor, the Pentagon

Admiral Mark Bradfield was doing his level best to become a civil engineer in addition to his day job as head of the United States Navy. Before him were reports and charts of comparable docks and harbors that had been constructed around the world in recent years.

What he needed were costs. The ballpark figure he had in front of him remained at around $1.4 billion, which interestingly was the precise figure Captain Bedford had reached.

The trouble was, there would be two groups who would ultimately approve or not approve the construction of US Navy Base Donegal. The first was the Senate Finance Committee, which might in this case be bypassed by the president of the United States. The second was the Irish government, which would be required to give formal approval for this binding contract with the United States.

All parties would wish to know the cost of the new base before they made a decision. The figure need not be totally accurate; neither would it need to be forever binding. However, it would need to be a hard, definite number, against which all of the parties could work.

Mack Bedford's $65 million for Killybegs was a bedrock—same kind of construction, same Irish bay, same labor force, same materials. But there were other projects with just as accurate numbers.

Admiral Bradfield had pulled up the details on a huge extension to the harbor at the Scottish port of Inverness, which lies at the mouth of the Moray Firth, just upriver from Loch Ness and that creepy old Scottish monster that no one had ever seen.

The Scottish government had paid almost $14 million to build the extension, a 650-foot steel-sheet pile wall, forming a brand-new quay and all the associated hard-standing area. Apparently, a new marina, almost entirely closed in from the waterway, was included in this cost, and Mark Bradfield thought it was extremely encouraging.

He also referred to Port Talbot, the gigantic tidal harbor that was constructed in South Wales almost fifty years ago, but had revealed a lot of heavy-duty facts—including the information that the harbor could take a hundred-thousand-ton vessel alongside. There was huge construction and dredging activity because the harbor breakwater was one and a half miles long. Even the lee breakwater measured one-third of a mile, and they used 2.3 million tons of stone to do it. Mark noted the breakwater core required stones of up to two tons each, but the main armoring on the south side of the main breakwater needed stones weighing *eight tons each!*

Unaware yet of Mack Bedford's discovery in the town of Mountcharles, Admiral Bradfield raised his eyebrows at the estimates for transportation of the stone. It had to be moved in dump trucks, thirty-five tons at a time.

They actually built, between the quarry and the harbor, a nine-mile road, which they completed in eleven weeks.

Admiral Bradfield also studied plans for Poland's biggest deep-sea harbor, built on the shores of the stormy Baltic Sea off Gdansk. This construction had a concrete pier that projected eight hundred meters into the ocean and a complete new container port, but it was all on a gigantic scale, nothing like the medium-size naval dock area they planned for Donegal.

The admiral did, however, make one note of a possible difficulty. Around the axis of the quay wall, the soil stratums were not able to support the load, and the huge Polish workforce had to excavate the earth to a depth of almost fifty feet with bucket-ladder dredgers and then pile sand into the gigantic hole to form a strong, hard base.

Mark Bradfield did not anticipate that happening on the rocky coastline of Donegal, but he was glad of the knowledge, glad to have grasped the rudiments of major naval construction of deepwater docks.

He was in no way concerned with the projected costs. All the numbers he was seeing were well short of the $1.4 billion Mack had suggested. Indeed, they had partially built a brand-new seaport off Great Yarmouth on England's east coast, with two enormous breakwaters, total length forty-five hundred feet, requiring nine hundred thousand tons of rock, and the whole contract was a mere $120 million.

The admiral thought Mack's estimate was on the high side. Even so, it was truly insignificant in terms of the annual defense budget for the United States of America, which was, for all security spending, $850 billion, and that was almost unchanged for eight years, despite valiant attempts to cut it. That number did, however, include $130 billion for other security-related agencies and an extra $80 billion for various global conflicts involving the United States. The Department of Defense base budget was around $530 billion, almost $300 billion of which was for operations and maintenance.

If a billion-plus was going to be spent on anything, Admiral Bradfield could not imagine a better place to do it than the coast of Donegal. And he summed up the plus side of the equation, the prime asset being, of course, the acquisition of a brand-new US Navy facility on the northeastern Atlantic Coast.

The jutting westward peninsula of Donegal formed a strategic masterpiece, in perfect position for a global naval listening station, a perfect site for a SOSUS hookup, a perfect retreat for any US warship in need of safe harbor, and a perfect location among friendly neighbors. Not to mention a deepwater base, thirty-five hundred miles from Norfolk, for refueling, repairs, and servicing.

Accompanied by Mack Bedford's boots-on-the-ground assessment of the local situation, the CNO could construct a terrific report for the project, one that Defense Secretary Simon Andre could present to the political powers with complete confidence in its practicality, accuracy, and viability.

Mark Bradfield took off his reading glasses, leaned back, and asked someone to bring him a cup of coffee. Studying the engineering reports had made his eyes tired, and he sat back and reflected for a few moments the pure chance of their present situation.

It had started way back in late January with Rani's contact in northern Russia, the suspicions, and the spying and lying, which had ended with the assassination of the Russian Naval officer. And how important was the outstanding mind of Rani himself, who had pieced it all together with his friend and contact, the one who had died for his beliefs?

So much of it was pure chance—the monastery, the visiting foreign rocket men, the Iskander-K, the secret missile tests, the Panama launch site, the suspect freighter from the Black Sea. All watched and observed by America's shadow operators.

And now there were only two mysteries left: how the Russians proposed to jam the US nuclear football and the date when they would launch their attack on Fort Meade.

Mark Bradfield had already advised the US missile systems departmental chiefs to realign certain defensive measures that would be activated in the event of any incoming missile attack. A response was much more difficult today than it had ever been, thanks to the advanced strategic mind-set of both Russia and China, and, to a far greater extent, the United States.

Gone were the days when great vertical silos connected to a missile-launch-attack control center were the accepted way of storing and launching intercontinental ballistic missiles against an enemy—when places like Vanderberg Air Force Base in California and the facilities in Wyoming and Montana were the prime locations.

Today there was still nuclear weapons assembly in Amarillo, Texas. The critical production of uranium 235 still took place in Paducah, Kentucky;

Portsmouth, Ohio; and Savannah River, South Carolina. And there were ground-based interceptors in Fort Greely, Alaska.

But the science of nuclear destruction, from static ground-based launch sites, had moved on. The United States continued to own a massive and brutally efficient nuclear arsenal, more than fifty-five hundred total missiles, with a comfortable range of eight thousand miles. But they probably would not launch from any of the land-based sites.

Today's US preemptive nuclear strike, or indeed response, would almost certainly come from a nineteen-thousand-ton Ohio Class submarine carrying twenty-four upgraded Lockheed Trident II Mark-5 missiles, with thermonuclear warheads packing a 450-kiloton wallop—enough to knock out half the solar system. With inertial guidance up to sixty-five hundred miles, these Mark-5s explode into twenty-four separate MIRVs (those are bombs or, more technically, multiple independently targeted reentry vehicles).

One of those Connecticut-built Ohio Class SSGNs was probably capable of keeping America safe, indefinitely, all on its own. However, just to be on the safe side, the United States Navy had fourteen of them, eight stationed in the Pacific Fleet in Bangor, Washington, and six more in the Atlantic Fleet at King's Bay, Georgia. Refueling, in the event of war, was not a problem. The Ohio Class GE Pressurized Water Reactor S8G (two turbines, 60,000 hp) ran for twenty years before running out of steam.

The deep, silent running of these supreme examples of US engineering gave the United States an indefinite range for its SLBMs (submarine-launched ballistic missiles). Anywhere was within easy range. And in addition to Admiral Bradfield's nuclear fleet, there were also long-range bombers and aircraft carriers from which the weapons could be launched.

It was, in truth, little wonder that a president like Markova was apt to have a nervous breakdown at the very mention of the word *Trident,* never mind *Trident II.* He knew as well as anyone that the Cold War had never really gone away.

Even after the 1994 Mutual Detargeting Treaty, which President Clinton declared would redefine the meaning of peace to children all over the world, nothing much changed. The treaty had absolutely no bearing whatsoever on the combat readiness of either the United States or Russia. And now, here was a highly intelligent US Navy CNO preparing to hit back at Russia if their secretive plan for a strike against Fort Meade was carried out almost thirty years after the Cold War had supposedly ended.

Mark Bradfield understood the detailed actions the United States must take if the Russians launched. The reprisal needed to be swift and utterly decisive. In the admiral's opinion, the first major US target, probably for an SLBM, fired from somewhere in the Norwegian Sea, should be Russia's deep-underground General Staff Command Post, sixty miles south of Moscow in the town of Chekhov.

This modern cyber center of military action represented the heartbeat of any Russian nuclear attack or response, and it's positioned deliberately away from the main city. The Chekhov Command Center is a colossal state secret, reputedly linked directly to the Kremlin by an underground rail line, Moscow Metro-2, administered solely by the Russian Federal Security Services, or FSB.

Chekhov, as decreed by Mark Bradfield, represented the prime US reprisal target, even though it would require an SLBM with a bunker-busting warhead capable of smashing into the ground and detonating a massive, "shaped," downward charge, not unlike the Israeli hardware that destroyed the nuclear bunkers in Iran.

The US admiral did not truly believe the Russians capable of closing down the president's nuclear football, any more than he thought the United States could close down the very similar device carried by the Russian president. But if they did, the US accent would need to be on high speed, nothing less.

The Russians themselves, after years of underfunding, were not the same fighting force as the old Soviet Union. Their nuclear arsenal was no longer well hidden, and the Americans could most certainly destroy a large part of it before anyone knew what had hit them.

These days the old Soviet missiles, while updated, were essentially stored in silos, garages, and dockside. Yes, they understood the need for mobile launchers, and they had their share, but they had nothing to combat the gigantic clout of the US undersea strike force. As such they had geared everything to speed.

The Russians worked against a ten-minute command-post deadline—that's ten minutes to detect, assess, and arrive at a decision on retaliation. By any standards, that represented a very small amount of time, but their missile launch sites were vulnerable, and Mark Bradfield had already issued a warning to his close associates that America's nuclear response to Russian aggression should be, in order, (1) the General Staff Command

Post in Chekhov; (2) the destruction of the Northern Fleet in the main yards of Severomorsk, Murmansk; and then (3) the shipyards of Severodvinsk and Archangel.

Only in the face of continued Russian missile attacks should the US Navy unleash an attack on the headquarters of the Supreme Command of Russian armed forces. The historic general-staff building is a Moscow landmark, a granite construction topped by a great square tower, bearing a huge engraved stone Soviet star above the old familiar hammer and sickle. It is situated on Znamenka Street in the Arbat District, just east of the Kremlin, where much of the widespread Russian military complex is also located.

Admiral Bradfield hoped it would not come to that because, like all modern naval and military chief executives, he was loath to inflict civilian casualties. No one was any longer sympathetic to that form of outmoded, outrageous twentieth-century warfare.

Markova was, however, inclined to make an exception in Fort Meade because the workers there might be civilians, but, to him, they were cyber warriors, and that put them squarely in his personal firing line.

While not yet on the CNO's prime attack list, there was just one Soviet nuclear base that Mark Bradfield advised should be satellite covered and, if necessary, hit and hit hard with a Trident II missile. The place that made him so critically aware was the ultrasecret Cosmodrome at Baikonur, formally a tiny village set in a remote outpost in the heart of the Kazakhstan Desert Steppes, 124 miles east of the Aral Sea.

Baikonur was a place both the Soviet and the Russian authorities had attempted for years to claim was merely a spacecraft station for peaceful exploration of the planets. Indeed, its history had been punctuated with now legendary missions—Vostok-1, the first manned spacecraft in human history launched from here in 1961 with the Soviet Air Force colonel Yury Alekseyevich Gagarin at the controls. The first man-made satellite, Sputnik-1, launched from Baikonur, and so did Luna-1. Generations of Soviet spacecraft, from Soyuz onward, made this isolated launch site their home base.

But so did the chilling R-7 Semyorka, the world's first intercontinental ballistic missile. And this was the primary purpose of Baikonur—to test liquid-fueled ballistic missiles. The secret name for the place was State Test Range No. 5, and it was known to only a select few, even in the Soviet

Union. The US Air Force U-2 high-altitude reconnaissance plane photographed the notorious desert missile test range on August 5, 1957.

Over and over, the Russian authorities had claimed it was dispensing with Baikonur as a military facility and intended to utilize it only for the peaceful exploration of space. But in 2018 it was still there as a missile base, although it was run as the Joint Venture Space Center with Kazakhstan. Nonetheless, even the Russian Air Force had never denied it might be deployed militarily under special circumstances.

Admiral Bradfield considered it was entirely his business to know all about the mysterious test range in the middle of absolutely nowhere. And he'd made certain the satellites were properly aligned to photograph it at all times.

He'd already made some fairly basic calculations: if America had to launch a retaliatory strike against an attempt on Fort Meade, he would, on reflection, suggest an immediate US strike not only on Chekhov Command and on the Northern Fleet bases *but also* on Baikonur. Because if Russia was *that* serious about conflict, the one surprise it might spring would be a sudden ICBM land-based launch, sending a cruise missile straight over the North Pole to Fort Greely, Alaska, home to some of America's most brilliantly engineered interceptors.

Mark Bradfield had no intention of putting up with that. He'd more or less decided on a preemptive navy strike on Baikonur, calculating it was only fifteen hundred miles from the northern reaches of the Persian Gulf to the significant part of Kazakhstan. There were constant US submarines patrolling off Iraq and Iran. It would take a well-targeted Trident less than twenty minutes to reach Baikonur.

And it was only two thousand miles from the eastern Mediterranean—and twenty-four hundred miles from the Barents Sea, both regular patrol areas for the US Navy. The Kazakh test range was such an obvious objective, in the event of a dire emergency, that it would be not much short of negligent to allow it to remain operational. No, a strike on that historic but sinister Russian facility was unavoidable.

It was a whole lot of history to blow up. But, in Admiral Bradfield's opinion, President Markova should have thought about that before he came up with this lunatic plan to hit Fort Meade.

The US Navy CNO picked up the telephone and asked to be connected, encrypted, to the chairman of the Joint Chiefs, General Zack Lancaster.

Office of the Northern Fleet Commander
Severomorsk, Northern Russia

Admiral Ustinov had run into a dead end halfway along Bolshaya Ordynka Street, south of the Moscow River. The Israeli Embassy, almost
under siege from officers of Russian Naval Intelligence and strong-arm
agents of the FSB, had resolutely refused to reveal anything about the
identity or whereabouts of Mr. John Carter, paint salesman.

Embassy officials had dealt with Russian inquiries with a combination
of deadpan ignorance, mystified disbelief, and mock helpfulness. They
had reacted to threats, persuasion, and even bribes with the same cool self-
righteousness.

I am so sorry, gentlemen, but I cannot tell you what none of us knows . . .
May I remind you that you are standing on Israeli soil . . . This is a foreign
embassy, and it must be afforded all the same privileges that your own embassy
enjoys in our country . . .

The Russian argument could loosely be described as loaded. They
wanted to know, in words of one syllable precisely, who was this Carter?
This British businessman who had arrived at Talagi Airport, Archangel,
and met for more than an hour with a Russian Naval lieutenant commander who had, that same evening, been shot dead for spying?

And not just regular spying. This hitherto trusted naval executive was
in the process of betraying some of the innermost secrets of the Russian
Northern Fleet. That included data about guided-missile ships, missile
tests, classified Russian plans to deal with their enemies, scientific devel-
opments in nuclear weapons, and top secret plans, known only to the fleet
commanders and the president of the Republic of Russia.

In fact, the Russian field agents were guessing about most of the above.
Their objective was not to be right or even correct about anything. It was
mostly to express outrage and to appear so furious with the naval spy that
they would stop at nothing to identify his Western contact.

None of this phased the Israelis in any way, their principal stance being
that Mr. Carter was British, and how could they possibly know, or even
verify, one fact about him? The counterattack of the Russians was that the
private aircraft used to transport John Carter out of Archangel had been

chartered by the Israeli Embassy, and did they normally go around chartering expensive Learjets for foreigners about whom they knew nothing?

Also, they wanted to know who paid for the aircraft. They had already checked with the charter company and ascertained for themselves that the embassy had paid the bill. Now they wanted to know who had repaid the money, and how, and from where, had the funds arrived?

Again, the Israelis had answered with practiced smoothness. The head of the paint corporation, in Birmingham, England, was Mr. Morris Goldman, a Jewish tycoon whose parents had fled Poland in World War II. Morris had been brought up in North London in the Orthodox faith, attended Carmel College in Oxfordshire, and served in the British Army as a lieutenant in one of the Hussar regiments.

When the Yom Kippur War broke out in 1973, Lieutenant Morris Goldman, now in the family business, had raced to Israel and signed on to help General Moshe Dayan in the Armored Division, as did many young Jewish officers from all over the world. As a former British army tank commander, he served with distinction and became a quiet supporter of the state of Israel, one of the *sayanin*—those of Jewish blood who would do anything in their power, at any time, to help their spiritual home in the Middle East.

The Israeli Embassy in Moscow had received, via Tel Aviv, a request from Mr. Goldman to assist his chief sales representative, John Carter, who was coming to Moscow for a few days. They had complied with the request and chartered an aircraft for him to leave Archangel at an awkward time.

Beyond that, they knew nothing. They had asked to see his travel documents, which were all in order. But they had never even spoken to him, having simply provided the aircraft and e-mailed the boss, Morris Goldman, in Birmingham. The flight was, of course, domestic, not flying beyond Russian borders.

This was an excellent labyrinth of extraordinary untruths, since Mr. Morris Goldman did not exist. Neither did the paint corporation in Birmingham, beyond being a shell company registered in London. The Israelis used it often to cover up various activities of a nefarious nature.

They fervently wished they could assist the Russian authorities. Indeed, they had tried to contact Mr. Goldman, but he was, sadly, unwell and convalescing at his home in Barbados. As for John Carter, he had left no trace after arriving at Moscow's international airport on that apparently fateful Sunday evening of September 2.

The Israeli cover story was watertight. The Russians could not crack it, no matter how they approached the problem. At the rougher edges of this strange encounter in Bolshaya Ordynka Street, the agents came very close to confirming that the men who worked in the Lubyanka did have the legal right to undertake "targeted killing" if they deemed it in the overall interests of Mother Russia.

To one or two Israeli officials, this did induce vivid illusions of their Moscow embassy being taken out with high explosive by the obviously very angry and very disbelieving Russians. But the ruthlessness of these Israeli guardians of their beloved country was a truth known the world over. Even the Russians understood that the chances of their own embassy in Hayarkon Street, Tel Aviv, surviving more than seven minutes after any kind of attack on Israeli personnel in Moscow, was, well, somewhere between remote and out of the question.

So the Russian intelligence chiefs found themselves quivering with fury in front of an opponent who was feigning peace and honesty, but for two bits would have opened fire, as it were. And just what did they know? If Nikolai Chirkov had reported to them before he died, did that mean the Americans now understood all of the ramifications of FOM-2?

Admiral Ustinov had promised Admiral Rankov he would find the identity of this John Carter. He had failed to do that. It was almost impossible to create a dossier on a probable spy when it was not even clear what country the man was in. Where to start? That was the question that plagued the head of Russia's Northern Fleet.

So far he had berated Military Intelligence, and Naval Intelligence, and the FSB, to no avail. The admiral had ranted on about a simple task, with all the mighty resources of Russian intel backing them, and the result was a "big, fat, fucking zero."

Admiral Ustinov informed them all that he had no wish to return to Admiral Rankov with this news, since it would require several of the agents and intelligence officers to start looking for new places of employment, and he understood how unsettling this could be.

He did not mention his own likely fate in this connection because, as a resident of sunny Volgograd, he did not wish to start contemplating Siberia and the probable discomfort of a salt mine. In truth, he felt sorry for all of the Russian investigators because this John Carter was one cunning foreign bastard, and these fucking Jews in the Moscow embassy were several steps worse.

The fact remained, whoever he was, this Carter had somehow made the journey north from Moscow to Archangel, almost certainly on the train, since station staff claimed they may have seen him, and Russian field staff had talked to a taxi driver, the one who had picked up Carter and driven him to Vaskovo Airport, where the Learjet was waiting.

They had, naturally, checked out the hotel where the cabbie had picked him up, and there they had drawn yet another complete blank. Yes, a Mr. John Carter had stayed one night, paid in cash, and left. No forwarding address.

Which left Admiral Ustinov wondering, like everyone else, who really was this fraud British businessman who had driven out to Talagi Airport and met the same Russian Naval officer the FSB had shot dead later that same night? The one thing Admiral Ustinov guessed he was not doing was selling paint.

And the great, shuddering question he had to face was precisely how much did Lieutenant Commander Chirkov tell the West about FOM-2? Maybe nothing, because the agents who tracked him to Café Lesnaya in Vologda had watched him every second and swore to God he had made only one call on his cell phone, and that had been to the Hotel Vologda, where he booked a room, confirmed by the hotel.

According to the highly experienced agents, there was absolutely no possibility he had revealed anything during his ill-fated stay in Vologda. They'd picked him up at the train station and never once let him out of their sight. The words they heard suggested, more likely, a girlfriend being informed Nikolai's boss had released him for a few days. The call could not have lasted more than five seconds before they blew his head apart.

It just didn't seem like a master spy's conversation. Nonetheless, thought the admiral, those agents were jumpy enough to kill him instantly, before he could say one more word. And the smashed mobile phone revealed nothing.

The key remained, as it had always been, John Carter. He had vanished and was likely to stay vanished. However, there was one aspect of the entire FOM-2 scheme that pleased Admiral Ustinov. If Chirkov had revealed anything about the mission, there would surely have been some reaction from the Americans.

Perhaps some complaint on a diplomatic level, maybe a clear and obvious example of US satellite interference, maybe CIA men being apprehended on the shores of the White Sea, maybe the sighting of a US submarine somewhere in the North, watching and observing. God knows, decided Admiral Ustinov, if we had been tipped off the United States was planning to hit the Lubyanka with a cruise missile, we'd have played hell . . . Foreign Office to US ambassador, Russian president to US president. We'd probably have gone to nuclear alert.

As a general rule, the admiral considered the West a complete puzzle. There had not been the slightest hint of US concern throughout the FOM-2 project. Not one of the vast army of Russian "spooks" in the United States had come up with one suggestion that the United States knew anything. Not even from the two Romanian moles, inserted into the CIA in the past two years.

The silence of the Americans was most unusual. And Admiral Ustinov was torn between two conclusions: (1) that they knew nothing, suspected nothing, and intended to do nothing; (2) that they knew plenty and were preparing a gigantic hit on the Republic of Russia at the first sign of aggression from his own hawkish president.

He knew as well as anyone that the Cold War was still here. He knew the size of the US arsenal of nuclear weapons. He knew that the Americans would be more quickly into their stride if it ever came to a conflict. He most certainly knew that almost every day American reconnaissance aircraft probed Russia's borders, trying to locate gaps in the air defenses.

A couple of times every year, his own Northern Fleet surveillance detected enormous US attack submarines, sometimes even the chilling Ohio Class Trident boats, patrolling the Barents and Norwegian Seas, armed, he guessed, with formidable weapons, a mere twenty-five-minute flight from submerged launch to Moscow.

Was it any wonder that a president like Nikita Markova should want to cut off the hand that threatened him, shut down US military communications indefinitely, and return Russia to its rightful place at the top end of world superpowers?

And his conclusion about the activities of the late Nikolai Chirkov and his phantom contact, John Carter? On reflection, he had to believe the Americans knew nothing. It was simply inconceivable to him, the most senior fleet commander in all of Russia, that Chirkov had somehow discovered the scope of fireproof-secret FOM-2 and disclosed it to the United States, which had proceeded to do absolutely nothing. No. That had to be impossible. FOM-2 was safe. And what's more, it could not fail.

Office of the Secretary of Defense
The Pentagon

Simon Andre had liked all that he had been shown. Captain Bedford's survey and subsequent visit to Ireland were revealing and enormously in-
formative. He had selected what must be one of the most perfect spots
ever for a US Navy base, in a country that could scarcely be more friendly
and sympathetic to all things American.

The north side of Donegal Bay had all five prime requirements: (1) an
ample main water supply, (2) ample national grid electricity, (3) easy access to diesel and petroleum fuel, (4) available local workforce suffering from
rampant unemployment, and (5) deep water, up close to shore. In addition, it was a mile and a half from probably the biggest stone-quarrying
corporation in Ireland.

Admiral Bradfield's cost estimates were wide ranging and well within
reasonable limits. Captain Bedford's high end, $1.4 billion, was accept-
able, but the CNO thought the project could be brought in for inside
$1 billion.

Considering its strategic importance, the price was modest for the
navy, where the cost of almost everything traditionally petrified even the
boldest of four-star admirals.

For instance, a hundred-thousand-ton Nimitz Class aircraft carrier cost
the thick end of $5 billion. These hundred-thousand-foot nuclear levi-
athans, named for the legendary World War II Pacific Fleet commander,
utilized a pressurized water-reactor four-prop propulsion unit generating
260,000 hp.

Simon Andre was an expert, one of those executives who grasped
numbers like Willie Mays making grabs in the outfield. He was probably the only man in the Pentagon who knew the three new Zumwalt supersonic guided-missile destroyers would cost, on average, $4.61 billion
apiece.

He thus considered the costs irrelevant and the initial plans for the
new base entirely acceptable. His own participation was strictly political,
and he did not think the project should require an act of Congress. It
was a reasonable part of the naval budget, necessitated by a succession of

unexpected changes in the political and military intentions of the United Kingdom.

Which left just one major hurdle: how to present, persuade, and, if necessary, cajole or bribe the Irish government into agreeing the base should not just be constructed but constructed right now.

On that, Secretary Andre had arrived at one or two very definite conclusions, the first one being that America's approach to the *taoiseach* (Ireland's prime minister, always referred to in Gaelic) should be one of a friend in need.

The Russian problem, which must affect all Western nations, now saw Moscow contemplating a strike against the United States. There was no help coming from the United Kingdom, which was penniless and saddled with welfare payments that would nearly bring down the national economy of China. Not to mention a National Health Service that was the third-largest employer on earth, right behind the Red Army and the Indian Railway system.

And that left America's most loyal and dearest friends—and indeed relatives—to help out as realistic working partners, rather than just spiritual ones. *We come to you as friends, and we come bearing gifts, with a proposal you will never regret . . .*

"That last part will get the bastards, see if it doesn't," said Andre with a devilish smirk. "I think we should consider the level of approach—perhaps start at ambassador status—and then be seen to bring in a real heavy hitter who can deal directly with the *taoiseach*. The Irish are a proud nation from top to bottom, and they won't like our dealing with them through some sundry government official."

"That could be difficult in terms of secrecy," said Captain Bedford. "Our top men tend to attract the goddamned media, and that's the very last thing we need."

"Agreed," replied Simon Andre. "We need a very special man, and I have not yet figured out whom it should be. But he needs serious qualifications, because he will certainly have to make the approach and then charm the life out of the Irish PM and his cabinet—give dinner parties and stuff. But he has to stay in the game, dealing with things on a daily basis. And for that he'll need to be in Ireland. Someone's got to move in. Of that I am nearly certain."

Mark Bradfield added, "Whomever we select must have navy experience, because any questions that arrive during the building of a small dockyard must involve naval warfare, far from the United States. It would be useless having some kind of a structural engineer answering military problems."

Simon Andre agreed with that, but told the small group in his office that he thought the most pressing issue was to reach a sound proposal that could be put to the Irish government.

"You mean tell 'em what they will get out of it?" said Mack Bedford. "Lay out our offer, make it attractive, and then help them overcome difficulties, probably of a local nature, and almost certainly a half-assed assault from the Green Party or whatever is the Irish equivalent?"

"Can we get a handle on the guys who might object to a brand-new base?" asked Admiral Bradfield.

"Probably not all of them immediately," replied Secretary Andre. "But you can count on the obvious groups—I mean the shellfishermen along those shores, men who work in that very cold water in all weather in search of mussels, clams, oysters, cockles and scallops, crabs and lobsters.

"Donegal has a couple of large shellfishing areas in the bay itself, and the deep-sea fishing industry operates from Killybegs, just along the coast. I expect we'll hear from the shellfishermen, and we'll just have to buy them off. But there won't be many."

"Have there been political problems there over fishing rights and standards?" asked Captain Bedford.

"So far as I could see, not very many," said the defense secretary. "A few years back there was some kind of a row over water pollution, and the government stepped in and solved it with a few new laws. But it seems pretty peaceful to me."

"There is a long tradition of commercial fishing in those waters, right?" said Mack. "I'm talking a way of life for generations, same as it is in my own part of the world."

"It's probably worth remembering we are not going into their waters and poisoning all the stupid fish, are we?" replied Simon Andre. "And we don't plan to be in their way, or snag their nets, or run over their fucking lobster pots. We're just conducting a safe harbor for the world's cleanest boats and attempting to be good neighbors."

"But they'll be looking for compensation, and they'll level every possible charge at us," replied Admiral Bradfield.

"Perhaps not, if the Irish government offers them a very fair deal," said

the defense secretary, "and informs them the prosperity of the entire country depends on the new project in Donegal Bay being completed and operated with the minimum of fuss and argument."

"That's a darned good point," said the admiral. "We really don't want
the Russians knowing that we are interested in building a new base in
northwestern Ireland. They'd have satellites trained on the place 24/7.

"When this thing is revealed to the Irish people, it ought not to be announced as a big deal, just a small, new ferry port or something to suggest
Killybegs is too busy with fishing and freight to house the passenger boats
any longer."

"Sounds like our new man, whoever he is, will be pretty versatile," said
Captain Bedford. "Some kinda combination of deep-sea fishing expert,
CO of a US warship, lobsterman, professional clammer, and social clam-
mer all at once!"

The SEAL commander could usually be counted on for a sideways
look at any situation, no matter how serious. Secretary Andre always appreciated that from one of his department's principal warriors.

But he deftly changed the subject and suggested they could do a lot
worse than come up with a good national package for the Irish government, a plan to help them deal with the huge financial debt that hung
over them. "I was thinking we could offer to take care of maybe half of
it," he said. "That would be in return for allowing the naval base and
granting us a long lease. This would not mean we suddenly had to find
a trillion dollars on their behalf. But that we would sort out the interest
payments, with a view toward Ireland, in time, becoming the fifty-first
state.

"Thereafter, perhaps in two years, we could take over the whole situation and collect significant taxation from Dublin to help pay for it. But it
would remove their financial burden because they'd only be paying us,
while we took care of their debts."

Mark Bradfield nodded in agreement. "I guess we'd allow the Irish government to keep what they needed to meet their national budget," he said.
"But we'd have some control and a big hunk of cash from them each year
to cover their share of the interest."

Simon Andre continued, "At the point when we decide to go the whole
hog, and nationalize the country into a US state, then we'd be responsible
for all of their debts. But we're easily big enough to let them get on with

being the prosperous little nation they always were—remember the Celtic Tigers?

"Either way, we'd both be on the pig's back. They'd get their enormous debt removed, and once the pressure was off their banks, they could start lending again, all backed by Uncle Sam. In return, we get a whole country, and one that most Americans have always loved."

"There are a lot of Irish industries that would do really well out of this," said Mack. "Like the stone-quarry company, plus the Irish utility firms—water and electricity. And once we get US Navy Base Donegal up and running, there'd be a lot of money to be made locally. We'd need workers at the base, plus all the associated businesses that spring up around a place like that—restaurants, cleaning, grocery stores . . . "

"Brothels," added Simon Andre, worldly to the end. But he quickly added, "There are no losers in this. Everyone wins, and a lot of people will get rich. But we must always return to the main point of the mission— that we get that critical navy presence in the northeastern Atlantic and no longer have to tiptoe around the broke and rabidly party-political British government."

"That's the heart of it," concluded Captain Mack Bedford. "We can zap FOM-2 so fast, and so quietly, the Russians will be baffled for years. Just so long as we have safe harbor in Donegal Bay and the fast-strike range that goes with it."

Simon Andre had arranged a highly classified meeting with the president and General Lancaster for 11:30 a.m. in the Oval Office. And as surprises go, this one would be about 240 on the Richter scale . . .

And the words *"You want to do WHAT!"* flickered across their minds, knowing, as they all did, how little this particular president enjoyed the unexpected.

9

Office of the CJCS
Second Floor, the Pentagon

General Zack Lancaster was attempting to achieve the outright impossible by doing seventeen different things at once while being interrupted, on average, every eight minutes by members of staff shining a glaring light on what he irascibly described as "the abso-fucking-lutely obvious."

He'd been in the office since six in the morning and had less than one hour left before he was due in the Oval Office for a possibly traumatic meeting with the president and the Pentagon's three resident fire-eaters, Andre, Bradfield, and Bedford.

Personally, General Lancaster thought it entirely possible neither he nor the president would survive the morning without having a heart attack, especially when the president heard they were planning to annex the Republic of Ireland as the fifty-first American state at the apparent cost of more than a trillion dollars.

At this point, his personal assistant walked into the room and told him there was yet another phone call he would want to take.

"I doubt it," growled the former Rangers C-in-C. "In fact, I will not be taking it or any other call before four o'clock this afternoon."

"It's from overseas, sir. Admiral Morgan."

"Well, put him on," snapped the general, his face lighting up into a broad smile.

Hey, Arnie! Where are you?

Clonna-what? Clonakilty? Where the hell's that, gotta be Scotland, right?

Ireland? What's going on there? She's what? Inherited a house . . . and you're in it. Jesus.

You haven't emigrated? No . . . I didn't really think that . . . You've got a what? A salmon river! Sure, we could come . . . Hell, this is the best call I've had this year . . .

When? Next month . . . No problem . . . I've got a week's leave coming . . . How long are you staying in Ireland? Back in November? . . . You must like the place . . . Can we have a chat tomorrow and fix a few dates? That would be perfect . . . S'long, Arnie. Hey, and thanks for calling . . .

Thus it was that General Zack Lancaster, the principal military adviser to the president of the United States, was able to sit in the Oval Office with calm indifference and listen to the long discussion about the annexation of northwestern Ireland and the endless wrangle about who could take charge of the operation, dealing on a personal basis with the Irish prime minister.

No one had any doubts that the proposition would appeal to the *taoiseach* on a purely financial basis. But it was a matter of approach, and prime ministers prefer to deal with decision makers who can say yes, no dithering.

Simon Andre had very swiftly outlined the Irish financial situation, which was essentially dire, but there was a gleaming silver lining. Ireland was a sound, exporting nation of only 4.5 million people. There were large fertile pastures for the production of cattle and the exporting of billions of euros' worth of beef and dairy to the UK.

There was a heavy mining industry—zinc, lead, alumina, gypsum, gold, silver, and barite—with two substantial natural gas fields at Kinsale and Corrib, the latter of which had almost 20 billion cubic meters of proven reserves. There was a steel industry, plus food, brewing, textiles, chemicals, and vehicles. There was an enormous service industry in the high-tech area, not to mention tourist millions pouring into the place every day.

Ireland, with a labor force 2 million strong, had a high value, and they were doing their level best to get out from under their debt—the best of any European nation. With a heavy injection of American cash within a very short time, Ireland would be back in profit and might prove to be one of the soundest foreign investments the United States ever made.

Simon Andre thought so. The American president agreed, but also understood the need for strict secrecy, since nothing must leak to the Russians about the new base in Donegal. Which once more left them with the same quandary they had always had—who would front the operation in Ireland?

At this point, General Lancaster made a somewhat theatrical move. He stood up from his chair and said, a little casually, "No need to worry about that, gentlemen. I have the man."

Even the president was slightly startled by that. "You have?" he replied. "Could we ask who?"

"Certainly," said the general. "Gentlemen, I give you the former head of United States National Security, Admiral Arnold Morgan."

"*ARNIE!*" exclaimed the president. "He's retired. Has been for five years or more. We can't send him to Ireland!"

"No need," said General Lancaster. "He's already there. Living for several months."

"What about Kathy?"

"She's there as well. In fact, she just inherited a house on the coast of West Cork."

"How do you know all this?"

"I've been talking to him."

"When?"

"About an hour ago."

"And you think he might step up and head the operation for us? Jesus, how old is he?"

"Arnie? Probably 73. And if you asked him to undertake a major project on behalf of the United States of America, he'd say yes, even if he was 147 years old."

"You mean the old flame still burns?"

"That flame doesn't ever go out," said the general. "Not with men like that."

"There aren't any men like that," mused the president. "Not quite like that. We're talking one of a kind."

"No argument from me," replied Zack Lancaster.

"Is his family from Ireland?" asked the president.

"No, sir. They're rock-solid Texans from way back. Kathy's folks were first-generation Irish immigrants. All four of her grandparents came here from County Kerry. She once told me all about it. They were Catholics, left the old country from Tralee during the Irish Civil War in the 1920s. Before the North-South partition."

All four men reflected for a few moments on the remarkable coincidence that suddenly found Admiral Morgan living, however briefly, in Ireland. There was no question he would be just about the perfect man for the forthcoming mission. He understood the navy through and through, he would swiftly grasp the financial intricacies of building a base on the Irish west coast, and he would certainly be a sufficiently big hitter to deal with the Irish president.

Also, he would not get bogged down in detail. He would conduct the negotiations with charm; he was a rich man, accustomed to grand living, at home with presidents and kings, and able to hand out the most ferocious tongue-lashings to those he suspected might be wasting his time.

Intellectually, he was like Margaret Thatcher in sea boots. He grasped facts, and retained them, within a memory the size of a Trident ICBM. And he never took his eye off the ball. Arnold Morgan, former nuclear submarine commander, would enter this project knowing that the United States wanted that naval base in Donegal to keep them permanently on top of the Russian situation.

He had been a major supporter of the SOSUS project and had made it clear on several occasions that he considered its general demise, during the years beyond the Cold War, a mistake that could only have been perpetrated by an imbecile.

He had never trusted the Russians in the past. He did not trust the Russians now. And he had no intention of trusting them in either the near or the distant future. "They can't tell the goddamned difference between an act of friendship and an act of war" was his view. "They think everyone's against them. The slightest perceived insult causes them to think they're in the middle of the Battle of Stalingrad all over again, besieged, hated, and threatened with extinction."

At a recent naval gathering in the Pentagon, Admiral Morgan had been asked to speak briefly on the subject of Russia's current stance on strategic fleet operations. His opening lines were memorable: "On a dumbest-nation scale," he had said, "the Russians are not yet on the chart. To them, everything is a threat. Right now they're trying to modernize that junkyard navy of theirs, devoting thousands of hours of research trying to produce quiet submarines instead of those rattletrap old Soviet nuclear boats that used to clank along the ocean floor like goddamned covered wagons."

The sudden revelation of FOM-2 would affect Admiral Morgan like no other. To those who really knew him, like Zack Lancaster, Arnold was never thoughtless. When this situation was carefully explained to him, his instinct would not be, surprisingly, to nuke the Solovetsky Monastery or Murmansk.

He would hope to smash the whole operation secretly and thoroughly and then sit back and watch Russia squirm in front of the international community. Arnold Morgan loved hanging the Russians out to dry, loved it when they were confused beyond redemption, but would not dare ask, *What just happened?*

It was impossible to think of any member of the US government or military who would relish the project of US Naval Base Donegal more thoroughly than Admiral Morgan. He would surely move heaven and earth in Irish political circles to make it happen, and happen fast.

All four men in the Oval Office knew instinctively that General Lancaster had hit upon the critical component in this tangled equation, the one element that would cause everything else to snap into position.

"If Arnie can be raised from his Irish lair," said the president, "then that would be my wish. Let's find out real quick whether he will once more take up the burden of high office and carry us over the line . . . "

"Guns blazing—just like old times," added Zack Lancaster.

1100, SUNDAY, SEPTEMBER 30

Ardfield House
Clonakilty, Ireland

Admiral Morgan's new Irish residence was an impressive white-fronted Georgian house in thirty-five acres of hilly countryside facing southwest, all the way down to the strong tidal waters of Clonakilty Bay. For some reason the property included a thousand-yard double-bank section of the Argideen River, three miles to the north.

It was all purchased by the Gallagher family in the mid-twentieth century, after selling a desolate three hundred acres of hitherto worthless woodland above Lough Leane near Killarney to a German hotel chain for almost $3 million, an enormous sum of money in 1960.

Thus, the Gallagher family members, who had not migrated to North America, became as prosperous as their US cousins and lived in some style above the bay, raising "store horses" for the Irish steeplechase community with periodic financial success.

However, as the years passed, the Gallaghers proved better breeders of hunter-chasers than people. And by the time old Seamus Gallagher headed for the great unsaddling closure above, there were no direct heirs left for what was remaining of the fortune.

The executors had located a couple of distant cousins in Vancouver and the former Kathy Gallagher in Chevy Chase, Maryland. The mansion in Clonakilty was valued at only $620,000 subsequent to the Irish property crash. This tempted Arnold and Kathy to fly over and inspect the place, and within a week, Arnold made an offer of $200,000 to buy out the two cousins, which they accepted with lightning speed.

Thus did Admiral and Mrs. Arnold Morgan become the owners of a deserted but strangely beautiful Irish property for the knockdown price of $200,000, right above the Celtic Sea, with views across the bay to Dunworley Head. In the autumn of his years, the admiral liked nothing more than to sit and stare out over the water.

"Keeping an eye out for Russian Oscar Class attack submarines" was Kathy's sassy opinion, never having quite grasped the thunderous weight of responsibility visited upon the chosen US nuclear submarine commanders, the men who patrol the greatest waters.

They'd owned the property for two years now and completely renovated it, repainted, recarpeted, rebathroomed, rekitchened, added stonework to the outside terracing, and, according to Arnold, installed enough curtain, sofa, and bedspread fabric "to cover the goddamned Pentagon."

The result was a marvelously comfortable house, with a willing gardener-chauffeur-housekeeper couple from the nearby village of Milltown to take care of the place fifty-two weeks a year. And now they expected guests,

General Zack Lancaster and his wife, Virginia, friends of the admiral's for almost forty years. West Pointer Zack and former midshipman Arnold always watched the Army-Navy game together whenever they were both in the Washington area.

"What do you actually plan to do with Zack during the next four days?" asked Kathy. "Virginia and I will almost certainly spend some time shopping in Kinsale. And you'll be stuck out here gazing at the ocean."

"I'll probably take him fishing," said Arnold decisively.

"But you don't know anything about fishing," replied Kathy. "You've never been fishing since I first met you."

"I'll catch up," harrumphed Arnold.

"But you haven't even got a fishing rod," she persisted.

"I'm having three or four delivered later today," he replied. "From the fishing store in Kinsale. All the gear—hooks, flies, line, and waders."

"But you don't even know how to tie a fly, or even cast," said Kathy. "Why do you always assume expertise in any subject?"

"I just happen to be a quick study," said Arnold. "I get it the first time—flick the old rod and line, and whip that baby straight into the stream. When it comes up, it'll have a big rainbow trout on the end . . . "

"Some people fish a salmon river for four days without catching one single fish," she countered. "I can just imagine how much you'd love that."

"That's because they don't have my expertise," said Arnold. "And because they don't have an expert with them."

"Don't tell me you've hired a teacher or someone to go with you?"

"Certainly not. I'll have my own private expert with me. Zack promised to teach me."

"You never even told me Zack was a fisherman," laughed Kathy, marching off to the newly renovated kitchen.

"Military secrets," said Arnold. "No gossiping about the head man in the Pentagon. But he does happen to be a very fine fly fisherman . . . Once landed four sharks in thirty minutes from the bank of the Hudson River when he was at West Point."

"Four *what!*"

"Tiger sharks."

"They don't even have tiger sharks in the Hudson River," she retorted.

"Just kidding," chortled Arnie, returning to the *Irish Times.*

Age had not wearied him. Admiral Morgan was precisely the same sharp, droll, and frequently irritating personality he had always been. He was not to everyone's taste, but he had a wide and loyal group of friends and followers.

In Ireland, he was rapidly becoming a countryman for the first time in his life. Like Captain Mack Bedford, he had purchased a heavy Aran Islands sweater and wore it with corduroy pants. The truth was he loved the pace of life here, the way people had time to stop for a chat, the easy way people slipped into conversation in bars and restaurants.

He loved the music, and the landscape, and the careless brand of "craig" the whole nation seemed to enjoy, along with the capacity to put a lot of things off until tomorrow. In terms of time, Arnold thought the Irish had a lot more in common with the Spanish than they ever did with the English.

And, perhaps surprisingly, the Irish loved the admiral, this straight-shooting, highly intelligent former US Naval officer, with his penchant for profound sarcasm, caustic wit, and quick, sharp jokes about almost everything. For the first time in his life, Arnold Morgan had found a place where nothing was expected of him except good humor, time for a glass of something, and friendship.

Zack and Virginia Lancaster showed up that morning, by US Embassy helicopter, landing right on the lawn roughly forty-five minutes after Air Force Two had touched down at Shannon Airport, eighty-two miles to the northwest of Clonakilty.

The visit unfolded predictably. Kathy and Virginia went breezily off to Kinsale, that legendary Irish seaport of narrow, winding streets, tiny houses, and boutique restaurants that have caused it to be labeled the "gourmet capital of Ireland."

Arnold and Zack, with a box of delicious wild Irish smoked salmon sandwiches and a few cans of Guinness, gathered up the newly arrived fly rods and headed for the Argideen River, driven by the admiral's devoted man, Finbar Murphy.

Zack had the most wonderful afternoon catching no fewer than four magnificent sea trout over a three-hour period on this tranquil Irish river with its deep pools and quiet riverbank. Arnie's fishing career was altogether shorter. In one half hour he hooked a bicycle wheel, an old sea boot, and no fish.

At one point, driven to barely controlled fury by his own lack of skill, he slashed the rod back and forth for a giant cast, hooked the right ear of an Irish cow grazing behind him, and would probably have been gored to death but for the solid protective iron fence that surrounded the pasture.

At this point, with the chairman of the Joint Chiefs laughing helplessly, Admiral Morgan, former head of the United States Atlantic Submarine Fleet, formally announced his retirement from fly-fishing on account of its being "entirely too goddamned dangerous."

In fact, there was nothing the admiral enjoyed more than to give a prolonged exhibition of mock anger, and he amused Zack Lancaster, as he had done for decades. His acute dislike of the newly discovered sport was genuine enough, but he cared nothing for his humiliation and thought it was as funny as Zack did.

They'd brought canvas chairs with them, and Arnie sat out the next couple of hours lounging in the autumn sun, ridiculing his buddy for the inordinate time he spent standing in the water with absolutely nothing happening at either end of his fly rod.

This level of banter ended when Sea Trout Number Three splashed into the general's net. And Sea Trout Number Four represented their forthcoming dinner, which would be expertly cooked by Finbar's wife, Mary, accompanied by a specially selected magnum of white burgundy from the admiral's Irish cellar, a 2010 Puligny-Montrachet 1er Cru, Les Pucelles, from the domaine of Olivier Leflaive.

For dinner that evening Mary Murphy wrapped each trout in separate tinfoil with just butter, salt, and pepper and cooked them on the hot outside grill. When she unwrapped each one, the outer skin seemed just to fall off, and she removed the center bone and served the fresh fillets with Irish potatoes and spinach.

For the first time Zack broached the subject of the Donegal base, and Arnold seemed slightly skeptical. But when Zack told the admiral precisely why they wanted it, to deal with the forthcoming Russian treachery, the whole atmosphere changed. Arnold glared at the mere thought of the Russian Navy and muttered, "I suppose that blowhard bastard Rankov's at the bottom of this."

"We don't think so," replied the general. "But I have no doubt he's in it up to his goddamned neck. For a short time we had an excellent spy, a

Russian Naval officer working right at the heart of the FOM-2 program. That's how we found out about it."

"And did he discover the causes of their aggression?"

"He placed it right at the door of President Nikita Markova himself. Apparently, he's never forgiven the USA for providing the hardware that helped the Israelis destroy the nuclear factories in Iran."

"Any more than the Israelis have forgiven Russia for arming the Syrians, so they could bombard them from the Golan Heights in the Yom Kippur War."

"Funny you should mention that, Arnie," said the general. "The Russian Naval officer was a contact of the Mossad, and it was one of the Israeli field officers who nurtured him."

"Is the Russian still active?" asked Arnie.

"He's dead."

"Jesus. Don't tell me the Russians had him taken out?"

"He was talking to the Mossad man when they shot him. We got the whole story pretty quickly. The Israeli's a real good guy, ex-IDF commando, who's an old friend of one of our SEAL Team commanders."

"Anyone I know?"

"Possibly. Captain Mack Bedford. SEAL Team 10 out of Coronado. He and the Israeli were in the Gulf together."

"Wasn't he the officer they court-martialed after that uproar on the Euphrates River?"

"He was. A goddamned disgrace it was, too."

"I remember it, Zack. And it was a goddamned disgrace."

"Mack flew here to Ireland with us," said the general. "He's gone up to Donegal to meet us sometime tomorrow . . . You girls can come if you wish . . . It's a beautiful coastline, and we're taking the helicopter, but we will be busy for a couple of days."

"I think we'll stay here," said Kathy. "I'll take Virginia to Cork City one day, and we can visit the coast here."

"Okay," said Arnold. "I had not quite realized that Zack was here to place me on assignment."

"Steady, Arnie. This is a request, not an order. You are perfectly at liberty to turn it down and mortify the president of the United States, while disappointing every one of the service chiefs in addition to the secretary of defense. Nothing serious."

"Then I guess I'd better do it," chuckled Arnie.

The subject of FOM-2 was subtly pushed aside, since neither the former national security czar nor the current head of the Pentagon was comfortable speaking on matters of the highest classification in front of anyone. And, knowing Admiral Morgan's preoccupation with all forms of military history, Zack asked him if he'd taken up local Irish folklore yet, especially their long struggle to kick out the British.

Unsurprisingly, Arnold Morgan was heavily into this heroic tale of the disorganized little island that took on the king's trained army—the same one that, with American help, had been about to slam the kaiser, never mind the near-defenseless Emerald Isle.

"Right here, old buddy," said Arnold, "we're sitting in the very cradle of the Irish Revolution. Just down the road, in Clonakilty, Emmet Square, there's a seven-foot bronze statue of the Big Feller—Michael Collins, the heartbeat of Irish Independence. He came from right around here, two or three miles up the road in Woodfield—the Collins family farm is still there. Not the whole house. The British burned that . . . "

"Michael Collins?" said the general. "Wasn't there a movie about him? I'm darn sure I saw one. It opened with the siege of O'Connell Street, the British army blasting the rebel headquarters in the post office with artillery shells."

"That's it, Zack. And you'll remember the Irish officer, standing high at a window, defying them with just his service revolver, firing back, refusing to surrender even though he couldn't win. That was Collins."

"He was some kind of a guy, and the Brits hated him, so he must have been a real pain in the ass."

"He was a lot worse than that," said the admiral. "Without him, the Irish would have caved in. But he kept rallying them, organizing skilled guerrilla warfare, attacking and harassing them, blowing them up, shooting from the hillsides, hurling bombs, killing and raiding.

"A lot more happened, but the truth is, the British army just got fed up with the grief, packed up, and left forever . . . Like all of Irish history, there's a song . . . and the last line goes, 'But the boys that beat the Black and Tans were the boys from the County Cork.'"

"And this is his country, these hillsides, these country roads—Clonakilty. Birthplace of Michael Collins." General Lancaster was genuinely taken by this Irish history. And he remembered from the film how the Big

Feller had died in 1922, ambushed in a County Cork lane, assassinated by men who had once fought alongside him.

"The whole thing disintegrated into a pretty good mess in the end," said Arnold. "Collins became a politician, and there were treaties, clashes, rows with the British, rows with each other, between those for the partition and those against. And they decided to kill him."

"I'll bet they regretted it."

"Christ, yes," replied Arnold. "He was the first commander in chief of the Irish Republican Army, president of the republic, the head of Sinn Fein, and the supreme patriot of his time. A lot of people never got over his death. And it took 'em a long time to build his statue, not until 2002."

"I'd like to see the statue," said the general.

"Soon as we get back from Donegal, I'll take you down there," said Arnold. "Collins and I had a few things in common, to tell you the truth."

"No doubt," replied Zack. "Patriotism and military know-how, for a start."

"And we were both heavy into intelligence," said the admiral. "You know about me in the NSA. Michael Collins founded the first Irish spy network, ran it himself, infiltrated the occupying army, drove the Brits mad."

"I guess we're a bit like that with the Russians," added the general. "And them with us."

1130, MONDAY, OCTOBER 1

St. Ernan's House
Donegal Bay

Captain Mack Bedford stood on the lawn out in front of the hotel and watched the US Navy helicopter making its approach across the eastern end of the bay. It came in low, banked hard left, and descended gently but with a deafening howl from its rotors as it touched down on the neatly clipped grass.

The copilot climbed down and opened the passenger door for General Lancaster and Admiral Morgan and carried their leather overnight duffel bags into the hotel. The two senior US commanders shook hands with Mack, and he led them into the front door of St. Ernan's House.

The helicopter took off immediately, flying northwest up to Donegal Airport, thirty miles away in Carrickfinn, another spectacular stretch of coastline on the shores of this wild and mountainous country. Meanwhile, Admiral Morgan and Mack Bedford met for the first time and over a quick cup of coffee aligned their opinions about dealing with the Russians.

At this point, Michael O'Malley showed up with the car. They set off down the road to the head of Inver Bay. Mack Bedford did not believe it was possible that any one man could ask as many important questions as those fired at him from Admiral Morgan.

How deep's the water at the mouth of the bay? . . . Is there a marked channel? . . . What about all those fishing boats from Killybegs and the passenger ferry? . . . How deep is it off St. John's Point lighthouse? . . . Does it stay deep? . . . I mean more than eighty feet all the way in, to our proposed jetties? We may need that much, if we have to get home underwater, out of the way of those rattletrap Russian satellites.

Mack answered everything, because this was not your average inquisitor. This was Arnold Morgan, probably the most feared admiral in the US Navy since the death, in 1959, of "Bull" Halsey, the fire-breathing Pacific War commander, Third Fleet.

It was clear to Mack that Admiral Morgan thought the ability to house, service, and protect US submarines was paramount to the requirements of the new base. But only once did Arnold mutter his personal view, "If these Russians cut up rough, in any way, we might have to put 'em right on the bottom of the goddamned Atlantic Ocean. We may have to hit 'em hard, hit 'em fast, and hit 'em low, below the waterline. And to be sure of that, we'll need a submarine out there ASAP. Right out of Donegal. Let's not fuck it up."

"Good idea, sir," said Mack. "No bullshit."

It was a short, crisp statement right out of the admiral's playbook. Mack was delighted to see the great man chuckling.

"When we attack, who's commanding it?" asked Arnold.

"I am, sir. SEAL Team 10. Scuttle the ship, retrieve the nuclear warheads, and take no prisoners."

"How do we know there'll be nuclear stuff on board?" he asked sharply.

"That's a definite, sir. The Russian spy found that out very early on and told my buddy in the Mossad. The missile to be fired at OPS 2A is a 'shaped' and controlled nuclear warhead, causing a massive explosion, but designed to knock down only the immediate target, no peripheral damage. I don't know if they can achieve that, sir. But they've hauled in experts from all over the world—and that's their aim."

Admiral Morgan grinned. He patted Mack on the shoulder and asked, "Can we stop 'em, Captain?" he said.

"Affirmative, sir. We'll stop 'em alright. And there won't be anyone left to discuss it, either. Russian sonsabitches."

Arnold Morgan *loved* Navy SEALs.

Michael drove them all over the area. They went down to St. John's Point and back to the village of Inver. The visitor from Clonakilty wanted to know every last inch of the plan, including the availability of granite from the quarry masters of McMonagle Stone in the little town of Mountcharles.

Arnold knew the weight of responsibility he would bear when he opened discussions with the Irish prime minister, and the one thing he detested most in all the world was being stumped on any technical question. Mack, anticipating this, had spent a diligent evening writing out meticulous notes and drawing diagrams.

He gave everything to the admiral, including the chart he had borrowed from the SPECWARCOM library. And for the second time, Mack visited the local electric substation and the water company's ops center near Donegal Town. Water had never been any kind of an Irish problem, especially in Donegal, where the ferocity of the rainstorms sweeping in from the Atlantic has to be seen to be fully appreciated.

Arnold Morgan never missed a beat. By six they were through and decided to return to St. Ernan's House to have dinner. All three of them would leave the following morning, Mack to Shannon by car to pick up the Aer Lingus midday flight from Dublin to Washington, the admiral and the general by helicopter back to West Cork.

It was immediately after dinner when General Lancaster finally asked the question that mattered most. "Arnie," he said, "may I take it you will accept this assignment and deal with it politically and practically from now on?"

"You may. I am honored to be asked, and I'll do everything I can to get the *taoiseach* on our side. I don't think that will be too much of a problem because it's a great proposition for him, and for Ireland. But I need to persuade him he doesn't need a new law or anything that will hang us up in the Irish Parliament for Christ knows how long."

As ever, the admiral had instantly cut to the chase. Speed was everything. The one thing that would scuttle this operation was a long delay in creating US Navy Base Donegal. Markova's navy was ready to load the missiles onto their freighter in Severomorsk, in readiness to proceed with all haste, south down the Atlantic Ocean to Panama.

The United States could not conduct the quiet, quick-reaction response they needed, the one that would give them both privacy and anonymity, unless they had that new base close to the action, with a secret submarine, hidden from the Russian satellites, and a secret plan, hidden from everyone.

"I guess we all understand the situation," said General Lancaster. "Unless we want World War III, we cannot just go charging out into the Atlantic and blow a Russian merchant ship sky-high. First of all, everyone would know, and the Russians would make it public, and probably slam a US Navy base with one of those Iskanders. That course of action would be purely primitive."

"But if I cannot persuade the Irish PM to come with us, instantly," mused Arnold, "that may be our only recourse. Markova is a dangerous sonofagun. He hates the USA, and he would seize any excuse to hit us, feigning innocence and telling the world he was truly aggrieved."

"The more you think about it," responded Zack, "the more subtle we will need to be. We just want that ship to vanish, no trace, no survivors, and no goddamned explosions shaking the stratosphere."

"If Team 10 is in place in Donegal," said Mack, "and SOSUS picks up that freighter, we'll get it done. I'll need a specialist team of four frogs and stickies. That way there'll be no mistakes."

"I suppose there's no way to avoid taking out the entire Russian crew?" suggested Zack. "I mean, that's kind of close to murder."

"Just so long as you don't mind Ivan Sneakovitch running to a Western newspaper," replied Arnold, "and then describing in graphic detail the barbaric action of the US Special Forces gunning down innocent civilian crewmen, women, children, cripples, and half-wits, with no mercy for anyone."

Zack Lancaster shuddered. "That, of course, is the very last thing we need," he said.

"That's no prisoners," confirmed Arnold. "And Mack, you'll remember who you're shooting, right? A group of villainous Russian murderers who intend to wipe out half the population of Fort Meade."

"We won't forget that, sir," said Mack. "We never forget the true character of our enemy. That's why we joined."

"Attaboy," said Arnie.

No two men in all the history of US conflict ever took to each other quite so rapidly as Admiral Morgan and Captain Bedford.

The three men talked almost until midnight, sipping Bailey's Irish Cream on the rocks until tiredness overtook them. Mack ordered breakfast for all of them at 7:00 a.m., settled the bill on his government charge card, and made sure there was a heavy-duty order of Irish sausages for everyone.

The following morning he was first away, driving down the west coast to Shannon. The helicopter for the other two touched down on the lawn at 8:30, and they took off instantly for Clonakilty, flying almost due south on the first stages of their 210-mile journey back to Château Morgan.

The fast US Navy helo took them straight over the heart of Ireland, over the counties of Sligo, Rosscommon, and Galway. They crossed the mighty Shannon River, leaving Limerick to their left, and then flew directly over four more of Ireland's great salmon rivers, the Blackwater, the Lee, the Bandon, and the Argideen, all of them in County Cork.

The pilot touched down on the lawn of Ardfield House before ten, and the two US military high commanders walked into the house to find Kathy and Virginia having breakfast.

"Good Lord!" said Kathy. "Where did you two spring from?"

"We're back from wild and woolly Donegal," declared Arnold. "And we've slept the whole way home on account of an Irish breakfast that would have fed a SEAL Team."

"Well, come and sit down while I give you some coffee to wake you up again," she replied.

Arnold added, "I'll have mine in the study. There are a couple of phone calls I need to make—in the national interest, that is."

He retreated into one of his new rooms, a brickred-painted, book-lined room with a huge partners desk at one end, green leather top, and a "captain's chair." Admiral Morgan went to work, putting in a call to the American Embassy in Dublin and asking to be put through to Ambassador Jack

Kirkpatrick, a southern newspaper and television owner with deep family roots in Ireland.

Their conversation was somewhat prolonged and, for Arnold, subtle. The objective of the old lion of the West Wing was to inform the representative of the United States in Ireland that he must effect a meeting with the *taoiseach* just as soon as humanly possible. He informed him that a thorough briefing was essential and that he and his houseguest, General Lancaster, were proposing to fly up to Dublin tomorrow for an urgent meeting that would probably last for the biggest part of the morning.

Meanwhile, could embassy staff organize a dinner party at the first opportunity to see the *taoiseach* in a social situation? No, the general would not attend that, as he was returning to the Pentagon in a couple of days, but Arnold regarded this particular exercise as a matter of the utmost priority, and Ambassador Kirkpatrick was to do everything in his power to make it happen fast.

The ambassador did, of course, know all about the towering reputation of Arnold Morgan and the massive role he had played in some of America's most dangerous times. And, quite frankly, the very sound of Admiral Morgan's name made him extremely nervous.

But today, the admiral was in a mellow and polite mood. He sounded understanding, aware of the difficulties in handling heads of government. He said he had full confidence in the ambassador's tact and ability to organize this critically important meeting.

Before he rang off, the admiral said warmly, "I'll wish you good-bye and the best of luck in this task. Look forward to seeing you tomorrow," which was most unlike him.

His sign-off statement was, however, more typical. "Don't fuck this up, Jack," he added. "Or there'll be all hell to pay."

Landing helicopters in the middle of the city of Dublin involved a labyrinth of regulations. Like most cities, special permissions were required, and the US Embassy offices, situated in Ballsbridge, could not be lightly exempted.

The arrival of Admiral Morgan might prove in the end to have been momentous, but right now, so far as Dublin Air Traffic Control was concerned, he could travel to Ballsbridge on the bus. US Embassy staff had to move swiftly and finally secured permission to land from the Gaelic Athletic Association, proprietors of the enormous Croke Park Stadium, the largest in Europe, on the north side of Dublin, between Drumcondra and Ballybough.

US officials had made one hell of a "pitch" to the association's chief executive to obtain his consent: that Admiral Morgan was probably the most commanding military presence in Washington, that his mission was hugely important for Ireland, that it involved discussions that would end in Irish PM to US president. The Gaelic Athletic Association would never regret this special hand of friendship offered to the United States.

And now the admiral was on his way, flying northeast on this bright Wednesday morning, crossing the River Suir south of the Rock of Cashel and then making a ten-mile detour around Coolmore, the world's greatest thoroughbred stud farm, where near-priceless stallions and broodmares roam in peaceful pastures. You can do darned nearly anything legal in Ireland except land helicopters in Ballsbridge and frighten the horses in Tipperary.

Arnold was flying to Dublin alone this morning, and thus far, as they clattered up toward Kilkenny, he knew nothing of the historic past of the eighty-two-thousand-capacity stadium where they would land. This was the place Dubliners call "Croker," the $260 million sports arena risen from the old Croke Park, where one of the most outrageous British massacres took place on November 21, 1920.

That was the day a small contingent of Royal Irish Constabulary and the British Auxiliary Division burst into the stadium and opened fire into the packed crowd awaiting the Gaelic football clash between Dublin and Tipperary. They shot thirteen people dead and gunned down the Tipperary captain, Michael Hogan, who died later at the hospital.

There were Irish families who never got over it. For nine decades the Gaelic Athletic Association would not permit players of a British game, like rugby or soccer or cricket, even to set foot on the hallowed turf of Croke Park. Eventually, they allowed the Irish rugby team to play England at Croke, while their own stadium at Lansdowne Road was being rebuilt.

Before the game, the head of the Gaelic AA had appealed to the huge crowd to appreciate that the young English players knew nothing of the events of the past. The great throng rose to them as sportsmen as they took the field. But the ghost of Tipperary's slain Michael Hogan prowled the touchline that day, and the Irish XV inflicted on the English their heaviest defeat ever in Dublin, forty-three points to thirteen.

In 1920 the king of England had made public his horror at what had happened on Bloody Sunday, as it would be forever known. And most of the world was appalled. Many people still think that was the end of the British in southern Ireland. The Irish War of Independence ended the following year.

In fact, Arnold would later discover what he believed was a close personal involvement in those events: the driving force behind this brutal battle of wills between the Irish and British was none other than the Big Feller, Michael Collins, C-in-C, Irish Republican Army, late of Woodfield, Clonakilty. On that very morning, November 21, 1920, Michael's feared Irish hit squad, the Twelve Apostles, had raged into the streets around Dublin's city center and slaughtered some of the most secretive British informers and spies, known as the Cairo Gang. In all, fifteen British intelligence officers were assassinated that day by Collins's elite troops.

Unrepentant, ice cold in triumph, he declared, "By their destruction, the very air is made sweeter. I have paid them back in their own coin."

The iron soul of this fabled Irishman seemed to Arnold to be as closely in tune with his own as it was possible to be. When finally he heard about Bloody Sunday, he accepted that the British action was a reprisal for the deeds of the Twelve Apostles, but nonetheless his man was still Michael Collins.

After just a few months living in Clonakilty, the former head of the US National Security Agency had lined up the IRA chief with his other hero, General Douglas MacArthur. The patriotism of both men touched him deeply, and the pure locality of Michael Collins made Arnold feel a part of it all. Spiritually, at least.

The helicopter was taking a long sweep around Dublin and coming in to land from the west. He could see Croke Park out in front, the lush green of the playing surface drawing ever closer. The pilot's descent was gradual, and the helicopter came slowly down in front of the Michael Hogan Stand, named, of course, in memory of the Tipperary captain.

An embassy limousine was awaiting them and drove the admiral through the busy city streets to Elgin Road, Ballsbridge, where Jack Kirkpatrick was ready with hot coffee and a couple of Danish pastries. He listened with nothing short of amazement while Arnold explained the scheme to bring Ireland into close partnership with the United States, sort out their debt, and construct a brand-new US Navy base on the north shore of Donegal Bay.

"Jesus, sir, you sure know how to wake a guy up," he said.

"I'm not finished yet," added Arnold. "If this works out well in the initial stages, we intend to go a step further."

"You do?"

"Yup. We'll probably turn the Republic of Ireland into the fifty-first state."

"Steady, sir. Don't do that—I'll be out of a job!"

Arnold pressed on, confirming that the financial package the United States would present to the *taoiseach* would be almost irresistible—taking care of half the national debt, assuming responsibility and paying the interest. And, of course, the extra business in and around the Donegal area would be very significant, unemployment being so high.

After an hour of discussion, the US ambassador understood the entire merit of the scheme and felt confident he could persuade the *taoiseach* that it was imperative he attend a dinner party, this week, in order to meet the American admiral Arnold Morgan.

"And please tell him," said Arnold, "if there is local difficulty among fishermen worried about their regular livelihoods, the US Navy intends to provide generous compensation out of its own budget. None of the American planners thought the presence of the US warships would have the slightest effect on the shellfish beds and that the compensation would, in the end, count as a mere bonus.

"Just impress upon him, Jack, that this is a win-win situation for everyone. But also let him know that the USA is trying to cope with a formidable threat from Russia, a possible nuclear hit on a critical part of our military establishment. I am imploring him to allow us to build this base in Donegal. Because it will change the world for us."

"Okay, sir. I'll get right on it. Will I assume you can come to dinner with us any evening I can fix it?"

"Absolutely," said the admiral. "Depending on how you visualize the situation, I'll either bring my wife or come alone. Whatever suits."

"No problem. I'll arrange it for the residence in Phoenix Park. That way there'll be no problem with the helicopter."

"Perfect," said Arnold, glancing at his watch. "I'll leave you in peace now. My car's right outside, and the helo's waiting over at Croke Park."

The admiral took his leave and walked, under US Marine escort, outside to the waiting limousine. On the way back to the stadium, the driver, Liam Mulligan, was delighted to regale his passenger with the full history of Croke Park and the legends that haunt the place still.

When they arrived, he parked the car and walked out onto the playing surface with Admiral Morgan, and there he pointed out a rising section of the modern seating. "That's Hill 16 over there, sir," he said, with an unmistakable quiet reverence, "and deep inside it there are fragments of the rubble from the 1916 Easter Rising, from the Irish city buildings the British artillery smashed, including stone from the General Post Office. It's a spiritual place."

The admiral gazed quietly along the playing field.

"You can't see it," said Liam Mulligan, "but every Irishman knows it's there. And what it means. And for sympathizers with the Sinn Fein party, that hill represents the two words we all carry in our hearts: Ourselves Alone."

The admiral turned to say good-bye, and he held out his hand in friendship. He said something that the Irishman did not fully understand, but nonetheless caught the drift. "We mentioned that to the Brits nearly 250 years ago," said Arnold. "So long, Liam . . . See you on Hill 16."

The helicopter took off immediately for the 165-mile journey home to the West Cork coast. They made it in just less than an hour, only to find the Lancasters and Kathy had gone to Kinsale for lunch and would not be back until late afternoon.

Arnold was happy to have the place to himself and settled down in his wicker rocking chair on the outside terrace with a book on the Easter Rising. But the traveling had loosened his concentration, and, on reflection, he preferred just to sit and gaze out to the long ocean swells of the Celtic Sea, alert, as ever, for the sighting of a periscope of an Oscar Class Russian submarine. He reached out for his old US Navy binoculars and focused on a distant Irish trawler that was driving home before a hard sou'wester, toward the Old Head of Kinsale.

Just then the phone rang on the white table beside him—Jack Kirkpatrick from Dublin. The news was excellent. Arnold and the *taoiseach* would meet at an informal dinner to be held in the ambassador's residence in Phoenix Park on Friday evening, 7:30 p.m., dinner at 8:00. "My wife will be there," he said. "And I invited Lizzie McGrath, so I think Mrs. Morgan should come with you."

"Couldn't be better, Jack," replied Arnold. "No problems landing at the residence?"

"None. Your pilot will fly in like a homing pigeon, drop you right at the front door. And I'm assuming you'll stay the night?"

"Perfect," said Arnold.

For an American naval commander and former head of the entire military intelligence network, Dublin represented an unusual gap in Admiral Morgan's experience. Until today, he had never even been there and certainly not to the great white Georgian mansion in Phoenix Park, which is home to the US ambassador.

Admiral Arnold and Kathy would occupy the magnificent suite on the second floor where President Kennedy and the first lady stayed. For a man accustomed for so many years to an iron-cased bunk in a nuclear submarine, this would not be too shabby.

And it slotted into Arnold's plans nicely. General Lancaster and Virginia were leaving on Friday morning and would fly to Shannon Airport at 10:00 a.m. The admiral and Kathy would leave for Dublin at 6:30 p.m.

When the Kinsale group returned, Zack Lancaster joined Arnold on the terrace for a cup of tea and a report on the day's action. He was of course delighted the admiral was dining with the *taoiseach* and was interested how quickly Jack Kirkpatrick had moved on the project.

"He doesn't think there will be a problem getting Neil McGrath onside," he said. "My biggest task is to persuade him he doesn't need an act of parliament just to get it all started. Because he doesn't. Ireland's government is perfectly entitled to enter into a financial agreement with the United States, and indeed to have a small dockyard built in Donegal, without actually changing the laws of the land. And this one has so many plus factors he'd be nuts not to help us."

"I agree with all of that, Arnie," said Zack. "But you know, the thing that will sway this is Ireland's endless affection for the United States. There's a bond there, and it's unbreakable."

The admiral, after these recent months living in the old heartland of the Irish Revolution, understood the very fabric that forever links the Emerald Isle to the New World: family to family, Irish village to US state, the shared bonds of unspeakable hardship that happened long ago, but still stand stark before everyone, the descendants of those who fled the terror and the starvation and the descendants of those who stayed, the survivors. The terrible beauty of Ireland, *still* not recovered in some remote places from the Great Hunger of the nineteenth century, still with its depleted population, yet still wishing the Americans well, with an undying affection for its blood brothers across the Atlantic Ocean.

There was a perfect example in June 1963, when Jacqueline Kennedy visited the village in County Wexford where the original Kennedy family still lived. Years later, she recalled the president's arrival and his motorcade outside the door of the house where his ancestors were born, including his great-grandfather Patrick, who emigrated to Boston in 1848. "We were all standing in the lane," she remembered, "when all these children came rushing out of the front gates—there must have been a dozen, all laughing and shouting. And every one of them looked just like my Jack."

As the thirty-fifth president of the United States felt on that Irish morning, so have millions of other Americans who, down all the years, made the pilgrimage home to Ireland. Admiral Morgan knew so much more about it now, and, frankly, it was inconceivable to him that Ireland would not step up to help America deal with the oncoming Russian threat. And he reveled in the fact that it was all up to him.

And so for the next couple of days the Morgans and the Lancasters spent their time sightseeing and dining, and the admiral even accompanied the general on another fishing trip, although he refrained from casting. And, in the late afternoon of Friday, October 5, he and Kathy took off from their back lawn, bound for the Phoenix Park, as the Irish always call it.

The landing, fifty-five minutes later, right on the lawn, almost took Mrs. Morgan's breath, staring down at the white mansion with its rounded twin ramparts on the front facade flanking a line of eight spectacular tall, arched windows. Arnold, who was by now a world expert on the history of the house, informed her casually that the Duke of Wellington, victor of Waterloo, had lived here when he was Sir Arthur Wellesley, Great Britain's chief secretary to Ireland.

"How could you possibly know that?" she laughed. "Three days ago you'd never heard of the place."

"I've told you," he replied, "I'm a quick study. See that copse of rhododendrons beyond the house? Winston Churchill used to ride his little donkey cart over there when he was a kid. His grandfather the Duke of Marlborough was viceroy to Ireland, and Winston's dad, Lord Randolph, was his private secretary. This is where the family lived."

"How do you know all this?" asked Kathy incredulously.

Arnold merely tapped the right-hand side of his nose with his forefinger, the way he usually did, when he knew he was well ahead of the game.

The uniformed copilot carried the overnight bags into the house. The US ambassador and the Irish prime minister were waiting to greet them outside the front door, but the rotors of the helicopter were making such a racket, even while just idling, that it was impossible to speak. The introductions had to wait until they had all entered the house. And since it had just started to rain, this was fortuitous.

Jack Kirkpatrick's wife, formerly an advertising executive from Atlanta, was southern charm itself and presented the admiral and Kathy to Neil and Lizzie McGrath, Ireland's extremely popular prime minister and his wife. The only other guests were the Irish finance minister, Jerry Mullins, who was already in the drawing room, and the extremely attractive president of Ireland, Mrs. Mary Russell (fiftyish), who was late, due, no doubt, to her living almost next door, across the park, and having access to an official car and chauffeur for only twenty-four hours a day.

In Arnold Morgan's opinion, Ambassador Kirkpatrick had done a thoroughly brilliant job of wheeling into the room perhaps the three most influential people in the country, certainly the three he most needed on his side: the PM, the money man, and the immensely well-respected head of state.

The butler served them each a glass of champagne, and, to Arnold's eternal gratitude, there proved to be no need for preamble and no need for lengthy explanations. Jack Kirkpatrick had spent two hours with the PM and Jerry Mullins that morning, and he knew they had briefed Mary over lunch.

Every one of them understood the context of the admiral's proposal but not the details. Neil McGrath, a former Dublin lawyer and a cousin of the famous McGraths who founded both the Waterford Crystal/Wedgwood and the Irish Sweepstakes empire, came right to the point. "Arnold, I have explained to Jack that I see no need to change Irish law in order for a new navy base to be built in Donegal Bay," he said. "So, therefore, if we reach agreement, we can move very fast. There are a lot of Irishmen who would love to work on a major construction project in that part of the country. We really need the jobs."

"Well, Neil," said the admiral, "our proposal is that we sign a long lease with the Irish government on the land we need up there. And that we make you a proposition for the United States to take a significant share in Ireland Incorporated, and in return we initially take care of 50 percent of the national debt, which I believe is in excess of a trillion dollars."

"You mean you're going to pay it off for us?"

"Not quite. But we are going to take it off your hands and assume all responsibility for it. We will start paying the interest immediately. Your national debt, so far as the Irish government is concerned, is thus cut in half at the stroke of a pen."

At this point, two things happened. Jerry Mullins started nodding so fast Arnold thought his neck might snap in half, and Mary Russell came elegantly through the door, apologizing profusely for her lateness and blaming the British prime minister for being so death-defyingly boring.

Yes, she would adore a glass of champagne, and God knows she needed it, after a half hour on the phone discussing "some tedious royal visit to Dublin by a couple of princes or princesses or whatever." Mary Russell could not understand for the life of her why the English thought "anyone in the whole bloody world cared what the devil their princes and princesses did, and indeed what they didn't."

Meanwhile, Neil McGrath never missed a beat. "And then?" he asked Arnold. "What then?"

"We start the new project, pumping even more money into the Irish economy, probably up to a billion dollars in construction alone, for jetties, docks, and buildings."

At this juncture, Arnold considered no neck could possibly stand the sheer pressure Jerry Mullins was putting on his, so fast was the finance minister nodding his profound approval for the building of the Donegal Base.

"And since at that time, the United States will effectively be 50 percent owners of the entire country," the PM observed, "what kind of a contribution will you want from us, in return for your generosity?"

"We will assess the budgetary needs of Ireland and place that figure right at the top of the equation. And that comes right off the top of all national income. Any surplus, we'll take half to help with the old interest payments."

"Aha, I couldn't quarrel with that," said Neil McGrath.

"And, thanks to the new base, there should be some sizable increase in government income during that first year," added Arnold.

"I imagine you've considered the long term as well as the short?" the PM suggested.

"Only to the extent that for a small country like this, a trillion bucks is one heck of a lot of money," said the admiral. "If, say, eighteen months from now, the partnership is proving financially successful for Ireland, you might consider going the whole way, handing over the debt for us to deal with and effectively becoming the fifty-first state. We'd love to have you!"

Neil McGrath smiled and whistled through his teeth, in that universal gesture that means, worldwide, *Holy shit! Are you kidding me?*

"Arnold," he said, "that would not take an act of parliament. That would take an act of God. I'm only in office for four more years—I can't just give away the whole bloody country!"

"You would not be giving it away. Neither would you be selling it," said the admiral. "It would be a simple merger between two compatible countries, and I venture to say it would signify unprecedented prosperity for Ireland."

The smile on the face of the finance minister would have floodlit Croke Park. But the prime minister was deadly serious.

"I do see that, Arnold. It would, I imagine, open up all kinds of trading lanes for us, and we would no longer be beholden to the European Union and to the UK for our exports, especially mining and agriculture."

"And with American money and engineering know-how," said Arnold, "we'd have those two huge gas fields in Kinsale and Corrib up and running in no time. There'd be more taxes flying around than Jerry here could spend."

"And I could visit my sister in New York without even a passport or a visa," said Mullins. "Same currency, same phone systems, same postage rates, and tax dollars to put this place right back on its feet. The old Celtic Tiger would roar again . . . "

"And wouldn't that be nice?" said the PM. "Jaysus, I'm sick to death of this nation being broke."

"Because it shouldn't be," added Jerry Mullins. "We have no need to import food, we have a welfare system about one-twentieth the size of London's, and the people here are educated properly."

"That's all occurred to us," replied Arnold. "I'm just surprised no one's thought of all this before."

"They probably have, but wouldn't hardly dare say it," said the PM. "The trouble is, this kind of thing may take years, and I need to ask you, just what is it that the United States wants to do in such a hurry, and can you tell me why?"

Thus, throughout most of dinner, with Arnold Morgan helped greatly by interjections from Jack Kirkpatrick, the two Americans unfolded the somewhat chilling story of Russia's proposed attack on the US military intelligence system as a straight reprisal for helping Israel to destroy Iran's nuclear program two years previously.

"We know what they're doing, and we know how they plan to achieve it," said Arnold. "But we do not wish to bring half the world to the brink of war. And this Russian operation could move out of the Barents Sea on a big freighter at any time.

"That would include missiles with nuclear warheads, guidance systems, mobile launchers, and electronic jammers to dismantle the president's communications. And we intend to destroy it, but quietly and secretly."

"At sea, presumably?" asked the PM. "Before the freighter gets to the launch site?"

"Precisely," replied the admiral. "And we have one major problem. That ship will pull out of Murmansk in the middle of the night. SOSUS won't pinpoint it for a few days. But when it does, we need to move real quick. And our hardware is just too far away. We need it right here on a northeastern shore of the Atlantic Ocean . . . "

"And that's where we come in, eh?" said Neil McGrath. "You want an American base, right here in Donegal, US warships within fast strike range of the rogue freighter."

"You got it," said Arnold.

Finally, the prime minister of Ireland made some kind of judgment. "Look, boys," he said, conspiratorially, "I have been asked for a major favor by the United States of America. And it's a favor I cannot refuse, because it's in the interest of world peace and prosperity. Whether we like it or not, we all live behind the powerful protection of the USA, and sometimes we take that for granted.

"No Irish government in my judgment could say no to the Americans on this. It's our duty; it's our chance to offer something for the common good. I'm going to say right now: that navy base can be built. It can start right away, because one of the undisputed powers I do have is that of compulsory purchase.

"The Irish government owns quite a lot of the ground you require, and I can make that available. Anything needs buying up, from anyone, I can do that—provided I have your word that the USA will compensate us for the cash outlays."

"You have our word," said Admiral Morgan. "Right, Jack?"

The US ambassador confirmed the deal.

Neil McGrath said immediately, "I will have contracts drawn up over the weekend, which will demonstrate that all the land you require is being placed in the formal ownership of the Irish government, and there will be a ninety-nine-year lease issued to the USA on that land, with full building rights and shoreline permits issued forthwith."

"You can do all that yourself?" asked Jack Kirkpatrick. "Without so much as a word in parliament?"

"The job of parliament is to change laws and pass laws," said Neil McGrath. "It does not need to concern itself with activities that require neither. I am empowered to enter into contracts with any nation, and I am certainly able to step forward to help our American friends, any way I may wish."

A full round of applause broke out for the Irish prime minister in the ornate and perfectly lit dining room.

And, from the high dining-room walls of the US Embassy, the superb portraits of two beloved Americans, both with unbreakable Irish roots, stared down with obvious approval . . . from Ballyporeen, County Tipperary, the fortieth president, Ronald Reagan, and from Dunganstown, County Wexford, the thirty-fifth, John Fitzgerald Kennedy.

10

By Tuesday morning, October 9, the Irish government had reacted with extraordinary speed to the American request. Along the Donegal shore at the eastern end of the bay every household was advised of the new development—that the Irish government was building a new ferry terminal to take the pressure off the Killybegs jetties.

There were only five occupied properties that were affected. And every one of them objected, until, under Admiral Morgan's edict, they were offered the full market price, plus $150,000 each, at which point every one of them changed their minds.

The government owned the rest of the required shoreline, and Neil McGrath had four lawyers working right through the weekend drawing up a lease for the US Navy, which allowed it to build initially a fifteen-hundred-foot jetty with a short seventy-five-yard stretch of tarmac road leading down to it.

It also issued permission for three major buildings to be constructed, though none of them could be more than two stories high, which would protect the water views from all the surrounding land. The government undertook to order the electric company, the Irish natural gas corporation, and the water board to bring central supply into the developed area immediately. All three utilities would stand by to lay pipes and cables, under Irish government instruction.

The lease further permitted two more piers to be built over time, one of them five hundred feet long that could be situated one hundred feet offshore, parallel to the main jetty, thus forming a narrow channel, which could be roofed to provide a submarine shelter from prying satellites. None of this would, of course, ever be made public.

Neil McGrath also recruited the chief executive of one of the major Irish waterfront heavy-industry corporations, Harris Pye Dry Dock, to come in and assist the Americans with advice on new buildings, naval repair facilities, dry-docking, and ultimately to harness a part of its one-hundred-strong workforce to lead the way in the construction. Harris Pye, located near Alexandra Quay on the Port of Dublin's North Wall, would be a regular calling spot for Admiral Morgan throughout the coming months.

Privately, Neil McGrath's old friend at the world-renowned Dublin harbor corporation believed the Americans would end up bringing in a floating dry dock—a huge pontoon with floodable buoyancy chambers. These are controlled by enormous valves that, when opened, cause the dock to stand lower in the water and allow a submarine to float in.

When the chambers are pumped dry, the water runs out, and the entire edifice rises up, leaving the ship on giant wood supports, ready for repairs or servicing. Harris Pye would undertake the construction of this dock because naval bases need one, especially the Americans, trying to operate so far from home.

The US Embassy in Dublin made copies of the lease to be sent immediately to Admiral Mark Bradfield in Washington and to the project chief, Admiral Morgan in Clonakilty. Subject to US approval, construction was to begin in the third week in October, with two huge cranes on floating barges hauling in the long steel piles, which would be driven into the seabed.

Tons of steel for the giant sheet-pile "walls" would be purchased from Irish corporations, all to be driven down into the water to form the ultimate "box" from which the water would be pumped out and refilled with stone and concrete. The speed at which this can be achieved is dependent entirely on the size of the workforce and the availability of heavy machinery, diggers, bulldozers, trucks, and jackhammers. So far as the US Navy was concerned, there was no limit, either financial or in gathering the major machinery.

Four senior consultants were there from Harland and Wolff, builders of the *Titanic* more than one hundred years ago in the Belfast shipyards, less than ninety miles away to the east. All four of them were experts on dock construction and crane capacity, Harland and Wolff being proprietors of the two largest gantry cranes in the world, "Samson" and "Goliath," which stand at well over three hundred feet tall in their cotton socks.

The orders snapped out daily from Clonakilty, mostly along the lines of, *Fine, just get it done . . . No delays . . . And I don't care if it does cost another fifty bucks a ton . . . Son, right here we're in a war situation . . . So far as I'm concerned, that jetty is life and death to the USA . . . Just build the sonofabitch . . . and build it now, hear me?*

In the end, everyone got Admiral Morgan's drift. There was urgency, which is sometimes rare in Ireland. They had the approach road down and concreted in ten days. The giant jackhammers were already pounding the steel piles into the floor of the bay; a convoy of trucks bearing thirty-five tons of rock at a time was coming in, thanks to some slick organization by McMonagle Stone of Mountcharles. The barges were moored offshore, laden with steel, and with cranes working from 8:00 a.m. to 6:00 p.m.

Diggers were cutting out channels for the utility supply lines. The great triumph of the operation was that the entire thing was, and seemed, Irish. There was no trace of a greenback or a US flag or a US corporation, and certainly nothing to suggest the United States Navy was anywhere near the construction site.

Deliberately, Admiral Morgan had ensured no US Navy personnel was in attendance. There were, of course, senior naval construction engineers visiting, but never in uniform, always in regular working clothes, wearing standard Irish hard hats on site.

So far as the US Navy knew, there was no Russian satellite surveillance trained on the Irish west coast, where there was no Irish Naval presence and never had been. A new local ferry terminal in Donegal was as interesting to the Russian Navy's Northern Fleet as the annual Galway Oyster Festival.

The first and only major setback came on November 3, one day after the first steel pilings were hammered into the seabed. That was the day the East Donegal Bay Oyster and Shellfish Association mutinied and turned up in force in Donegal Town's District Court Office on Bridge Street.

Armed with two lawyers and a petition with twenty-three names on it, they sought an injunction to prevent any further work on the proposed ferry terminal that, they claimed, would endanger their livelihoods, pollute the crystal waters of Donegal Bay, and destroy shellfish life in the immediate area. The terminal, they claimed, was illegal, unnecessary, and a blight on both the land and the seascape.

By early afternoon they had succeeded in getting their case before a magistrate, who reminded them they were coming up against the owners of the land, which happened to be the Irish government. "I cannot allow an application for an easement on this project on the basis that it's against the law," he told them. "Not when the defendant will be the government of Ireland, which, indeed, is the law."

He informed the petitioners there would be a one-month adjournment while he sought advice on the possible damage to the environment and whether there was a chance of compensation for the five principals, the shellfishermen who believed both the mollusks and their livelihoods would be gone.

While the clerk to the magistrates informed the government of the problem, the petitioners made their way to the village of Bruckless, where, in the shadow of the great round church tower, they unfurled banners and marched to the construction site, led by the oysterman Tom O'Toole from Mountcharles.

They stood for a half hour and chanted *FERRY PORT . . . FERRY PORT—NO! NO! NO!* while the massive JCB hydraulic buckets hauled sand and shale out of the foreshore in readiness for the two-ton hunks of granite that would replace it.

At this point it started to rain, and Tom O'Toole immediately led his little army of protesters directly to the village pub, the Mary Murrins, to celebrate a day of "mighty achievement."

"We showed 'em today, lads," he said as the barman drew their pints of Guinness. "Showed 'em that ferry port will be completed over our dead bodies, so it will."

His deputy, Padraic Treacy from Dunkineely, added darkly, "And if they ignore us, we'll start blowing the place up." Padraic was essentially unaware of the small company of United States Marines, currently on their way to act as permanent guards to the new facility—just as soon as Mr. and Mrs. Ronan O'Callaghan moved out of their sizable house and provided the first accommodations for non-Irish residents. This was expected in the next few days, the Irish couple having accepted a full two hundred thousand dollars over the market price to be gone within ten days.

Meanwhile, Neil McGrath had informed Admiral Morgan of the mutiny in Bruckless Town (population 184) and asked him whether he'd pay to bring in lawyers and have them mount a legal defense. The courts would hold the civil case up for a minimum of six months.

"Hell, no," replied the admiral. "Buy 'em off."

"There are about five of them involved in the main part of the claim," said the PM. "The estimate is they make forty thousand euros a year, except for last year, when the oysters got some bloody affliction called red tide and dropped dead in their shells."

"Okay, we'll buy them out," said the admiral. "Offer each man a half million for his business. And tell 'em we'll rent it all back to them for a dollar a year. If they can still fish, that'll kill the charge we've screwed up the shellfish beds."

"Good idea," said the PM. "I'll send someone up there to make the offer on behalf of the government."

And so it was that an Irish government lawyer arrived at the world headquarters of the East Donegal Bay Oyster and Shellfish Association, the Mary Murrins in Bruckless, to try to sink the protest beneath a rising tide of cash.

Tom O'Toole rose to introduce the lawyer to the small gathering, but could not resist a small, impassioned commercial before he did so. "We realize," he said, "you will have come here with various propositions intended to despoil our magnificent Donegal coastline. But I should issue this warning right now, that no amount of money, intended as either a bribe or compensation, will be acceptable to any of us. This is a protest of conscience, in defense of our beautiful and historic land, and there are not enough dollar bills in all the world to wrest from us this priceless asset and this traditional way of life."

At which point, the government lawyer, Dermot O'Brien, rose from his chair and stated, "Then this meeting will end very swiftly. But I am instructed to offer each one of you the sum of five hundred thousand dollars to cover your losses."

"I'll take that," called out Padraic Treacy, the local czar of the periwinkle flats. "That'll do very nicely to stave off the coming hardship."

"I'll take it as well," added Tom O'Toole. "That's a fair offer, sir. You're a gentleman."

The Great Environmental Mutiny, which began with such fervor in the tiny parish of Bruckless, ended where it had started, in the Mary Murrins, over a couple of pints of stout. It petered out before an avalanche of US cash, after a protest meeting that lasted just one minute and thirty-seven seconds.

The shellfishermen were not the only local businessmen to start profiting from the oncoming presence of the United States Navy. Admiral Morgan ordered the local gas station to be given the franchise for the dockside fuel pumps that would be built in the new base. This more or less ensured that Raymond O'Connell and his family would become millionaires inside a year.

He also ordered the village store to begin preparations to provide all supplies to what would become a busy terminal in the coming months. No other store would be involved. Arnold also ordered a donation be made by the Irish government to the local school and a new emergency wing to be constructed for the nearest local hospital.

He made a five-thousand-dollar donation for new gear for the local soccer team, and by Christmas, with the main jetty almost complete, the Irish government and its new construction partners were the most popular organizations in the history of Donegal, whoever those new partners might be.

0900, THURSDAY, JANUARY 3, 2019

HQ SPECWARCOM
Coronado, California

Captain Bedford and Admiral Andy Carlow were in deep conference on the shores of the Pacific Ocean, inside the compound where the Navy SEALs practice their daily exercise regimen—the one that ensures they remain the hardest men who ever lived, at least since the Stone Age when the cave dwellers needed to throttle a wild mountain lion in order to have lunch.

While lines of would-be SEALs slogged it out, pounding along the edge of the surf, Mack and Andy walked slowly along the dunes in the early sun, wrestling with a tricky naval warfare problem that would surely unfold in the next few months, half a world away.

The task that lay before them seemed to belong to the eighteenth century, to the days of sail when great wooden ships of the line battered each other into submission with heavy cannon fire. In that era, boarding a crippled warship was an essential part of ocean warfare, especially if you happened to be a pirate or any kind of privateer.

The normal tools of the trade involved grappling hooks, ropes, lines, ladders, and cutlasses. The musket men tended to stay in the sail rigging and fire down on the enemy as the ships closed together for the short-range stage of the battle. Admiral Lord Nelson, victor of Trafalgar in 1815, lost his life in that way, shot down on his own quarterdeck by a French marksman, within sight of his greatest triumph.

Andy Carlow was not altogether sure the coming mission in the North Atlantic was going to be a whole lot different. If there was one thing the SPECWARCOM boss hated, it was losing his SEALs, especially having them shot by snipers or any other foreign marksmen lurking in the rigging.

The plan for the forthcoming action was already refined. The target was the big Russian freighter that US Naval Intelligence suggested would steam from Murmansk to Panama with a lethal cargo on board specifically designed for a nuclear-missile hit on the United States' most precious building at Fort Meade.

The guided missiles were already on the ship. The huge TELAR mobile launchers were also on board, plus all the electronic guidance and jamming equipment required for such an outlandish plan. To Admiral Carlow it still seemed unreal. But Captain Bedford knew better, since it was one of his oldest friends, the Mossad agent, who had uncovered the plot. SEAL Team 10, Mack Bedford's command, had been chosen to stop that ship dead in its tracks, to put it on the floor of the Atlantic with no survivors, no one to talk, no one to run to some newspaper or magazine with stories of US brutality on the high seas.

This required a boarding. The powers in the Pentagon had decreed that this Russian intruder, steaming south to an unannounced missile launch site, could not be hit hard with a torpedo, or missile, or bombs, and sunk. Too darned noisy, too darned messy, and too darned public. In this modern world of satellite surveillance and electronic eavesdropping, that kind of thing is very nearly prehistoric, especially among nations as big as the United States and Russia.

Everyone who was aware of the Russian treachery understood that freighter, with all of its deadly cargo, had to go. But it had to go quietly. Very quietly. As if it had never been there. And that was the task that now faced SEAL Team 10—how to get rid of it, silently and without a trace, in such an icily clandestine manner not even the Russian Navy would ever know what had happened.

It was, by any standards, a tall order. But then Navy SEALs hardly ever attempt anything that is not a tall order. "And the fact is," said Mack Bedford, "we have to board the goddamned ship. And there'll be Russian military guards, armed and permitted to fire at will in the event of an attack. Andy, we'll be sitting ducks, worse than Admiral Nelson was."

"Then we'll have to take out the guards first, right?"

"Correct. We'll flood the buoyancy tank on the starboard side of our ship, so we're heeling maybe thirty-five degrees, appearing to sink. We'll come in toward them for the rescue, port side nearest, which will be the high side. Our own marksmen will shoot to kill with silenced rifles, picking off every Russian guard and any crew members who have strayed topside.

"Then we'll use grapplers and rope ladders, hurling them upward over the rails, and all the while our marksmen will unleash covering fire as we board the vessel. At the same time, we'll send four frogs over the side to get under the freighter and place four big stickies on the underside of her hull, timed for, say, thirty minutes.

"First SEALs over the rails must slam the radio room before it can be used for any kind of satellite transmission. Then we'll search the place and get the nuclear stuff off, if it's possible. If not, we'll just sink the sonofabitch and fuck off. They can work out what happened any way they like. But there won't be a trace. That I can promise."

"I like it," replied the SPECWARCOM chief. "What do you need now?"

"A darned great freighter, four thousand tons minimum, to practice boarding."

"And how many SEALs for the operation?"

"Ten marksmen, four frogs, fifteen boarders, and four seamen able to handle the crane. That's in addition to a twenty-man Irish team to handle the ship."

"No problem," said Admiral Carlow.

"You hope," grinned Mack.

SAME DAY

Northern Fleet HQ
Severomorsk, Russia

The *Koryak* was moored alongside one of the biggest jetties in the Russian Naval yard, right next to the heavy-duty crane. Work on her hull had continued for weeks, and as the new year dawned, the two TELAR mobile launchers were on board, with the twin Iskander-K missiles already embarked on the flatbed of the giant trucks, bolted into position for the voyage and the disembarkation in Panama.

In fact, they were both ready to be fired, the erectors all set to come slowly from horizontal to vertical. All that was required for a major launch was the electronic guidance system to be activated and the homing device locked on, with GPS numbers punched in, accurate to about four feet . . . not bad after a couple of thousand miles.

One more week, and it would be impossible to see those missiles anywhere on the tank deck of the former Russian Navy landing ship *Korolev,* with her new name, new paint, and new gunnery system. This was a last-minute single 76mm deck gun, 120 rounds per minute, fitted to the for'ard forecastle. By modern naval warfare standards, this did not make her by any means lethal to an enemy, but it did mean you'd want to be darned careful before you got into her line of sight.

The new, improved *Koryak* was 370 feet long and stood quite high off the water. Loaded, she displaced forty-seven hundred tons, and right now she was being fitted with a false wall at the aft end of the tank deck that would render the TELARs invisible. The wall would be painted dark blue along with the inside of the entire hull in that section.

No one, unless they were searching and had studied a detailed plan of the ship, would even dream there was anything behind that carefully fitted section of the hull—never mind four missiles, designed to pack a big-enough nuclear high-explosive wallop to knock down the towering Building OPS 2A in Crypto City, Maryland.

Parked on the dockside, not yet embarked, was an eighteen-wheel red-

and-white Mercedes truck, with hard, high sides and rear doors but a soft top. Down the side of the truck were the words *LYON GENERATEUR L'ÉLECTRONIQUE.* On the driver's side door: *400 Boulevard Laurent Bonnevay, Lyon, France.*

Admiral Ustinov had ordered this leviathan to be parked and anchored, so it almost obscured the blue wall, which would discourage even the most zealous Central American customs inspectors from prying too deeply into the hidden secrets of the eighteen-wheeler.

Anyone wanting to search the truck on its long journey north from the Balboa docks in Panama would hardly notice the relatively small jammer attached electronically to an industrial-size generator bearing the correct metal identification plates of the French corporation that built it, plus a set of papers, instructions, and sales documents showing it was bound for the University of Colorado Hospital in Aurora.

The *Koryak* would also transport a detachment of Russian Navy guards, armed but with weapons stowed, in case the vessel should be boarded at any stage by customs or military officials.

The most secretive section of the *Koryak*'s cargo, however, contained the four hidden nuclear warheads, which would eventually be fitted to the Iskander missiles. Admiral Ustinov's advisers suggested it would not be too smart to subject them to a long and possibly rough sea voyage of many thousands of miles.

Nuclear weapons do not go off on impact, but need their computers to be programmed. Nonetheless, all nuclear weapons scientists dislike rockets being transported around the world with their nuclear warheads fixed. There have been accidents, and it was infinitely preferable to have the warheads completely disarmed and, if possible, hidden.

This precaution also represented the difference between being accused of transporting forbidden missiles and transporting obviously harmless ones, merely going for test firings, to test guidance systems.

The biggest problem of all was that US warships, and probably even US satellites, seemed to be able to locate any nuclear cargo stowed inside any ship. The Americans steadfastly denied any such thing and claimed they could not see straight through the steel hulls of the world's heavy cargo ships.

But no one believed this. There were a good few instances of ships being apprehended by warships—not necessarily American—and thus being caught red-handed moving weapons-grade uranium around the world's oceans.

Sophisticated naval organizations were certain that somehow the Americans could penetrate cargo ships with X-ray beams sensitive to nuclear material and that if anyone wanted their intentions to be kept secret, they'd better take serious steps to camouflage their uranium 235.

Admiral Ustinov's men had been working on this for several months and had constructed two boxes made of solid lead almost six inches thick. Each side was around five feet long and three feet high. The box was almost three feet across. It was so heavy, Admiral Ustinov thought it might "sink the damn ship." It was so heavy no one ever weighed it. Each of the boxes would carry two of the Iskander-K nuclear warheads.

The project to hide the critical components was nothing short of brilliant. The boxes were to be situated right below the main deck hatch and both lowered and raised by crane. They would be bolted to the hull and a false-front elevation fitted to make them look like storage lockers.

More important, the massive strength of the lead casing, similar to that surrounding the nuclear reactor in a US warship, would surely fend off prying beams and rays, from either US satellites or patrolling warships.

So they lifted the boxes, both empty, off the dockside and lowered them into the hold of the *Koryak,* directly below the main foredeck hatch. The next step was to transport the nuclear 'heads onto the dockside and have them, too, lifted, lowered, and fitted into their transport casing.

Everything went extremely smoothly. Except for one problem. The Americans caught them red-handed, with their devastatingly effective military spy satellite US-224 KH-11 sliding through space twenty-two thousand miles above. This optical masterpiece, constructed in California by Lockheed, was the size of the Hubble Telescope, hurled into space in 2011 by a Delta IV-H heavy rocket at a staggering cost of around $4.4 billion, courtesy of the colossally secretive National Reconnaissance Office.

Firing off photographic shots every five seconds, KH-11, its secondary mirror moved to take in unusual angles, lasered in on the Severomorsk dockside almost right on time and collected one of the best selections of totally incriminating snapshots ever received by the NRO. The data were transmitted through a network of US communication satellites to an NRO facility so secret it's known only as US Area 58, a kind of lost land of cast-iron military secrets. No one had ever guessed the location correctly, although some believed it was located at another rigidly classified US military establishment, Fort Belvoir, Virginia, south of Washington, DC.

The data ended up in the top-priority section of Air Force general Jack Myers's desk in Chantilly, Virginia. And there, before him, was incontrovertible evidence that nuclear material was being loaded onto the very Russian freighter everyone had been watching for many weeks, the one out of the port of Sevastopol on the Black Sea, the *Koryak*.

They'd watched the TELARs go aboard, they could watch the work being carried out on the hull, and they could see the big French road freighter standing by on the dock. They'd seen components being loaded into that. But now there was nuclear material, almost certainly warheads, judging by the shape.

They also had a couple of shots of two big metal boxes being loaded down the foredeck hatch. General Myers instantly hit the direct line to Admiral Mark Bradfield in the Pentagon.

The two men agreed on one shining truth—that Russian Naval officer, the one the FSB shot down in cold blood on Galkinskaya Street last September, had been right on the money with just about every piece of information he had provided.

0900, MONDAY, JANUARY 7

HQ SPECWARCOM
Coronado, California

Delta Team 10 was, as ever, at operational readiness for deployment for any task the US Navy elected to throw at them. From the moment their commander, Captain Mack Bedford, was reunited with them, every man could sense there was a new mission forthcoming and that it was something top secret, highly dangerous, and extremely important.

Mack had already decided to take as large a group as possible to Donegal, even if there was no room on board the attack ship for everyone to make it to the ops area. He had by now refined the personnel he required—the four-man diving team and a team of at least three medics who could be used as a reserve. He wanted a fifteen-man assault force to board the Russian ship and ten marksmen on board his own ship, all of whom could double as members of the assault force if necessary.

He would take a total of eight SEALs with prior experience in the surface navy. These men would assist the Irish crew in maneuvering the ship through the likely rough North Atlantic. All of these were hard-trained combat warriors, and they were ready at a moment's notice to step in as replacements or, possibly, reinforcements.

Mack knew the mission needed the forty-man team because it was hard to assess how many personnel would be on board the Russian freighter.

Mack reasoned there were only about thirty crew in the biggest oil tankers, so the *Koryak* should be around the same. But if there were a lot more Russians on board, that would represent big problems after the SEALs boarded—like Russian sailors, possibly with cell phones, locking themselves in rooms.

The principal objective of this mission was top secrecy. If these Russians were permitted to make phone calls home, the US Navy may as well bomb the goddamned ship, since one phone call home to Severomorsk meant the whole world would find out in the next twenty minutes. The more he pondered the personnel problem, on both ships, it seemed to Mack the more difficult this mission became.

Too many SEALs might mean chaos; too few might mean unnecessary death and mission failure. Team 10 would have to fight its way through the *Koryak*'s interior, and there would be enough danger from ricocheting bullets inside the steel hull without having to use high explosive to blast open steel doors in order to confiscate cell phones.

In any battle situation a lot of problems rise up unannounced and get solved on the spot. It was Captain Bedford's job to subdue and silence that Russian crew in the preplanned way, board and capture, destroy radio contact, every SEAL free to fire at will. All Russian guards on deck as the ships closed to be eliminated by SEAL marksmen the moment the lines were secured.

Right now what Team 10 needed was practice at boarding. If this operation went pear-shaped after the initial boarding, every team member would transform instantly into a fighting warrior. They would need to seize the grappling lines and scale the hull of the *Koryak* like a swarm of armed orangutans.

Mack was taking his tried and trusted SEAL leaders, guys he had known and fought with, the very heartbeat of Team 10. Several of them had grown up under his command. There was Barney Wilkes, from the salt marshes of North Carolina, who had joined him as a twenty-four-year-old petty officer/2, the best swimmer in Coronado. He was thirty now and, having passed Officers' Training School with brilliant grades, had become Lieutenant Barnaby Wilkes, team leader. He was also very handy with a machine gun and an RPG (rocket-propelled grenade).

Also going to Donegal was Cody Sharp, now thirty-seven, son of a North Dakota cattle rancher and a chief petty officer. Cody was formerly with SEAL Team 1 in Hawaii and had fought with Mack in Iraq. He was a gunner by trade and an exemplary boatman, the precise kind of seasoned SEAL leader you need when operating several hundred miles from shore in the North Atlantic.

A long-serving CPO, Brad Charlton, would also be going to Ireland. Mack Bedford never went anywhere without his right-hand man. Brad was now a master chief petty officer.

Shane Cannel had been with Mack for six years, first as a PO/2, but he would go to Donegal as a chief.

Mack's 2/IC would be a young officer who had fought with him in Somalia, Josh Malone, now a lieutenant commander. They went together to see Admiral Carlow, trying to get hold of an old merchant ship they could borrow for a couple of months' training, practicing their boarding techniques.

Admiral Carlow instantly put twenty men on the case, scouring the immediate southern California coastline for a suitable ship, calling shipping corporations, asking for help. Everyone knew, of course, that if the navy did not get it, the admiral would commandeer someone's freighter for a couple of months, with or without their blessing.

It took exactly four hours to find the ship. It was moored in a small harbor north of the Port of Long Beach. A five-thousand-ton freighter called *San Natale* had been plying the coast from California to Bogotá for many years, especially during the time the United States blacklisted Colombia for failing to curb its drug-growing activities.

The *Natale* was owned by an outfit called Panama Steamships and sailed under a Panamanian flag. It was probably the only ship in history that was suspected of smuggling bananas. But that was its mission in life, running ripe Colombian blacklisted bananas into California for the past thirty years.

When the Port of Long Beach authorities made contact, the captain of the ship was so terrified the United States might put him in jail for banana offenses from twenty years ago that he willingly handed the *Natale* over to the navy in return for a two-month charter fee.

Thus was Mack Bedford's trial horse floated in San Diego Bay in mid-January, when the weather was still warm but with a brisk wind gusting under the towering arc of the Coronado road bridge.

All forty members of the team had been briefed as to the requirements, but not provided with details of the actual target, nor indeed the location of the ops area. Admiral Carlow had also commandeered the three-thousand-ton US Coast Guard cutter *Bertholf,* a twin-shafted, fast twenty-eight-knot Legend Class vessel, which would "double" for the Irish ship they would use when the *Koryak* hove into sight.

On the opening morning of training, Mack sought out the ship's handlers to undergo the first detailed practice—bringing the *Bertholf* alongside the old banana boat, close aboard, and ready for lines to be attached, holding the ships together.

Mack's crew was then informed that the real ship they would use in the operation would be fitted with flooding tanks, which would heel her over to thirty-eight degrees during this exercise, giving the appearance of imminent sinking, a disaster about to happen.

For the first two days this was not possible, but coast guard engineers quickly organized something very similar, and a couple of passing yachtsmen, out in the ocean, did indeed believe the *Bertholf* was about to meet her doom, which Mack considered to be a "darned good sign" of the training authenticity.

There were a few SEALs who thought it likely the coast guard ship really would sink at this diabolical angle and jokingly asked permission to abandon. Which Mack impolitely declined.

It took four days out in the Pacific before they could comfortably approach the old freighter, cutting the engines back and drifting in with the wind and tide, several huge navy fenders made of synthetic rubber hung protectively over on the port side. Every time the *Bertholf* bumped the starboard-side hull of the freighter, six Navy SEALs hurled the grappling irons up and over the gunwales with expertise being honed daily both on-shore and at sea.

This skill, the bedrock of all pirate operations in the Indian Ocean, was hard to perfect, but for the SEAL assault force preparing to hit a Russian ship, it would be a matter of life and death. And this entire element of the forthcoming attack needed to be planned with precision, timing, athleticism, and marksmanship.

When those grappling irons grabbed and held, the SEALs in the upper works would open up with withering fire on any Russian who appeared on deck. The aim was to extinguish any attack on the climbers, still hauling themselves up the ropes, hopefully unseen by anyone still alive on the *Koryak*.

It took three weeks before Mack Bedford was confident that his team could hit that Russian ship with speed and ruthlessness. At this point he reduced oceangoing practice to every other day. This was especially welcome among those SEALs who had been seasick, tossing around out in the Pacific, and those who had managed to fall into the ocean off the side of the banana boat, four of them more than once.

Mack now designated every second day to the CQB (close-quarter battle) range, especially constructed inside the compound, wood rather than steel, but built to replicate the confined areas of an ex-Russian warship. This also led to intense fire-control drills, since any kind of a blaze after an explosion could jeopardize the entire operation.

The frogs who would place the limpet mines on the underside of the hull of the *Koryak* came under the command of Lieutenant Barney Wilkes, and they had already gone over the side of the *Bertholf* many times. But they too had much to practice. No one knew quite what the hull of the Russian freighter would look like, whether it would be covered in barnacles, impossible to make a limpet mine stick.

If this was the case, the SEAL divers would need their long combat knives to scrape a section clean in order to clamp the magnetic bomb base onto the steel. This is all very well in short sentences on dry land, but deep under the freezing Atlantic water, breathing carefully to conserve oxygen, being moved by the current, and working in the most uncomfortable environment—well, this wants a lot of concentration. SEALs need to know exactly what they are doing before going over the side.

There are only a very few people on this entire planet who would dream of taking on such a task. But one of the great SEAL mottoes is *For almost every fighting force, tackling water, ocean or river, is nothing short of a pain in the ass. For us, it's a haven.*

From the moment new applicants join a BUD/S class, they are plunged into the enormous Coronado pool and drilled for months on end, until swimming, diving, and working underwater are second nature to them. Pool Comp, it's called. And each of the three men who would accompany Barney Wilkes under the *Koryak* had finished class honor man in the underwater section.

Each of them had also been among the 11 or 12 men selected from an intake of around 165. They don't just take anyone into the US Navy's most elite fighting force. You need to finish in the top 8 percent to get through. And if you intend to be a frog commander, you probably need to make honor man underwater. And this coming mission was what they all came for—basic underwater demolition.

Throughout the Donegal training program, the frogs routinely checked their underwater gear, making sure everything was in top order, especially the diving tanks and the lines that provided them with air. When the nondiving group was in the close combat zone, the frogs moved to a specially constructed area under the hull of a boat and practiced every phase of their preparation.

Over and over, they unhooked the limpet mines from their backs, removed the bombs from their knapsack holders, and rammed them tight against the steel, checking the timers, examining the mechanism, ensuring there would be no mistakes when those lethal weapons clicked into place under the *Koryak*.

As they moved into the second month, they fired at targets daily: they practiced firing from the hip in narrow corridors with sharp turns, they climbed, they threw the grapplers, they ran, and they staged hard, close races in the huge SEAL pool. The days of accidents, even near accidents, were eliminated. No one broke an ankle, and no one else fell off the hull of the banana boat. No one nearly got shot; no one nearly drowned in the Pacific. Mack Bedford's men were almost ready.

The final phase, before departure for Ireland, involved drawing their equipment and storing it for transit—"packing down" in SEAL parlance. Each man was taking his personal weapons: combat knife, SIG Sauer

9mm pistol, and M4-A1 rifle, with three magazines, each holding thirty 5.56mm rounds. Packed in separate boxes was a thousand-round reserve.

They also took a couple of heavy weaps (machine guns) and ammunition belts. SEALs feel only half-dressed without the ever-present ability to blow the living hell out of someone, or something, should it be required.

In addition to the limpet mines, there were three M203 grenade launchers (including a spare), together with a box of sixty hand grenades, just in case they had to fight their way out against an overwhelmingly greater force. They took their regular medical kit, mostly bandages, dressings, and morphine. Plus communication gear, camouflage cream, and a couple of laptop computers with navigation software, showing shorelines, depths, rocks, sandbanks, early warnings for anything that might get in the way of the coming SEAL assault.

The specialist equipment, personally owned, was packed down separately . . . that's wet suits, diving tanks, air lines, goggles, and those big SEAL-grade flippers, which can propel an operator like Barnaby Wilkes through the water like a pent-up porpoise.

In the final days of training, Mack's senior men tried to assimilate the precise conditions they would meet as they drifted in toward the Russian freighter. But the difficulty was height. They had diagrams of the ship's interior, adapted from the priceless world almanac of ocean warfare, *Jane's Fighting Ships*. But they were uncertain about the precise distance above the water the *Koryak*'s stern rails would be. And the heaving surface of the Pacific was, at best, capricious.

The equation also involved the height of the Irish ship they would be aboard. Mack had put the entire Department of Naval Intelligence on the case, trying to ascertain whether the *Koryak* would be slightly above, or below, the high side of the heeled-over Irish patrol boat. But he doubted they could finalize any of these stats until they moved to the eastern end of Donegal Bay.

SEAL Team 10 flew to Ireland on March 10 in their regular turboprop aircraft, the giant C-13O Hercules freighter. The navy had already dropshipped twenty-four American-built vehicles from the port of Southampton in southern England to Dublin—a dozen Jeeps, four trucks, four vans, and four staff cars.

All of them had been driven across Ireland to the Donegal area, where an Irish body shop and repair service had worked for five nights, under the strictest cover, repainting and disguising anything that might suggest American military. The SUVs were all black with Irish license plates and insignia. The rest were resprayed in a variety of colors—silver, white, and blue—again with Irish plates.

Four vans drove down to Shannon Airport to await the arrival of the SEAL Hercules and then to transport all the gear back to Donegal. The SEALs themselves were traveling north in a luxury white Volvo bus, said to be the last word in "executive travel."

SEAL Team 10 drove down to the new complex just before lunch. Mack was tempted to take Lieutenant Commander Malone and drive over to the St. Ernan's House hotel for lunch. But he decided he had better get his team squared away as soon as possible. There were now four houses available, all of them renovated for the Irish government. This took care of the senior sixteen of the SEALs.

Brand new and constructed a couple of hundred yards along the shore, the first new accommodation block provided individual rooms for up to forty SEALs. It was set back but with views across the bay and contained a recreation room and large communal bathrooms on each of its two floors. The marine security guard was already ensconced in here. A separate "chow hall" had been built right behind the main jetty and was fully staffed by Irish caterers, with all supplies provided from the Bruckless village store.

The commanding officer of NAVFAC Donegal was Lieutenant Commander James Mills, who had flown in from Norfolk, Virginia, on short notice and was now resident in the newly renovated house vacated by Mr. and Mrs. Ronan O'Callaghan. But the bucolic view from their house was not what it once was.

Since the barges carrying the steel piles and sheet "walls" were already in place, the jetty construction corporation, under the auspices of Harris Pye of Dublin, had decided to build immediately the second jetty, 125 feet offshore from the new construction's seaward side, thus creating the narrow channel between the concrete jetties, which everyone wanted.

This entire area could be covered, and the holes for the roof girders were already in place. The result was one of the fastest covered docks ever built. Even before the completion of the floating dry dock, Harris Pye was constructing the side structures and the steel roof.

It was complete by mid-March. In under five months, a safe US Naval harbor had been built on the shores of Donegal, and there was no way any Russian satellite could peer down from space and ascertain what the Americans were doing. The deep water washed in so close to this part of the shore, it was unlikely they would ever see a prowling US submarine in the area.

US underwater boats could get within twelve hundred yards of the dock without surfacing and then make another four hundred yards at periscope depth. Which meant that even if the US submarines came in at only five knots, no Russian satellite had more than a six-minute window to hit a photographic target on which they had never been focused.

Mack Bedford could not believe his eyes at the transformation of this place since the first day of October. He could never claim it was made more beautiful, and in fact it was infinitely less beautiful, but there was a strong, functional aura about it.

The new harbor launch, a huge, red-and-black, disguised SEAL inflatable flown from Norfolk and trucked from Shannon, rode easily on her lines out between the jetties. Only the presence of two barges, anchored inshore and loaded with pilings and sheet steel to strengthen the foreshore, betrayed there was still work in progress along this once pristine land.

There was also shipping activity in Irish waters. The seventeen-hundred-ton *LÉ Róisín,* a lightly gunned Irish Navy coastal patrol ship, was currently buffeting her way through long, breaking seas off County Derry, past the Giant's Causeway, on the far northeastern corner of Ireland. At a steady fourteen knots, she was about halfway around the 260-mile north route from Dublin and was expected to dock on the brand-new main jetty, under the roof, in US NAVFAC Donegal, at around nine o'clock this evening.

The *Róisín* was the ship SEAL Team 10 would use to stop and then capture the Russian Navy's *Koryak,* as soon as clearance came through. At present she carried a crew of forty-four, six officers, but many of these were gunnery men, and personnel who were required only if a naval action was fought. This would be novel, since Ireland had never in its history fought such an engagement, at least not since they saw off a couple of Viking raiders in the Middle Ages.

With the arrival of their ship so imminent, Mack Bedford decided upon a thorough briefing of his full team starting in the afternoon. And there, in the accommodation block's recreation room, he assembled his forty personnel to explain the rudiments of the plan and why it was considered necessary.

They listened in silence as he unfolded the long saga of the forthcoming attack on the main building at Fort Meade. Several of them looked very surprised. It's hard to accept the grim reality of the Russian mind-set until it's made clear, chapter and verse, what they really stand for.

Mack told them about the spy who'd given his life for this mission. He told them how accurate Nikolai's data had been and how he had carried out this high-level spying task, with no consideration for his own safety, but out of concern for his own people, and the dangerous, impossible path down which Nikita Markova was leading them.

He described how Nikolai had been gunned down by the Russian Secret Service. And how the Mossad had done so much to reveal Russian intentions. He told Team 10 how Nikolai Chirkov's information had been pinpoint accurate at almost every turn in the road. And he told them how they, Team 10 alone, had been selected to smash Markova's plan.

He then explained the need for total secrecy and that the Russian freighter would be carrying the full complement of equipment for the attack on Fort Meade. But it must be taken out without anyone ever knowing, because it was critical the president of the United States must not be implicated.

Mack worked from a wide blackboard at the far end of the room, demonstrating how the Irish ship with the full team embarked would be fitted with an enormous flooding tank that would tilt them to almost forty degrees. At that moment they understood for the first time why they had trained as they had, off San Diego.

The *Róisín* was to act as if she were sinking, wallowing in the water, imploring someone to help them. Under international maritime law, any approaching ship, military or merchant, is obliged to steam immediately to the rescue. The Russians would have no choice, once they had received the SOS from the *Róisín*.

The SEAL ship would drift slowly in and wait for lines to be secured. They would immediately attack, capture the ship, and, with the aid of the crane fixed to their foredeck, lift two heavy lead boxes out of the *Koryak*'s hold, because in there were four nuclear warheads, photographed by the US satellite KH-11 several weeks ago.

The attack would be conducted on the precise lines they had practiced so many times off San Diego.

"How big's the *Koryak*?" asked one SEAL.

"Five thousand tons," replied Mack. "I am hoping it will feel exactly the same as that banana boat we worked with.

"Only one thing's changed. I have given a lot of thought to the advantages of a daytime attack, but I've concluded that it's better for us to attack at night, to achieve surprise. I am still open to suggestions from senior men, but I was swayed by the difficulty of (a) appearing to be in genuine distress in broad daylight and (b) trying to conceal our key groups of assault troops on the decks as we make our approach.

"I understand it would be much easier to see where the hell we're going in the daylight. But I am always drawn to the issue of the surprise attack. And it's much easier to achieve that at night. I think we'll get aboard more quickly and safely in the dark, and that gives us a great chance of imposing ourselves from the outset. Remember, the Russians will think they are just moving in to assist some sinking Irish boat when, suddenly, in the pitch-dark, they find themselves in the middle of a sea battle.

"That surprise element is critical—it gains us the initiative. Tomorrow morning you'll see two big searchlights being fixed onto the Irish boat's upper works. As soon as we attack, those lights will switch on and blind anyone on the *Koryak*'s deck. We'll have a man on each light, so we can get light where we need it and use it as a weapon when we don't. Our marksmen will provide covering fire to the assault party, while we climb the hull, hopefully not too high."

"You coming with us, sir, up the side of the ship?"

"Sure I am. If I'm not there, you might fall in the friggin' Atlantic," said Mack.

Everyone laughed, remembering that the guy who had asked the question had fallen straight into the water the first time they scaled the rusting old beam of the banana boat.

"We'll have two fire teams, sited separately on the upper deck, where they will remain throughout the contact phase. They will each be armed with their M4s. But we cannot yet tell whether the marksmen will face a sparsely populated deck or a more substantial defense force. We'll decide that on the night. Each fire team will hold one grenade launcher, and both teams will come under the command of Chief Sharp."

The tall SEAL gunner from the Badlands of South Dakota gave a little half salute in confirmation.

"There will be two further four-man teams on the railings," said Mack. "They come under the command of Chief Cannel, and in position throughout the approach phase. They will all be wearing long, hooded oil-skin coats and be ready to help secure the boat alongside the Russian ship. Under those coats they will be in full combat gear, rifles slung around their necks. They should be ready to use those weapons the moment the situation warrants it.

"Should the opening assault force secure the Russian ship quickly, Chief Cannel's men will withdraw into the shadows—his first team will remain on call as a reserve, to be used as and when required, or to provide medical support if needed.

"The remaining team will go below, change into their diving gear, and wait for the moment to go over the side, under the command of Lieutenant Barney Wilkes.

"Remember, no one's going into the water before the Russian ship is secured and the nuclear material has been removed. Even then, the divers do not go in until the lines are off and the *Róisín* has retreated maybe thirty or forty yards.

"This is a vital safety measure. If there were any kind of accident, and the *Koryak* blew up, we do not want to be attached to her. Agreed?"

All forty SEALs signaled their mass approval, punctuated by a few *Hell, no*s, and a couple of *Fuck that*s.

Mack concluded his talk with two further warnings. The first was the importance of getting those four nuclear warheads off the Russian ship and onto the *Róisín*.

"The NSA believes we're gonna find 'em in two big metal boxes. I have pictures. But we cannot leave them aboard and then blow up the ship. If anyone found out we'd dumped a half-ton of uranium 235 in the middle of the Atlantic, there'd be all hell for young and old. Guys, we gotta find it and find it quick. I'll show everyone the pictures later."

"Sir?" asked one young SEAL. "Are you saying we hoist the boxes with the warheads inside or get the warheads out and leave the boxes behind?"

"That's a good question, kid," replied Mack. "Especially since I don't know the answer. But I do think it will come down to weight. Those boxes are probably lead, or at least lead lined. And that stuff's heavy.

Master Chief Brad Charlton will be in command in the *Koryak*'s hold, so he'll decide.

"My own instinct is to get the warheads out. That way we can lift them over to the *Róisín* one at a time. If we leave them packed, the weight will double, maybe triple . . . We don't want to break the fucking crane, right?"

Mack Bedford had a way with a phrase that always touched a laughter button with his men. Partly out of the oncoming stress, and partly out of genuine amusement, they gave him a spontaneous *"HOO-YAH, CAPTAIN MACK!"*

Mack's final point was equally serious—the problem of close-quarter fire inside the ship and the danger of engaging their own men by failing to recognize them in the dark. "That's one reason you must maintain tight fire control at all times, because in this Russian ship, belowdecks, we'll have a real problem with ricocheting bullets, so don't loose off ten rounds when one will do it.

"I do understand it's likely to be more difficult in the dark, and it will take us longer. But in terms of safety and victory, we wanna go in at night.

"In addition, all members of the assault teams will wear helmets with special mounted lights at all times. These are being constructed in Dublin right now and will be with us by tomorrow night. In the *Koryak* environment we have the beginnings of mass confusion. Remember, we are taking out the radio, satellite communications, electronic masts, and the entire comms system, if we can get at it.

"During this time we may hit a main electric circuit or any other power point. That's just a hazard of our trade. Those helmet beams will be valuable to us, showing the way and lighting up both the enemy and our own guys. If anyone's interested, they were personally designed and ordered for us by Admiral Arnold Morgan."

At least five *"WOW!"*'s could be heard in the hall. "When they arrive, you will also see each helmet contains a built-in radio and ultraslim microphone," said Mack. "That will enable any man to communicate with any other individual, anytime during the operation. You'll be issued with small cell phones, and you just punch in the first couple of letters of anyone's name.

"It's quick and simple. You hit *CH* and you'll hear, 'Chief Charlton,' right inside your helmet. *CA* gets Shane. *SH* gets Cody. *BE* gets me. And remember, *BE* also stands for 'bedlam,' and that's what it's likely to be. But

I know you guys, and you'll stay cool. Just remember your training, and, when you have to, shoot to kill.

"Questions?"

Silence, as expected. All SEALs think that kind of pontification is for the lower orders (anyone who's not a SEAL). They pride themselves on getting it the first time. And they believe their commanders have told them all that they need to know. If you're confused after a brilliant briefing by Captain Mack Bedford, go work in a bank or somewhere where the pace is slower. That's the philosophy.

Their creed, preoperational, is curt: *This is no place for men in short pants. In the next few weeks every one of us will put his life on the line for the United States of America. We don't have weak links. And we don't have guys who need to ask damn fool questions.*

THE FOLLOWING DAY, TUESDAY, MARCH 12

Quayside, NAVFAC Donegal

The Irish patrol ship *Róisín* rose and fell on her lines, moored alongside Jetty Number 1, beneath the steel roof of the covered dock. Not even a local passerby could see her. You needed to be in a boat out in the bay to get a look at her, and even then identification was more or less impossible. And the sudden appearance in the bay of an Irish Coast Guard cutter, appearing to guard St. John's Point, was a somewhat off-putting presence.

There was a small group of SEALs all wearing civilian clothes on the dock, talking to the Irish Naval CO, Commander Joe Farrell. The issue here was how many of the Irish crew would accompany the Americans on the mission. There had been an edict from the Irish government that the navy should provide all possible assistance to the US Special Forces.

However, the Irish Navy, like the rest of the armed forces, had always been neutral in any conflict involving a foreign enemy. The truth was, Commander Farrell's crew had not signed up to engage in some kind of bloodbath in the middle of the Atlantic with a boatload of mad, homicidal Russian nuclear scientists.

Commander Farrell said he would ask his men for volunteers, but that Captain Bedford would have to explain to them precisely what the mission entailed. Meanwhile, the SEALs offered him six or eight sailors to occupy critical positions in the *Róisín*'s crew, helming and navigation, during the approach and contact phases.

Commander Farrell was more than glad to have them and said he would work on a final crew list sometime in the next twenty-four hours. He would command his ship throughout the mission.

He suggested the Americans come out for a trip down the bay later, to familiarize themselves with the ship and to work alongside other members of the crew. Right now there was a team of engineers aboard, fixing four heavy tanks down the starboard side below the waterline, so they could be flooded with seawater. They were also fixing pressure pumps to get rid of the ballast when they started for home.

He'd given thought to the problem of accommodation and had the ship's small gymnasium emptied to provide space for sleeping. He intended to dispense with half of his crew and to find room for all of the forty SEALs.

He wanted to know if Mack thought they would need the mounted gun on the foredeck, but the SEAL boss thought not, as there would be plenty of American firepower on board, and the sight of that mounted weapon might be like a red sheet to a bull in the opening moments of the attack. Mack thought the *Róisín* should look like a stricken and harmless vessel for as long as possible.

"Are you restricted to small arms, Mack?" asked Farrell.

"No," he replied. "We have a couple of heavy machine guns, which we do not intend to use except in a dire emergency. I would, however, like to have them mounted up there, firing from our port side directly at the *Koryak*'s upper deck. I might use one of them to blast their comms mast if the circumstances are right. Otherwise, we'll slam in with an RPG.

"I just don't want to alert the whole fucking ship too early. The guys've got to have the best possible shot at getting on board, and it's not going to help them by making a diabolical din before the Russians know what's hit them."

"No, I see that," said Commander Farrell. "May I assume you've done some of this stuff before?"

"Coupla times," said Mack.

"I was getting that impression." He grinned. "You want to go aboard now, and we'll find a spot for your heavy guns?"

"Good plan," said the SEAL commander. "I'd like 'em high and out of the way, difficult to see."

"No problem. I'll have the water guys fix 'em up, soon as they get done with the tanks."

With that, the two commanding officers headed up the gangway to the Irish warship. Mack Bedford cast his mind back to that late-September day, only six months ago, when first he had chugged down the bay in company with Michael O'Malley.

He'd checked the water depth every few yards, and he'd swum through the clear waters, examining the undersea terrain. And the Royal Navy's Admiralty chart of the seabed had shown him that this was indeed the ideal spot for US Naval Base Donegal.

This was the tiny spot on the map where President Nikita Markova's grandiose plans for world supremacy would begin to crumble.

11

They trained in secret all along that lonely stretch of Donegal coast, running in formation at night. Prime Minister McGrath ordered the N15 road along the shore under police control at 2:00 every morning. With three patrol cars holding up traffic and escorting the very occasional late-night local car home, the SEALs were hardly seen by anyone.

In the daylight they underwent the traditional iron regime of push-ups, and despite the coldness of the water they ran in pairs, splashing through the shallows along a lonely part of the shore, which was now virtually inaccessible because of the base.

Every other day selected groups went out in *Róisín* for a couple of hours, familiarizing themselves with the layout of the ship, standing in tight formation in the precise spots they would occupy when they foundered into the attack, the boat listing heavily to starboard, tanks flooded, SOS signals flashing, rifles and grapplers at the ready, SEAL marksmen at Action Stations.

It continued, day after day, night after night, every man maintaining a level of fitness and strength beyond the comprehension of ordinary mortals, more on the level of a Bengal tiger than a human being. There's a compulsory exercise all SEALs undergo called a straight pull-up, where the man grasps an iron bar fixed above his head. A normal fit man in his twenties or thirties might do two of these, possibly three, pulling himself up until his chin rises above the bar. A trained athlete might do eight, or maybe nine. SEALs do thirty-four, minimum. As previously mentioned, they are not like other people.

The vagaries of Russian intentions were beginning to wear on everyone as March turned into April, and US surveillance was still observing the *Koryak* moored alongside in Severomorsk. The electronics truck from Lyon, France, was now aboard, along with the TELARs and the warheads. They had watched the ship being supplied, with crates of food, drinks, weaponry, and most likely clothing.

The *Koryak* would be traveling from a bitterly cold northern Russian spring, nine thousand miles directly to the tropics. If US intel was accurate, the voyage would take twenty-eight days, from the Murmansk Inlet to the great port of Cristóbal at the Atlantic end of the Panama Canal. This superefficient harbor comes under the Panama Port Authority, in association with the Chinese-owned corporation that administers it.

The Russian ship was then scheduled to make its way up through the three giant canal locks, across the Gatun waterway's tropical forest, and on through the narrows of "the Cut" to the port of Balboa, where the Lyon Generateur l'Électronique truck would disembark, along with the "jamming" staff, in search of the US president's nuclear football.

But the calm of the huge navy yard's northern dockside area remained undisturbed through the first three days of April, except for a heavy snowfall, which required a convoy of snowplows to clear the jetties.

On the evening of April 4, however, shortly before midnight, US satellites picked up an unusual number of lights on the dockside where the *Koryak* was moored. The poor weather obscured visibility, but one satellite picked up at least eight uniformed Russian Naval officers moving on and off the ship. Unknown to the Americans, Admiral Ustinov had issued an order so all-encompassing it not only achieved Russian purpose, but achieved American purpose as well.

Admiral Ustinov had banned cell phones from being used by anyone aboard the ship—and that included Captain Gromyko, the entire rocket-launching staff, the ship's crew, the electronic technicians going to Colorado, drivers, cooks, and deckhands. The admiral understood that one careless phone call home to Russia could cause a forest fire of information—*the Russians are staging a nuclear strike against the United States.* That was a chance he could not take, and officers stood by, on the dockside, as every cell phone was handed over.

The *Koryak* would be without personal communications, and the only way to make contact was through the ship's main comms center, which had been expensively transferred ten yards forward from its own room to the bridge, where Captain Gromyko and his second officer were personally responsible for every word spoken. The entire system was encrypted; every call was hooked up to a recording device and permanently connected to a direct satellite link to Northern Command HQ.

No ship had ever traveled in such silence, so cut off from the outside world. Aside from the regular ship-to-shore radio system to harbormasters, docking facilities, and coast guard call centers, there would be no contact with anyone, all the way to the Panama port of Cristóbal. There was just one cell phone on board, and that was locked in a desk drawer on the bridge, and only the commanding officer had the key. Only in the event of a dire and life-threatening emergency was he authorized to use it.

The US satellite could photograph the crowded dockside activity clearly enough. But the angle from space was not quite good enough to pick up the navy commander in chief, Admiral Vitaly Rankov, and the Northern Fleet C-in-C, Admiral Alexander Ustinov, who were both there.

Neither could the satellite see them on the bridge saying farewell to Kapitan Sergei Gromyko and his staff. When they finally left and stood back on the dockside to watch the departure, Admiral Ustinov perceived his ultimate boss, the former Olympic oarsman Vitaly Rankov, was in the best possible spirits. He was treating this stupendous international mission as if it were a sports game.

"This, Alexander," said the admiral from southern Russia, "is probably the world's ultimate power play." Ustinov knew enough about Admiral Rankov's near-fanatical devotion to Russian ice hockey to recognize the warm glow of certain victory that dwelt within him.

"The power play, Alexander," he said determinedly, "when you have the big advantage, when your opponents cannot match you. That's when it matters. That's when you strike."

All Admiral Ustinov knew about "power plays" was that they happened when one team on the ice had an extra player or two . . . and needed to turn on the heat. He wasn't at all sure that Rankov was correct about the Americans being shorthanded. But if the idea made the C-in-C happy, then that was just fine.

Even as Admiral Ustinov pondered the intricacies of the power play,

KH-11 was still whispering through space, snapping the *Koryak,* over and over, for the Americans. Recording the wide Russian tugboat, pulling her off the dock and turning her north, out toward the icy Barents Sea, bound for the Panama Canal.

The American surveillance system was on high alert, as it had been for weeks, and the data from KH-11 whipped into the satellite grid and flashed down to the National Surveillance Office, Chantilly. It was 4:50 p.m. in Washington. General Myers sounded the alarm to both the NSA in Fort Meade and to the office of the CNO in the Pentagon. Within moments Admiral Bradfield had Admiral Carlow on the line in Coronado, and the message was flashed instantly to Captain Bedford in Donegal:

Captain Bedford NAVFAC Donegal. Russian freighter Koryak *(heavy) cleared Severomorsk 2345 (local), Thursday, April 4. Now headed northwest three-one-five, at 14 knots, Barents Sea. 70.29N 34.00E. Satellite tracking—* Koryak *ETA latitude 55, 230 miles west of Arranmore Island, Donegal, 2100, Wednesday, April 10. Carlow.*

It was a little after ten o'clock in the Donegal SEAL compound, and Mack saw no point waking everyone on this Thursday night when no one was going anywhere until next Wednesday. The *Koryak* was almost six days away, buffeting through the notoriously rough Barents Sea in deep water, off the far-north coast of Norway.

The Russians had almost two thousand miles still to cover, and the *Koryak* would be well in the sights of US surveillance all the way. Mack and his team were trained to the minute for this. Mack would have a conference with Commander Farrell in the morning, and he'd give the guys the weekend off, since there was no way the Russian ship could get anywhere near them until next week.

Wednesday night was the very earliest they could make contact. They'd store the ship on Monday and Tuesday with fresh produce and water. Departure time: 0600, Wednesday. ETA ops area: 1800 hours, same day. Contact *Koryak:* 2100.

Time was on Mack's side because the *Róisín* was a fast patrol boat, highly streamlined, and even in a heavy sea would cut through the water at twenty knots, all the way out to meet the killer freighter from the North.

While the Russian freighter fought its way over vast ocean depths, south past the endless islands and fjords of the twelve-hundred-mile Norwegian coastline, Team 10 tried to relax. The SEALs were thousands of miles from home and still in lockdown mode, since the mission was imminent. They had not been permitted phone calls, e-mails, or any contact with the outside world, so highly classified was the project.

They spent Sunday night watching movies and eating pizza, sent in hot from the Bruckless village store. On Monday they went back to work, helping with the final organization of the ship. They were also packing up their personal gear. When they pulled out of Donegal Bay at first light Wednesday morning, they were not coming back.

Not one of them truly understood the escape plan. And the prospect of rampaging into an armed Russian vessel, capturing it, ransacking it for its most valuable cargo, and then sinking the bastard, was quite sufficient to occupy the minds of most of them.

Mack Bedford received a computer printout of the route taken by the *Koryak* every day from the NSA via Admiral Carlow's office. The mission had been planned as well as any mission ever could be. They went to bed early on Tuesday night and were awakened by Cody Sharp and Barney Wilkes at 0430.

Every man, carrying only his personal knapsack, reported to the *Róisín,* where Captain Farrell and Mack Bedford were already on the quay. Mack took the roll call himself, and SEAL Team 10 was officially embarked at 0530. Right on time, 0600, they pulled off Jetty Number 1, into the sunrise, leaving behind the roofed dock and the little villages they had never really seen.

No one saw them leave; there were no cheerful ships' horns or farewell waves as they stood fair down the channel to outer Donegal Bay. There was an element of sadness to the entire scene, as the unknown warriors from Coronado set off on their mission to put the world back on its proper axis, safe once more from the ravings of the unbalanced Russian president.

Some of these Americans may die, others may be shot or otherwise injured, but no one in the villages of Killybegs, Dunkineely, Bruckless, Inver, and Mountcharles would ever know who they were, or that this naval facility had been built in Ireland, essentially for them.

In years to come, in times less stressful, members of SEAL Team 10 would perhaps visit and sample the Guinness and the local salmon and the Irish whiskey and maybe even fish the local rivers gushing out of the

Donegal mountains. But today, the visitors from California were going to war, and no one knew. Or ever would. That was the stark and deadly nature of their business.

There was a chill in the air as they pushed on west, running close to the north shore, out past Carrigan Head. The *Róisín* was a good ship in this short, choppy sea, made less freezing by the ever-present western tides of the Gulf Stream.

Right now Mack Bedford plotted the *Koryak* some 180 miles north of the fifty-fifth parallel and still steaming on an unvarying course, straight through the GIUK Gap, and picked up electronically by the brand-new SOSUS listening station, which was dug hard into the hillside on land a half mile before St. John's Point.

This was a low building on the windward side of the peninsula, where only the roof and a few aerials could be seen from the road. It was staffed by ten US Navy electronic technicians, radar and sonar, and they lived as civilians in the Central Hotel, Donegal Town, their work so secret not even Mack Bedford knew of their existence or of their building.

The US SOSUS men reported all contacts and findings directly to the NSA, Maryland. If Admiral Alexander Ustinov, back in Severomorsk, had known how much these intercept experts knew about the *Koryak,* he would probably have shot himself, just to dispense with the oncoming grief.

The *Róisín* was 6 miles south of the fifty-fifth parallel, pushing west about 180 miles from the ops area. The weather was overcast with a hard sou'wester gusting across the ocean. But the horizon looked very gloomy, and Captain Farrell thought it might "rain like the blazes, before we're much older."

The sea was iron gray in color, but the wind proved a blessing, blowing the distant storm system away to the north and leaving the surface relatively calm, choppy but still easy going for the *Róisín.*

Mack's main preoccupation remained the battle for control of the Russian ship's interior. He was certain his SEALs would conduct the assault phase of the operation impeccably, getting aboard and taking out any Russian personnel on the decks.

The next phase was the difficulty, because the companionways inside the *Koryak* were narrow, too enclosed for four-man SEAL teams to work. The teams would need to split in two, working in pairs, moving forward to the front of the ship, covering each other, firing very deliberate shots at any target in their sight.

Mack's fear had been, and remained, the danger of loose bullets ricocheting off the steel walls of the hull and hitting his guys. The last thing the SEAL commander needed was wounded men, lying in the ship's passageways, needing to be evacuated before they could enter the final phases of the operation.

He called a briefing right after lunch and once more tried to evaluate the forthcoming mission inside the ship. "Look," he told them, "the big sections of the operation, capturing the bridge and taking the hold, seizing the nuclear warheads and getting them out of there, well . . . that's all out in the open, and clear to everyone.

"It's those fucking companionways that bother me, and I can't stress too much how careful the first assault troops need to be. Their job is to clear the way, to intimidate the Russians, take out anyone who gets in the way, and carve out a path for our attacking troops to charge through and get control of the bridge and the cargo hold."

Mack talked to the men who would scale the hull on the grappling irons. Once aboard, they must regroup and then advance slowly through the passages, two at a time, with special care at the corners, opening every door and tossing in a hand grenade to stun or wound.

"Your meticulous work will decide whether this mission succeeds or fails," he said. "So don't, for Christ's sake, leave any cabin unchecked. Clear the way for the complete capture of the *Koryak,* and then fall back to guard what you've done and keep the escape route open, just so we all get off safely."

At this point one of the junior team members, a twenty-three-year-old already assigned to the opening assault group going up the side of the ship on the knotted ropes and grapplers, asked, "Sir, are you in the first climbing party, soon as the ships are secured together?"

"Correct, Charlie. I'm going up the ropes with you four guys. At the top, I peel off and organize the safety of the ropes on the rails, and then I fix and drop down two more rope ladders that I'll carry up the hull with me."

"Jesus, sir. They're heavy."

"Tell me about it."

Mack then described the SEAL Command Center, which would be on the bridge of the *Róisín*. "Lieutenant Commander Josh Malone will be in there. As the mission moves ahead, he'll be the only man who knows where everyone is. He'll have an assistant, our comms guy, Robbie Damon, and that's where you check in . . . Punch in *CC* on your phone, report your name and position, and then state your problem.

"Josh will also man the heavy machine gun in an emergency. Captain Farrell has it rigged on the port side of the bridge aimed at the Russian ship."

By 1700 the *Róisín* was still cutting through the water at twenty knots and was now within 24 miles of the ops area. Hour by hour Mack Bedford was receiving satellite communications direct from the NSA, pinpointing the precise position of the *Koryak* as it steamed south down the Atlantic.

It was four hours from the fifty-fifth line of latitude—56 miles. Sometime during the next sixty minutes it would show up on the new, high-powered American radar screen on the *Róisín*'s bridge, specially fitted under orders of the Irish prime minister, under heavy urging from Admiral Morgan.

The two men had become good friends, and Neil McGrath loved his knowledge, particularly enjoying the bewilderment of his own colleagues when he displayed deep understanding of naval warfare.

The cooks prepared sirloin steaks for everyone at 1830, and immediately afterward, Mack Bedford and Captain Farrell went to take a long look at the position of the approaching Russian freighter. Her speed and course remained steady, and Mack's graph showed she had been holding course southwest, ever since she'd angled slightly away from the mountainous southern peninsula of Norway.

Koryak had left the Faroe Islands 45 miles to starboard, with the Shetlands 150 miles to port. She'd pressed on past the remote and mysterious jutting hunk of granite named Rockall (83 feet long), at which point she was 162 miles west of County Donegal.

At 1900, she was less than 30 miles from what Mack believed would be the datum—55.00N 13.48W; 190 miles due south of the Rockall rise. *Róisín*, heading in dead-slow now on an east-northeast course, was a mere 4 miles out, and now it was clear the Russian ship, at this speed, would cross the bow of the Irish patrol boat about 3 miles ahead, a little more than two hours from now.

Captain Farrell ordered the buoyancy tanks to flood down, and the sea valves were opened at 1910. They increased speed slightly and began to make a racetrack pattern, before moving slowly forward toward the datum. Captain Bedford was watching the approach of the *Koryak* on the screen and resolved to do nothing until darkness fell shortly after 2000.

The boat went to Action Stations at 2030 with the Russians still 10 miles from the datum and *Róisín* now less than 2 miles away.

At 2040 the Irish patrol boat, now wallowing forward at a thirty-degree angle as the tanks grew ever heavier on the starboard side, issued an urgent SOS distress signal to all shipping in the area.

The ship's radio officer opened up the 500kHz radio frequency used for distress signals and began the time-honored Morse code sequence—SOS (. . . – – – . . .) *dit-dit-dit-daah-daah-daah-dit-dit-dit*—all run together, an unmistakable sound in any comms room, the *only* Morse signal with *nine* elements.

Immediately, he broadcast a full signal: *SOS—SOS—SOS—This is Irish cutter* LÉ Róisín—*PSN 50.00N 13.48W—Ship holed starboard side after engine room explosion—Sinking fast—Will abandon in thirty minutes—One lifeboat damaged badly. AR and K. Dit-dit-dit-daah-daah-daah-dit-dit-dit.*

On the other radio transmitter the *Róisín* operator sent out a Mayday signal, again to all shipping in the area, calling out the old French phrase—from *M'aidez!* (Help me!), dating back to the days when French was the international language in the early twentieth century—*MAYDAY! . . . MAYDAY! . . . MAYDAY!*

In the comms area of the *Koryak* (the back wall of the bridge), the signal came through loud and clear. But with a ship carrying illegal nuclear warheads, Captain Sergei Gromyko was not overjoyed at going to anyone's rescue. But he understood clearly that if anyone ever found out he had totally ignored a distress signal from a sinking vessel a few miles away, he would probably be jailed for twenty years in an international court of law and never be granted license to command any ship ever again.

If there's one cardinal sin in international shipping, it's to turn a blind eye to fellow mariners in peril. Hardly anyone has ever tried it. No one has ever got away with it. Kapitan Gromyko instantly ordered his engines all ahead, course now more southerly. The *Koryak* accelerated to the aid of the "stricken" Irish Navy patrol boat.

Night falls very quickly in the northeastern Atlantic, and it was pitch-dark, under lowering skies, as the two ships steered onto an intersecting course. In broad daylight the *Koryak* could probably have picked up the Irish ship on the horizon at around seven miles. It was no more difficult in the dark, but the distance would be a lot closer before the Russians could pick up the Irish running lights.

Gromyko's lookout was seeking a port-side red off their port bow at around three miles. He planned to knock off the first seven miles in a little less than twenty-five minutes, which should give his crew time to start the rescue before the Irish ship went down. Also, he was carrying lifeboats for more crew than he had on board, and he had the deck crew immediately begin preparations to lower away as soon as they made contact.

In one way, Kapitan Gromyko found the entire exercise a gigantic pain in the ass, but another part of his brain was telling him, this was no bad thing. In time everyone would know the merciful Russian freighter had steamed to the rescue in the middle of the Atlantic and heroically saved a stricken Irish crew.

His ship would be known and remembered for that mission of mercy, and that would surely put off interfering US customs officials from giving him a hard time. With his radio operator announcing, in English, that the five-thousand-ton Russian freighter was making all speed toward the sinking ship, he raised his night-vision Red Army binoculars and stared straight ahead, out of the wide bridge windows. His pale-blue eyes scanned through the darkness for the red running light he knew was out there, somewhere.

The Irish radio operator called over to Captain Bedford, almost unrecognizable in his combat gear, face blacked up with cammy cream and his green-and-brown camouflage-colored bandanna, the headgear SEALs fondly describe as their "drive-on rag."

"Sir, they got the signal," called the operator. "Russian freighter *Koryak* making all speed dead toward. We should pick up red-and-green running lights in about ten minutes."

Mack Bedford punched the air with delight. That signal represented the one part of this mission over which he had no control. He could order the SOS to be broadcast over and over, but there was nothing, repeat *nothing,* he could do if the Russian CO chose to ignore it.

"Beautiful," he said.

The SEALs were at *Action Stations!* Chief Sharp had the marksmen in two strict teams of four, strategically placed on the upper decks, facing out over the high port side. The boat was rocking and rolling in the choppy sea, and everyone knew the task of the gunners was way beyond the capabilities of ordinary troops. But these men had trained for literally thousands of hours, as no other combat troops on earth.

At 2110 the *Koryak* spotted the Irish cutter and made radio contact. At the same time, Mack Bedford's two SEALs on the bow spotted the lights of the Russian ship. Mack told the operator to speak in English and to inform the Russians they should slow down to ten knots and the *Róisín* would limp forward at five knots.

At the RV point, could they turn to the northeast? That way the Irish cutter would attempt to come in, high port side to the Russian starboard, and hook up. They had lines, big fenders, and plenty of crew. If the Russians could just help secure the ships together, they could evacuate before *Róisín* finally went down.

Kapitan Gromyko's operator sent a confirming message. The SEAL team could see the big Russian freighter up ahead, well lit and moving slowly. Captain Farrell immediately observed that she was not particularly high in the water, more a result of her old-fashioned Russian design than cargo weight.

In fact, in Joe Farrell's estimation, the ships would close together with only about five feet difference in height, from *Róisín*'s rails to *Koryak*'s big cleats. This would make a major difference to Mack Bedford's opening assault party, which was prepared, if necessary, to rope-climb twenty feet to the point where their grappling hooks gripped the dark-blue rails on the Russian hull.

At this moment the climbers were well hidden in the shadows of the upper works, but they wore their helmets, the ones with the lights and radios, and their M4s were slung over their backs. The six men charged with securing the lines were now dressed in their oilskins, with four of them positioned aft and two for'ard.

The first moment the ships were locked together, all six would retreat into the shadows and cast off their foul-weather coats. Four of them, the Special Forces frogs, would move inside to pull on their wet suits, ready for the dive under the hull to fix the limpet mines.

The other two would stand in reserve to assist the attack party at a moment's notice, but, for the first twenty minutes of the assault, they would prepare one end of the crew dining room as a hospital, fixing cots and

laying out bandages, dressings, blood transfusion bottles, sterile hypoder-
mics, and morphine.

The two SEALs designated to work the searchlights were already in
place, dressed in full combat gear and helmets, ready, if required, to climb
the rope ladders and join the fight. This may seem like detailed planning
to the umpteenth degree. But to SEALs, this is a way of life. They are
trained to fight every day if necessary, and they know precisely what to do
at each stage of the battle: *to move forward, to fall back (rare), to provide
covering fire for the assault leaders, to engage the enemy, to search, rescue, attack.* It's all second nature to them.

The avowed creed and philosophy of the Navy SEALs are not carried
into combat in any handbook, or set of rules, because that would be su-
perfluous. It's written, in letters of pure gold, on their hearts:

*I will never quit. I persevere and thrive on adversity. My nation expects me
to be physically harder and mentally stronger than my enemies. If knocked
down, I will get back up, every time. I will draw on every remaining ounce of
strength to protect my teammates and to accomplish our mission. I am never
out of the fight.*

Thus, Mack Bedford's SEAL Team 10 stood poised for action, in the
shadows, weapons primed, certain of their personal tasks, certain of their
mission, and certain of their duty to their nation. They were enormous
men in every sense, including the iron master chief, Brad Charlton, who
stood "only" five feet, ten inches, but whose men would follow him into
the fires of hell.

Right now he had his left arm slightly raised, signaling absolute still-
ness, until the moment when they all charged for the grappling lines and
rope ladders and then toward the freighter's for'ard hold, where the nuclear warheads were hidden.

Slowly, the two ships closed together, Captain Farrell on the helm of
the *Róisín,* edging the heeled-over cutter forward, along *Koryak*'s starboard hull, until they were almost aft to aft. The two sets of seamen were
facing each other, and the Russians were waving, although this gesture of
friendship was not returned, mostly because the Americans were nervous
about dropping their light machine guns in the middle of the joyous
greeting.

"STAND BY FOR THE LINES!" yelled the Irish boatswain, staring
across the few feet of ocean that separated the two ships. Together all six

lines were thrown, grabbed, and cleated off on the big cast-iron fittings on the *Koryak*'s main decks.

Mack Bedford swiftly counted a total of six working deckhands, and there must be a couple more up for'ard, the guys who had caught the lines. He could also see two seamen at the aft end of one of the upper decks. No one else.

He hit the buttons on his cell, just *SH,* and Chief Sharp answered instantly. "I got six aft," said Mack. "And there's gotta be two for'ard. See those two guys on that upper deck? I think that's all. Ten total."

"Roger that, boss," replied Cody.

He immediately sent one of his marksmen to deal with *Koryak*'s foredeck, and only four more seconds elapsed before Mack Bedford's right arm, briefly illuminated by a spotlight, swept downward, and the devastating SEAL attack opened up.

High above, the two big searchlights burst into life and sent a brutal beam straight into the eyes of the Russian deckhands.

Chief Sharp's sharpshooters opened fire and gunned down all six of them in the aft area. Up front, a single SEAL gunner hit both Russians on the foredeck, and Cody's Assault Group 1 cut down the two sailors on duty in the upper works.

Simultaneously, the grappling irons flew across the narrow waterway between the ships and clanked onto the high railings. The opening SEAL assault group, led by Mack himself, tested the knotted ropes for strength and then swung through the air like acrobats, the soles of their feet slamming into the hull with a dull and decisive thud, as precise as any corps de ballet, but a bit heavier and not quite so graceful.

"FUCK!" growled one of them, scraping his knee on the hull, but then his boots gripped the knot, and with two heaves he was up and over, standing on the *Koryak*'s deck surrounded by dead Russian sailors and lining up with his three fellow climbers.

Without a word they raced for the aft entrance to the fo'c'sle, leaving the boss to check the grappling irons and then throw each rope back to the waiting members of Assault Group 2. Mack tightened the special cast-steel shackles he'd brought with him to attach two new rope ladders to the rail posts, and he tossed them, too, to the waiting SEAL climbers.

A half minute later he had a total of ten combat warriors on board the *Koryak,* and once more he pulled up the grappling ropes and threw them down to the final six climbers, one of whom, Mack's bodyguard, would remain with him while the others fanned out and helped to capture the ship. This was a very dangerous time because it was not possible to ascertain how many Russians now knew they had a hostile enemy force on board.

At this point the two big SEAL searchlights were scanning the aft deck, while the fifteen-strong huddle of SEALs awaited final orders from Mack. Swiftly, the team commander joined them and ordered them inside the ship, taking the port and starboard doors into the passageways.

Simultaneously, Mack went through to Command Center and ordered the *Koryak*'s comms system destroyed. Two RPGs ripped across the deck and smashed into the radio masts, including the giant air-surface search radar. Chief Sharp himself could still see another mast jutting into the night sky, and while he was uncertain what it was supposed to do, he slammed it anyway, with another RPG, magnificently aimed.

Also, from Cody's vantage point, it seemed the outside lights, all over the fo'c'sle, could not possibly be doing anyone any good except the Russians, who could see from anywhere their ship was under a heavy and murderous attack. There must have been a dozen areas that were brightly lit, illuminating secret places, and spilling light out, all over the place.

He ordered his SEAL marksmen to punch out every lightbulb on the ship, and that included running lights, mast lights, and automatic lights over the lifeboats. No one with a Russian passport was going anywhere tonight. The accuracy of the silenced M4s, firing from the darkened *Róisín,* would have made an Olympic shooting judge blink with admiration. There were sixteen bulbs, and it took four shots each, from four men.

The core action of the operation was now taking place inside the ship. Brad Charlton led his team along the starboard edge of the interior, watching for a downward companionway. The SEALs moved two by two, and the first problem came after only twenty yards when two young Russian officers, both armed with service revolvers, suddenly burst out of a cabin and faced these terrifying, black-faced, bearded, and armed intruders.

No one spoke, but Brad Charlton's M4 spat fire, one short volley, and the two Russians would never speak again. With a sharp, beckoning movement to his team, following along the passage, Master Chief

Charlton pressed right on toward the for'ard hold where his objective was hidden.

They trotted through the narrow ship's corridors, in that half crouch SEALs adopt when moving to attack. There was only one door on the left side, and Brad wrenched it open and threw in a grenade, which blew almost instantly and ensured no one would run out of there in much of a hurry.

By now almost the entire ship's company was aware they were under attack; even away at the farthest point, the officers in the bridge control room knew something very serious had happened. They'd heard gunfire, and they'd heard the explosions as their comms system was blown to high heaven.

All lines seemed dead, except for the one emergency open line to Northern Command, and instinctively Kapitan Gromyko made for it and hit the connect button. Too late. Captain Mack Bedford came rushing through the door and shot the CO dead before tossing a grenade straight at the desk in front of the comms keyboards.

There was just time for the SEAL commander to duck out and jump down onto the stairway that led to the bridge. The grenade exploded and blew the back wall of the control room to smithereens. In a split second Mack was back in, thrilled there was no further possibility of any kind of communication with the Russian ops room in Severomorsk, and even more gratified to see there was no one left alive on the bridge.

All five members of Kapitan Gromyko's afterguard had died in the blast, and the CO himself had not had time even to regret embarking on this lethal mission of mercy. Mack wondered whether there was a Russian version of the fable *No good deed goes unpunished*.

Outside he could hear a commotion as at least three Russian crewmen came stampeding up the stairs toward the bridge, shouting and yelling, *"Kapitan . . . Kapitan!"* Mack let them keep coming, stood behind the door, and cut them down one by one as they entered the remains of the shattered control room.

By now he was confident Team 10 had the ship. Listening carefully, he could hear from deep in the hull scattered bursts of machine-gun fire as the SEALs methodically cleared the place out, extinguishing even the semblance of a chance that someone might decide to put up a fight.

Outside it was very dark now, and the decks were no longer under

lights. Only the two SEAL searchlights still pierced the blackness of the
Atlantic night, scanning slowly across the ship, like the satanic beams of a
Nazi concentration camp, searching for weakness. Or defiance.

Mack Bedford's raiders had smashed forward with their mission, elim-
inating all opposition. There had been no major outside noise since Cody's
boys had knocked down the masts. The outer steel of the big Russian
freighter had muffled her own death throes.

The radars of both the *Róisín* and the *Koryak* had revealed no other
shipping anywhere near. It was just possible there had been another vessel
within range of that SOS, that the instantly recognizable *dit-dit-dit-daah-
daah-daah-dit-dit-dit* had been heard on some remote airwave somewhere
in this vast ocean.

But neither captain nor *kapitan* had believed there was anyone within
range to hear the whole message and move in to the rescue. If there had
been, Gromyko might have attempted to get out of it, given the secrecy of
his mission. Captain Farrell had seen only empty seas.

By now, Brad Charlton and his team had taken the entire tank deck
without a fight, six unarmed Russian seamen having surrendered immediately when the master chief and his five black-faced warriors, machine
guns leveled, came bursting into the area. Brad ordered his 2/IC to march
them back to a dining room where there were already twenty-three Russians, crew and missile technicians, secured under padlock and key.

Brad himself, with two SEALs, was measuring the distances from the aft
end to the French truck, on which he could plainly see the words *Lyon Generateur l'Électronique.* But it was backed hard against the hull, and it was not
possible to get inside the rear section where the jamming gear was stowed.

It was the big wall on the truck's left-hand side that was baffling Brad.
It was newly painted, and without encumbrance, just one high, wide sheet
of metal, without a blemish or a scratch. Brad banged it with his rifle butt.
The distant echo was obvious.

These days, when rogue freighters were routinely apprehended by customs and warships, false walls were commonplace. And in Brad's opinion, he'd just found one. Also, the distances on his diagram and the long
measurement did not tally. The one on the *Jane's* diagram was at least forty
feet longer.

It was possible the nuclear stuff was sealed behind the wall, and Brad
was uncertain whether to have a hole smashed through it with axes and

crowbars or to blast it with a hand grenade. But they were not that far above the waterline, and he sure as hell did not wish to "blow a darned great hole in the friggin' hull and drown everyone."

Just then Mack arrived, with two SEALs and two prisoners, Russian missile technicians whom he had persuaded to show him the stored nuclear warheads. That had been done by sign language: Mack's bodyguard shot their colleague, and they agreed to cooperate.

Both of them had nodded keenly when Mack showed them his pictures of the TELAR truck, and now they were pointing at the blank wall, and one of them raised two fingers, which Mack took to mean the information he expected—the two big missile launchers were in there, obviously behind the wall.

Brad told him it would take a well-placed hand grenade to blast a hole, but he was wary of such an explosion in this enclosed space. Mack decided they did not need to see the TELARs, since the warheads were not installed, and he ordered someone to return to the *Róisín* and bring over a limpet mine, which they would place at the base of the wall. Brad would set it to detonate the same time as the ship's hull, when the Americans were all well clear.

Both men had a picture in their minds of the *Koryak* going to the bottom of the Atlantic, with this watertight cavern behind the wall still housing the TELARs, which would somehow remain intact, with their missiles, until the end of time. Both men could not accept that. That TELAR cavern needed to be flooded, the TELARs destroyed. Mack Bedford had just sorted it out in quick time.

The question was now the warheads. The two Russians walked along to the companionway on the starboard side of the hull. They led the way down to the for'ard cargo hold, walking carefully to a row of lockers. They went to the large one at the end of the line and pulled open the door, which fell right out with a metallic clang on the floor.

Behind it was a dull gray box constructed of thick lead. One of the Russians pointed to it, and Brad ripped away the rest of the thin outer casing, easily tearing off black-painted sheets of metal to reveal two containers. They were heavily closed, like treasure chests, but not locked, and Mack and Brad heaved one of them open.

Inside the first they found what they'd come for: two cylindrical containers, three feet long, with rope handles on each side. There was a skull-and-crossbones maritime danger symbol painted in red on the side. They exactly matched the photographs taken from the great lenses of the US satellites. Mack and Brad heaved, carefully removing the first of the two cylinders from its thick lead cocoon.

In a few moments the foredeck hatch would be opened from above and ropes lowered to lift all four of the cylinders to the deck. There they would be attached to the *Róisín's* specially fitted crane and then swung slowly over to the Irish patrol boat.

Right here was the incontrovertible evidence of Russian intentions— nuclear warheads, to fit into the big missiles in the hidden TELARs. This was the moment when everything Lieutenant Commander Nikolai Chirkov had forecast actually came true. This was the moment when the SEALs' brutal and apparently murderous acts could be utterly justified. There was enough atomic power in those four missiles to flatten half of Fort Meade, where thirty-two thousand Americans worked every day and where the loss to US military intelligence would be incalculable.

While the heavy-lift operation went ahead, Mack and Brad Charlton went back to the tank deck and between them clamped a magnetic limpet mine to the bottom of the new wall. The master chief took personal charge of the detonator, checking with Mack, "Say, one hour?" he asked.

"Yup," replied Mack. "We'll be out of here in thirty minutes, and that gives us another half hour to clear the datum. It's almost 2200 now. We'll set that mine, and the ones on the hull, for 2300."

By now the ship was dark and quiet. No more machine-gun fire. On his cell phone Mack called his senior men into a huddle for 2215 on the aft deck, and then he watched while the deck crew slowly hauled the last of the nuclear warheads up and out of the *Koryak's* cargo hold.

They were moved with delicate care once attached to the crane. Two SEALs had lines on each warhead, and when the lifting gear swiveled back to the foredeck of the *Róisín*, they very slowly played out the rope, allowing each warhead to cross the twenty-foot gap without undue movement. They all knew the uranium would not detonate upon impact, but that did not lessen the creepy, sinister atmosphere that always lurked around the very word *nuclear*. They all knew that if one of them went off by mistake, the impact of the explosion would take both ships and everyone on board to Davy Jones's locker.

The transfer went without a hitch, and Mack vanished into the darkness to speak to his senior men. His question was simple: "Is the ship secure—no chance of anyone getting free?"

"Not now, sir," replied one young SEAL. "There are quite a few dead."

"I know there are, son," replied Mack. "But there was no other way."

"Sir, quite a few of the guys are not real happy about killing any more unarmed sailors," he said, "but they will, of course, if you ask them."

"I'm not real happy about it, either," said Mack. "But you guys know the problem. We cannot let news about this operation leak to the outside world . . . because it would be highly detrimental to the United States, and hugely embarrassing for the president. And that means no survivors. The Russian ship has to sink without a trace. No one can be allowed to live, to tell the story."

"I know, sir. We all know. But it was still hard to see these guys as real enemies. They didn't know who we were, or what they'd done, or why we were killing them."

"Let me help you out on that," said Mack. "This ship was carrying four of the fastest guided cruise missiles ever built. They carried nuclear warheads and were headed to a secret launch site, halfway along the Panama Canal, in the fucking jungle.

"With Chinese help, the launchers were headed for some clearing in the trees, and, on a given day, the missiles were to be unleashed at the US National Security Building in Fort Meade, Maryland. The Russians have already test fired them successfully over the optimum distance, two thousand miles, Panama to Fort Meade.

"Not only that, but the Russians were planning to fuck up our president's emergency communications, rendering him helpless, unable to launch a retaliatory move. Every single one of the big Russian brains who masterminded and built this wicked fucking operation is right here on this ship.

"You shot someone? You probably shot the guy who was launching the missile. You probably blew the brains out of some crazed Russian scientist who checked out the codes to wreck the US president's system. I just hope it was one of President Markova's best friends. And I hope you shot him dead.

"This ship, the one you're standing on, represented to us the biggest single danger our nation has faced since Pearl Harbor. US casualties would probably have been twenty times worse. Americans vaporized in a nuclear blast.

"Well, you guys just fucked up those Russian plans. And I hope you fucked 'em up real good. Right now, I want every one of you to get around the ship and slash all of the ropes and lines holding the lifeboats. Anyone gets free, he still isn't going anywhere.

"And at 2300 hours, this ship dies. And if we do it right, no one will ever know what happened. When you're all done, head back aft. That's where we evacuate back to the *Róisín*.

"And I'm telling you, even if no one else knows, there will be big muckety-mucks in the Pentagon, not to mention the White House, who understand precisely what you achieved. And for us, that represents undying personal glory. Now *LET'S GO!*"

The SEALs once more fanned out and headed for the lifeboats. Ten minutes later they were on the rope ladders and climbing down the *Koryak*'s hull, to the huge cargo nets the SEAL deck crews had rigged between the ships for the fastest possible escape.

They had suffered no casualties, principally because no one on the Russian ship had shown any intention of fighting. When the last man was aboard, the lines were cast off and the Irish cutter began to pull away.

Barney Wilkes and his team all wore on their backs light harnesses carrying the heavy limpet mines, which resembled industrial-strength Chinese woks without the chop suey, just compressed TNT, sufficient to knock down a Shanghai street market. All four SEALs were lined up in wet suits on the port side of the ship, which was almost upright now, since the buoyancy tanks had been pumped nearly dry and the *Róisín* was back on her correct lines.

With the engines running, Captain Farrell stood off about forty yards, and Barney's men attached air lines and flippers and jumped into the water, swimming immediately to a depth of around fifteen feet and heading right back to the hull of the *Koryak*. And there they kicked forward under the keel, to their allotted places, where they tested the deepest part of the hull for barnacles.

It was pristine clean, principally because the ship had been in dry dock for its refit and repaint, moored in freezing water thereafter, and moving swiftly ever since, none of which was in any way appealing to the deepwater mollusks that fasten onto ships' keels when they're parked in warmer, still waters with peeling bottom paint.

When Barney's men unclipped their limpets, it was pure routine to snap them magnetically to the underside of the hull close to the keel. But it was dark, and the working conditions were grim and awkward. Because of the mines, they wore their small oxygen tanks on their chests, and it was obviously restricting for working divers. The frogs needed to fix the mines in an agreed pattern, because the "shaped" charge was designed to intensify and focus an upward blast, which would cut through several inches of steel.

Each one of these "sticky bombs" would put a major hole in the hull, which would be fatal in the end, but probably would not sink her for several hours. The trick here was to detonate four of these powerful explosions quite close together, causing four good-size holes, maybe six or eight feet across, to become one whacking great gash, thirty feet across, the keel obliterated.

That would sink her. Fast. The aging Russian warship was not compartmentalized, and the onrushing ocean water would cascade right through the decks. She'd be gone in less than twenty minutes.

But the main task, always the most difficult, was for the SEALs to ensure the detonators were correctly set to blow simultaneously. Most of the normal procedures had been carried out on the ship, unscrewing the black plastic "bung" in the casing of the mine, to reveal the priming well, and then to fix the mechanism. But each underwater timing clock must be set for 2300 hours, and every second was critical for one big bang, not a series of average explosions.

It's difficult to curse and swear underwater, but the level of frustration was high down there under the *Koryak*'s keel. The four SEALs struggled, turning their screwdrivers, twice dropping them, and thanking God they each had two spares. Their hands were cold in the freezing water, and that added to the slowness of the operation. Also, they were trying to breathe slowly, to conserve the oxygen, and this too required a major effort.

One by one they completed the bomb-laying phase of the operation. Each frog waited for the last man to finish, treading water in the dark, and then kicking back together, two by two, SEAL standard practice, no one on his own, to the *Róisín,* to await the result of their labors . . . the death of the *Koryak.*

When they arrived, the cargo nets were down, and they pulled off their flippers and clipped them to their thighs. Then they climbed back up the hull of the Irish cutter, where Captain Farrell had arranged for hot cocoa and sandwiches in the dining room.

It was 2245, and the *Róisín* was already retreating, moving back to a point one thousand yards east of the Russian freighter. No one doubted the forthcoming triumph of the mission, but many of the SEALs could not stop thinking about the fate of the men on board. It did not seem to matter whether they were missilemen or electronics technicians: their fate would be the same. Drowning. And every man in any navy has an innate sympathy for that.

Mack himself was affected. He didn't even know how many personnel were still alive on the *Koryak,* but they were all going to drown, and that made him uneasy. He had, after all, issued the commands that would end their lives. All he could do was to recall the final words spoken to him by the SEAL C-in-C, Admiral Carlow. "Mack," he'd said, "this is not going to be easy. But the people on that ship are collectively planning to launch a murderous strike against the United States. They intend to wipe out thousands of innocent Americans, many of them servicemen, some of them friends. And it's taken millions of dollars of our resources to buy a chance to stop them.

"You are the man chosen to pull the trigger and save our world. So don't shy from it, old friend. And don't doubt the rightness of our cause. The goddamned Russian operation had to be stopped. We could not bomb the ship publicly. So you must blast it privately. Mack, however it may seem, this is a mission to rescue Fort Meade from a near-unstoppable attack, a massacre. Just imagine the heartbreak if it happened. The place would never recover. I know you won't let anyone down."

And so Mack Bedford sat with his team, sipping hot cocoa and reflecting on the long journey he had traveled since first Rani Ben Adan had contacted him. Mack knew how much the Israeli would have loved to be here, right now, to see the culmination of his very brilliant assessment of Russian villainy, risking so much to hear the observations of Lieutenant Commander Chirkov.

He could hear the ship slowing, and he could feel it making a hard port-side turn. He stood up and moved out to the deck, followed by almost all of the SEALs who had taken part in the operation. They spread out, along the rail, and Mack checked his watch: 2258.

It was difficult to see the *Koryak* now, except through night glasses.

There were no deck lights, and most of the electronics inside had been wrecked by hand grenades, especially the one that smashed the comms system on the bridge. That had ruptured a main cable.

Mack's watch flicked to 2259. And just about every SEAL on deck was glancing back and forth from the dial of his watch, particularly Barney Wilkes. The seconds ticked on, and there was a sudden muffled yet thunderous jolt as if coming from the ocean floor . . . *BAH-BOOM!*

"That's two," said Mack.

And then BOOOOM!

"Three," he added.

Four seconds later came the fourth, a stupendous underwater *THUMP!* that shuddered the *Róisín's* hull.

"That one's for you, Nikolai," said Mack, staring up into the starless night. Through his night glasses he could see the *Koryak* already beginning to sink, bow down, as thousands of tons of green water gushed into the keel deck.

Moments later there was another mighty explosion, and the flash from this one lit up the interior of the tank deck. Mack could see the blazing white light, as Brad Charlton's "sticky" blew the hell out of Admiral Ustinov's dark-blue wall, the one that hid the TELARs and the Iskander-Ks.

"Nice shot, Brad," said Mack.

"Thank you, sir," replied the master chief. "No mistakes, right?"

"No mistakes."

No one went inside. Everyone just stood there watching the death of the *Koryak,* watching it sink lower and lower in the water. Soon there was just the upper works, and she tilted inexorably for'ard, and the bridge dipped under the ocean. And then, for a split second, her stern rose up, and, just briefly, her twin screws could be seen above the surface.

With what sounded like a mighty sigh, the Russian freighter plunged forward, spearing into the surface of the ocean. Then she was gone, taking what remained of her crew and their notorious cargo to the oblivion of the ocean bed.

There was nothing more to see. The *Róisín* turned to her new southeasterly course, steering one-four-zero, at fifteen knots, the short Atlantic chop right on her starboard bow. They'd enter the mouth of the Shannon estuary, 230 miles away, at around three tomorrow afternoon, Thursday.

With midnight approaching, there was little else to do except sleep, and the SEALs who had fought the action were monumentally grateful for the opportunity. There were bunks, sleeping bags, and cots for all forty Americans, and no one begrudged them one inch of their space. Some of the young Irish crewmen were in awe of these ruthless SEAL combatants from across the ocean and would have sat up all night talking to them if anyone had been able to stay awake.

By first light, they were running only 70 miles off the coast of County Clare, but still several hours from the Shannon. The first land they would see would be the Aran Islands on the port side, since Captain Farrell intended to come inshore and then swing south down to Loop Head, which guards the estuary. That way, they'd leave the Arans on their port quarter and the Cliffs of Moher on their beam.

All morning they lounged about the ship with Mack Bedford, listening to every news bulletin they could pick up on the Irish news radio channel. But there was no mention of the vanished Russian freighter. They came in from the northwest and passed the lighthouse just after three and steamed into the mouth of the Shannon.

It was 10 miles up to the choke point that lies between Kilcredaun and the cliffs of Kilconley, and another 20 miles up to the old seaplane port on Foynes Island, which lies on hilly land on the south side of the Shannon River. These days Foynes is a major deepwater seaport, and space had been allocated to bring in the Irish warship, direct orders of the prime minister.

They came alongside at half past five, and swiftly disembarked, each SEAL with his own bag and combat gear. The area had been cleared and deserted save for the big luxury Volvo coach on the dockside. They climbed wearily aboard for the short journey around the estuary and over the Limerick town bridge, to Shannon Airport, where a US Navy Hercules awaited them, engines running.

By seven SEAL Team 10 had taken off, climbing west above the Shannon River toward the open Atlantic, bound for US Naval Air Station North Island, which adjoins their Coronado base in San Diego. It was a nonstop direct flight home to the West Coast for Mack Bedford's SEALs: a very secret mission accomplished.

No mention was made of any disaster in the North Atlantic on any of the international airways. No one reported an explosion, or a sinking, or anything unusual. The US National Security Agency combed every possibility for even the suspicion of a missing ship, and thus far there was zero.

Headquarters, Northern Fleet Command
Severomorsk, Russia

Koryak's call-sign was "FOM-2," bestowed upon her in anticipation of overwhelming victory. She was treated by the high command as the most dangerous and important Russian ship on the Seven Seas. And, like the gigantic Typhoon Class nuclear submarines, with their embarked ICBMs, she was required to check in every twenty-four hours.

The Typhoons, of course, needed to make a special trip to the surface, to make satellite contact, reporting course, speed, and position. The *Koryak*, which could be contacted anytime since she was already on the surface, was under ironclad orders to make no communications to anyone. Fleet HQ, probably Admiral Ustinov in person, would come on the satellite link every afternoon around five o'clock (local Severomorsk) for the briefest confirmation of her speed and whereabouts.

The *Koryak*'s was a near-silent voyage, and at five on Wednesday, April 10, her check in took a total of twelve seconds. On Thursday, April 11, however, eighteen hours after she was sunk, the silence was deafening. The sat/comms operator in Severomorsk could not raise her. Over and over he went through on the link, requesting the same thing: *Freighter "Koryak," come in, please, FOM-2 calling . . . Report your position . . . Repeat, report your position.*

Nothing. This was disturbing, but not yet a five-alarmer. Submarines can vanish completely, but not surface ships, at least not without an absolute uproar involving air-sea rescue, coast guards, various navies, and heaven knows what else.

And a lot of things could have gone wrong. The *Koryak* could have an electronic problem. There could be a glitch on her satellite mast, maybe a stalled generator, perhaps even her duty-comms officer missing for a half hour. She was, after all, a civilian ship now, and they did not necessarily follow the strict codes of military discipline.

The trouble was, in Northern Fleet HQ, everything to do with the *Koryak* was on a hair trigger of nervousness. The comms operator was terrified of reporting anything to Admiral Ustinov except good news. The admiral regarded the blue freighter in the same worshipful light he regarded the gigantic 272-foot *Mamaev Kurgan* figure, with its mighty raised sword representing Mother Russia, in his home city of Volgograd.

By the operator's calculations, the *Koryak* should be 250 miles south-west of her last-known. "Jesus Christ!" he muttered, because that was a shockingly long way by anyone's standards. The question was, should he raise a major alarm by announcing the ship had vanished? Or take it calmly and announce there were electronic problems aboard the *Koryak*?

He went for the former, on the basis that if he settled for option two, and the ship really had vanished, he would be blamed for not making everyone aware of the crisis at the first possible moment.

Subsequently, Admiral Alexander Ustinov practically had a heart attack. *"WHAT DO YOU MEAN, VANISHED?"* he bellowed.

"Er . . . not really there, sir."

"HOW THE HELL CAN SHE BE NOT REALLY THERE? SHE WEIGHS FIVE THOUSAND TONS, AND SHE HAS BRAND-NEW ENGINES AND A VETERAN CAPTAIN AND NAVIGATOR!"

"I don't know, sir. But I cannot get a reply from her."

"Have you checked . . . "

"I've checked everything, sir."

"WELL, WHERE THE HELL IS SHE?"

"I'm not quite sure, sir."

"Have you checked the international airwaves, coast guards, and every other damn thing, to find out if anyone's seen anything?"

"Not yet, sir. It wasn't my place to raise an alarm on that scale."

Admiral Ustinov was nothing if not very smart. And the phrase involving alarms, and raising them, struck home with him. The last thing he wanted was a public panic involving the Russian Navy looking for a civilian ship, especially one carrying illegal nuclear warheads.

His attitude softened, and he said, "Listen, kid, give me your opinion. Is there any point waiting twenty-four hours, see if she makes contact with us at five—in case they've put the fault right?"

"Sir," said the young operator, "we have no satellite photographic cover in that part of the Atlantic up to the coast of Ireland. But, as you know, there are three or four ways to make contact with a surface ship. I've tried them all, including the cell phone the captain has for emergencies, the only mobile on the ship. It's dead—not unavailable, or busy, or switched off. Dead. Nothing. In my view, that ship has sunk."

Which left the admiral just a few seconds to gather his thoughts before making the worst phone call of his life—the one that would alert Admiral

Vitaly Rankov to the undeniable fact that FOM-2 had died, and with it the exultant hopes and dreams of President Nikita Markova.

The greater tragedy was, no one could share the problem. There was no one to help solve it, or investigate it. Both he and the commander in chief would have to suffer silently, and Ustinov imagined the coming fury, which must surely emanate from the Russian Navy's Main Staff HQ in St. Petersburg.

But nothing much happened at all. Admiral Rankov went very quiet, and, since they could do nothing about it, not even discuss it with anyone else, he accepted their fate. The dream of FOM-2 was over. Vitaly had his suspicions, but he chose, right now, to keep them to himself.

Meanwhile, the US cleanup phase of the mission continued. In the Far North of Russia, at nine o'clock on the following morning, Friday, April 12, the nine-thousand-ton Los Angeles Class submarine *Cheyenne* suddenly surfaced 120 miles northwest of the Murmansk Inlet, in full sight of two Russian warships, one of which was the eleven-thousand-ton guided-missile cruiser *Varyag,* which the Americans had been tracking for five days.

The US crew knew precisely who she was and was fully aware this Northern Fleet–based ship had also served in the Pacific and had, not so long ago, visited San Francisco on a goodwill tour. And right now the Americans were out on the casing, waving to the men from Severomorsk, asking if they wanted to come over for a cup of coffee.

The Russians gave serious thought to this, and especially to the inevitable Boston cream doughnuts, but decided they'd better get back to base before dark and cheerfully yelled their farewells from the upper decks . . . *Da svidanya! Da svidanya, Yankees! Da svidanya, "Cheyenne"!*

The *Varyag*'s logbook would, of course, record that at 0900 in the Barents Sea, they had spotted a US submarine, the *Cheyenne,* heading northwest around the Norwegian coast and been respectfully greeted.

As for the *Cheyenne,* she pressed on down the long seaway that washes past a thousand Norwegian islands, and then continued through the GIUK Gap, across the fifty-fifth parallel, and made a hard left turn into Donegal Bay.

On April 19 she became the first US submarine to pull into the covered dock at US NAVFAC Donegal, right alongside the Irish cutter *Róisín.*

And there they transferred the hottest cargo in all the world: four nuclear warheads, lifted across from ship to sub, and lowered with the *Cheyenne*'s davits deep into her hull, ready for immediate passage across the Atlantic to New London, Connecticut.

Thus, the US Navy had heeded the advice of Admiral Morgan, who considered it would be "goddamned rude" to embarrass the Irish prime minister by unloading live nuclear warheads onto Irish soil. The republic was, after all, reputed to be strictly neutral during all forms of conflict between international powers.

And Ireland was neutral. That nation never took sides in two world wars. She would assist no one in the grim art of international warfare. Except for her cousins in North America. Because, in the end, the Emerald Isle, with a million blood ties, would refuse the United States nothing.

1700, FRIDAY, APRIL 19

Naval HQ
St. Petersburg, Russia

Admiral Rankov could contain himself no longer. He picked up the telephone and asked to be put through to his opposite number in the Pentagon.

Admiral Mark Bradfield came on the line immediately, not with the old informality of Admiral Morgan and the tirade of insults that usually accompanied such calls, but with a polite, "Good afternoon, Admiral. What a nice surprise."

Vitaly would almost have preferred an Arnold Morgan beration for Russia's "junkyard navy" than listen to this obvious American smoothy. But he pressed ahead anyway. "Admiral, a week ago we lost a freighter in the middle of the North Atlantic. I wondered if any of your patrol ships may have seen anything of her. She was a five-thousand-ton vessel, dark-blue roll-on, roll-off, vanished without a trace."

"Can't say I've heard anything," replied Bradfield. "But I don't think we had much in the North Atlantic this month. Certainly not surface ships."

Rankov recognized this as one of the two or three biggest lies ever told. The US Navy *never* dropped its guard.

"Perhaps you could check for us?" he replied. "We think the accident happened on the fifty-fifth parallel, around 14 West."

"Certainly," said Mark Bradfield. "Be glad to. Hold on for one minute. I'll be right back."

Admiral Rankov waited.

When the US Navy's CNO finally returned, his answer was as predicted. "As I thought, Admiral," he said, "we had nothing in the North Atlantic that week."

"Not even a submarine?" asked Vitaly.

"Not really. Only the USS *Cheyenne,* and she was a couple of thousand miles north, close to the ice cap, on a scientific exploration."

Vitaly inwardly shuddered. They had not fed him just a pack of lies. They'd laced it with a truth they did not have to reveal, confirming the complete honesty and goodwill of Uncle Sam.

"Thank you, Admiral," said Rankov, putting down the telephone. His polished jackboots clicked on the marble floor of his grandiose office as he walked out muttering, "I just hope they understand, I know what they did. I absolutely know. And I shouldn't be surprised if that bastard Morgan was involved, retirement or no fucking retirement."

EPILOGUE

Dublin, Ireland

The financial arrangement between Ireland and the United States worked out extremely well for both countries. The US Navy was more than happy with the new base on Donegal Bay, for what it believed was a reasonable cost, and the place thrived as soon as it was completed.

American commanding officers came in regularly and regarded the advent of a home port on the eastern side of the Atlantic as pure luxury, instead of the thirty-five-hundred-mile slog back to Norfolk, Virginia, often in rough weather.

The removal of 50 percent of Ireland's national debt was an enormous boost to the economy. Almost immediately, Ireland's fortunes improved, as American industry and finance kicked in, bringing prosperity to many places, especially Donegal.

The gross national product improved. Debts were paid. Ireland voted overwhelmingly to adopt the US dollar instead of the euro. The government, under the shrewd and affable Neil McGrath, ensured that all of Irish industry and agriculture took advantage of the opportunities on the far side of the Atlantic, now that trading tariffs into the United States were zero.

The proposition that Admiral Morgan had suggested to the PM nearly three years ago in Phoenix Park had proved tempting in the extreme, month after month, as the US connection seemed always to open the doors to the sunny side of the street.

Neil McGrath's personal popularity was a key ingredient. He was from a wealthy family, substantial in his own right, universally admired for not being in politics for personal gain, a state of grace not always adhered to by politicians of any nation.

He took his government with him on almost any major issue. And his view was well known, that Ireland was so much safer and wealthier by remaining firmly in the American camp, rather than with struggling European economies with massive welfare programs and very few resources.

Today, a spring afternoon more than two years after the unspoken events of April 10, 2019, Admiral Morgan and Prime Minister McGrath had lunched at the Shelbourne Hotel, and were strolling companionably back along Kildare Street toward Leinster House, home of the Irish National Parliament.

Arnold still loved his home in Clonakilty, and Neil McGrath and his wife were regular visitors. It was an easy and warm relationship between an Irish politician and a US Naval commander, both of whom wished only the best for their respective countries.

McGrath loved America's willing generosity to Ireland. And Arnold Morgan was gratified to see American financiers hauling the Emerald Isle ever closer to a debt-free economy, like Switzerland.

The place was running at a profit, not least because the iron-souled austerity measures of earlier years had been obeyed and carried out stoically, by a people to whom relentless hardship was an ever-present memory.

Ireland was surely at the dawn of a new era. She was in close partnership with her oldest and truest ally, the bighearted powerhouse across the water, which, not so long ago, had stepped up and offered the hand of friendship . . . a safe and welcoming haven, and rescue, for this tearful, dying nation from the cruelest of famines.

As they turned into the great Dublin mansion of Leinster House, the American admiral glanced up, as he always did these past few weeks. He sharply saluted the joyous sight of Old Glory, fluttering boldly above the Irish Parliament . . . the Stars and Stripes, for the fifty-first state.